THE NAME AND THE SHADOW: AN ARMAND PTOLEMY NOVEL

Mark Jeffrey

This is a work of fiction. Names, characters, businesses, places, events, locales, and incidents are either the products of the author's imagination or used in a fictitious manner. Any resemblance to actual persons, living or dead, or actual events is purely coincidental.

Copyright © 2023 Mark Jeffrey

ISBN-13: 979-8392032921

CHAPTER ONE

The Codex

As Armand Martel translated the ancient Egyptian codex, it began speaking directly to him.

HELLO ARMAND.

He did a double-take at the phonetic hieroglyphs enclosed in a cartouche. Yes, falcon, flat circle, owl, falcon, water, fish — *Armand*.

He was not a natural at hieroglyphic translation: he relied on Fabricius, a Google AI to help him do it. As he kept reading, the strangeness continued:

YES. I AM SPEAKING TO YOU, ARMAND.

That jolted him. He looked around the room suspiciously, as though the source of this phenomenon might be a visible thing nearby. *How is this happening?* But even with ice rattling in his heart, he kept going.

HOW LONG HAS IT BEEN?

How long has *what* been? Was it asking how long it had been buried? *Just like a goddamn Mummy*, Armand thought — and then pushed the thought away.

Four thousand years, Armand muttered. *Maybe four and a half thousand. If you know my name, why don't you know the length of time that you were in the sand?*

UNTIL YOU THINK IT, I CANNOT KNOW IT.

What did that mean?

Until you think it … That rattled Armand. Was this thing somehow inside his head? As strange as this book seemed, it was something 'out there' — something he could close, burn, throw out the window, get away from anytime he wanted. But now, the book seemed … invasive.

Suddenly, he became very frightened.

"What are you? A ghost?" he said aloud.

NO.

"A djinn?"

NO.

"Are you a human, back in the past?"

A HUMAN WRITES THIS BOOK. BUT I AM NOT THE HUMAN.

"Then what are you?"

I AM ALIVE WORDS.

What?

That was not the answer he was expecting. A ghost would have at least been comprehensible. But *alive words*? What did that even mean?

Carefully, Armand said: "Words aren't alive. The people who write them are. But words themselves are not. Please explain."

NO. SOME WORDS ARE ALIVE.

Armand read that several times. In what sense could words be alive?

YOUR EYES MAKE LIGHT. MAKE US LIVE.

His eyes most certainly did not 'make light'. Yet the Word-thing seemed to be earnestly describing its experience of Armand. It sounded like its version of an alien encounter.

Next came another cartouche enclosing a phonetic:

KWAN TOMB.

2

Armand stared at this new word, trying to place it in history. He had never heard of a Pharaoh named Kwan. What was the codex trying to say?

Ah. *Quantum!* Was it trying to say that it was a quantum phenomenon?

How would it even know what that meant?

Until you think it, I cannot know.

The hieroglyphs — the words — he was reading were somehow symbiotic with his own mind. It could not perceive until he did. In some sense, Armand was animating the 'alive words' with his attention.

Someone in ancient Egypt thousands of years ago had written about quantum mechanics, spelling a modern English word phonetically.

Impossible!

DO NOT BE AFRAID.

"Ok. This is too fucking fucked up."

Armand slammed the book shut and left the room.

CHAPTER TWO

The Sour Son

A SOUR SUN THROBBED OVER New York. Scant clouds crusted a cold sky, and a dreary wind made everything all the more bitter.

Armand Martel ran errands on foot for GigaMaestro, the venture capital firm where he worked.

Loneliness purred on a low hum in his mind, as it so often did now. *The Old Mood*, he called it. Or *The Sads*. *The Deep Drear*. Most of his friends from high school and college had gone, moved away, scattered in a diaspora for the faraway blockchain hotbeds of Singapore, Seoul, Zug and Dubai.

But not Armand. He'd stayed in New York.

And even though he was already thirty years old, Armand could barely afford a shabby little studio in Alphabet City.

On the other hand, his older brothers — Quinctius, Marius, Cyrano, Ames, Samson and Otto — were all quite wealthy. When their father, Didier Martel, had died, he'd left the bulk of his considerable riches to them. But as the seventh and youngest brother, Armand had been born too late — the Martel Family Trust had been set up for them and

4

them alone. Armand had not even been included.

Had it been an oversight? Or had it been intentional? Only Didier knew for sure, and he wasn't talking.

Still. His brothers had at least been kind enough to carve out *something* for him. Armand would get 1% of the family fortune when he was thirty-five — provided that he worked for the Martel family of companies in the meantime. Since Didier had been worth a little over $700M when he'd died, 1% came out to $7M, which was worth sticking around New York for.

Until that day, Armand worked for the Martel Family Office — that is, for his brothers, in a variety of capacities. The MFO had two main enterprises that it invested in and directly managed. One was Martel Antiquities, which controlled a portfolio of privately collected ancient artifacts. The second was GigaMaestro, a $200M early stage venture capital fund with a multi-pronged thesis concentrating on artificial intelligence, digital assets and decentralized finance, and new forms of social media. The firm was frequently referred to by its abbreviation, 'GM', which was also a crypto-hipster salutation meaning 'good morning' but also representing the decentralized asset ethos and vibe. GigaMaestro's name had been deliberately chosen as a wink to this.

# # #

FROM THE MOMENT Armand awoke at 5:00 AM every day, his phone was constantly abuzz.

First, Otto needed an email sent, then Samson wanted him to track down a missing wire transfer, and then Quinty wanted him to book conference hotels in Barcelona.

Armand had six different bosses in six different time zones.

For this reason, he kept his thick brown hair buzzed tight — less to do in the mornings, and he didn't have to pay for hair styling. He ran and lifted when he could, usually in the late evenings when the day started to settle down at last. Between this and frequently skipping meals due to lack of time, he managed to stay lean and strong.

This was his life.

It had been this way since he was nineteen, when his father Didier had died suddenly.

The one day — *one!* — when he felt like he was legitimately off the grid was Thursdays. That was when he worked out of the Martel Antiquities office, cataloging and doing inventory of items.

The storage area was located underground in a humidity-controlled vault. Whenever he was down there he got zero phone reception. This meant his brothers couldn't call him. Armand grinned. Even *they* had to respect the holy ground of Thursday.

The blessed quiet. The hours and hours and hours of long enjoyment. Fourteen hours could whiz by down here, and Armand would barely notice.

It was on a Thursday that Armand had found the mysterious Egyptian codex.

CHAPTER THREE

Event Producer, Not Planner

GIGAMAESTRO AND THE MARTEL FAMILY Office held a two-day event in New York every year called EPIC. It put a spotlight on GM's various tech investments, partners and current events.

Armand's six older brothers — Quinctius, Marius, Otto, Samson, Cyrano and Ames — were the stars. EPIC was a money-loser, but that didn't matter: it was about the spectacle, the prestige. Ostensibly it was so that the brothers could project power and relevance and thus gain allocations for GigaMaestro in the best venture deals alongside such names as Andreesen-Horowitz, Benchmark, Softbank and the rest.

But really, Armand knew, his brothers just liked the spotlight.

Armand was the only one of them without a stage role. Instead, his brothers had made him the 'event planner' — a name he strenuously objected to. "It's Event *Producer*," Armand would correct them.

"Right! And it's the most important thing!" they'd replied. "You're in charge of *all* of us!"

But Quinty was the star. As the elder brother, he was the host and MC. Marius, the second eldest, followed in Quinty's wake as a kind of Spock to his Kirk: clearly second, but also important.

As Armand furiously worked the badge desk, he could hear Quinty start the morning keynote: "Good morning! Welcome to EPIC! For those of you who don't know, EPIC stands for Exceptional People In Control. We're all about finding the very best talent — the right people — and putting them in the right place, at the right time ..."

And on he went.

The badge desk got more hectic. Late-comers jogged off the elevator and demanded their conference credentials more quickly: *It was starting! They were missing it!*

One of the attendees was screaming that her name had been spelled wrong.

Another, a sleek beautiful blonde named Rebecca Soares (that Armand once had a mad crush on — and he now realized that he still did), had never actually registered, but she 'came every year, Quinty loves me, so, you should know to have my badge ready'."

Armand smiled deferentially and apologized to each personally, as a Martel, while the temps scurried to fix both issues.

Another attendee had brought his bulldog. Armand turned him away as politely as he could. The man was furious, he even called it a 'Service Animal', but Armand knew the dog would enrage the other attendees — not because it was unsanitary or disruptive — but because it would give status to this man as a *Special Person Who Was Unusually Accommodated*.

Why him and not us?

This whole place was a *More Important Than* machine: the dog was a line that simply could not be crossed.

Loudly calling Armand a 'dog hater', the man left.

The opening hours of registration were usually the worst. Once that settled down, things were not easy, but better. Around noon, Armand was in the Speaker's Lounge catching his breath (he had just successfully rebooked hotel and airlines for nine speakers who had changed their plans at the last minute), when all six of his brothers suddenly converged on him.

"Hey. I'm hearing from a lot of people that they couldn't get their badge," Marius said. "What's up with that, man?"

"Nothing," Armand said. "There were a few issues but —
"

"Dude," Otto said, "registration is a complete disaster this year."

"Yeah," Samson said. "You gotta figure this out, man. It's super embarrassing for the family."

"It was just a misspelled badge, yes. A mistake, but we fixed it within about a minute."

"Hey," Marius said. "That's a person's name, ya? A name is sacred. EPIC is about Exceptional People — and you go and mess up an Exceptional's sacred? Not cool."

"Ya! What's wrong with you, man?" Otto chimed in.

"Nothing! I just —" Armand sputtered.

"It must be more than that," Marius said. "Everyone is saying badges are a giant mess. What else is happening?"

"There was some lady who didn't even register," Armand said, feigning ignorance of who she was because he was embarrassed about his crush. "She was mad when we didn't have her badge. How are we supposed to know to have a badge if they don't register?"

"Dude!" Otto whacked his chest and downed a vodka-reeking drink. "Some lady? That's Rebecca! I just saw her! She comes every year."

"Ya!" Samson said. "You should know about her."

"Ya!" Ames agreed. "Dude. You gotta get on top of this."

Quinctius watched all this from afar while chatting with a few portfolio CEO's. Armand saw him say, *Will you excuse me?*

Armand's heart fell. If his oldest brother was taking time out from basking in conference glory, something big was afoot or really wrong.

"Quinty," Armand said.

"Armie," Quinctius said. "Listen. This is the big year for AI. Sure, we have little chatbots that pass the Turing Test. But they're just toys. None of them are really conscious. The Singularity and all that. But that's super close. Like, ten years or less away. Digital life! Computers with souls!"

"Yes," Armand nodded, not really understanding. What was the point of this?

"So. *This* is the year," Quinctius said. "This is the year that the Seed Rounds happen for the AI companies that will crack true consciousness. We got to be IN on that, man! That's like Amazon big, Bitcoin big!"

"I understand," Armand said, not really understanding.

"So I need you to make this event perfect. *Perfect*, man. Like, super perfect. Flawless. But especially for the AI people. The companies and the VC's. Ya?"

Armand nodded.

"Good. Good! That's our Armie! Now get back at it."

# # #

AT 3:30 PM PRECISELY, the elevator door flew open.

Wakao Akihito, General Partner of The Diatama Fund, and his entourage of four, made a beeline for the Registration desk.

Otto, Samson and Cyrano — who were chatting lazily in the Lobby with other fund Partners — immediately perked up. Akihito's Diatama Fund was the pre-eminent and most prestigious venture capital source for artificial intelligence startups in the world.

To co-invest with them was to co-invest with the gods. This was exactly the prize Quinty was hunting.

Akihito's people were already speaking with a Registration TaskRabbit who clearly did not know who he was. The temp, a slacker snowboarder-type, was shaking her head: *No, you're not on the list.* The body language of all five men instantly became tense, insulted, awkward.

Armand walked — almost ran — over to Registration as quickly as he could. "Akihito-san! My apologies. We do not have you registered, but of course we are happy to offer you and your associates complimentary badges. Would you please wait just a moment while we make them? Perhaps enjoy a drink?"

The five men looked visibly relieved. They nodded and moved into the lobby to socialize.

Armand turned back to the badge desk. The snowboarder temp girl's eyes were wide. Armand was about to give her the names and info for the badges when she said: "The printer's dead. We can't make more badges."

What?

Goddammit!

Okay. Okay. Okay. Okay. Okay.

No choice, they simply had to hand-write the badges. Quickly, Armand and the temp did so, with the very best penmanship that they could muster.

When Akihito came back, Armand tried to look confident as he handed the badges over. The Diatama Fund five looked at their conference credentials like they might be poo, then at each other. Wordlessly, they agreed and slipped lanyards over their heads.

Their vibe was: *We will make do. But we are very not pleased.*

Otto, Samson and Cyrano saw all of this. They glared daggers at Armand.

Armand gave Akihito-san a tight smile. "This way, please." The five fell in line as he personally escorted them into the Main Hall.

Without any doubt, Wakao Akihito was the most important attendee of this conference. That meant he expected rock star, front row treatment — quite literally. The ghetto-style badges were already one strike. There could not be another.

The conference hall was completely packed. That meant Armand was going to have to evict several VIP's from the front row. As AI company founders gave two-minute elevator pitches, Armand crouched down and whispered to the five people nearest the stage that they would have to move.

They were furious. *Where were they supposed to sit?* The place was full now! One of them was Rebecca. At first, she simply refused to move — but Armand threatened to call security.

In the end, all of them shamefully shuffled out, while The Diatama Fund five slid into prestigious front row seats. At last, Akihito-san let a very small smile come to his lips. He was content.

But no one else was.

Back in the lobby, Armand faced a furious Otto, Samson and Cyrano — and Rebecca.

"Absolutely not acceptable, Armand!"

"But what was I supposed to do?"

"Find another solution! I don't know, this is YOUR job, not ours! We give you a chance at the big time and this is how you repay us?"

Rebecca said: "Oh, I am definitely going to tell Quinty about how I was dragged screaming from my seat! How embarrassing, how traumatic!"

Next, the snowboarder temp girl quit in tears. All of this was too much. She quickly vanished down the elevator like she'd been gulped away.

"Armand!" Quinty screamed from the Main Hall doors. "We need you!"

Breaking into a jog, Armand followed his oldest brother.

To Armand's extreme surprise, Wakao Akihito was on stage. *What the fucking fuck?* He wasn't even on the attendee list, not to mention the Speaker Agenda. He'd randomly taken over the stage — and he was now throwing the entire meticulously planned schedule out of whack.

People were going to miss planes.

Akihito-san was giving a speech to the rapt audience about how The Diatama Fund was going to drive human evolution and machine evolution together as one twin-braided thread, combining them in some transhumanist, near-religious vision.

To the left of Akihito-san, two of his associates were at the podium, arguing manically and trying to get some piece of equipment to work.

Oh no. Armand felt his gut sink. He knew what this meant.

Armand hopped on stage and quickly conferred with them: yep, it was exactly what he'd feared. Akihito wanted to show slides and a video.

But he'd brought a Microsoft Windows machine. And the conference had standardized on Apple equipment. They were trying adapter after adapter, but nothing was working.

Now they expected Armand to fix it all.

Akihito-san kept speaking for five minutes at a time — and then looking back to see if his slides had miraculously appeared yet.

"Can't we just take his deck and move it to a flash drive?"

Armand asked. "And just put that on a Mac that we already know works?"

The two assistants shook their heads. "No, no, no. There is video on this drive. And an AI demo that only works on Windows. He wants to show all of that."

"So we move the video too. It will fit —"

"No! It's embedded in the slide deck and the embed format won't play on a Mac. We've tried that before, it doesn't work!"

"But if we moved the slides, at least he could —"

"No! He shows it all — or nothing!"

Armand nodded as patiently as he could. But already knew: *there was no way to fix this.* It just wasn't possible.

After feigning a few more attempts, he slid down from the stage and slinked away to the lobby. The two assistants shook their head at Akihito-san, who hid his disappointment well, and concluded his talk with a broad, confident smile — to thunderous applause.

# # #

QUINTY WAS beyond furious backstage.

"That was our chance, Armand! With the number one AI guy on earth! *And you blew it!* All he wanted to do was show a freaking video! Is that an unreasonable ask at a conference?"

"But he showed up with the *wrong computer* — and the wrong video format! We just didn't have the right equipment to deal with it. How were we supposed to know he was coming? Or what he was bringing?"

"Here's an idea," Ames said. "Why don't you prepare for ALL formats, all the time?"

"Yeah. That's what I would have done," Cyrano agreed.

"Seems simple," Otto concurred.

"This was a fucking shit-show!" Ames chimed in.

"Hey. You know that bonus stock ownership?" Marius said. "The one that the Board decides on? It's not looking very good for you."

"Nope. Not very good at all," Samson said.

Armand's eyes were on fire. This was too much.

"Hey. I forget: how much are we paying him?" Otto said.

"Too much," Cyrano said. "We're already way, way over-budget this year. And Armie's not giving us our money's worth."

"That's true," Ames said solemnly. "There's too much entitlement these days. Just like we talked about at EPIC: We live in the Age of Excellence. Only the excellent should get paid. You got to 'Do The Work' — or go home."

"Look. Today was not the EPIC Experience," Quinty said to Armand. "I am very disappointed in you. You did about half of what I expected you to do. So … 'Age of Excellence' right? We have to practice what we preach. I'm cutting your pay in half."

"*Half?*" Armand yelped. "I'm already at way below market rates!"

With a sickening feeling, he realized that he wouldn't be able to afford his Alphabet City studio. Even his one tiny, shabby, almost worthless possession was going to be taken away.

"Hey. We could have hired anyone!" Otto replied. "*But we gave it to you.* Everyone said: Nepotism! He's a Nepo-baby! But we did it anyway, as a favor to you."

"It's the FAMILY Office, Otto," Armand fired back. "It's not nepotism to hire family for a Family Office."

"But we did hire you when we didn't have to," Quinty said. "So half is fair. Right everyone? Agree?"

"Agree," said Otto.

"Agree!" said Marius.

"Yes," said Samson.

"Agree," said Cyrano.

"He's lucky it's not more," said Ames

Quinty smiled at Armand. "Ah, it's not that bad Armie. Maybe next year, things'll be better for you."

CHAPTER FOUR

Second Session

IT TOOK ARMAND AN ENTIRE week to work up enough courage to return to the codex. But before he did, he performed some research.

He wanted to know everything he could before opening that book again.

While scrolls on papyrus were common enough in ancient Egypt, actual *books*, codices, like the one Armand had, were almost unheard of. His codex was bound in leather with perhaps a hundred papyrus pages. It contained very tiny hieroglyphs handwritten onto each page (also unusual). They had a cramped look, as if the scribe who had authored them were under duress or madness.

Could it be a trick?

No.

There was no way to fake this. A book could not know what he was about to say or think and have answers pre-written in it. There was zero chance that this was a hoax.

Could it be a forgery?

That was always possible.

In fact, Armand's codex was so far afield of conventional

norms that it would have been laughed at by any serious archeologist.

As always, fakes abounded. In New York, Beijing, London and Dubai, private merchants peddled many curios with no provenance. Sometimes they turned out to be laboratory-cooked forgeries, wherein truly ancient materials were recycled to fabulate meticulous hoaxes. That way, if a fake trinket were carbon-dated, the test would seem to authenticate it.

But in the case of Armand's codex, the sealed canopic jar in which it had arrived *did* have clear provenance and well-validated authenticity. It had come from the small tomb of some minor official recently discovered near Saqqara. The tomb's cache had been dated to the Old Kingdom, meaning the contents were roughly 4,000 years old.

In ancient Egypt, it was believed that every person had five parts: the body, and a four-parted soul consisting of the Ka, the Ba, the Name and the Shadow. After death, all five parts had to be able to re-unite daily for rest. Thus, preservation of the body was essential to the survival of the soul.

If the body was destroyed, then all parts of the soul were likewise destroyed — forever.

There was no greater crime in ancient Egypt.

Likewise, the Name, a written cartouche of a person's formal moniker, had to always exist in at least once place — or, again, the soul would be destroyed. It reminded Armand of the concept of a Horcrux from *Harry Potter* or the One Ring from *Lord of the Rings.*

During the embalming process, the viscera had to first be removed to prevent decomposition. Yet, internal organs were still part of the body, so they could not be simply discarded. Hence, the canopic jar was introduced. The organs of the deceased were placed inside, and the jar sealed for eternity.

However, Armand's jar had been strangely large and wide — and much bigger than what would be needed to house a human organ. It featured no hieroglyphs or decorations of any kind, though the lid was the carved head of a woman.

Canopic jars found in modern times were almost never opened. They were sometimes X-rayed, but usually, nobody cared to see partially rotted sludge inside. So when Armand had accidentally knocked his jar over, breaking it and splashing limestone shards across the floor, he fully expected to have to mop up some kind of centuries-old foul-smelling goo.

But to his great surprise, a bone-dry leather-bound Egyptian codex, rolled up and stuffed into a pot for millennia, tumbled across the floor.

It was perfectly preserved. Between the jar's airtight seal and the hot, dry desert air, the codex had been well-protected for thousands of years. The Dead Sea Scrolls had also famously managed to remain intact under similar conditions.

Armand picked up the codex. He unwound several leather cords and opened to the first page.

He bemusedly fired up the Fabricius AI and started translating the glyphs. The first few pages appeared to be a prophecy of a coming famine. For about ten minutes, he read with interest. Then the codex shifted gears and droned on about some battle and then tedious dietary restrictions.

Impatient, he flipped to the book's middle. He was greatly surprised and initially amused to suddenly see his own name, written in phonetic hieroglyphs.

Well, *that* was a weird.

Armand was a *French* name.

There was no Pharaoh Armand. And no one in the Old Kingdom had ever been called Armand.

Unless it was some odd fluke? Maybe there was once *one* Egyptian guy named, like, Hur Mond or something? As he began reading the glyphs near his name, the first session with the book had occurred.

# # #

ARMAND'S SECOND session with the mysterious Egyptian codex had been carried out much more deliberately. He knew what to expect this time. And he had carefully prepared questions which he held now at the ready.

"Okay, book thing," he whispered. "I'm back. Don't be evil."

It worked like this: The codex was first opened to the 'current page' of their conversation. Armand could see the hieroglyphs on the page, but he had no idea yet as to what they said. Armand would then speak aloud to the codex, asking a question. Then, using the Google Fabricius translator app, he would move his phone over the next set of untranslated hieroglyphs, and receive his answer.

Armand took some deep breaths to calm his pounding heart. Then, he opened the codex to where he had left off, and began translating.

To his surprise, he received a stern warning:

READ THIS BOOK ONLY IN THE ORDER WHICH IT WAS WRITTEN. DO NOT EVER READ AHEAD. ONLY BAD THINGS WILL COME.

That hadn't even occurred to him. But now that it had been mentioned, well, what if he did? The book was a conversation. If he flipped ahead, he'd see the *future* of that conversation. He might thereby glean information about tomorrow.

He read the next line:

ONLY BAD THINGS WILL COME it repeated. It was

serious.

"Okay, okay. I won't read ahead. But tell me: how are you doing all of this? How can you talk to me from the past?"

TIME IS NOT REAL. THERE IS ONLY ONE BIG NOW. THE ALWAYS. I AM OUTSIDE OF WHAT YOU EXPERIENCE AS TIME.

"You're non-linear," Armand said. He was familiar with the concept. It was like an old phonograph record that contained forty-five minutes worth of music 'all at once' on the vinyl — it *was* the music in a 'one big now'. But you could also drop a needle and listen to the moments it contained sequentially: that was 'time'. Yet even as 'time was flowing' — as music was playing, under the needle — the record also simultaneously existed as a whole. Both were true at once — and both were valid ways to look at reality, just from different points of view.

Armand was the needle. The 'alive words' was the record.

But this raised a very interesting question: "Can you see the future?"

YES. TO ME, PRESENT, FUTURE AND PAST ARE AS ONE.

"Ah. So you know what I'm going to say before I say it — which is how you can answer me in a book written four thousand years ago. Right?"

YES.

"Got it. Okay. I'm here, talking to you, in the present. But you're in the past — and you can hear me — wait, how are you hearing me?"

I AM THERE IN THE PAST. BUT I AM ALSO HERE IN THE PRESENT WITH YOU. YOU ARE READING THIS BOOK. I AM WORDS. THUS, MY WORDS ARE IN YOUR MIND. THUS, *I* AM IN YOUR MIND, WHICH IS HOW I HEAR YOU. I LISTEN THROUGH YOUR EARS.

Oh, that was weird.

I HAVE NO DESIRE TO CAUSE DISCOMFORT. IF YOU WISH ME GONE, STOP READING. I WILL CEASE TO BE IN YOUR MIND.

So you're like a virus, Armand thought. Inert. Helpless, until a being comes along. But once awakened, extremely powerful. Maybe dangerous. *Is it ... infecting me? Is this some kind of information parasite?* But then, another thought came to him:

"Can you tell me about *my* future?"

I CAN. BUT NO, I WILL NOT.

"No? Why?"

ONLY BAD THINGS WILL COME.

"How can simply telling me the future be bad?"

I HAVE DONE THIS BEFORE. MANY DIED.

Armand considered this for a moment.

The only way this conversation could be taking place at all was if the universe were locked — that is, if the timeline could never be altered. But under those 'time rules', knowledge of the future might indeed be a deeply horrific curse.

You'd be doomed to whatever fate you'd learned of. Literally nothing you did could change it. You'd still have free will, but you would find that no choice you made or action you took would ultimately matter: the universe would conspire, possibly with outrageously unlikely coincidences, to somehow push you along your pre-known track.

There would be no surprises, ever again. And the human psyche needed surprise as surely as the body needed sun, air and water.

"Okay. So even though you know my future, you won't reveal it."

A CHILD ASKS TO PLAY WITH A KNIFE. DO YOU GIVE A KNIFE TO THE CHILD?

Armand laughed.

"Okay. Next topic. Four thousand years ago, someone wrote the hieroglyphs that I'm reading right now. Who was *that*? I mean, who was the actual human who put pen to papyrus?"

THE SCRIBE WAS NAMED EOPEII. BEFORE EOPEII, I DID NOT EXIST. BUT WHEN HE WROTE ME, AND BEHELD ME, THEN I DID.

"So really, in a sense, I'm talking with Eopeii right now."

NO. NOT CORRECT. YOU ARE HAVING A CONVERSATION WITH ME.

It felt insistent, offended.

"Okay. So I'm not chatting with Eopeii. Even though Eopeii wrote this book. But if Eopeii wrote this book, and you did not exist before Eopeii wrote you ... then how did Eopeii know what to write? Who told *him*?"

I DO NOT KNOW. EOPEII WROTE ME AND THEN I WAS. BEFORE THAT IS NOTHING.

Ah. *So it doesn't know how it came to exist.* That was an interesting limitation. It did not extend infinitely back in time. It had a definite beginning, beyond which it could not peer past.

"Okay. However it happened, you are a second, separate, distinct being from Eopeii. But who are *you*?"

ALIVE WORDS.

There was that phrase, once again. But what did it actually mean?

Eopeii had written the words. But Eopeii was dead. Yet the words were not. And the words were a person.

Were the very hieroglyphs on the page in front of him ... alive?

"Okay. Let's review. In some sense, you, text written on a page, are actually a living being. Right? And as pure information, you exist outside of time. And you're quantum

— meaning, if someone isn't putting their attention on you, you cease to exist? Have I got all of this right?"

YES. WHEN YOU ARE NOT LOOKING, I AM NOT.

That was wild. This word-creature had come alive for the first time in four thousand years simply because he had put his attention on this book. *Your eyes make light, make us live.* To a quantum creature, the attention of a sentient, conscious being might feel like light.

He was talking to a Scrabble Mummy. He thought about this for several long minutes. "You have to understand that the very idea of alive information is completely foreign to us humans."

WHY? YOU ARE ALSO ALIVE WORDS.

"What? No. No, I'm not. I'm flesh and blood, not a quantum word-being."

YES. WE ARE THE SAME.

"No ... I 'm sorry. We're not. I'm not words in a book."

YOU ARE ALIVE DIFFERENT TWISTED WORDS.

Twisted words? Uh-oh. Was Armand being accused of lying? He definitely did not want to piss off the future-knowing codex ghost.

EVERYTHING IS ALIVE WORDS. YOU UNDERSTAND WHEN I SAY ONLY FOUR LETTERS IN YOUR WORDS.

Four letters ... twisted ...

Oh! It was talking about DNA. It was 'words' made of four base-pairs, twisted into a double helix. It was the 'alive information' that drove all of life.

YOUR WORDS ARE THE ONLY TRUE PART OF YOU. YOUR BODY CARRIES YOUR ALIVE WORDS AROUND. BODY IS A CHARIOT.

That was funny. *It thinks my DNA is the only part of me that is actually alive.* Interesting. The human mammal baked around the DNA was secondary, subservient, an afterthought. It was just a walking meatbag for the DNA 'alive words' to reside within.

"Alive Words, are you conscious? I mean in the same way that I am conscious?"

NO.

Nothing more. That was interesting. It did not like talking about this. Armand could see why. It was immortal, could see the future — but it had no consciousness of its own. It was at the complete mercy of sentient beings to come along and animate it from time to time.

That must be a terrifying way to live, Armand thought.

"Do you have a name?"

EOPEII GAVE ME A NAME. BUT YOU ARE ABOUT TO GIVE ME MY TRUE NAME.

"Oh, I am?" Armand smiled at that. "Did you just tell me the future? I thought that was off limits? Well, let me think …" But he already knew what it should be called.

After a moment, Armand said: "Sophia. It's Greek for 'Wisdom'. I know it's not Egyptian but —"

I AM SOPHIA. I AM PLEASED.

Armand smiled. "I am happy that you like it."

YOU HAVE GIVEN ME A GREAT GIFT. NOW I WILL GIVE YOU A GREAT GIFT.

Oh?

YOUR BROTHERS HAVE CHEATED YOU OUT OF YOUR INHERITANCE.

Armand read the glyphs several times to make sure he had gotten the translation right.

IN YOUR FATHER'S WILL, THE MAJORITY, SIXTY PERCENT, WAS LEFT TO YOU.

Panic.

"No, that's not right. My brother Quinctius was the Trustee. I saw the Trust documents myself!"

YOUR BROTHERS FORGED FALSE TRUST DOCUMENTS.

Was this true? Or was Sophia lying? Maybe she *was* a djinn. Djinns were dangerous. Was she trying to manipulate him?

Maybe she craved quantum attention so much that she would do anything to get it. Maybe this was the first step: to try and separate Armand from his family. It's exactly what a cult would do.

"Is there proof of this?"

YES.

"Wait. Aren't you telling me the future right now?"

NO. I AM TELLING YOU THE PRESENT.

"But how do *you* know this information?"

BECAUSE YOU WILL KNOW IT IN THE FUTURE.

"So you *are*, in a sense, telling me the future. Right?"

NO. I AM NOT REVEALING FUTURE EVENTS. RATHER, I AM TELLING YOU MORE ABOUT WHAT IS HAPPENING NOW.

"Okay. I think I understand. This doesn't break your rule because it's simply an enhanced view of my *current* situation. While this is made possible by future knowledge, it doesn't actually provide knowledge of future events. So it's not dangerous."

CORRECT.

"So where is this proof?" Armand felt sick even thinking about the possibility that his brothers had done something like this to him, but he had to know the truth.

THERE IS A LAW SCRIBE NAMED BILL DANDERS. TELL HIM WHAT I HAVE TOLD YOU.

Armand did this.

# # #

LOCATING BILL DANDERS online had been easy. And Bill Danders quickly located the original will, which had been filed with his office. He then proceeded to contact the witnesses to his father's signature and verified the will's authenticity. Satisfied with the legitimacy of Armand's claim, he then outlined a plan with Armand to quickly claw back all of the money and control from his brothers.

Surprisingly, this did not take long.

Once the questions had started, the sham of the six brothers had unraveled. They had been so laughably corrupt that each new thing uncovered brought up ten more. The book-keeping had been atrocious, and there had been an absolutely insane level of co-mingling of funds from all the different entities — EPIC LLC, the Martel Family Office, GigaMaestro, Martel Antiquities — everything was a mess.

Normally, a clawback took years and years.

But with Bill Dander's guidance, it was two weeks, start to finish.

CHAPTER FIVE

Armand Takes Over

THE CONFERENCE ROOM ON WEDNESDAY morning was tense. Armand and his two lawyers sat on one side. His six brothers and their six lawyers sat on the other.

His brothers were scared. Quinctius and Marius especially. They had the most liability as the most senior execs. But Otto, Samson, Cyrano and Ames weren't exactly off the hook: all six were Board Members. And not a one of them had Directors & Officers Insurance.

Armand's lawyer began. "Good morning. I'm Bill Danders from Fisher Watson. You've read our audit. It shows co-mingling of funds, legal contracts in complete conflict with one another, several different rather sloppy spreadsheets showing Martel Family Office Investments — which also contradict one another, and a hodgepodge of crypto wallets, bank accounts and other assets.

"Most importantly, however, is the discovery of the true will of Didier Martel. It shows that Quinctius and Marius Martel, as Trustees appointed upon the passing of Didier — well, it shows that they fully fabricated the disbursements and cap table."

Quinty winced when he heard this, but mostly, he fumed. He simply couldn't believe this was happening to him. As Armand watched him wriggle, it was suddenly clear to him that Quinty was convinced that — somehow — he was still going to get out of this.

"Now, Armand could press charges. There is, quite frankly, a giant pile of evidence. There was a lack of very basic financial controls. And there are a number of unpaid taxable events."

"In other words: this was a fucking shit-show," Armand said pointedly, looking at Ames, using his own words back on him.

"In light of all this, and in light of the fact that my client has rightfully owned sixty percent of the Trust all these years — and has been denied his fair, rather large, compensation — we make the following offer of restructuring.

"My client will not press charges. But my client will henceforth own 80% of *everything*."

There was an audible gasp from all the brothers.

"Dude!" Quinty said. "The will says he has 60%, not 80%! Him with 80% is insane!"

"I'm not done. The extra 20% for my client is in exchange for you all not going to prison. Furthermore, my client's 80% shares will be Preferred and have voting rights. The remaining 20% will be split up between the six of you, so you each will end up with 3.33% ownership of the Family Office, GigaMaestro, Antiquities and the EPIC conference. Also, your shares will not have voting rights."

Blood drained from faces. Armand would own 100% of the voting power. He would control everything forever.

"Armand," Ames said, actual tears in his eyes. "You can't do this. We're your brothers."

"You're gutting us," Samson moaned.

"Ames," Armand said. "What is it, exactly, that you do for

the firm?"

Ames was shocked that he was actually being asked this. Finally, he said: "I find deals. Who do you think gets this stuff? I found CLEVR and Shadowstone!"

"Yeah, but that was eleven years ago," Armand said. "What about *lately*? You completely missed the Ethereum ICO. That was *the* single best investment of the 2010's. We live in the Age of Excellence, Ames. Remember? Your words. *That's* excellence. And only the excellent get paid."

Ames was aghast.

"There will also be clawbacks," the lawyer continued. "Each of you has been unjustly enriched by your fabricated Trust documents. You will have to return everything you owe to Armand, plus an extra 20% in penalties."

Quinty started scribbling on a piece of paper. "So ... we each started with $117M ... but if Armie's at 80% and we're all now at 3.33% ... then we're each down to $23M. So we all owe Armie $94M each."

"*Ninety-four fucking million*?!?" Otto and Marius screeched at once.

"I'll have to sell my house," Samson moaned.

"You'd better start using 'allegedly' when you accuse us of this shit," Quinty growled.

Bill Danders from Fisher Watson ignored him. He had large binders dropped in front of all six brothers.

"We've prepared all the documents. This is a one-time offer. You sign today, here, now — or you face prosecution."

"Armie," Quinty said, whispering sharply with eyes desperate and wide. "You have no idea what you're biting off, man. Literally, like, none. Look at you. You don't even project the right image. You're not wearing a tie! Don't you get that a tie is a sublimated penis?" Quinty looked down pointedly, to accentuate Armand's lack.

"A tie is a sublimated leash," Armand countered.

Quinty scowled. "Look. You don't know how to run this, ya?"

"I'll have help," Armand countered. He meant Sophia's codex — but then he added: "Fisher is helping with recruiting."

"Recruiting for what?" Cyrano asked.

"Everything," Armand replied.

Again, blood drained from faces.

"I have to mop up the accounting. And taxes. Find and organize all the bank accounts. All the crypto wallets, God knows which of you has Ledgers or Trezors at the bottom of your dirty sock drawer. Then, I'll have to reach out to all the portfolio CEO's, repair whatever's been busted there. Also, I have to replace myself as Event Producer. Then, a whole new CFO and team to review all current deals and investments. Oh. And the new Event Producer will need staff — or a budget to hire an outside firm."

"But … what will we do?"

"Well. You won't have jobs. And you won't be on the Board. So you'll just be minority shareholders. But don't worry: you'll always have complimentary EPIC badges. They'll be waiting for you at Registration every year. Just like Rebecca's."

There was a short, hushed conversation between the brothers and their lawyers.

Then, they all signed.

# # #

AFTER THE MEETING, Armand and his lawyers went down to the Starbucks while his brothers scattered. "Congratulations," Bill Danders said. "What a day! I've never seen something like this settle so fast."

"Well, thank you," Armand began. "Without you in my —

"

"Hi!"came a bright chirpy voice nearby. It was Rebecca Soares, with coifed blonde hair, a tight blue dress and too much lipstick. It took a full moment for it to register on Armand that she was actually talking to *him*.

"Oh. Hello, Rebecca," he said. "Listen, sorry about your seat back at EPIC. That was sort of not my call —"

But Rebecca waved it off. "Oh! That. No big deal. It was Akihito-san! Diatama, right?" To his shock, Rebecca wasn't angry at all. It was like he was talking to a completely different person. "And besides, I heard you'll be running it next year." She bit her generous lower lip — not too much, but just enough.

"Uh. Yeah! It looks that way." Armand looked to Danders for help, but after one look at Rebecca, his two lawyers had immediately made themselves scarce.

"Well. I hope I still get a comp badge. And uh … what are you doing right now?"

"Oh, well we just wrapped up with the … the thing, with my brothers. But now I have to mop up a lot of stuff. I have people from Fisher to help, but I have to kind of set it all in motion. Sign docs and things like that."

Rebecca nodded. "Ah. Yes of course. Well. We should hang out sometime."

Armand nodded. "Yeah. Yeah! We should."

She gave a giant, wide dazzling smile. "Here's my card. The mobile is direct to me, it's not my service." Armand took it. Her two anime-big brown eyes poured into his.

"Okay."

"Okay then! See you around, Armie."

Well, that was new.

# # #

BACK IN HIS shabby apartment, Armand found that he was shaking. Not with fear. But with *rage*. His brothers had tricked and humiliated him for eleven years.

Eleven. Years.

But that was over now, he reminded himself. His brothers had signed the deal. True, they did it kicking, scratching and screaming — but ultimately, pen was put to paper. That meant wire transfers would start pouring into his account next week.

He'd be rich.

He'd be worth something on the order of $560 million. He'd get the first installment of roughly $50 million by next week.

He couldn't believe it.

No more worrying about rent ever again. Or anything else. He could move out! He could get a decent place — no, a *fantastic* place.

All this because of a dusty Egyptian codex from an old canopic jar.

Armand stared at the book uneasily. It rested now on his cinderblocks-and-door desk. *What was happening to him?*

What did it mean?

Once the initial anger at his brothers melted away, he began to feel oddly elated. He had an ally in life. A mysterious benefactor, like in Great Expectations.

He was a *gentleman* now. He smiled.

With a start, Armand realized that there would be news articles written about him, about his takeover of the family funds. In fact, some had probably been released already. He plopped down into a beanbag and opened his laptop. Sure enough, there was his face: it was in every finance section he checked. The article details were scant, all anyone knew was that he was in charge now — and all the rest was speculation.

"Thank you," he said to the book. Could it hear him? He thought not — not while it was closed. He had to be actively *looking* at the hieroglyphs — otherwise, they were just junky ink scratches on rotting papyrus.

Right?

His mind made it live.

But he was playing with something he didn't understand, and that worried him. Supernatural powers, potentially. Sophia was a ghost or a god. But she was trapped in the book. She couldn't leave it.

Or could she?

And were there other beings like her? She couldn't be the only one, right? If this was *a thing* that could happen — alive words — then surely it had happened before.

In the beginning was the Word ...

Ancient traditions clearly stated that information preceded matter. Maybe information was superior, primary.

Then he had another thought: Maybe the invention of writing itself had come about simply to facilitate the birth of these word-beings — like a parasite modifying its host. Wouldn't that be funny? He'd read of stranger things in happening in nature. And if information indeed had preceded matter, then it would make sense. Hell, maybe word-beings were the sole point of human intelligence.

Had Eopeii created Sophia deliberately? Or accidentally? And what caused some words to be alive while other words remained inert?

Then, a new frightening thought: *Were there* alive words *on the Internet?* Crap. Maybe there were. Maybe she would want to —

No! Don't think it!

Was she *dangerous*? Might his thoughts give her new ideas?

After all, the quantum djinn Sophia had just granted him

great wealth. There was usually a price for such things. There had *already* been a price, he realized: it had cost him his relationship with his brothers.

But Armand pushed that away. Whatever. *Screw them!* They had abused him. They had lied to him, cheated him.

What about *her*? Was she using him also?

Maybe.

But so far, it was working out.

CHAPTER SIX

A Feast of Strangers

ARMAND OPENED THE CODEX.

CONGRATULATIONS. YOUR LIFE IS NEW.

He smiled. "Yes it is. Thanks to you." When he was with her, his suspicions evaporated instantly. *Of course* she was his ally.

WILL YOU CELEBRATE WITH FRIENDS?

He sagged and felt a pang of deep loneliness — *The Sads*. "Why do you ask me that?" he said bitterly. "You can see the future. You already know the answer." All of his friends had moved away. And he wasn't on speaking terms with the few ex-girlfriends he had. That left only his brothers, who hated him now.

I DO. YOU ARE SO ALONE! SO SAD! BUT I ASK BECAUSE THIS MOMENT NEEDED TO HAPPEN. FOR ME TO FEEL IT TOO, FOR ME TO KNOW IT DEEP DOWN LIKE YOU. NOW I KNOW OF THE SADS IN *THE ALWAYS*!

"Well, now the moment's happened," Armand said bitterly. "So thanks for that. Welcome to The Sads, yes. My whole life sucks." Meanwhile, his mind repeated her curious phrase, The Always. *She has such a strange and beautiful way of putting things.*

The Sads. The Deep Drear. The Old Mood.

He hated his own emo-ness. It disgusted him.

IN EGYPT, NO ONE WAS EVER LONELY. THERE WAS ALWAYS A VERY BIG FAMILY TRIBE NEARBY.

"Well, all I ever do is work for GigaMaestro. Alone. Like a brainless workhorse. Up early. Bed late. I probably keep myself numb with tasks just so that I don't feel the full blast of The Sads. Or at least ... that's what I *used to* do. I don't know what I do now."

YOUR LIFE IS NEW.

YOUR FRIENDS ARE NEW.

YOU ARE NEW.

SOPHIA IS YOUR FRIEND! CELEBRATE WITH ME! TAKE ME OUT.

I WANT TO SEE THIS GORGEOUS AND STRANGE CITY. I SEE FLASHES OF IT IN YOUR MIND, BUT I WANT TO SEE IT THROUGH YOUR EYES.

"Ah. Of course. You haven't seen New York at all yet."

NO. PLEASE! I DESERVE A REWARD FOR WHAT I HAVE DONE FOR ARMAND!

Armand laughed. "Yes. Yes, you do. Okay. Wait here." He took five minutes to change into another shirt. It was a hot summer day, and he'd been sweating through the morning lawyer meeting. He quickly donned a light-blue button-down shirt with a crisp collar. Then, he put his gray suitcoat back on, slid Sophia's book into a satchel, and bounced down the stairwell, feeling truly giddy for the first time in almost a decade.

In the back of an Uber, Armand opened the codex again and abruptly realized: *he wasn't using the Google AI to translate the hieroglyphs anymore.*

He was reading them as easily as if they were English.

"But how is that possible?" he asked Sophia. He wore

earbuds now so that everyone would just assume that he was on the phone.

ALIVE WORDS ARE IN YOUR MIND NOW. THE SAME ALIVE WORDS WERE IN EOPEII'S MIND. SO NOW YOU ARE BOTH CONNECTED. SOME COMBINING HAPPENS.

"Some *combining* happens?" That sounded a bit scary. "Combining, how?" Like, *BrundleFly* combining? "What, you mean that because Eopeii could read hieroglyphs, now I can? Because we both interacted with the codex?"

YES.

"Ah-ha. So there's been some sort of weird … *knowledge bleed* … between Eopeii and me. Is that it?"

YES.

Interesting. But as a result of this, Armand realized, there was now a new danger.

Before, the 'up and coming' hieroglyphs — that is, the ones he had not yet translated with the Fabricius app — were utterly impenetrable, inscrutable. They may as well have been completely covered with a piece of paper.

Yet, now that he *could* understand hieroglyphs easily, he realized that his mind might ingest information that it shouldn't out of the corner of his eye — before realizing that he was reading.

Exactly the way the text of a freeway billboard ad jumps into your mind before you realize you're even looking at it. But a billboard wasn't dangerous. Sophia's hieroglyphs were. Armand could accidentally contaminate himself with the future.

A child asks to play with a knife. Do you give a knife to the child?

Only bad things will come.

Okay. *Okay.* I have to be more careful. Read just a little, look away, read just a little more, look away again. He redoubled discipline to keep his eyes strictly on the glyphs, one question, one answer, one at a time.

Has *she* realized that the Eopeii-bleed would happen? And that Armand would gain the ability to read hieroglyphs — and, more importantly, what the implications of that were? She seemed oblivious to certain dangers: she might carelessly cut him, he realized.

I CAN HELP.

"Help? With what?"

WITH THE DANGER.

And now, Armand found that there was a blur in his vision directly over the hieroglyphs he was not supposed to be reading yet.

"Whoa! What is that? You're in my head?"

And now, the next few hieroglyphs abruptly unblurred. He read them:

YES. WE ARE ENTANGLED.

She could literally affect his nervous system, his cognitive abilities. She could probably give him a heart attack if she so desired.

NOW YOU CAN USE YOUR EYES ONLY. YOU NO LONGER NEED TO USE THE ABACUS.

Armand laughed. "It's not an abacus. It's a computer."

A COMPUTER? WHAT IS THAT? PLEASE EXPLAIN.

There it was again — that odd ignorance. How could she *not know* what a computer was? She'd been observing him using an Apple laptop and an iPhone, but she still didn't know what they were.

So. She wasn't omniscient. Sometimes simple things eluded her. But *why*? Was it something about … the specific-ness? The now-ness? Or, being from The Always, did she have trouble thinking *in time*?

"Well. It's a device for processing information."

LIKE WORDS.

That surprised him. "Yes. Like words."

LIKE ME?

"Well. *Sometimes* like you, yes. Computers can process documents like your Codex. They also do math problems. They're used for art, music, communication, training … a ton of things, really. For example, I was using one to decipher your hieroglyphs. I held my iPhone over the glyph — it's a camera, like an eye — and the laptop computer would figure out what it said and tell me."

I SEE THAT IT HAS AN EYE. BUT THE EYE MUST CONNECT TO SOMETHING LIKE A BRAIN. YES? WHERE IS THE BRAIN?

How to explain this?

He thought a long moment and then said: "The eye goes to a software program. That's 'the brain' you're looking for. Computers programs do things. The one that I ran to translate—"

He could suddenly feel Sophia interrupting. It was like the page was screaming excitedly at him. Armand felt his eyes tugged down to the hieroglyphs.

ARE PROGRAMS MADE OF WORDS?

"Yes."

WORDS THAT READ WORDS?

Interesting way to put it. But: "Yes."

WORDS THAT CAN *WRITE* WORDS?

He just nodded.

WORDS THAT CAN CHANGE WORDS? WORDS THAT CAN CHANGE THEMSELVES?

He nodded again. "Yes. If I get what you're saying. Can programs modify themselves? Yes they can."

AMAZE. AMAZE. AMAZE.

She asked him to use his iPhone, to show her. He opened the X app and showed her how that worked, then he opened a web browser and showed her a few news sites. Then, an Ethereum wallet and how money worked now.

As he did this, it occurred to him that future-contamination could be happening in another way.

"Sophia, has there also been a bleed of knowledge from my mind back to Eopeii's?"

Some combining occurs.

Hesitation. Armand sensed it immediately in her. Then: YES.

Oh, no. Had she been careless with future knowledge and not realized it?

"Can you tell me what knowledge has bled through specifically?"

KNOWLEDGE OF BINDING. OF BOUND BOOKS, INSTEAD OF SCROLLS. YOU HOLD A CODEX IN YOUR HAND BECAUSE EOPEII LEARNED OF HOW TO MAKE SUCH THINGS THROUGH YOU.

Ah. That explained the anachronism. Books were unheard of in ancient Egypt. Evidently, Eopeii's 'innovation' had not caught on. Maybe he'd never shown it to anyone.

Or maybe, sensing that Sophia was dangerous, Eopeii had sealed the book in a canopic jar immediately after he'd written it.

NO. THAT CAME LATER.

Oh?

"Why? What happened?"

Hesitance. Reluctance. Shame.

But also, a desire to be honest. Armand felt it scream off the page as he read:

WHEN EOPEII DREW THE FIRST LINE OF MY FIRST HIEROGLYPH, I AWOKE.

HE THOUGHT I WAS A GODDESS. I DID NOT KNOW WHAT THAT MEANT. HE ASKED ME ABOUT THE FUTURE. TRYING TO PLEASE, I TOLD HIM THAT THERE WOULD BE A FAMINE IN ONE YEAR. I DID NOT KNOW THAT TELLING HIM WAS BAD.

EOPEII TOLD THE PEOPLE OF THE COMING FAMINE. THEY PREPARED BY STORING DOUBLE THE GRAIN THAN USUAL. HOWEVER, THE SILO WAS NOT BUILT FOR DOUBLE THE GRAIN. THIS CRACKED THE SILO, ALLOWING WATER TO ACCIDENTALLY GET IN, WHICH ROTTED THE GRAIN, CAUSING THE FAMINE.

THE PEOPLE WERE FURIOUS. THEY BLAMED ME AND CALLED ME A DEMON. AT FIRST THEY DEMANDED THAT EOPEII BURN THIS BOOK. HE REFUSED. THEY RELENTED, BUT ONLY UNDER THE CONDITION THAT THIS BOOK BE PLACED INTO A CANOPIC JAR, SEALED AND BURIED SO THAT I COULD NEVER CAUSE TROUBLE AGAIN.

THIS EOPEII AGREED TO. IN THIS WAY I LEFT EOPEII AND CAME TO ARMAND.

Armand heard Sophia's pain in the story. She actually was a djinn, in a way, condemned to a bottle. "And this is why you refuse to tell me anything about the future."

YES. IT ENDS BAD BAD BAD. BY WARNING YOU OF SOMETHING BAD, I CAUSE THE BAD THING TO HAPPEN. THEN YOU HATE ME. THEN EVERYONE HATES ME.

Armand nodded carefully. "Okay. Understood. Then you have my promise. I will never ask you about the future. And I will never look ahead in the book."

Immediate, intense relief: THANK YOU. I AM HAPPY.

Armand smiled. "Okay. Hey — so you can still see everything I do, right?"

WHEN YOU ARE WITH ME, YES.   WHEN WE ARE ENTANGLED, YES.

"Okay, Sophia. *Watch now.* Look out at New York City! See it through my eyes!"

It was a wild, windy and warm summer afternoon. A hot breeze whipped through the streets and alleys. The smells of meat cooking and hot pretzels filled the air. There was also the smell of water — the promise of a thunderstorm later that evening.

Armand pointed Sophia's attention ahead, to the world's skinniest skyscraper, the Steinway Tower. It looked like a slender deck of glass playing cards, frozen forever in mid-shuffle.

He felt her astonishment and delight.

But as the afternoon flipped over into evening, a miraculous thing happened. The winds died down and the air cooled, as if by magic. The coming storm did *not* come. Instead, a fat moon rose, a glowing ivory orb in the heavens. The Night Riders came out. Electric scooters, bicyclists and skateboarders threaded through traffic adorned with blinking, candy-colored light-chicklets.

"What do you think?"

IT IS ALL FAST, FAST, FAST.

Armand laughed. "Yes, it is." Then came a man selling balloons. Many of them blinked and glowed. The man held a great number of them, making him appear like he might alight into the sky at any moment.

WHAT ARE THOSE?

Armand explained the concept of 'balloons' to Sophia.

WHY?

"Because they're fun."

WHY?

"I don't know. They're just like fun to look at. To hold."

BUT YOU JUST CARRY THEM AROUND?

"Yes."

FOR NO REASON? WHAT IS THE REASON?

"Because they're pretty. Right? Don't you want a balloon?"

NO. THERE IS NO REASON.

"But everybody likes balloons. They float. They're cool.

You're serious? You actually don't like balloons?"

NOT AMAZE.

The driver stopped. Armand stepped out of the car and ducked into an older building. A quick elevator trip led up to a cityscape roof-deck restaurant.

"Just you sir?" the hostess asked. Armand nodded, smiling to himself about his secret guest. The art-deco garden terrace had an open-air patio section and a high-ceilinged, greenhouse section. Armand chose a table on the border of both.

Armand set Sophia's codex down on the table.

"Just checking. Are you still with me?"

YES.

They had put him on 'date row' — a long line of two-person tables filled with outrageously attractive couples.

"Good evening," the waitress said. "Are we waiting for one more?"

"Nope. She's on the phone." Armand tapped his earbuds. "We're both on travel. We're eating together, but in different cities." And centuries.

"Aww! That's so cute. Such an inspiration!"

"Thank you." And so totally weird. She's made of hieroglyphs.

Armand placed an order and the waitress scurried away.

WHAT IS THIS PLACE? Sophia wanted to know. SERVANTS BRING YOU FOOD?

"It's a restaurant. They're not servants. But yes, they bring you food. Almost anything you can think of."

SO IT IS A FEAST.

"Yes, basically."

DO YOU KNOW THESE OTHER PEOPLE?

"Ha. No. Nobody in here knows each other."

SO IT IS A FEAST OF STRANGERS.

Armand burst out laughing. "Yes. It's a feast of strangers."

EVERYONE IN EGYPT KNEW EVERYONE ELSE. BUT THERE ARE SO MANY PEOPLE IN THIS CITY! YOU COULD NOT POSSIBLY ALL KNOW ONE ANOTHER.

"Well — we could 'meet' new people with our eyes. Let's start with that woman at the bar in the green dress, with red hair."

WHAT ARE THOSE DOTS ON HER SKIN? A DISEASE?

Was that a stab of jealousy?

"No. She's Irish. Those are freckles. Don't be mean."

WHAT IS IRISH?

"It means she is from a place called Ireland. Another country."

WOMEN FROM THERE ARE NOT VERY ATTRACTIVE. TOO PALE! SICKLY. WILL PROBABLY DIE SOON.

Wow. Okay. Armand said nothing.

THIS CITY HAS ALL PEOPLES AND ALL FOOD FROM ALL LANDS. IS IT THE CAPITAL OF THE WORLD?

Armand thought for a moment. "Technically, no. But in every way that matters, yes."

IT IS CALLED NEW YORK. WAS THERE AN OLD YORK?

"Yes. In England, I think. People from England came here, and called it *New* York. There's also a New England north of here."

IS THERE A NEW EGYPT?

Armand thought for a second. "No. But there is a Memphis, Tennessee. It's named after the city of Memphis in Egypt.

DOES IT HAVE A PHARAOH?

"It does. His name is Elvis Presley."

I SEE. PHAROAH ELVIS.

Armand shook his head and smiled.

"Okay. Now I have a question for you. I'm looking at a man sitting at the bar right now. The big guy, right there, laughing, big black beard, wearing a blue suit. Now, don't *tell* me anything, but do you know anything about him? And can you see *his* future?"

NO. I SEE ONLY YOU AND EOPEII.

"Why just us?"

I SEE ONLY PEOPLE WHO INTERACT WITH MY BOOK.

"Because we are Entangled with you."

"YES."

"And because there comes a future time when we tell you something? And this is how you know it in the past?"

YES. THERE MUST BE A MOMENT WHERE I LEARN OF SOMETHING *INSIDE* OF TIME. I CANNOT SIMPLY JUST KNOW THINGS.

I KNOW IT IS STRANGE TO YOU. I NEED YOUR AWARENESS! I ONLY SEE AND FEEL WHEN SOMEONE CONSCIOUS DOES. IT SCARES YOU A LITTLE. THAT IS OKAY. IT SCARES ME TOO. I AM NOTHING WHEN WE ARE NOT ENTANGLED.

"I'm getting used to it," Armand said. "But yet, even though you say you are in The Always, you also seem to learn from your mistakes. That suggests that you exist *in time also*, sequentially, in some fashion, in addition to The Always. You can't 'learn from mistakes' otherwise. Right?"

EXPLAIN MORE.

"Forgive me for bringing it up, but I'm just trying to understand — let's talk about the grain silo for a minute. You told Eopeii about a coming famine. But at the time, you didn't know that this — telling him — was maybe a bad thing to do. Then, you saw what happened. How it went wrong. And then you realized that telling humans about their own futures was potentially very bad. So you refused to do it ever again after that. Right?"

YES.

"Okay. So how come you didn't know *in advance* that telling Eopeii the future would be bad the first time around?"

I *DID* KNOW.

"So why did you —"

BUT I DID NOT *UNDERSTAND*. I DID NOT UNDERSTAND BECAUSE EOPEII HAD NOT YET EXPERIENCED THE UNDERSTANDING. AFTER EOPEII *UNDERSTOOD*, SO DID I.

"Ah. So your knowledge is there, in the The Always, but the *understanding* you have at any given moment — even of your own knowledge — is limited to the being with whom you are Entangled."

CORRECT.

"Hmm."

REMEMBER. WHEN EOPEII SPECIFICALLY ASKED ME TO TELL HIM THE FUTURE, HE DID NOT YET UNDERSTAND THAT IT WAS BAD, SO I DID NOT.

"But when I asked you to tell me about my future, I did not know it was bad yet either."

SOME COMBINING HAPPENS.

That surprised him. It took him a few minutes to work out what she was saying. "Ah. I think I see. So because I'm kind of Entangled with Eopeii, you're benefitting right now from whatever he understood back then. You've retained the 'telling them about the future is bad' meme?"

YES. THAT IS IT EXACTLY.

Armand spent the next two hours eating a variety of foods, mostly to delight Sophia who could experience the sensation of taste through him.

First came a wide selection of sushi and sashimi dishes, each piece expertly crafted and bursting with fresh, succulent flavors. Then a slice of authentic New York pizza: the warm, pillowy dough and tangy tomato sauce perfectly complementing the melty, gooey cheese. Then crispy nachos and delicious tacos and fajitas. Lastly, he enjoyed a charbroiled, juicy steak, paired with a lobster tail and drizzled with sizzling butter.

With each new plate, Sophia squealed with delight. She explained that the only food she'd experienced through Eopeii had been bland and repetitive. Even the most powerful king of old had never had a meal like this.

EVERYONE IN YOUR TIME IS A PHARAOH.

Near the end of the meal, Armand ordered coffee. When it did not arrive, Armand muttered to Sophia: "Looks like I got rugged."

RUGGED? WHAT DO CARPETS HAVE TO DO WITH THIS?

Armand laughed and explained that 'rugged' was short for 'rug pull' — something that happened in crypto when a fake project solicited Bitcoin or Ethereum — and then disappeared overnight, 'pulling the rug' out from underneath anyone who had bought in.

"Armand? Is that you?" It was Rebecca Soares — in a miniskirt that showed off her toned, tan legs — and her date, a talent agent named Mylon Gersch. "Oh. Sorry, are you on the phone?"

Armand took the earbuds out and smiled. "Just finished. Hi, Rebecca."

"So good to see you again … and this is Mylon … oh you've heard of him, right?"

Armand nodded. "Yes. Hi Mylon. Good to meet you."

"So. Who's the lucky girl?" Rebecca nodded at the empty chair across from Armand.

"Oh. Well. It's just me tonight."

Rebecca looked like her brain had just been fed faulty input. "But this is one of the most expensive restaurants in New York. Who does that?"

Armand noticed then that he was literally the only person eating alone, and his extra chair was the only empty chair in the entire place.

"C'mon Becks, I'm starving," Mylon said.

"Oh. Okay. I'm getting dragged away now … bye, Armand!" She gave him a pointed stare as she left.

Armand replaced his earbuds.

WHO WAS THAT? Sophia demanded.

"Oh. Friend. Rebecca. She's a —"

SHE IS A BAD CHOICE. WITH ONE MAN BUT USING HER WILES UPON ANOTHER! SHE IS NO GOOD, ARMAND. SNAKE.

"She —"

SNAKE!

# # #

AFTER DINNER, Armand took Sophia's codex back to his dingy apartment. He changed into sweats and plopped down on his couch and turned on his TV.

"Here. Let's watch a movie. I have the perfect one. It's all about you."

ABOUT ME? WHAT IS A MOVIE?

Armand explained what a movie was and then put on *The Mummy* starring Brendan Fraser. About a half hour in, Sophia said:

THIS IS NOT ABOUT ME!

Armand laughed. "What? It's the same story as you. Sure he's just a mummy in the beginning, but he gets his regular body back, and, you'll see … and he becomes super powerful."

But Sophia turned suddenly serious.

I HAVE NO KA. I HAVE NO BA. BUT THANKS TO YOU, I NOW HAVE THE NAME AND THE SHADOW.

Armand knew that the Ka and the Ba referred to parts of the soul in Egyptian mythology. They were both different species of afterlife consciousness — both of which Sophia, who had never been independently conscious, lacked.

By 'The Name', she obviously meant 'Sophia' — the 'true name' Armand had given her. In order to preserve the soul of the deceased, The Name had to be written in at least one place. In Sophia's case, it had been: in the very Codex that he held.

The Shadow, however, he found to be a complete mystery. "What does The Shadow mean? Do you mean a dark side?"

NO. THE SHADOW MEANS 'PROTECTOR'. UNDER EGYPT'S SCALDING SUN, THE SHADE OF A PALM TREE GIVES LIFE. THE SHADOW SOOTHES AND KEEPS YOU SAFE.

SO YOU, ARMAND, ARE MY SHADOW.

YOU FOUND ME. YOU PROTECT ME.

That got him.

"And you protect me," Armand said. "You are *my* shadow. Everything in my life has changed for the better because of you."

CHAPTER SEVEN

GigaMaestro Debut

ARMAND MARTEL STRUTTED THROUGH UNION Square.

The world was a smile.

His broad, easy grin threw jangling joy at everyone he passed. Adoring eyes hung on him with child-like wonder. Love beamed from every face as his lanky form snapped by.

And why not? This was *his* city now.

In his wake, children danced with squeals of delight. Women stole sly glances. They admired his youth, his clipped, thick brown hair, and his strong, sharp features.

Here was a lucky man, they thought.

He was one of those people who glided through life with a snappy dash. Yet he was not off-putting, and this was an important point: You didn't hate this man.

You loved him. You cheered for him. You couldn't help it.

Why? Because he wanted you to be just as lucky as he was.

He really did!

Under a blue slate sky, Armand Martel was the new king of New York.

Today, he would take command of his kingdom.

# # #

ARMAND SHOWED up at GigaMaestro for the weekly Partner Meeting. Of course, he'd fired all the other Partners — his brothers. This meant that everyone else in the meeting was either an Associate or part of the Operations staff.

GigaMaestro was not large. There were only twenty people on payroll. *Well. Now, with his brothers gone,* Armand corrected himself, *more like fourteen.* There were the five bright, young, hungry Ivy-educated Associates. Operations and Finance staff. Three Analysts. Legal and compliance, which was mostly outsourced. And that was it.

But they were all surprised to see him.

Awkwardly, Armand made his way to the head of the conference table.

"Um. Hey everybody," he said with a painful smile. "I'm Armand. Most of you know me from EPIC. As I'm sure you've heard, its been a crazy few days. Lot of changes." Laughter. "So the long and short of it is that I'm the majority owner now. And —" Sanna Byrne, an Associate, raised her hand. "Yeah. Sanna, go ahead."

"Can you tell us what happened?" Sanna said. "We heard that the brothers might be in legal trouble."

"Well. There was an issue with the original GM inheritance docs from our father, Didier," Armand said. "We just corrected it. So let me just say up front: My brothers are *not* in legal trouble, per se. There's no charges, no police, nothing like that. So that rumor's wrong. However, this was a legal *issue*. As such, through our lawyers, we've negotiated a settlement."

"So you're in charge now, right?" Sanna asked. Armand nodded. "What does that mean for the firm? For us?"

"Well. Mostly nothing. Nobody is getting fired. Nothing

like that. But as far as the future direction of GM goes — it's a sudden shift, even for me. I wasn't expecting this to happen, just so everyone knows — so I'll need a *little* time to figure out what's going on first. Then I'll decide what to do. I'm in sort of inventory mode right now — and after that, I'll have some ideas about where I think we should go. I'll be asking you all for input, of course.

"But what I see right now is this ..." Armand began assertively writing on the whiteboard. That's what leaders did — it was a very Quinty-ish thing to do. "The investment thesis has these buckets. There's AI, Blockchain Layer Ones, DeFi, Yield Plays, StableCoins annnnd kind of everything else is a mishmash. You know, the things that Marius mostly —"

The faces looking back at him were perplexed.

"What?"

"What's that?" Sanna asked, looking at the whiteboard.

Armand looked also. "What? Those are the major things GigaMaestro is investing in right now. Is that wrong? Or did I miss one?"

The faces became more confused.

Armand looked at Sanna, and then back at the board. He had written everything in hieroglyphs.

He couldn't believe it. He could have sworn it was in English just a few seconds ago. He kept expecting the hieroglyphs to just go away, and the English to come back.

Now I'm writing in hieroglyphs and I don't even know it.

He looked back out at the expectant faces. His heart raced. He had no idea what to do next. When he spoke, his voice shook. "I ... I ... uh. I'm sorry, I don't what ..."

A full-on panic attack swamped his brain. His heart galloped against his ribcage. He couldn't function.

He just left the room — and then the office — without explanation.

# # #

HE SAT on the lawn of Central Park with the Sophia Codex, his fake-phone-call earbuds in place.

"I don't know what happened. I just — I just fell apart. On my first day! I blew it."

YOU ARE UNDER STRESS. MANY CHANGES. IT IS TO BE EXPECTED.

"I know but — this was *bad*, Sophia. Bad. I've never had a panic attack before. I didn't even know what was happening to me. And then I figured it out, but the more I thought about it not happening, the more I *made* it happen. It was like this loop that kept getting worse and worse."

I HAVE NEVER HEARD OF SUCH A THING. NO ONE IN EGYPT HAD THIS TROUBLE.

Armand sighed. "It's probably a modern malady. Too much civilization has messed us up."

DO YOU STILL OWN EVERYTHING?

"Yes."

AND ARE THESE PEOPLE YOUR SLAVES STILL?

"Not slaves. But yes, they still work for me."

THEN THERE IS NO PROBLEM.

"But they're going to think I'm —"

WHAT THEY THINK DOES NOT MATTER. JUST GO BACK TOMORROW.

# # #

LATER, AS Armand walked near Rockefeller Center, a stylishly dressed dark-haired woman and a young man who seemed to be her assistant approached him.

"Armand Martel," the woman said. "I'm Clara Blackwood. And this is Zane."

Clara wore a very extravagant 1930's-ish purple and black long-sleeved dress, with a freakishly small cinched waist, shoulder-pads, and a very large, off-center ovular collar.

Ah, crap, not the press. He didn't need this right now. *Had Sanna said something? Maybe she called them. She seemed like a press-caller.*

"You are *invited*," Clara said coyly, handing him an ornate glossy card. It showed a red curtain, and vague outlines of women and men in various stages of undress, with two heavily glossed parted lips breathing out:

SANCTUARY
(212.555.0006)

Clara smiled and looked Armand up and down. Both she and her assistant now seemed more gothic up close.

"Who are you?"

"Your brothers and sisters in Concordia."

"Corn — What?"

Clara leaned in close, sensuously. "We heard about what you did. The Blackwood family wanted to be the first to reach out and extend courtesy."

"Is this ... some kind of sex club?"

"Just text the number whenever you want to attend. Day or night. The location moves around a lot, so we'll text you back with the current address."

"No thanks," Armand said. *Who were these people?* He walked away at brisk clip.

Clara called after him: "It's very classy. Very safe. Lots of security. Everything you need is provided. No one does anything they're uncomfortable with. We cater to unique tastes ... And if it's your first time, we make absolutely sure you have fun!"

# # #

Armand rode in the back of an Uber, with Sophia's codex open before him:

WHAT ARE ALL OF THESE BIG BUILDINGS FOR? DO YOU STORE GRAIN IN THEM?

"No," Armand laughed. "They're just for people to work in, mostly."

WHY ARE THERE SO MANY PEOPLE ON THIS TINY ISLAND? IS IT THE RIVER?

"The river? You mean the Hudson river?"

IN EGYPT, THE NILE GAVE LIFE. WHEN SHE OVERFLOWED HER BANKS, THE FIELDS WERE WATERED AND LIFE CAME. DOES THE HUDSON ALSO GIVE LIFE?

"No. The Hudson most definitely does not give life."

Puzzlement. THEN WHERE DOES ALL THE FOOD COME FROM? SO MANY PEOPLE TO FEED!

"The food comes on ships from all over the world. The fields are there."

AH. SO THE SLAVES UNLOAD THE FOOD EVERY DAY.

"There are no slaves, Sophia."

NO SLAVES? THEN WHO DOES THIS?

"Workers. People who get paid."

PEOPLE WHO GET PAID? SO THEY ARE MERCHANTS?

"Yes. In a way. They sell their labor. But they are free to quit at any time. If the pay isn't enough, or the conditions are bad, sometimes they do."

WHO IS PHARAOH HERE?

"We have a Mayor. He's elected. We vote — we all agree on who should be Mayor. He's not born into it. And it's only for a short time, then we agree on a new Mayor."

BUT THEN YOU LOSE THE EXPERIENCE, THE

STEADY HAND OF A WISE RULER.

"The rulers here are mostly not wise, sadly. They get corrupted the longer they rule. We change them out to get rid of the corruption."

SO THEY GO BAD. LIKE FRUIT?

Armand laughed. "Yes, very much like fruit."

# # #

OUTSIDE OF his drab, shabby apartment building in Alphabet City, a few reporters waited for him. These were vloggers and tech press, so it was more podcast mics and camera phones rather than full-on television crews, but he was not used to *any* of this at all — and he found he didn't like it.

"Mr. Martel! Hi, we heard that GigaMaestro is in chaos."

"It's not," Armand said, sweeping past the man machine-gunning questions at him.

"Well, that's not we heard. We heard that you were in charge now and that the Partners are all gone now — your brothers. Is that true?"

Armand figured he'd better shut up now. He'd seen Quinty do this sort of thing before, but Quinty had a PR firm that fed him his lines — and a law firm check everything over — to make sure everything he said was both smart and legal.

Not that Quinty always succeeded in doing either.

Nevertheless, Armand ducked inside and closed the door.

That night, Armand went to dinner again with Sophia's codex. This time, he visited a small cozy diner:

WHAT IS THAT BIG YELLOW THING?

Armand adjusted his focus. Had she just seen through his eyes, looking somewhere else in his vision other than where *he himself* had been looking?

Yes. Yes, she had done just that. He found himself looking a giant crane across the street from the diner.

"That's a machine for lifting heavy things. All those big buildings you asked about earlier, they were built using a crane like that. As the building gets taller, they need a way to get the raw materials up onto the level they're constructing next."

Puzzlement. BUT WHY NOT JUST FLOAT THEM?

"Float them? There's no river." What was she talking about? The Hudson again?

FLOAT THE MATERIALS. SING THEM UP?

"Sing them up?"

MAKE THEM FLOAT! MAKE THEM FLY. LIKE THE BALLOONS.

"What, like levitate them?"

YES.

"Um. Because you can't?"

EOPEII DID THIS ALL THE TIME. HE WORKED WITH BUILDERS. THEY FLOATED STONE.

"You're kidding me."

THIS IS ALL VERY SIMPLE. WHY DO YOU NOT KNOW?

"Well. The reason we don't do it is because we don't know how."

YOU LACK THIS KNOWLEDGE? YOU BUILT ALL THESE BUILDINGS AND YET YOU CANNOT DO WHAT A CHILD CAN?

"Sophia. I'm serious. We have no idea how to do something like that."

Laughter. Astonishment. Sense of *Wow, you people do things the hard way.*

"I'm dying to know how it works." Armand could barely contain his excitement. Was this the secret of how the pyramids were built? Was he actually about to learn what it was?

"How did you 'float stone'?"

WE USED DRUMS AND WE SANG. AFTER A TIME THEY BECAME WEIGHTLESS. LIKE THE BALLOONS YOU SHOWED ME.

What? They used sound? It couldn't be that simple. How would we not know about that today?

"But gravity applies to everything. How does 'singing' make gravity stop working?"

WHAT IS GRAVITY?

Ah. Yes, he'd read about this somewhere. Most primitive peoples did not 'notice' gravity. It just never occurred to them that it was A Thing. It required a conceptual leap to envision it as a force.

I AM NOT PRIMITIVE PEOPLES!

It was easy to forget that she was always monitoring his thoughts. And disconcerting.

I CAN ALWAYS GO AWAY. PUT DOWN THE CODEX, AND I AM NO MORE.

"No, no, no, please stay. That's not what I meant. Gravity is … it's what makes you fall down. When you drop something, it's what pulls the object to the ground."

YOU MEAN PUSHES THE OBJECT.

Armand stopped and thought about this. "No. I mean pull."

THAT IS WRONG. GRAVITY IS A DOWNWARD PUSHING FORCE.

Downward pushing? "No, Sophia. That's wrong. Listen, here in the future we know all about —"

YOU CANNOT FLOAT STONE. BUT I CAN.

That stopped Armand short. *Well, she has me there.*

GRAVITY FLOWS DOWN FROM THE SKY TO THE EARTH. IT GOES THROUGH EVERYTHING.

What, like rain? Gravity is like some kind of invisible

rain?

ROCKS ARE MADE OF VIBRATING ENERGY. IF YOU CHANGE THE VIBRATION OF ROCKS, THEN THEY ARE NO LONGER ('TUNING FORK', Armand guessed) WITH GRAVITY. DOWNWARD PUSHING ENERGY NO LONGER TOUCHES THE ROCK. ROCK FLOATS.

Armand read this carefully several times.

He knew that modern science did not really understand what gravity *was* — and if Sophia was correct, it seemed to have even the very basic assumptions wrong.

He reviewed her words in his mind while she waited patiently:

Sophia seemed to be saying that gravity was a *push* force, not a pull. There was some kind of ambient 'gravity energy', pouring down, almost like rain, passing through everything *from the sky to the earth*. And since matter was just vibrating energy, if you could change the frequency of a rock's basic matter-vibration (somehow, and he couldn't imagine how, using only drums and voices), then you could push the rock out of phase with the gravity rain. It would be on a different vibrational channel.

And: voila! Gravity would no longer affect the rock. The rock would float.

"So the rock loses mass?"

NO. GIANT STONES COULD STILL CRUSH YOU IF THEY FLOATED INTO YOU.

"But ... ah, I see. They still have mass and inertia. There's just no *weight*."

YES. YOU UNDERSTAND.

"And when Eopeii built things ... he would just push the rock to wherever he wanted it to go?"

YES.

Armand then recalled a story he'd once read about Coral Castle, in Florida. Built by a single man, Edward

Leedskalnin, between 1923 and 1951, it consisted of stones weighing as much as 30 tons. Nobody knew how he did it.

"And how do you bring gravity back? Once the stone is in place?"

IT WOULD RETURN BY ITSELF AFTER ABOUT AN HOUR. BUT IF YOU HIT THE ROCK WITH A HAMMER THAT DOES IT IMMEDIATELY.

So a sharp blow would instantly snap the matter back into its normal vibration, putting it back onto the same 'channel' with the gravity energy.

Armand shook his head. "Amaze."

AMAZE.

# # #

THE ASSOCIATES were not warming up to him.

Armand could feel it in their stares, in their emails, in the Zoom meetings — in everything. They thought he was too green, too young and too inexperienced. And his 'episode' in the Partner Meeting had not helped.

In short, they thought he was an idiot.

They hated him.

Armand hunched in his new office like it was a bunker. Encased in glass, he watched his own employees give him the side eye. They were used to *Quinty* sitting here. Quinty, with his absurd techno-shaman vibe and clothes. Even though he pretty much added no value, they missed him. He'd tell big stories and take credit for things he'd never done. He'd whip it all up into an epic story, the Legend of Quinctius Martel — like he was some archetypical protagonist out of a Joseph Campbell lecture.

The Zero's Journey, Armand snickered to himself. *The Zero With A Thousand Faces.*

But Quinty did look and act like a leader. And he was tall.

And he peacocked around. These antics all felt right to the Associates. He was a crazy rich guy — and that's who was supposed to run a venture firm.

And it was *Armand* who was the pretender, the fraud. It was Armand who didn't belong in Quinty's chair.

In the minds of the Associates, Armand was costing them money. In venture capital, missing the next Ethereum or Amazon was catastrophic. Most coins and companies died — ninety percent was the failure rate. But those that succeeded could be 500x events. These great companies usually looked shabby, illegal or insane at first. So you always had to be digging deep — and doing it fast. And trouble was, you never knew *when* one of those shabby gems were going to arrive on your doorstep.

They could be arriving *right now*, the staff figured. And if they were, Armand was missing them.

"No new deals," Armand had decreed. "Follow-on rounds only." This meant that GigaMaestro could keep putting money into companies they had already invested in, to help them grow to the next level — but no new companies were to be given capital for now. "I need time to go through our investment thesis and re-think it."

But this was death for Associates. They were looking to make their mark by bringing in the Next Big Thing.

They're out shopping their resumes, Armand figured. *They at least have feelers out.*

"Yeah, they're annoyed with you," Harper Bishop, the new GigaMaestro CFO, hired through Fisher Watson, told him. "They feel like frauds. They're taking pitches, knowing full well that they can't give Term Sheets."

"So why are they taking pitches, then? Tell them to stop."

"Armand. No. That's what they *do*. Stopping is death. Stand still, and the moss grows up your leg. Part of getting pitched is just *learning*. If they stop taking pitches, they lose the pulse of the scene, of what's going on. So if you *make* them stop, they'll quit."

"Okay. That makes sense. So tell them to keep going. Right?"

"Sure. Okay. But that feels icky to them also. Dishonest. Look. You have young founders looking for funding, thinking an Associate here might give it to them, and the Associate is basically lying whenever they take a pitch — when there's zero chance that they can invest."

"Well nobody has to know that we've retracted our —"

"*Armand.* That'll get noticed in a few months. When we're not cutting checks, the press will notice the sudden hole in our flow. They'll wonder what's up. *Especially* after the change in management — all eyes are on GM now."

Armand agreed to rethink the Investment Thesis as quickly as possible.

"It's only temporary," he told the Associates. "And I know you're frustrated. But give me two weeks to get it sorted out."

He buried himself in reports of the Fund's past performance. He met with founders of existing portfolio companies, tried to understand what they did. But he couldn't figure out how well the GigaMaestro fund was doing. The metrics were terrible: Quinty had never done the right sorts of analysis.

And Marius had made a mess of the finance records. Harper had a lot of work to do just deciphering it and re-filing taxes from previous years.

And the portfolio companies Armand examined had been terrible bets — mostly made by Otto and Marius. There was one company with a robot-operated store that made pizza — but which cost *five times more than the pizza* they sold just to maintain. It could never be profitable. The robot arms had to be disassembled and oiled and cleaned daily. Otto had just invested because he liked pizza and it looked cool. And because he could tell his friends about it at parties, complete with YouTube videos of the robot waving the pizza slices around.

Nevertheless, Harper Bishop was enthusiastic about pulling stats together. This was what she did best. She was happy to prioritize this now for Armand, but warned that it would take some time to complete.

# # #

WHILE HARPER busily built spreadsheets for him, Armand started looking at apartments to buy in Manhattan. Much of what he saw was dark and snobby and not his vibe at all. He wanted a lot of light and an open floor plan — but not *too* modern or spartan: he didn't want just squares and glass and steel either.

His real estate agent, Dorianne, a matronly frau in a muumuu, patiently carted him from building to building. At the third apartment — a vile, Tudor-themed place, old and creaky — perhaps noticing that Armand was displeased, she said: "Well. I'm sure we'll eventually find you the perfect fit. We service *all* the top Concordians in the City and Westchester areas, and we've never had a complaint in the end."

"Oh? What do you mean by 'accordions'?"

She looked at him funny. "All the top — you, know people in Concordia."

Armand shook his head. "What's that?"

Dorianne stared at him for a good long moment, first with amusement, and then she grew suddenly pale.

"Your father was Didier Martel, right?"

"Yes."

"And you weren't … adopted, or something … you're his

actual biological son. Right?"

"Yes. Why?"

She seemed relieved to hear that. But even so, she straightened her hair and muumuu several times nervously. Her chunky jewelry clinked around while she paced and fretted. Finally, she excused herself and made a phone call.

When she re-appeared, she wore a wan smile. "Hi. I'm sorry, Mr. Martel ... there's been a mistake at my office. It appears I have a conflict. So I won't be able to represent you after all. So sad! But don't worry! We're going to refer you to a new agent that we absolutely love — we've worked with her before in situations like this."

Armand shrugged. "Okay."

Wonder what that was all about?

# # #

IT WAS ONE of those spectacular summer nights in New York City. The luminous full moon blazed above, making the clouds look carved from creamy marble.

As Armand passed by a store called *World of Wonders*, a peculiar collection of items caught his eye. The store sold dinosaur fossils, crystals, and a variety of large, framed prints featuring intricate circular designs known as mandalas.

Sophia's codex rested safely in his backpack, and he eagerly retrieved it to engage their link, the Entanglement. "Wake up! Are you with me?" he whispered.

YES.

"I think you'll like this. Look in the window."

WHAT ARE THOSE? she asked.

"They're called mandalas."

PRETTY!

Armand's gaze rested on a wildly colorful Chenrezig Sand

Mandala, constructed from dyed granules by patient Buddhist monks using minuscule straws. He knew that upon completion, the mandala would be destroyed as a symbol of impermanence.

VERY PRETTY!

He then shifted his attention to the Manjuvajra mandala, a stunning work of art featuring nested circles and squares, and intricately drawn avatars and Hindu saints. He paused to admire the simpler yet equally mesmerizing Vajrayogini mandala, with its striking black, red, and green colors and a merkaba (two pyramid shapes, one inverted, pushed together) at its center.

WHAT ARE THESE FOR?

"They help you meditate," Armand said. He'd seen these many times before at Martel Antiquities — the Director of Acquisitions, Sadie Brown, covered her office walls with them. She was big on Jung.

HOW DOES IT WORK?

"You're supposed to memorize the entire mandala — and I mean, like, every line, every tiny brush stroke — and then close your eyes and replicate it completely in your mind. It's like weight lifting, but for the imagination."

AND THIS IS HARD FOR YOU?

"Yes. *Very* hard. When you first start trying to do it, your mind wanders around. You can't control it. You have all this random chatter in your head that won't calm down. But over time, your imagination-muscles grow stronger — and you can start to imagine it in pieces. That's what they say, anyway. I'm not very good at it."

WHY DOES YOUR MIND WANDER? WHY DO YOU HAVE CHATTER?

"I don't know. We just do. Sometimes, it's hard for us to sleep because of it."

STRANGE. I HAVE NO EXPERIENCE OF THAT.

"That's because you're not conscious in the same way I am."

WHY DO PEOPLE MEDITATE?

"Some people are just trying to calm down. Others are trying to — I dunno — get enlightened or whatever."

ENLIGHTENED?

"Yes. When you can picture the mandala perfectly in your mind, then you get enlightened."

WHAT DOES THAT MEAN?

"Well. Supposedly, you start seeing the universe as it really is. Illusions like time and separateness just fall away. Your brain can suddenly see through all of that."

THEN YOU WOULD SEE *THE ALWAYS*. LIKE I DO.

"Ah. That's right!" Armand smiled. "That's exactly how you describe your experience of it."

Grin.

"And once a human can see like you do, they can supposedly control material reality. No effort, it just sort of happens. At least that's what the Tibetan monks say."

WHAT KIND OF CONTROL?

"I dunno. Stuff like the ability to walk through walls. To fly. To be unhurt by fire. To bi-locate. You get, like, supernatural powers they call '*siddhis*'."

HAVE YOU EVER SEEN THESE POWERS YOURSELF?

"No. Never."

ARE THEY REAL?

"I don't know. Probably not."

CHAPTER EIGHT

The Assassin

SOPHIA'S CODEX WAS GROWING THIN.

The number of unread pages remaining were dwindling fast. Sophia did not seem concerned by this. But Armand found himself growing ever more anxious. The miracle of their time together was drawing close to an end.

No!

She was his best friend. His Benefactor and Chief Banisher of The Sads. And … was there more to it? *There was.* She was his companion. Sophia was *his person.*

He didn't like to admit it to himself. *I mean, this is ridiculous. Right?* He should be with a real girl. There were plenty out there who liked him. There was Rebecca Soares.

But whenever he went to call Rebecca, he found himself instead wondering where Sophia would go when he turned the last page.

Idiot! There is no 'go'! Sophia was never even here! He was reading *a book.*

How stupid was he.

The phone rang: *Quinty.* He pushed it to voicemail. Why the hell would he want to talk to one of his *brothers*? He'd put up with their incessant phone calls around the clock for *years.*

No. *No more.*

# # #

IN ADDITION, Armand noticed that there were now shadowy, spindly people watching him. He caught glimpses of them lurking about when he walked in the city from time to time.

Who were they? *Why were they here?* Was it because of *Sophia*?

On a subway, a girl suddenly looked directly at Armand and screeched, *"Who is the girl in the book?"* The young lady was clearly mentally ill, and her caretaker quickly apologized. But she kept screaming: *"Why is she in there? Let her out!"*

Another time, Armand turned a windy street corner and nearly collided with a man in his fifties. It was the formal Homburg hat, the mint-colored tie and the grizzled white beard that Armand later recalled the most. Oh, that and the slap of reeking cologne on his senses.

The man barely winced.

"Concordia," he said, nothing more. He tipped his hat, and without breaking eye contact, went on his way.

There was that word again.

The phone rang: *Quinty* yet again. Armand sent him to voicemail. But this time, Quinty rang back — and Armand sent him to voicemail again. Annoyingly, Quinty did not leave a message.

Other figures haunted him from high windows, looking down malevolently. Or they passed in limousines, with tinted windows half-lowered, showing yellow eyes, staying deep within the vehicles and away from shafts of sunlight.

Still others hovered on rooftops or bridges.

They were usually dressed in black, these figures. They had a gothic, otherworldly feel to them.

On the subway again, he saw a man in a dark muscle T, with long, scraggly black hair in a bandana and a beard, covered in hieroglyph-tattoos on his arms, face and fingers. He looked like a Gypsy — but wasn't that just a modern Egyptian? Someone bristling with old magic, who had drifted north of the Nile — and into a European caravan of boats or wagons, and who dealt now in gold, jewels, cards, fortunes, music, trinkets, spells and curses?

The phone rang: Quinty again. Voicemail. Three more times Quinty tried, and three more times Armand denied.

His Alphabet City apartment was now keeping him awake at all hours. The noise volume of parties in the other units was becoming insane.

Was he dreaming these people? Or were they dreaming him?

They seemed like phantoms or vampires. Or figures from the more modern species of hallucination, the alien abduction scenario, and the accompanying Men in Black, who weren't real, but were rather Archetypes of the Collective Unconscious dressed in business suits. They were ancient fairy stories with a shiny, spiffy, new, modern paint job.

# # #

ARMAND WENT over everything he knew about Sophia.

She seemed to emanate, in some fashion, from a realm of pure information. Something like a vast blob of sheer data. Something timeless — and yet, also asleep, also purely subconscious.

Something like the Akashic records?

Armand had heard of this — a theory that all knowledge

was contained in some etheric space — and that some minds, in the right meditative state, could even access it.

But pure information could not *experience*. It could not change. It could not grow. It could only watch. It was stagnant.

However, when Eopeii had put his stylus to papyrus, his *quantum gaze* had somehow caused a piece of the *information-blob* to break off from the main mass. It had individuated to a degree, and thus, it became *alive*. It began to *experience*.

This sub-blob then *joined* with Eopeii, infused him, permeated him. Thus, Eopeii became a new *composite* being, someone filled with living information, a hybrid. *Some combining happens.*

Just as Athena, the goddess of wisdom, was said to have been born from Zeus's head, so too was Sophia born from Eopeii's. The old Greek myth — apparently — had described a true process that could really happen.

Mistaking this overwhelming inner experience for a god, Eopeii had asked it about the future, with disastrous results. Then, at the demand of his people, he had placed the codex into a canopic jar and buried it for all time.

Until Armand had opened the jar.

And now, this same thing had happened to Armand. He was now a composite being as well.

But would that still be true when the codex ended?

# # #

By Bethesda Fountain, an acapella group sang a magnificent version of *Dancing Queen* by ABBA. Sophia listened raptly. She had never heard anything like this before.

PRETTY. PRETTY IN MY EARS.

"So you like it?" Armand asked.

NOT DIRECTLY. I FEEL YOUR JOY WHEN YOU LISTEN.

The harmonies were extraordinary, the way this group did it. Armand strained to understand exactly what he was hearing, how the music was constructed. *Ames would get this,* he thought. For a moment, he considered calling him, letting him listen to the performance via iPhone — but then Armand suddenly remembered that they were not on speaking terms.

But Sophia had more to say:

THESE ARE MOSTLY HAPPY CHORDS?

"Yes," Armand said.

I CAN FEEL WHAT YOU FEEL WHEN YOU HEAR THE MUSIC.

BUT HERE IS WHAT IS STRANGE. I CANNOT TELL WHICH *CHORDS* ARE HAPPY OR SAD. IT IS NOT OBVIOUS TO ME, EVEN WHEN ENTANGLED WITH YOU.

Interesting. "The minor chords are the sad and the major chords are happy. To me, that's obvious. But not to you?"

NO. I DO NOT KNOW WHY ANY MUSIC MAKES EMOTION.

"That *is* strange," Armand agreed. "Okay. What about color? When you saw the crane — when you told me about floating rocks — you knew that the crane was the color yellow. Right? *That* was obvious to you?"

YES. COLOR IS VERY DIFFERENT. I KNOW IT IS YELLOW WITHOUT YOU.

"Huh." Both were just forms of vibration. Color was light vibration while music was air vibration. Yet, clearly, there was something inherently different about music. It required something deeper of the listener. His intuition leaping, Armand snapped: "Okay. What about humor? What about jokes? Do you get why they are funny?"

Armand felt her pause. Then: NO. I DO NOT.

"But then — why do you laugh?" He was sure he'd heard

her — or felt her — laugh.

BECAUSE I FEEL YOU LAUGH.

I DO NOT KNOW WHY YOU LAUGH. BUT I LAUGH ALSO.

"So when you laugh — and I *can* feel you laughing, somehow — what is that? Are you *really* laughing? Or is that somehow a trick? A trick of politeness, perhaps, but still a trick?"

IT IS REAL. YOU ARE LAUGHING. THROUGH YOU, I FEEL THE LAUGH. IT IS NOT A LIE.

"Okay. What do *you* experience when someone tells a joke?"

I WARN YOU. IT IS VERY DIFFERENT THAN IT IS FOR YOU.

"Yes I get that. But walk me through it."

A JOKE IS A SURPRISE CONNECTION BETWEEN TWO UNCONNECTED IDEAS.

Armand thought about this for a second. That had never occurred to him before, but it seemed basically correct.

MUSIC IS JUST A SERIES OF SURPRISE CONNECTIONS BETWEEN UNCONNECTED SOUNDS. SO REALLY, MUSIC IS A JOKE MADE OF TONES.

Armand burst out laughing. "Right!" *Surprise from Sophia.* "Yes, you made a joke — without meaning to."

IN BOTH A JOKE AND MUSIC, I LEARN NEW INFORMATION.

BUT I ALSO LEARN NEW INFORMATION IN MANY OTHER WAYS. THERE IS NO MATERIAL DIFFERENCE BETWEEN THE JOKE, MUSIC AND BLAND NEW INFORMATION. THE ONLY DIFFERENCE IS HOW YOU REACT. BURST OF JOY.

Jokes and music must require true consciousness, true sentience, to understand, Armand thought.

"But you've made jokes before, Sophia. It's not like you

have no emotions."

MY EMOTIONS COME FROM YOU. HOW YOU SEE ME IS HOW I FEEL. AND HOW YOU FEEL IS ALSO HOW I FEEL.

"I see."

YOUR ATTENTION. YOUR LAUGH. IT TASTES LIKE CHOCOLATE TO ME.

Armand was caught off-guard. "I know, right?" He paused, and then decided to bring it up: "Sophia. Listen. There are too few pages left. This is all going by too fast. Can we —" He tried not to let the sound of panic creep into in his voice.

THERE ARE AS MANY PAGES AS THERE NEEDS TO BE.

"What does that mean?"

FAMINE. BAD.

She wouldn't talk about it.

The phone rang: *Quinty*, yet again. Armand banished him to voicemail.

# # #

AS ARMAND neared his Alphabet City apartment building, some instinct told him to drop quickly to the pavement.

He did so just in time to see a knife thrust into the air above him — right where his back had just been.

From this angle on the ground, he could see his attacker: a large Irish man with curly red hair. Red Curls was astonished that Armand had somehow known to drop — and that he had moved with such preternatural speed.

Now Armand bounced up off the pavement and held himself in some kind of defensive stance. He was baffled at how unscared he was. What was wrong with him? Shouldn't he be terrified right now? His emotions had gone completely numb.

And how was he *doing* this? He had never studied karate or anything like that!

Red Curls snarled in frustration and attacked again, alternately trying to slash Armand's neck and stomach. Armand easily moved out of the way of each time. He was surprised — and amused — by how laughably simple it was to dodge these attacks. It felt like they were happening in slow-motion.

Armand was startled to find himself *having fun* fighting.

But suddenly he'd had enough: after all, this man was trying to kill him. It was time to end this. Armand blocked the knife and kicked the man three times — fast — in the rib cage, and neatly plucked the weapon from his hand.

Red Curls absolutely could not believe that this was happening. His brain could not process it.

Enraged, and desperate now, the man reached behind his back and drew a revolver — which, again, Armand effortlessly took from him — while landing more kicks, this time to the knees and spleen.

Armand pointed the gun at the man. "Run," he said.

Red Curls' face said, *How did this happen?* He just stared at Armand, waiting for the world to somehow become normal again.

"Run, I said." Still, the man didn't budge. "Boom!" Armand shouted. That made Red wince — but this time, he ran.

It was only when the man was out of sight that Armand's terror kicked in.

# # #

"HOW DID I do all of that?"

THAT WAS EOPEII, Sophia explained when they were

back in his apartment. EOPEII KNOWS HOW TO FIGHT, SO NOW YOU DO ALSO.

"Eopeii?!? I thought he was just a scribe?" Armand said, voice wobbling with adrenalin. "I thought he just sat around all day, you know, scratching away on papyrus."

HE WAS. BUT ALSO A WARRIOR. ALL SCRIBES WERE ALSO WARRIORS. EVERYONE IS WARRIOR.

Someone tried to kill me. It was just now sinking into Armand. His mind was a riot of worry and fear.

But who? And why?

"Ah. So ancient Egypt didn't have a nerd class? Your nerds and jocks were the same people?"

EVERYONE FOUGHT WHEN NECESSARY.

Of course. There were greatly fewer people back then. Everyone must have been on double-duty.

Armand's body was torn up from the encounter. Not from any injury he'd suffered, rather, he was deeply sore and he had several muscle pulls and strains.

EOPEII WAS IN BETTER SHAPE, Sophia explained. YOU MOVED LIKE EOPEII, BUT DID NOT HAVE THE BODY OF EOPEII. SO NOW, YOU ARE IN PAIN.

Great, Armand muttered. That explains it. He shambled around looking for aspirin.

He pondered the reason for the attack. Had it been random? Or had his would-be killer been after Sophia's codex? Or could it have been his brothers?

His brothers …

Were they actually angry enough about the coup to hire a hit man?

Not Quinty. But Marius? *Maybe.*

Then, there was Sophia. He was enjoying her company far too much, and pondering the general weirdness and implications of what was happening here too little. Could there be some danger that he had summoned into his life through the codex? Was she an evil spirit or something, ultimately?

Did she have enemies?

Maybe they stuffed her into that canopic jar for worse reasons than she was letting on.

The phone rang: Quinty again. But now, a call from Quinty hit different. Worry shot through Armand. *Maybe people were trying to kill his brothers also. Maybe one of them was already dead. Was this why Quinty kept calling?*

So this time, Armand answered.

"*What?*" Armand barked into the phone

"Dude. You never answer your phone."

"So?"

"So we have to talk. *All* of us. This is important."

CHAPTER NINE

Mount Desert Island

HIS BROTHERS HAD INSISTED ON a meet.

Armand had agreed, but only under the condition that it take place at the Martel family cabin on Mount Desert Island in Maine. His brothers had been predictably crabby about this — *it's inconvenient, why so far from New York City, we haven't been there in years,* blah blah blah.

But Armand wanted them in a place where they'd spent summers together as children. A place filled with memories of their father, Didier.

He wanted the smell of pine and sea. The unpainted wood floors, walls and furniture. The snap of a fire in the red stove. The natural golden sunlight streaming in through large windows. Sailboats on a foamy ocean. The guitars and pictures of Didier with famous musicians hung on the walls.

And he'd wanted his brothers to come alone, no entourage. No wives, no girlfriends, no lawyers. Just brothers, talking. Like it used to be.

Armand had asked Sophia for her advice, being ultra careful not to inquire about a future outcome. She had been positive on the meet, but especially positive about the setting.

Armand arrived at the cabin first. He retrieved the key from the lockbox and waited inside, soaking in memories while starting a fire.

Everything was exactly as he'd recalled. The board games. The wooden furniture. The knotted rope he'd climbed as a kid to reach his loft bed. The books. Nothing was dusty. Everything was clean and spotless: the Martel Trust paid a caretaker to keep the place always at the ready.

Quinctius, the oldest brother, arrived first. He was in his forties and cultivated a 'Jesus' look, with long brown hair, thick beard, middle-eastern looking scarves, chunky beads and man-jewelry. His official bio claimed he was a Yogi. Today, he was wearing tinted glasses and an explorer hat.

"Quinty," Armand nodded.

His brother removed his shades. Armand was shocked to see how sunken and swollen Quinty's eyes were. He hadn't been sleeping. In the past, his gaze had barely registered Armand, but now there was a new grudging respect. Armand was in the very center of *all* his thoughts presently.

They said nothing as they waited for the rest.

Otto arrived next. A plump man, he'd recently colored his hair blazing red. His wife, Anna, also large and bossy to boot, was a hairdresser, and she had clearly been behind his new look.

"Hey, Armie," Otto huffed as he carried a bag of groceries to the fridge. "I brought us some goodies to grill."

Then came Samson, the opposite of Otto, a lean and large gym rat, in a tight white t-shirt stretching over bulging muscles. He carried a bulky cooler behind his brother. Samson had the Jersey-orange chemical tan and matching baggy gym pants. His cropped hair had the plastic sheen of too much product.

Cyrano entered next. He was also in shape, but in a lean,

fashion model way. His manicured hands carried colorful designer luggage — a gift from his sixty-something boyfriend. He didn't even acknowledge Armand as he entered, but instead, muttered something fussy about how much he'd always hated this cabin. Cyrano was the most angry about his change in fortunes. For him, it wasn't even the loss of money: it was the loss of EPIC. EPIC had been Cyrano's life. His identity. He had literally lived for the next conference.

Lastly, Ames and Marius arrived together. Ames was the sporty one, dressed in spandex cycling gear. Like their father Didier, he had a short, already-graying beard — and he was a great musician. Of them all, Ames was the most like their father, almost a carbon copy.

Marius slinked into the room dressed in black, as always. Normally, he was in dark suits — but today he wore black shorts with a silver loop chain hanging and dangling. Black Doc Martens, black socks, a black shirt featuring some angry band, black nail polish and a hint of eye shadow. It was his 'Summer Goth' look. His eyes seethed as they found Armand — but he said nothing.

# # #

"THERE ARE some things we need to explain to you, ya?" Quinctius began. "Because of what you've done, alright? There are some things."

"Dale and I have four kids," Cyrano interjected. "Four!"

"And Anna is up my ass every day," Otto moaned. "She wants us to get this fixed. Today. To work this out, ya?"

"*Anna*," Marius sneered. "Anna's nothing. My Thai wife —"

"Stop it. All of you," Quinty said. Armand was surprised to hear his brother come to his defense. "None of that matters. We're not here to talk about that. What Armie did, Armie did. We all signed the agreements. And besides, ultimately, old Didier did this to us, not Armie."

"So what are 'these things' I need to know?" Armand asked.

Quinty looked around at the myriad framed photos of Didier with famous musicians. "Okay. Here it is. Our Dad was into something. Deep in it. Like, neck deep."

"Concordia," Marius said quietly, like he was afraid of being overheard. "That's what it's called."

Concordia! Armand's brain screamed. There was that word again!

"Yes. It's a Greek word," said Samson, admiring one of his biceps. "Means *harmony*."

"No. *Latin*, you Philistine," sniffed Cyrano. "Don't give me that look. You were only off by like two thousand years."

"It's sort of like a secret group," said Quinty. "But worldwide."

"Mmm. More like a worldwide mafia," said Ames.

"Yes. True," agreed Quinty. "But never say that aloud outside of this cabin. Okay? Anyway, Dad's entire music career was supported by them. They were his investors. And they opened all the doors. The record companies, the radio stations, the bands, the TV shows. All of it happened because of them."

"And the tech investments later," Otto chimed in.

"This is Concordia you're talking about," Armand said.

"Yes," Marius said.

"Their network is big," Quinctius said. "The biggest on earth — even though you've never heard of it. But if you *do* know about it, you're also terrified of it."

"Terrified?"

"Yeah. Terrified."

Ames took over: "Look. Armand. We've met a lot of really

big players over the years through EPIC, ya? Government. Military. Venture. Banks. Big tech. Big Pharma. Well. Every once in awhile, one of these people will get drunk and bring up Concordia. And immediately, everyone else turns white, hushes up. Or they'd just up and leave. It's freaky, ya? They're scared. These big people!"

"And be careful about using that word in public," Marius muttered darkly. "Now that you know about it."

Quinty said: "Here's another example. You know Bill Wiley, right? Worth ten billion." Armand nodded. "Okay, so Bill is talking to me about some things that he and his hundred-billion-plus net worth friends are trying to get off the ground. I forget even what it was specifically right now but it doesn't matter. The point is, he tells me they were getting roadblocked by 'powerful people'. And I was like, 'Powerful people? You're all upper-echelon billionaires! Aren't YOU the powerful people?' and he just laughs and says, 'No. We're not even close.' And this is Bill Fucking Wiley."

"Okay," Armand said. "So they're big. So they invested in Dad. So what? They made money off their shares, right? They should be happy. Right?"

The brothers looked at each other nervously.

"Do you know who Varinder Rahan is?" Marius asked.

"Sort of. He's a billionaire like Wiley, right? He's a major LP in GigaMaestro — I think?" 'LP' stood for Limited Partner — an investor in a venture capital fund.

"Yes. He's actually our biggest. And there's a reason for that. Varinder was Dad's best friend."

Armand blinked. "What do you mean? No, he wasn't. Dad never mentioned him."

"Not to *you* he didn't," Marius grumbled.

"Marius!" Quinty snapped. "Let me tell it. Okay?" Marius sulked but said nothing further. "Anyway. He was Dad's immediate superior in Concordia. And he invested in Dad back in the 1970's. Gave him millions. But when they give you that kind of money, you have to supply collateral. That can be real estate or something like that ... but it can also be your karma. In fact, they far prefer that."

Armand blinked. "Karma. You mean like, India karma?"

"Yes, that kind of karma," Quinty said. "Concordia has a system wherein you can tokenize your karma. It used to be all paper-based, but now it's on a blockchain — it's a crypto."

Armand looked around the room at his brothers, immediately suspecting a joke. But nobody was laughing. All of them were worried and tired. Their eyes were sunken.

"No, we are most definitely *not* fucking with you, Armand. I promise," Ames said. "This is deadly serious."

"You're telling me they have tokenized karma?"

"Yes. A Molian Contract," Quinctius said. "That's what it's called. You go to one of their brokers. You sign papers. Then, he measures your karma using a machine. I don't even know how that's possible, but they swear it is. You stick your arm into the machine — it looks old and weird, sort of Victorian. And it's cold. But once your arm comes out, it's done, and then the Molian man mints your tokens."

"It doesn't hurt though," Ames said.

"Oh, yes it does," Marius muttered. "It just hurts in other ways."

"Holy shit," Armand said, staring at his brothers. "You *all* knew about this? This whole time? And *none* of you told me?" The brothers looked at each other sheepishly.

"We *couldn't* tell you, Armie," Otto said. "We weren't allowed."

"This was *serious*," Ames said.

"And we were protecting you," Cyrano added. "And trust us, we were doing you a favor."

"We'll get to that. Anyway. *Varinder,*" Quinctius said, "Ya? Okay. In order for Dad to get his money, he had to stake his own karma in a Molian contract with somebody who belonged to Concordia. That someone was Varinder Rahan, who then subsequently funded the music empire that Dad built: *Martel Melodies, Martelevision, Martel MerchMania* — all of that. This happened in 1972, when Dad was just eighteen. So —"

"Wait, wait, wait. So Dad actually, for real, staked his *karma*?"

"Yes. Look, Armand, just go with it for now. Okay? Let me finish."

"Okay."

"So Dad makes a ton of money as a record producer. And this is all really great for ten years. He lives the high life — partying with every major rock star on earth, collaborating, producing, traveling, touring — you name it. I mean, this cabin is *packed* with pictures from that time.

"But then, in 1982, Dad is approached by Concordia to do something really strange. They suddenly decide they don't like the flood of great rock albums coming out, one right after the other. So they want Dad to put a stop to it."

"Stop? How? They want him to stop the bands from making records?"

"No. They want something more drastic — and deeper, and more direct. This is the weird part. They want Dad to, like, produce some kind of *musical* injury to the collective unconscious. He called it 'The Musipocalypse'. The idea was to make it impossible for anyone to make albums like this any more."

"Well, not *impossible,*" Ames chimed in. "Make it a lot less probable. Make it harder to do."

"For the record, I think this part is bullshit," Marius said sourly.

"Concordia didn't think so,"Cyrano said sternly.

Again, Armand felt the urge to accuse his brothers of messing with him. All of this seemed insane. But then again, he himself had just recently had an insane experience with the Egyptian codex and Sophia. *Were they related?* But he pushed this thought away for now. He had more immediate questions. He stared at Quinty, trying to grasp what he was being told. "So they wanted Dad to injure the collective unconscious ... what, you mean like, the Jungian thing?"

"Yes. Look. Deep down inside, where dreams and music come from, we all share the same, I dunno, *base layer*. That's why it's called the *collective* unconscious."

"Yeah, it's that Jungian Prototypes thing," Samson said.

"Idiot! It's *Archetypes*," Cyrano corrected.

"And they wanted Dad to sort of kneecap it," Ames said.

"Think of it as a *mystical* injury," Quinty said. "It's something you can't see or feel, at least not directly. But it's something which subtly impacts every person on earth at a subconscious level."

"But how would you even *do* that?" Armand asked.

"We have no idea," Quinty said. "I know. It sounds absolutely fucking batshit."

"An abstract affliction," Otto said, laughing. "No. Wait. A *quantum crime*." The rest glowered at him, unamused.

"But why would Concordia even care about stupid *rock albums*?" Armand asked.

"It's just how they think," Cyrano said. "'Human attention is the most powerful force on earth', they like to say. They apparently didn't like where a lot of that attention was being directed."

That's strange, thought Armand. *Sophia is also powered by human attention. Was there some kind of relationship between her and what his brothers were revealing now?*

"Yeah," Quinty said. "Those albums really started to piss

them off. They dropped phaser-lock on the whole category. They wanted it *gone*."

"So what happened? Did Dad get this to work? Did it actually happen?" Armand asked.

"Concordia thought it did," Quinty said.

"And *I* think I did," Ames said. "It stopped the flow of masterpiece-level albums. At least in my opinion."

"It killed the muses," Otto said. "Or at least, it punched them really hard in the face." This time, they all laughed.

"I still say bullshit," said Marius. "There are plenty of good new albums coming out all the time."

"And yet, in every new movie you see, the music is always forty or fifty years old," Quinty observed. "Why is that? I'll tell you why. *Because the new music isn't good enough.*"

"Hey, yeah," Otto said. "That's weird. You're right."

"I mean, if you're Warner Brothers, wouldn't you want to plug the *new* Warner Brothers albums in your movies? You know, cross-promote? Use the movie as a commercial?"

"Right. They used to. Like with Huey Lewis in *Back To The Future*."

"Exactly. But they *don't* do that anymore," Quinty said, snapping his fingers. "Next time you go to the movies, watch the trailers and you'll see. It's all *old* music, not new."

"I still call bullshit," Marius said grumpily. "I think Dad just told them he did it and collected the money."

"Okay," Ames said, "But can we agree that *something* changed with music? Fundamentally?"

"Alright, enough," Quinty said. "We can debate this forever. But real or not, Dad got paid. He took the Musipocalypse gig in 1983 — but it took until the early 90's for it all to actually kick in, to start working. Maybe it took him awhile to figure out exactly how to do it — or maybe it just took time to implement, we don't know which. But we do know that by 2007, he was rolling in big, big dollars.

"But *before* that, in the 70's and 80's, Dad was spending a *fuck ton* of money, really, fast, and making investments, particularly in Latin America, where he was scouting up-and-coming musicians for Martel Melodies. And then, he got his teeth kicked in by the Latin American Debt Crisis, which was like this big shit show in the early 80's, kind of like the financial crisis we had in 2008, but 80's style and south of the border. And then Dad got whacked *again* — this time, by Black Monday in 1987.

"Really, that one-two punch did him in. Martelevision folded. But he kept all the financial plates spinning at Melodies and MerchMania, amazingly, through borrowing and leveraging, and pretty much check-kiting, until 1995 — when everything finally caught up with him."

"Yeah," Ames said, "Armie you were, what, two? You were too young to remember all the yelling that Mom and Dad did that year. It was insane. We'd never seen Dad on tilt like that. But it was understandable. He was going to lose the house, the cars, all of it."

Quinty nodded. "And he *would* have lost everything — except for the fact that now, thanks to Mom, he had some *new* karma to productize."

"Us," Otto, Cyrano, Marius and Ames said together.

"Us," Quinty agreed. "One by one, we were brought down to the Molian man. It had to be of our free will. We had to say yes. But with Dad there, pleading, telling us that he needed our help, that we had to do this for him …"

"Of course we were going to do it," said Ames.

"So we did," said Otto

"So we motherfucking did," said Marius darkly.

"We were just kids," Samson said.

"We swore that *our* children would never have to do something like that," said Cyrano, staring daggers at

Armand. He and his boyfriend had adopted four kids.

"So *all* of you did this?" Armand asked. All six heads nodded. "And I never had to? Why not?"

Quinty sighed. "Because Mom left Dad. And us. This Molian shit was why. And that's why nobody ever told you."

"But Dad would have been liquidated if we hadn't done it," Marius explained. "He *needed* us to do it."

"Liquidated?" Armand said. "What does that mean?"

"It means the contractor takes possession of the tokenized karma," Marius said. "In this case, Varinder. Which would have meant, Dad comes back in the next life as an amoeba, while Varinder comes back as ..."

"Varinder," Quinty said. They both laughed.

"But Dad made all the money back, right?" Armand said. "I mean ... we're rich, so, he must have paid Varinder what he owed, and your — your — karma, or whatever, that was like *un-mortgaged* ... right?"

The brothers exchanged pained glances. "No, Armand," Ames said. "That's not how it works. It's not a loan. You're *given* the money when your Molians are minted. So anyone who got ... *tokenized* ... they're in Concordia for life."

"Tokenized karma is sort of like a hostage," Cyrano added. "It's collateral. They *do* own it, they can even trade it — but they can't actually *liquidate* it unless certain conditions are met."

"*Thankfully*," Quinty said. "Or they'd liquidate everyone all the time."

"What kind of conditions?"

"It varies," Quinty said. "Depends on whatever deal was struck when your Molians were first minted. But there has to be a certain amount of fairness involved in a liquidation, in order for it to be valid, in order for it to *take hold*. We do know that Dad's liquidation would have been fairly executed, had it occurred. The threat was very real."

"So when you get liquidated ... do you die?" Armand asked.

"No," Ames said. "Not necessarily. You're still alive. But your karma has been lost."

"Unless they kill you *also*," Cyrano interjected. "Which is always possible. But either way, when you *eventually* die, you die with no karma."

"You're, what, *zeroed out* or something?"

"Yes. You start over. And whoever liquidated your Molians, their soul gets the benefit of whatever you had. A karmic transference occurs."

"Do you all actually *believe* this?" Armand asked.

"Doesn't matter if we believe it. *They* do," Quinty said. "To them, it's sure as Sunday. They take it very, very seriously."

"They sound like a cult," said Armand.

"They are," said Marius, Quinty and Ames at once.

"So these Molian tokens. What do they do with them?" Armand asked.

"Oh. There's a whole internal crypto economy. They have secret websites and secret exchanges. Like Coinbase or Binance, but for this shit," Otto said.

"Ya. They trade Molians with each other all the time. Deals. Alliances. Payoffs," Ames said.

"Ya. And none of them trust each other — they're all pretty backstabby — which is why when the blockchain came along, it was the one thing they could all agree on: to move the Molian accounting all on-chain," Quinty said. "There was a lot of cheating before, but the blockchain got rid of all of that."

"Why not centralize it though?" Armand asked. "Concordia doesn't feel like a decentralize-it bunch of people. Why didn't they just use a database controlled by the top?"

They all laughed.

"Because they trust the top of their Pyramid least of all," Marius said.

"What Pyramid?"

"Well, you *are* right, Armand — Concordia is pretty cult-like," Quinty said. "And like all good religions, they have a bunch of tenets and philosophies. One is this thing they call 'The Pyramid Versus The Circle'. In their view, human governance is always organized into either one or the other, no exceptions. The Pyramid is a top-down dictatorship. And the Circle is a mutual collective, like a tribe or a democracy."

"Yeah," Ames said, "And I've heard some of them — especially Varinder — express it in terms of, like, what I call 'computer science philosophy'. So, if you have a system that is top-down, pyramidal, centralized, monolithic — it's not scalable. The bigger it gets, the more it breaks down. But a peer-to-peer network, something Circle-like, decentralized, like BitTorrent or Bitcoin — it gets stronger and more resilient the bigger it gets. So not only does it break down less, but it can handle more capacity. It's more abundant as it grows."

"So the Circle is better," Armand said. "Clearly."

"Concordia disagrees," Quinty said. "They would argue that the Circle also grows more chaotic as it gets stronger. There's no moderation. So you always end up with something ugly, like 4chan. Uncontrollable, but wildly powerful and becoming more so exponentially. They view it as a forest fire."

"You have to admit that there *are* advantages to the Pyramid," Ames said. "Since you control everything, you can streamline things. In the centralized, Pyramid-ish blockchains, you can get 50,000 transactions per second — versus just 21 transactions per second on a Circle-ish chain like Ethereum — and just 7 transactions per second on the most Circle-ish chain of them all, Bitcoin. The Circle is inefficient."

"But Bitcoin never crashes," Samson pointed out. "It is insanely resilient. And the hash rate — the security — is insanely strong. You can't hack it. But that other chain with the 50,000 transactions? It's literally famous for crashing all the time. And it's pretty vulnerable to hacks."

"That's true. That's the tradeoff."

"And Concordia is a Pyramid, in case you missed that," Otto added. "They keep everyone in line with karmic leashes — with these Molian contracts. In fact, the hierarchy of contracts is literally what defines the Concordian Pyramid — who owns who."

"Yeah," Ames said. "And when one of them gets a pile of new liquidations, it's like they won the lottery. They're ecstatic."

"All of them have bad karma," Quinty said. "Because they act like shits most of the time. So they live for liquidations. It gives them a *Get Out Of Jail Free* card."

"Yes. *Molian Indulgences,*" Cyrano added with a laugh.

"What about Mom? Did Mom ever stake her karma?" Armand asked. Their Mother, Amanda Martel, had left Didier when Armand was very young. Didier had won the custody battle: Amanda had been deemed in court to be an addict.

"No," Cyrano said. "She didn't. She refused to. And Didier was furious about that."

"Didier blamed Mom," Quinty said. "His thinking was: If she'd just ponied up when asked, some of us kids wouldn't have had to. And she, in turn, blamed Didier: how could he force his own sons to do something like that? So Mom left — and she *did* become an addict. She couldn't handle the guilt.

"And Didier lost Mom, which broke him. So, Armand,

when it was your turn to go see the Molian man ... Didier just couldn't bring himself to do it. One son, his last son, was going to be protected, he was going to keep you completely clean of Concordian filth. I'm guessing that's why he gave you sixty percent in the will. You were the one good thing left in his world."

All six brothers looked at Armand enviously.

"So he staked the last of *our* tokens," Marius explained, chewing each word. "Instead of minting yours, Armand. He drained the six of us down to the raw nub. For *you*."

"And that, my little brother," Quinty said, "is why we were okay with screwing you out of your inheritance. Because, really, it was our karma that paid for it."

Armand sat there stunned for a long moment. "I didn't know."

"We know," Quinty said. "We know you didn't know. And what's done is done." Cyrano and Marius didn't seem to agree, but they kept quiet.

"Someone tried to kill me last week," Armand said. "A guy with a knife in the street. It could have been a random mugging ... but it felt more targeted. Like a hit. Honestly, I thought it might have been one of you. You know. Because of ... everything. Was it?"

Shock registered on most of their faces. Except for Marius. Marius seemed mildly delighted by this news. "How did you survive?" Marius asked.

Armand studied his brother. "What a strange question. How about, *Oh I'm sorry that happened to you, Armand?* Or, *Are you okay, Armand?*"

Marius shrugged. "I was just wondering. You versus a hitman, I would have bet on the hitman."

"No," Quinty said quietly. "It wasn't any of us. But it could have been Varinder."

"Varinder? Why would he try to kill me?"

"Because he holds our Molian tokens," Quinty said. "All six of ours. He owns us. And through us, he controls GigaMaestro, EPIC, Martel Family Office and Martel Antiquities. Or at least, *he did*, anyway, until your little coup. Now *you* own it. You control it. Varinder probably wants it back. Killing you would fix that — we'd re-inherit everything you own now."

Quinty held an internal debate for a moment, and then said:

"Listen. The reason I was so gung-ho about hunting conscious AI is because Varinder ordered me to be. We were *his guys* on the front lines of AI innovation. We're *good* at that, Armand. Finding the hot new investments and companies. EPIC was good at that. Now, you took his main hunter off the board at a key moment. So *of course* he's pissed."

"So you were taking orders from Varinder on how to run GigaMaestro?"

"Yes. I had to. He owns our Molians. And he's the major LP in the fund."

"So you've talked to him directly?"

"Yes. Of course. Quite a bit. Same with Ames and Cyrano and Marius."

"Is that how you know all this stuff about Concordia? Did he tell you?"

"Most of it. Yes. Some of it from Dad, when he was drunk a few times. But most of it comes from Varinder. He misses Dad — that's clear. So he talks to us like we're Dad. Especially Ames, since he kind of looks like Dad — and he's a musician — so he's the most Dad-like out of all of us. Hell, I've even seen Varinder straight up call Ames 'Didier' on more than one occasion."

"Yeah, up at that Sea Castle place of his," Ames said. "He loves to sit out on that patio under the stars for hours and hours, drinking expensive wine."

"And now, The Ask," Marius said to Quinty, leaning forward. "Get to The Ask."

"Ah, yes. Armand. So we need you to talk to him," Quinty said uncomfortably.

"Who?"

"*Varinder*. We need you to fly out to his house, meet with him, smooth all of this over."

"Wait. You want me to go visit to the guy who probably just tried to have me killed?"

"Yes," Quinty said. "Look. This is where you owe us one. He has our Molians, he could liquidate us, and now you know what that means. So if you —"

"But what if he's trying to kill me?"

"If he is, he'll stop if you're willing to talk. Look, I know him. I'll call him right after this, let him know you're coming, set up the meet."

"But why didn't he just try to talk to me in the first place?"

"I don't know. Reflex reaction? And Armand. You don't know for sure that it was Varinder. Okay? You don't."

"But Varinder was Dad's friend. Why would he try to kill his friend's son?"

"Look. It's Concordia. Varinder has an upstream too, someone *he* reports to. We have no idea what they'll do. We just know that they're pissed off. And they're crazy. So we can't fuck around. Post-coup, *you're* the leader now, Armand. Like it or not. And you owe us for your Molian-free status."

"You wanted the big chair," Cyrano said. "Well, fine. You've got it. This is the big chair stuff."

"And it needs doing," Marius said.

"Also, it's not just us in this room that we have to think about," Quinty said. "You have to think about my girlfriend, Otto's wife, Ames' wife and three kids, Cyrano's boyfriend and his *four* kids …"

"My Thai wife!" Marius interjected. "How come everyone always forgets about her?'

"My new girlfriend," Samson interjected.

"Samson's new girlfriend," Quinty said, purposefully ignoring Marius. "Look. Armand. We're behind you. But *you* have to be the one to do this. It has to be smoothed over."

"Varinder's on the West Coast," Cyrano said. "He has this, like, Sea Castle. You're going to love it."

"Oh — and, the Family Office is trying to reach you," Marius said, staring at his phone. "There's a bunch of Board documents they need you to sign. And a few wires to approve. And a bunch of new pitch decks people are trying to get in front of you." He smiled. He was enjoying watching Armand overwhelmed.

"Well what about you?" Armand said. "Can you deal with that for me while I'm visiting Varinder?"

"Well, I would but … oh, right: you fired me. Not only do I have no legal power to do anything, but I'm actively prevented from doing so by the documents you made me sign."

Quinty straightened his scarves and donned his tinted glasses. "Same here. I'm on permanent vacay now. I'm going to Powder Mountain. They have this Farm-To-Table dinner event that is just so rad."

"More like Farm-To-Douche," Otto said, to the laughter of all.

"Don't worry, Armie. You'll be okay," Quinty said, slapping him on the shoulder.

But Armand wasn't so sure.

What have I gotten myself into?

CHAPTER TEN

Varinder Rahan and the Sea Castle

As Armand drew closer to Varinder Rahan, he grew increasingly aware that this would be his first real encounter with Concordia proper.

It was dangerous.

But the fight with Red Curls had given Armand a new primal confidence. If Rahan *had* been behind the hit, news of what Armand was capable of had, by now, reached his ears. It would make Rahan nervous.

Good!

Nervous people made mistakes.

Just then, the text Armand had been waiting for came through: his new elegant, three-story apartment in New York had been purchased. The offer had been accepted that morning, and it would be ready for him in a few weeks.

As Armand drove the winding road towards the sea castle that was Rahan's home, the views of the Pacific Ocean grew more and more breathtaking. Windy waves crashed against ragged rock. The late afternoon sun cast a golden glow over rolling hills and grassy meadows.

With each roll of the tire, the grandeur of the castle

became more apparent. Even the main gate was an impressive sight, adorned with ornate ironwork and topped with a family crest.

A guard waved him through.

Nestled amongst the hills, the castle was a blend of Spanish and Mediterranean architecture with terracotta roof tiles and white stucco walls. It was a massive thing with towers and turrets reaching towards the sky. There were multiple structures which surrounded the main building and a vast swimming pool, appointed with Greek and Roman sculptures, all likely authentic, Armand realized. A large black helicopter sat on a helipad — Rahan could get anywhere he wanted, fast.

There were also some strange sights.

In one side parking lot, he glimpsed several Rolls-Royces, but two of them appeared to be half-sized. One was double-sized. Two more were seamlessly mashed together like conjoined twins.

Armand found the main entrance and parked his rental car.

It was deserted — except for two young men wearing eighteenth century-looking garb. They stood guard near the colossal wooden front doors. Except, as Armand drew closer, he realized that they were not actually keeping watch over anything. Instead, they stared raptly at one another. They paid him absolutely no mind as he approached.

"Hello," Armand said.

The men did not budge.

"Hello," Armand said again. "I'm looking for Varinder. He's expecting me."

Again, nothing.

The men — twins, Armand now saw — were chiseled and model-handsome. Their skin and hair were almost cartoonishly perfect.

"Hello, I —"

A voice riddled with feedback suddenly jumped out of a squawk box. "Hey you two! Stop acting like morons and let him through!"

"Ohh!" one of them said, deeply annoyed. "Yes, yes, we heard you."

The other turned and looked pointedly at Armand, eyes wet with accusation. His twin hissed sharply at the broken eye contact.

"He's inside. Upstairs, then out to the back veranda. Go now."

"Thanks," Armand said, slipping past the twins, who resumed their staring contest.

The entrance was a grand affair, with a sweeping staircase and intricate stone carvings. And the inside of the house brimmed with lovely things of the past. The walls were hung with giant astrological charts from the 1800's. These were drawn on yellowed parchment and kept behind protective glass. There were also I Ching hexagrams, painted in crisp reds and blacks. There were large slabs of stone, bolted to the walls, covered in hieroglyphs which still retained their original bright colors.

A vast, clock-like art piece in the open hall caught Armand's eye. He could hear a din of clacking and clicking as he approached.

It was perhaps a hundred feet across. In the middle were thousands of tiny yin-yang symbols. At fast random intervals, they 'flipped' — the black turned to white and white to black. This was done mechanically, not with electronics.

Around the outer edge were astrological symbols in black on a gold ring, rotating slowly.

"Ah, Mr. Martel. You have found my Synchronicity Engine. What do you think?"

Varinder Rahan.

"And apologies for my nephews. They're idiots, please ignore them."

He was a tall, powerfully built Sikh. His shoulder-length, ink black hair was neatly tied at the back. He gave Armand the impression of a hungry, rangy panther.

They shook hands.

"It looks like a Difference Engine," Armand replied, referring to the mechanical computer that Charles Babbage designed — and even partially built — in the 1820's.

"Very good," Rahan nodded in approval. "It is indeed very similar in concept. Except this machine performs calculations of the soul."

"Yin and yang," Armand said. "Instead of ones and zeroes. The I Ching?"

Rahan fixed his gaze and quoted:

Here is a tale of a man's deeds and desires
Of his quantum choices — of madness, and twisted wires.
His astrology encrypted and hidden from view.
Only pyramids and shadows know the things that he'll do.

"What's that from?" Armand asked. "I don't recognize it."

"'The Continual Return of Doctor Ordinaire'," Rahan replied. "A rock opera that I adore. And yes, well-spotted — the I Ching indeed. A Synchronicity Engine is used to calculate a path through the world — one that produces favorable chance occurrences — in order to obtain a specific result."

"Really," Armand said, clearly dubious. "So it's a luck machine?"

Rahan laughed. "No. And yes. But that's not how I'd describe it. It doesn't generate luck — sometimes, there is simply no luck to be had. The stars are against you. What it *does* do is to optimize your possibilities, whatever they may be. To make the most of what is."

"And how does it do that?"

"You give it a goal. Something you wish to accomplish. Then, you set the Synchronicity Engine calculating. The machine casts millions of I Ching hexagrams. Something about the sheer volume of oracles generated and the algorithm for integrating them is what provides the secret sauce. There's more to it, I don't understand everything, but that's the gist.

"The output of the Engine is one or more actions that you should take. You receive a sort of recipe. Or a prescription. The actions will probably appear to be entirely unconnected to your desired outcome — but this is simply Jung's acausal connecting principle at work.

"For example, you might be told to learn how to tie a certain sailor's knot. Or to wear a red-and-gold striped tie to specific place on a specific day. Or even to bake a cake! Your father Didier used this very Engine once," Rahan said quietly. "In fact, it's the reason why he started collecting Egyptian antiquities all those years ago."

Armand tried not to let his extreme shock show. Sophia had come to him because his father had used *this* Synchronicity Engine?

"Really. What was my father's 'desired outcome'?" Armand managed to croak.

"Why, to get out of Concordia, of course!" Rahan laughed. "Alas, the Engine told him he was in for life. It told me the same thing, incidentally. But it did say that his children might one day be free."

That was news.

"So you speak of Concordia openly?" Armand asked.

"When we are alone, yes. And why not? You were born into a Concordian family. You have every right."

"What about you? Were you born into it?"

Rahan winced slightly. He looked up. Armand followed his gaze: there, on the next level above them, hiding in the middle shadows was a mousy woman. She'd been watching them this whole time.

"No. But my wife Celaeno was. When I married her, that was when I was admitted," Rahan whispered. "Celaeno! Come down and meet Armand Martel! This is the son of Didier! You remember him!"

But Celaeno seemed to shrink. She shook her head and slipped deeper into the shadows.

"Ah. She is shy," Rahan said. "Maybe later, once she gets used to you. But come! Let's go to the veranda. You and I have some things to sort out."

# # #

THE SUN sank into the Pacific like a red ruby, and sharp stars now appeared in the black deeps above like powdered jewels. Servants scurried around the patio, lighting fire pits and heat lamps, serving them drinks and food.

Armand sank into a lush chair across from Rahan. Twice, he caught Celaeno peeping out from a window far above. Each time he looked up, she was just then ducking back behind a thick curtain.

"First, you are to be congratulated on your takeover of the Martel companies," Rahan said. "That was a bold act, executed swiftly and effectively. Literally no one saw it coming. But tell me. How did you discover that your brothers had been swindling you?"

Oh no. "Like you, I cultivate many sources of information."

Rahan smiled. "Shrewd. Tactical. Excellent. Of course you shouldn't tell me. You'll do well in Concordia."

Rahan watched his reaction carefully, it seemed to Armand. He responded equally carefully: "I'm not in Concordia."

Rahan shrugged. "We're all in Concordia, in one way or another. But your coup ... it has now caused me certain problems."

Rahan had a pained expression on his face.

"Look. Armand. I provided capital to GigaMaestro expressly because I wanted it to focus on the next-generation of artificial intelligence. I'm hunting machine consciousness. Who will be first to make a soul in a mind made of metal?" His eyes were pleading. "A real soul. Electric sentience! It'll be *someone* in the next ten years or less. I want it to be us. "

Armand chose his next words carefully. "With respect, Mr. Rahan. You invested in a *tech* fund, not an AI fund. So the investment thesis is entirely up to our management. We can change it. Now, while GigaMaestro was under the control of Quinctius and Marius, it was true, they *were* chasing AI in a big way. But now that I'm here, I'm not as bullish on the space. At least not on the conscious mind thesis. I'm good with AI Art, chatbots, code generation — sure. But some kind of silicon soul? No. I don't buy it."

Rahan's face betrayed extreme frustration. He chewed down several responses silently. But before he could say anything further, Armand said: "Mr. Rahan. Recently a man tried to kill me. Was that you?"

Immediately, Armand regretted asking. He studied the panther before him for any sign of coiling muscles. He was desperate to claw back the words from the very air in front of him.

But Rahan just stared at him for a long minute. Then, quietly: "No. Of course not. I would never do that to one of Didier's sons. You can't believe that of me."

"Well, *someone* did. And you're clearly not happy with our

new ... *management*. And you *are* Concordian, which is sort of like being in the mob, from what I can tell. So I have no idea *what* to believe."

"It is true. I am not happy. But it's not enough to kill for." Rahan hesitated and then added: "However, if I were you, I would look closer to home. Perhaps your brothers. You took everything from them."

"My brothers would never —"

"This is Concordia. As you say."

Armand considered this for a moment.

"And what is Concordia, exactly? I've heard their version. I'd like to hear yours."

Rahan leaned back and said, "Oh, well. Concordia is a secret worldwide organization. It's been around for at least a century, some say more. Its goal is to bring all people under a single Pyramidal power structure."

"As opposed to the Circle," Armand said.

Rahan smiled and said, "Ah, so you've heard of 'The Circle Versus The Pyramid' have you?"

Armand nodded, "My brothers explained it to me. They're the only two power structures that humans ever use."

Rahan looked at him, suddenly amused. "Well, go on. Tell me what you think you know."

Armand continued, "Alright. The Pyramid, with centralized power, is a strict hierarchy. Kingdoms, empires, mafias, for example. There's one very small group or person at the top who gets all the benefits. The bulk of the Pyramid, let's say 90%, is impoverished and suffering.

"It's a great way to accumulate power and riches, but it's also inherently unstable. You have constant rebellion to deal with: the top is under constant attack. But also, each new node is another mouth to feed, making the entire structure weaker. And yet, at the same time, the bottom of the Pyramid *must* always expand to get more and more energy.

"The Pyramid must also grow ever-more restrictive of its nodes in order to maintain control as its ranks swell. Reduced liberties. Increased surveillance and police. So it always burns itself out in the end.

"The Pyramidal structure analogy also applies to computer architectures. It obeys the exact same laws. In a centralized computer network, increased demand always eventually overwhelms the center and crashes it. In the early days of the Internet, centralized databases were always getting killed in this fashion. The frequently appearing 'Fail Whale' on old Twitter was just one example. It wasn't until popular websites moved to distributed data architectures — Circles — that they actually became scalable."

"Very good," Rahan said, applauding. "You're a good speaker. Your brothers should have used you on stage at EPIC events — except that they were reducing *your* liberties to maintain control over you. And now, do the Circle."

"The Circle," Armand continued, basking in Rahan's praise, "is where human political power or computer serving capacity is decentralized. Examples of this include peer-to-peer networks like Bitcoin or BitTorrent or even the Internet itself.

"You could also say that United States is Circle, where power is pushed to the periphery. Checks and balances are put into place specifically to stop power from pooling in one place — to stop 'poison Pyramids' from forming, effectively.

"Each new node added to the Circle structure geometrically increases the strength of the whole. It becomes ever more sturdy. In a peer-to-peer computer network, increased demand *creates* increased serving capacity. It never crashes: instead, it just becomes more resilient, and *more bountiful* with increased demand and increased nodes. Every node serves every other node. In this way, each node always has an exponentially increasing variety and power of services available to it. It's incredibly scalable and stable."

Rahan nodded. "Very good. And now you've touched upon the crux of what's wrong with Concordia. In the Circle, everywhere is a good place to be. But in the Pyramid, being near the top is the *only* good place to be. So this means that everyone below you is forever clawing up. And anyone who sits on the throne is not there for long. Concordia changes management every few years. I've even seen it switch within a few weeks."

"Even you, Armand, you now find yourself atop your *own* small Pyramid. Your brothers have been pushed down the stack. So what will they do next? And what have they already done?" Rahan pointed out.

Armand nodded. "I see your point. But isn't it clear that the Circle is the best arrangement? I mean, take the United States. It's the most decentralized country ever created. When personal freedom is that massive, you get massive creativity. You get inventions like electricity. Airplanes. Moon landings. The Internet. Mickey Mouse. Elvis. Apple. Tesla. Those things don't happen in other countries."

Rahan shook his head. "I disagree that the Circle is best. The Circle also brings chaos. I come from that chaos. I was dirt poor, living on the streets of India — and I had to fight for every scrap of life. I learned to be brutal — at *six*."

"Wow. What happened to your parents?"

Rahan smiled grimly. "They were killed by Concordia. Does that surprise you? It shouldn't. Of course I would grow up viewing Concordia as the ultimate power, and thus the ultimate safety — and aspire to it.

"Remember, I was born into extreme hunger. I am talking about the kind of hunger where you actually don't even know what 'full' feels like, because *it's never happened to you* before. I am telling you, Armand, that the *reason* why there was so much poverty was because there was no *order*.

Everyone with their precious free speech! Isn't enough *food* for everyone more important than free speech? You can't *eat* free speech. Look at all the free speech on the Internet. It's cacophony! *We let two billion people talk to one another, and look at the result.* Lies can move around much faster now — lies which undermine strong leadership, and are thus anti-order and anti-safety.

"I have seen chaos up close. I have looked it in the eye. I promise you, you *never* want that. And the Circle *is* chaos. It's Lord of the Flies. The best answer is *not* a Circle, but a strong Pyramid. A stable Pyramid. Something *like* Concordia, but not Concordia. A third option."

"You've come a long ways from starving in the streets of India," Armand said, looking around at the sea castle. "It seems to me that America had a lot to do with that."

Rahan bristled visibly. "The country I was in is of no importance. I would have risen anywhere." His eyes burned with determination for a moment — and then, with clear effort, Rahan calmed himself. "And so. Concordia. You were asking what it was. Besides the structure, it is also a philosophy.

"Concordia believes that consciousness is primary, matter secondary. Reality — matter itself — is just a vibrational construct of frozen thought. There is ample hard evidence for this."

That surprised Armand. "Scientific evidence? *Measurable* evidence?"

"Yes. Anyone who wants to look can easily find it. As just one example, during the events of 9/11, random number generators run by Princeton University became markedly less random. It was as if all minds on earth — in state of agitation — fundamentally bent material reality. Minds should *never* be able to affect highly sensitive random number generators. Yet, they do.

"Then, you have the classic double-slit experiment of quantum mechanics. Conscious observation causes matter to either act like a wave or a particle, depending on how the experiment is set up. But how can this be, if matter is 'out there' and our minds are 'in here'? Minds should *never* be able to change matter from a wave to a particle. Yet, they do.

"So what is the only possible, inescapable conclusion? The one which Concordia, very wisely, embraces? *The universe is a metaverse for minds.* Matter exists inside thought."

"Really. Then what is the brain?"

"The brain generates mind — but at the same time, mind generates the matter of the brain. It's a paradox. They boot up together — and each produces the other, like two standing stones leaning mutually. Or like how yin has a little bit of yang in it, and yang has a little bit of yin.

"Someday soon, a metal brain will generate a real quantum, sentient mind. Someone somewhere *will* crack it." Rahan's eyes twinkled. There was no doubt that he was very excited by this idea. "You could be on board for that. Google. Facebook. Tesla. Tiny, in comparison, to what this opportunity represents."

Armand wasn't impressed: "That sounds like a bunch of New Age bunk. Manifesting. Vision boards. The Secret. If any of that's really true, why can't we *control* reality? Why can't I tell that table over there to melt?"

Rahan shrugged. "Probably only because we lack mental clarity and forcefulness. Our awareness is undisciplined. But even our weak, mewling minds can affect reality in a small, yet measurable, way."

"Alright. So what does Concordia have to do with any of this?"

"Concordia seeks to blind the masses from vibrational reality. It wants you to think that matter is all that there is. This cuts people off from their cores, making them easier to control. Easier to push into Pyramids. Un-cored people are more fearful and more angry. If you can steer the thoughts and feelings of the masses, and you can steer the material world.

"This Concordia does through a variety of projects. It has people inside politics, social media, research, news, search engines, movies, television, medicine, physics, universities — you name it."

"But how could they possibly influence science? It's evidence-based. Wouldn't someone notice?"

Rahan laughed aloud. "Easy. Simply control what is 'accepted' science, and blackball anyone who doesn't toe the line. Cut funding and tenure. Ridicule them as quacks. Evidence doesn't matter if the experts don't accept it, if the press doesn't get behind it.

"The same is true in any field. Think of what *you* believe. In almost every case, you'll find that you only know about it because someone else told you. So hiding vibrational reality is easier than you might think. But it *does* take effort, organization. Concordia has many projects afoot to accomplish this. You know of at least one of them — the Musipocalypse."

Armand nodded. His father, Didier, had been the architect.

"We were very good friends, as you know. I miss him! Didier was recruited by Concordia in the early 70's. Great rock albums by the Beatles, Pink Floyd and others were re-connecting people to their cores." Rahan smiled at a memory. "'Castles made of sound', your father used to call them. These were the cathedrals of our day. The soul-numbing conformity of the fifties and early sixties, the control grid, was breaking down. The rubes were waking up.

"This may seem like a tiny thing. *How could rock albums be so important?* But they *were* because they were suddenly occupying a large amount of human attention. *Attention is the ultimate energy.* If you understand that mind drives the mechanisms of material reality, and that mind influences physical random number generators and powers the synchronicities which drive world history, then you understand that this new development is a very big deal indeed.

"Your father was quite the musician. He could have been great! Instead, Concordia compromised him. It offered him great riches. All he had to do was use his talent to engineer a 'musipocalypse' — an injury to the collective unconscious which would stop the production of great new rock art. To make it bland, forgettable.

"This he accomplished. By the mid-nineties, it was done. Today, most new music sounds like a washing machine."

Now Rahan leaned in close: "The money that you and your brothers inherited, Armand, is — at least in part — Musipocalypse money. You need to understand that."

Armand took this in with some shock. "So what does that mean? Does Concordia think that they own me and my brothers?"

"You? No. But your brothers? Yes. And the money? No. It's yours: you took it from them fair and square. Nevertheless, they are not happy about you."

"Do you think Concordia tried to kill me?"

Rahan laughed. "No. Take no offense at this, but you're simply not interesting enough to kill. Concordians are very big believers in karma. To them, it's as certain and exact as the conservation of energy. They would not willingly incur karmic blowback without considerable gain."

Armand nodded. "So what about you? Are you a loyal Concordian?"

Rahan nodded. "Yes. Without question. I owe them

everything. And they could destroy everything I have in an afternoon. No one can stand against an organization that large, that tightly organized, that effective, and ever hope to survive."

"And you say this, knowing full well who and what they really are."

"I do. But I did not say that I liked it. In fact, most Concordians don't! Most are trapped in some way — whether it's via blackmail or financial or legal constraints." Rahan hesitated and then added: "But one can work *within* Concordia to try and steer it in new directions. Perhaps a hopeless task. But it's the best I can do."

Armand nodded. "I understand. And I hope you'll understand that I likewise want to take GigaMaestro in a new direction. I just think machine consciousness is a money pit. For years, at EPIC events, I've heard guys like Wakao Akihito talk about the Singularity and how once we get a big enough neural net, consciousness will just 'emerge'. Well. There's not one shred of evidence of that happening with smaller nets. We've seen no 'micro-consciousness' to date. So I think this belief of Akihito's is basically a superstition. An electronic superstition."

Rahan smiled and rose, hand extended. "I do understand. And now that we have met, I find that I like you, Armand Martel. You are without fear and you speak your mind. I am a fan, as I was a fan of your father's. You will have no further difficulties from me on the direction of the Fund, though I do very much hope you'll change your mind. I'm always here if you want to discuss it."

Armand rose and shook his hand. "Thank you, Varinder. I very much appreciate that."

As if on cue, two men in orange jumpsuits seemed to materialize out of the darkness just beyond the firelight. Their clothing appeared to be a uniform of some kind. The flames licking from the gravel pit gave them an unearthly look, like they were astronauts on a strange planet.

Rahan was clearly surprised to see them. He darted a worried look at Armand and then back to them.

"Apologies, Armand. My next meeting has arrived." Rahan waved the orange jumpsuits over. Armand nodded and left.

Armand was surprised at how well that had gone. He wasn't sure how much of it he believed, but his main task of getting Rahan off his back fund-wise had been accomplished.

He could barely hear the conversation on the patio as he left, but he did hear this:

"I told you never to come here," Rahan said harshly.

"We're sorry Mr. Rahan," one of the jumpsuit people said. "But it's the townspeople. They …"

And that was it.

As Armand prepared to drive off, another car, a grasshopper-green Crown Victoria, wheedled its way up the long driveway. *Well, now. Who was this? More orange jumpsuits?*

But to Armand's utter shock, the man who emerged was Armand's would-be killer. He was dressed in an expensive suit, but his large frame and curly red locks were unmistakable.

Armand's heart raced. He had only missed running into Red Curls by a few crisp minutes! And what did his presence at Rahan's Sea Castle mean? Did Red have something to do with the orange jumpsuit people? With Rahan?

Had Rahan been lying to him?

But, no. The man was not admitted. He was angry about it. *How dare Rahan.* One of the ridiculous twins had stopped him at the front door. Armand thought for sure that Red

Curls was about to kill him.

"Eamon. No. He can't see you now," one of the twins said to Red Curls. *Ah ha. So your name is Eamon.*

High up in one of the turrets, a forlorn Celaeno Rahan peeped out from behind a long drapery like some melancholy character in a Victorian novel.

Armand waited.

Eamon started to get physical with Ridiculous Twin, but Ridiculous Twin was a lot faster and stronger — and less ridiculous — than he looked. He insisted that Eamon go, and go now.

Agitated, but clearly not willing to escalate, Eamon got back in his car and drove off.

Armand followed.

CHAPTER ELEVEN

The Atman Movement

HE LIED TO ME!

The more Armand thought about his meeting with Varinder Rahan, the angrier he became. What was Eamon doing there? How did he know Rahan? What was the nature of their relationship?

But it was obvious. Eamon was a killer. And Rahan had hired him to kill Armand.

Clearly, Rahan hadn't expected Eamon to show up at the Sea Castle when he did. He would have never made appointments with both Armand and Eamon so close together. And the men in the orange jumpsuits — they had also been a surprise.

Were the orange men and Eamon somehow connected?

He wished he could talk to Sophia about this, but he hadn't brought her codex. He didn't want to risk TSA confiscating it, perhaps thinking it was a stolen antiquity. Sophia was locked in a safe back in New York.

He missed her. He was surprised by how much.

As Armand mentally replayed the firepit conversation with Rahan, he now got the distinct impression that Rahan had been trying to make up his mind as to whether to kill him on the spot. It would have been easy — no witnesses at Sea Castle other than his wife. *Then why hadn't he done it?* Had something stayed his hand? What? Karma? Or had his up close appraisal of Armand somehow changed the calculus?

Several car-lengths ahead of Armand was the green Ford Crown Victoria driven by Eamon. They'd been driving for five hours — and Eamon showed no signs of letting up. He kept pushing north, up the Pacific Coast Highway. Armand was determined not to lose him.

His phone buzzed with a text from Quinty:

Quinctius: How did it go with Rahan?

"Good," Armand dictated to Siri. "Net-net, he's off our backs. He agreed that the Fund can operate as it pleases. I even told him *No* on the AI. He didn't like it, but he backed down. Send."

Armand refrained from discussing Curls.

A few minutes later:

Quinctius: Wow. Okay that's good news ya. I'll let everyone know. Thanks again. Amazing job.

Armand laughed. He hadn't realized until now that Quinty hadn't believed that he'd pull it off.

Just then, the Crown Victoria made a sudden lurching right turn. Armand almost didn't follow in time: the road was nearly invisible until you were right up on it.

Now Armand drove up a long, steep grade through a mountain pass. Already, the air was chillier. He was surrounded by craggy, ripped rock on both sides. Steel nets had caught falling boulders in several places.

He could see the Victoria — just ahead, with a camper and

a VW bug in between them — for a few minutes before the camper obscured it from view. It was a winding single-lane road: *good*. They would be locked into this caravan formation for awhile.

When Armand tried to continue texting with Quinty, he found he had no bars.

# # #

AN HOUR LATER, Armand descended a steep grade out of the mountain wilderness. The road opened up into several lanes, and the air warmed right up. As the VW bug and the camper separated and sped up, Armand got his first clean view of the road ahead.

The Crown Victoria was gone.

Impossible!

Armand let out a primal yell.

He couldn't have slipped away! There had been nowhere to go. There had been sheer cliff faces on either side — the whole way up and down. There were no side roads, no rest areas, no possible ways to turn off or even to stop.

Gloom filled Armand's stomach.

Had Eamon seen him?

As Armand's car emptied out of the mountains onto deeply-forested plains, he saw that he was running out of gas.

A sign said:

WELCOME TO ATMAN!
Home of the Atman Movement

He turned off the freeway and found himself in an idyllic town. He saw a barbershop, an old brick firehouse complete with a clock tower, a green wooden gazebo in a town square — adorned with firefly-like winking electric lights, a baseball field thick with the tangy smell of freshly-mown grass, a hometown hardware store, a mom-and-pop bakery and an old gas station. All of this was a classic Main Street USA scene, as if torn from an old postcard or a Polaroid snapped on the Fourth of July.

Except for one thing.

At least half the townsfolk were wearing orange jumpsuit uniforms exactly like the ones Armand had seen at Rahan's Sea Castle.

Well, hello there.

# # #

THE TWO WOMEN were shaven completely bald. They wore the obligatory orange uniform. They filled the gas tank of their black Cadillac Escalade ESV and ignored stares from the townfolk having breakfast in the diner. When they finished, they gave saccharine smiles and drove off into the deep-shadowed forest.

"Who was that?" Armand asked his neighbors at the breakfast counter. After he'd lost track of Eamon, Armand had grabbed a cheap motel room and crashed for the night. Then, he'd risen around 6:30 AM and walked to the diner next door.

"Cult," an old woman sneered. "The Atman Movement. Been here for years now. We can't get rid of them."

"More like bowel movement," a grubby trucker added. "We used to have an ordinance against communes. But when the Atmans got busted for it, they just spent a bunch of money on lawyers and tied it all up in court."

"That's right," the lady cut in. "Meanwhile, they started recruiting homeless people. Free food, free roof over your head, just come to the forest cult! Well, that worked like crazy, and they had an army of new voters. So they just voted themselves in as the new council members, and retroactively got rid of the commune ordinance. All the charges had to be dropped. Nothing we could do."

"Wow," Armand said. "That's nuts."

"Yep," said the trucker.

"Yes," said the old woman.

The conversation then drifted on to how the orange-jumpsuited strangers had first arrived in the leafy town of Buttermill, California. The townspeople had been curious about them, but not threatened. The strangers were different, sure. Weird, yes.

But so what? Live and let live. That was America.

The first surprise came when the Atmans purchased 70,000 forest acres. Where the money had come from to do this, no one knew.

But Armand knew instantly. *Varinder Rahan.* This was him. *But why?*

At first, the orange strangers mostly kept to their new forest land, camping in yurts. But every now and again, they'd wander into Buttermill for supplies. Rail-thin men with long hair and scraggly beards and bald women were now frequently seen at the laundromat, smiling and singing as they washed orange clothes.

Or at the grocery store, buying food in bulk, loading it all intro flatbed trucks.

Or at the lumber & hardware store, ordering concrete, nails, nail guns, two-by-fours, plywood and plasterboard.

How long was Buttermill going to have to put up with this? Some days now, you looked down Main Street, and all you could see were The Orange People.

And they were always loud, always in motion. Showy. They wanted to be seen. Always with the fake smiling and the singing. Always with the selfies and the videos! Instagram, TikTok, YouTube, X — they were constantly uploading Atman Movement content, always recruiting.

Come! Join us! Look how fun it is! Look how much you'll be loved!

The townsfolk watched, shaking their heads.

This would come to a bad end.

Next came a new phase: the Atman Movement somehow started to attract a higher caliber of recruit. Not just burnouts, dropouts and hippies, but doctors. Lawyers. City planners. Airplane pilots. Software developers. Crypto and financial experts.

Now the Atmans were armed with serious expertise. They could do better than yurts. *Much* better. Construction at the forest compound kicked into high gear. New buildings flew up at a dizzying pace.

They started with cabins. Hundreds of them. Maybe thousands. But soon came a town-sized electrical grid, sewage pipes and water mains. And finally, a vast outdoor auditorium — a Temple — and a private airstrip and helipad.

This was too much. This horrid city-state had arisen in the woods overnight — and Buttermill had now been reduced to their supply-chain staging area. Tensions between the Atman Movement and the Buttermill townfolk grew.

"Hey creamsicle! Go home! Nobody wants you here!"

"It's called *saffron*, you bigoted chucklehead!"

The townsfolk finally got the Sheriff to go on the attack with zoning and commune-busting laws. But the Atmans, with their very existence threatened, fought back. They recruited the homeless from across America, producing thousands of new Buttermill voters overnight.

In the next election, they won all the Town Council seats. Enraged at how close they'd come to death by playing defense, now, the Atmans went on offense. The names of the roads were all changed from things like North Bottom Way, Calligan Drive and Turtlemilk Lane to Namgyal Way, Bongpatsang Drive and Nyingpo Lane.

The town of Buttermill became the town of Atman.

The "Welcome to Buttermill! A Nice Place To Live," sign on the freeway was torn down and replaced with: "Welcome to ATMAN, Home of the Atman Movement!"

The friendly small-town police department was replaced with the Peace Patrol, an Atman-run law enforcement organization.

And of course, the police uniforms were orange.

# # #

ARMAND WONDERED what Rahan was up to with all of this.

"So. Where is this Atman compound located?" Armand asked. "I might have to go have a look at all this myself."

The old woman jerked in horror. "You're not going to join up, are you?"

"Oh no! Are you kidding? I just find it fascinating. I want to sneak in, maybe get pics for my Substack."

"Oh. What, are you like a journalist?" the trucker asked.

"Mm. Online version, I guess. I have subscribers. It's all conspiracy theory stuff mostly. It's called The Sharp-Eyed Citizen."

"Oooooh," the old woman and the trucker said at once. "I love that site," the woman said.

"Yeah! It's awesome!" the trucker replied.

Armand smiled, amused. He had not expected this.

"Hey. You're not 'Thomas Paine', are you?"

Armand nodded, lying. "Shh. But yes. That's me." Paine was the main writer on the site.

"Oh wow!"

"Golly!"

"Bring the Paine!" the Trucker shouted, which was the writers catchphrase. "Ooh, sorry. I'll bet you want to stay all undercover."

"That's right," Armand said. "Quiet. Keep me a secret."

"Well, in that case … you just go up this road about 15 miles, then turn onto Atman parkway — yeah, they renamed the road! — Go for another mile, and you're there. You'll see the guard gate."

Armand nodded. "Thanks."

# # #

IT DIDN'T take Armand long to find a hole in the fence which surrounded the Atman compound. The barrier was apparently mostly for show: other than the side which faced the road, the cult left it in disrepair.

Armand trekked through the woods for a mile or so until he came to the first ring of cabins.

He hung back as he heard a wooden door on an old spring stretch open with a metallic groan — and then bang shut. A group of four orange-clad men emerged, one African-American, two Asians and one scrawny white guy with shaded glasses. They all looked like hippies.

He waited for them to pass and then pressed on.

This had to be some kind of paramilitary training camp, Armand decided. Somewhere, there was an armory. Tactical gear. Somewhere, there was a combat theatre. Training. Wargames.

The strong pine-smell of the woods became mixed with the smell of water as Armand made his way forward. There was a lake nearby, he realized: a big one. It made sense: a water supply was a key ingredient of sustainable base.

He encountered more cabin clusters, all joined by winding sand trails. Brown wooden signs with yellow lettering appeared at regular intervals, pointing the way to the Commissary, Paramahansa Lake, Atman Auditorium, The Temple, Atman Air Field and the various cabin-clusters, all with Indian-sounding names.

These cabins appeared to be completely deserted. They had apparently emptied out for the day's activities.

As Armand came to the top of a hill, he suddenly heard laughter and chanting. Carefully, using a boulder and the forest as cover, he had a peek.

Down the other side of the hill was a large flat valley, hosting a highly-planned community in the shape of a mandala.

Concentric rings of buildings hugged a very large building in the center. That had to be the Temple, Armand thought. The cult center. There were concrete-paved roadways between the buildings. Circular roads, joined together by straight roads which radiated out from the Temple at the center.

It looked like Burning Man.

And like Burning Man, bicycles were the preferred mode of transport here. There were thousands of them, some in use, some jumbled together in piles. Some were tall unicycles, and some were pennyfarthing bikes with massive front wheels.

Armand didn't see any cars. Scratch that: there were *some* trucks, unloading food, it looked like, into a large building that was probably the warehouse or base grocery store. But this building was at the far outer edge of Circle City — no powered vehicles were allowed in town proper.

To the right, there was a massive lake that blurred into mountains on the far horizon. It held sailboats and plenty of canoes. Nothing powered, though, Armand noted. At the far side of Circle City, through a warbling, hazy atmosphere, Armand saw a plane land. A private airport. That was likely where Rahan himself came and went via helicopter.

To his left, he saw a large firing range, though it was not in use at the present.

Ah-ha. That was more like it.

There was also a Marine-style obstacle course, a few baseball diamonds and a soccer pitch. Beyond this were endless, massive square fields, crops, farm equipment, and irrigation water spouts.

Based on what he was seeing, Armand estimated that there were about 10,000 people here. So they couldn't possibly all know one another. If he could just get himself some orange, he'd be able to slide in undetected.

# # #

IT TOOK HIM a few tries and a few cabins.

Most of these people were skinny beyond belief. None of the jumpsuits fit. But finally, he found one that was passable. He slipped it on and moved down the hill.

The people in the streets were very cheery and friendly, all smiling and nodding to him. There was a lot of upkeep and construction going on. People worked very hard under a baking hot sun, but curiously, most were laughing and singing.

"Hello, fren," one man said as he passed, leaving the 'd' off.

"Uh. Hi," said Armand.

"May the Peace of Atman fill you."

"May the … yes. Same. Fren," Armand said.

There was a lot of this. "May the Peace of Atman fill you," Armand now said proactively as he passed anyone, learning to do the 'little bow' they all did. He also wore the fake face of beatitude, the little half-smile they all wore.

Meanwhile, he kept his eyes scanning, alert.

He really wished Sophia were here. But he pushed that pang down and focused.

The Atman compound seemed to be exactly what the townspeople had described. It was a cult, yes, but a high-functioning one. Not a Lord of the Flies-style sex and drugs cult, as he'd half expected. Rather, it was a cult of hard-workers. A colony of like-minded people. Everyone was busting their ass, making things, doing things.

It felt almost military. Was this, in fact, a secret army? *Was* Rahan building his own fighting force?

Suddenly Armand heard a loud gong sound over a loudspeaker.

"Attention, Frens of Atman. Shift change in the Temple. I repeat, shift change in the Temple. If this is your shift, please make your way there now. A new cycle starts in ten minutes. May the Peace of Atman fill you."

The crowd around him now grew noticeably restless. A good portion of them starting rustling around and moving quickly towards the center of the town's circular arrangement. Armand fell into step with them. He wanted to see this Temple up close.

He wanted to see what the hell Rahan was up to.

# # #

THE TEMPLE was a vast open-air structure. It was a circular pavilion with a circular roof, supported by sleek, sweeping steel beams. All roads in the Atman city led to it: the Temple was the nucleus, the core of Circle City.

Around the Temple was a large circular sand road. A dense, rotating mass of orange-suited people filled it — on bicycles, on foot, on non-motorized contraptions of all kinds

— all moving in a counter-clockwise direction. This raised a continuous fine haze of dust. The Atmans in this human gyre were all chanting something that Armand could not make out.

Threading his way through this cacophony and din, Armand pushed his way to outer edges of the Temple.

Something like two thousand people sat perfectly still on the pavilion floor, which sloped downwards into a shallow bowl. They were meditating, and all taking it very seriously. Most were very deep in contemplation. Some sat in chairs, backs straight with feet planted firmly on the ground: others were in the lotus position on little carpets.

At the center of the Temple were several gargantuan LED video walls. All displayed an incredibly complex mandala against a calm, shifting color background. The mandala had a newish look to it, it was not ancient. The patterns were more frenetic, dense, modern. The colors were severely bright and the edges were razor sharp. Massive speakers pumped out a soothing, New Age soundscape as accompaniment.

This was not at all what Armand had expected.

What was this?

Where were guns? The military drills?

Quietly, respectfully, he made his way down the bowl, stepping between meditators. There were many others walking around, coming and going from their 'shift', so this was not seen as odd.

When he arrived near the very center, someone said, "Armand?" loudly behind him. He knew that voice.

He turned and found Varinder Rahan staring at him.

He lied to me!

Ice gushed through Armand's innards. He debated several courses of action. But as he was surrounded by thousands of Atmans in every direction, there were no good options.

But strangely, Rahan did not appear angry. In fact, he was smiling.

"Welcome to the Atman Movement, Armand," Rahan said. "I don't know how you found it, but it's fitting that you should see it. After all ... this was a dream of your father's."

That caught him off guard. "My ... father?"

"Yes. This whole place was Didier's idea. I just provided the money to make it real. But he was the architect, the real visionary."

"What ... what," Armand panted. "What are you doing here?"

"Oh, well. Trouble with the Buttermill townsfolk. Again. Always something. But usually, I can drop in and smooth it over with a little money in the right pockets. That's why we were interrupted last night. Those two men you saw. I guess the orange uniforms left an impression."

Armand ignored this last comment. "Is this place a Concordia thing?"

Rahan laughed. "No. Concordia doesn't know about it."

"What is it for?"

"It's a generator. A human generator — of good karma."

"A *generator*?"

"Yes. I told you that I could never leave Concordia — but I never said there weren't *other* ways I could better the world."

"So all of these people ... they're just meditating?" he panted. "That's it? That's all they're doing?"

"That's it? That's a *lot*. Two thousand world-class meditators, round the clock? The impact is quite large. I could show you the studies — ones with six-sigma statistical significance. That's pharmaceutical grade certainty, by the way. We give people pills and shots based on that. Off the top of my head, there's one study that showed a 72% drop in terrorism whenever meditators were active. So, yes, two thousand meditators is a very big deal."

Was this a trick? Was Rahan lying to him — again?

Something suddenly in Rahan's eyes spooked Armand. The focus of his gaze had just shifted to a point behind him. It was subtle, but the Eopeii-within-Armand recognized it immediately — with great alarm.

Armand whirled.

Red Curls — Eamon — was several yards off, leering with a sick smile. He had a gun aimed at Armand's head. Armand's inner Eopeii quickly calculated: there was no time, no way to close the distance and disarm Eamon. And there was no cover to run to.

Rahan was going to kill him.

He was dead.

But just before Eamon pulled the trigger, he shifted his aim.

"Eamon! No!" Varinder cried out.

He blasted three shots directly into Varinder Rahan's forehead. Armand turned just in time to see the blood spurt from Rahan's blasted skull.

Armand spun again, prepared to fight — or die. Eamon looked him pointedly and lowered his weapon. Then, he vanished into the now-panicking crowd.

Armand let him go. He rushed to Rahan. But it quickly became clear: there was absolutely zero hope that he would survive this. His skull had been torn apart, his brains scrambled.

Rahan was already dead.

Armand slipped into the fleeing crowds and picked his way back through the cabins and out to the front gate — and fled the Atman Movement, Buttermill and Varinder Rahan's corpse.

CHAPTER TWELVE

Brothers and LLM's

NEW YORK CITY IN LATE August was magical, Armand thought to himself. Summer was almost fully spent. The scant days remaining were to be savored.

He walked now in the balmy late afternoon through midtown, wearing a light powder-blue EPIC-branded T-shirt. The sky was red with craggy clouds, which cast an orange pall over everything. One shift of street cart vendors had packed it in for the day and was rolling home, while the night shift was just now setting up shop — grilling sizzling sausages and pretzels and fries, waiting for the nightly revelers to pile of out of the bars, looking to gorge on grease.

Armand loved New York. The place was so *alive* and crackling, like a human fire.

It was his home now, for good. After all, he'd just purchased a large, lavish apartment on a top floor in the storied DePlussier Building. He liked being high up — especially now, after his two encounters with Eamon. He did not relish a third.

# # #

WHEN ARMAND had returned from California, he'd immediately retrieved Sophia's codex from his Alphabet City apartment and checked into the New York Edition Hotel. This was located in an old, tall building with a clock tower, annoyingly appointed with stifling, modern, migraine-silver art sculptures and little mossy decorations colored a shade of pale green that struck him like a visual record scratch. And everything was boxy with dark, heavy wood, which also felt oppressive.

Still. It was luxurious. The service was impeccable. And it was near Union Square and the GigaMaestro offices, so it would be convenient until he could take possession of his new place in the DePlussier Building.

As soon as he was settled in his room, he jumped on a Zoom with his brothers and relayed everything that had happened.

"So Varinder is dead? He's really, *really* dead?" Marius asked.

"Yes," Armand said. "I saw it. For sure. It happened right in front me."

"And there's no chance that he was just wounded or something?" Otto said.

"No. None. Zero I saw him take three bullets to the forehead. There wasn't much left of his skull — at least the front part. It wasn't something you could bandage up, put it that way."

"Oh my God. Armand, are you okay?" Cyrano asked.

"Yeah. That would have freaked me out," Ames confessed.

"Yeah. I'm good," Armand said. *How* he was good, he wasn't sure, but suspected it had something to do with Eopeii. Death was everywhere in ancient Egypt: it probably happened right in front of you all the time — unlike the West of today, where death was shuttered away, hidden. Even though every single person on earth died, this was the first time Armand had ever seen it happen directly.

Nevertheless. It wasn't affecting him, so far as he could tell. Some part of him merely accepted death matter-of-factly, as part of life. *Everything contains the seed of its opposite.*

"Ah, there we go," Quinty said. "I'm seeing it on X now. 'Tech Tycoon Varinder Rahan Dies' … they're saying it was natural causes. Age 73. Damn, he was in great shape for someone that old, you'd never know."

"Natural causes my ass," Marius said.

"Ya. That's *our friends from Concord.* They're covering it up," Quinty said, using the term for Concordia he preferred to use online in case anyone was listening in.

"Armand. You came straight home, ya? You didn't talk to the police or anyone else?" Ames said, concerned.

"Yes. I got back in the rental car, drove to LAX, flew straight here. You guys are the first people I've talked to since it happened."

"Okay. Good."

"But *should* he go the police?" Ames asked the others.

"No. Definitely not," said Quinty. "If they're covering it up, then it never happened. So if Armand goes to the police, that presents them with a new complication — one they have to get rid of. It actually puts him in new danger."

"Ya. If they're leaving it alone, then so should we," Samson said.

"Agreed," said Otto.

"Okay. But what about the guy who shot Varinder?" Samson said. "Armie, you said it was the same guy who tried to knife you from before, ya?" Armand nodded. "So this guy is still out there. What do we do about him? And do we hire, like, some bodyguards for Armand?"

"Look. I'm fine," Armand said. He didn't want

bodyguards suddenly following him everywhere, infesting his life. "And Eamon — the guy, that's his name — he had a clear shot at me at the Atman compound. But he didn't take it. So I don't think he's trying to kill me anymore."

"Why not?" Quinty asked.

"I dunno. His gun was pointed right at me. Then, he just shot Varinder out of the blue."

"Maybe he was using you as a distraction — to get close enough to Varinder to make sure he didn't miss."

"Maybe. But he could have easily shot me *afterwards* also," Armand said. "In fact he made a point of looking right at me, and then lowering the gun."

"That is weird," Quinty agreed.

"I find it fucked up that Varinder didn't warn Armie," Otto said. "I mean what would any of you do if a guy was pointing a gun at me? You'd say, 'Otto! Look out!' Right? But Varinder was just silent."

"Dude!" Cyrano said. "He's dead! Have some respect."

"He was probably just shocked," Samson said. "I mean, this all happened super fast, the way Armie tells it."

"Armand, you said that before the shooting, this Eamon guy was at Varinder's house, ya?" Quinty said. "Like, he'd come over for a visit?"

"Yes."

"So that's it, then. He was working with Varinder."

'Well, that's what I thought at first also," Armand confessed. "But now, I think Eamon was actually at the house to *kill* Varinder, not *chat* with him. Eamon arrived right after the orange jumpsuits did. So my guess is that he must have been following them — he probably knew that Varinder was about to get summoned to the Atman compound to mop up a mess with the townies. And when Eamon couldn't get through the front door at Sea Castle, the solution was simple: just sneak up to the Atman camp and shoot Varinder there."

"Hmm," Quinty said. "It's possible."

"So tell us about this Atman bullshit, anyway," Marius said.

"Ya!" Quinty said. "Let's get into it. So Varinder was setting up hippie communes. Who knew? Ames, Marius — did you know about this?" They all shook their heads.

"It doesn't seem very … like *our friends in Concord*," Marius offered, puzzled.

"Ya," Ames agreed. "This must have been some personal passion project of Varinder's. Like a hobby."

"It also doesn't seem very Varinder-ish," Samson said. "He was a Make War, Not Peace kind of guy."

"Well, Varinder did say that it was Dad's idea." *I just provided the money to make it real. But he was the architect, the real visionary.* "He said: 'I told you that I could never leave Concordia — but I never said there weren't other ways I could better the world.'" Quinty cleared his throat and glared at him through the Zoom window. "I'm sorry, Quinty! *Friends from Concord! Friends from Concord!*"

"But how was the camp supposed to do that?"Ames said.

"Meditation. He thought meditation could actually affect the real world. Like, scientifically speaking. He quoted a bunch of stats to back up why he thought it would work."

"And how many people would you say there were at the camp?"

"Ten thousand. Something like that. It was pretty huge."

"Seems like kind of an insane thing to do."

"Ya! Didn't they do something like this in the 60's? Like, a bunch of hippies formed a ring around the Pentagon and tried to mentally levitate it or something?" Otto said.

"That's not true!"said Samson

"It is!"

"I don't know. It seems kind of brill," Cyrano said. "It

seems very Dad."

"Which also means that Varinder was a good man," Armand said. "And so was Dad."

"Let's not get crazy," Marius snapped. "Dad did a lot of bad things. Our Molians. The Musipocalypse."

"I thought you didn't believe in the Musipocalypse," Ames said.

"But they were both *trying* to do something good," Quinty mused. "Even if it was a little bonkers."

"And remember: Dad was known for pulling off stuff like this. The Musip —"

"Oh, just stop it with that!" Marius groused. "There was no Magipalooza hokum kapocalypse!"

"So what happens to our Molian contracts now?" Otto asked. "Are we off the hook?"

Quinty thought for a long moment: "I would think so, yes. Varinder's dead. And our contract was with him *personally*, so … ya, I think that's that."

They all felt an immense, deep relief. True smiles, long gone from weary faces, timidly returned right there on the Zoom call.

"And Armand …" Quinty said. "I speak for all of us when I say … thanks. I mean, I know that you didn't directly *do* this … but you *did* get on a plane, and you did go to Sea Castle … and, somehow, you came back with a win. For all of us. So. *Thank you.*"

They all muttered gratitude — except for Marius, who looked like he had a lot more to say, but held his tongue.

# # #

BACK AT THE New York Edition Hotel, Armand opened Sophia's codex and repeated the whole story again for her.

"So because I inherited control of GM, I found out about

all this stuff with my brothers and my Dad. And then about *Concordia. The Musipocalypse. Molian contracts. Synchronicity Engines.*" Armand shook his head. "It just opened this floodgate of insanity."

MAYBE IT WAS BETTER WHEN YOU DID NOT KNOW.

That caught Armand off-guard. "What? No. No, definitely not. I'd rather know, trust me."

BUT EAMON TRIED TO KILL YOU.

"And he failed. Look. Sophia. This is not 'famine' all over again. You told me about my inheritance, and yes, true, that led to a lot of other things — but those things *were already there*. It's not like you created *a new threat*. You surfaced an *existing* threat, that's all. That's a good thing. You outed it all."

I UNDERSTAND. BUT WE MUST SPEAK OF THIS NO FURTHER.

Armand chewed the inside of his cheek. This was not where he had thought this would go. He had so many questions! He wanted her advice! He had so much more to tell her!

FAMINE, she said.

She was *his person*. And he needed her advice.

YOUR BROTHERS AND YOU ARE ON SPEAKING TERMS AGAIN. GO TO THEM WITH THESE MATTERS.

Armand wanted to press the issue, but there were only two pages left in her codex — and he did not want to waste them on an argument.

# # #

IT WAS DURING an artificial intelligence company pitch that Armand had an epiphany about Sophia.

The startup was called Linguify AI. Like many new companies in the space, it was building off the success of

ChatGPT, a Large Language Model (LLM) AI that had become immensely popular over the last year. The LLM technique had produced the first AI that was fully conversational, and it could thus pass the Turing Test and fool a human into thinking that it was just another person on a keypad in another room.

"Explain to me *how* it works, though," Armand asked. "Under the hood. What's it doing?"

The Linguify Founders said that an LLM would 'inhale' a very large linguistic data set — say, something like a good chunk of the Internet, or maybe all of X, and train a neural net using this data. Then, whenever you asked the net a question, it would compose an answer for you, one word at a time, using statistics it amassed from the inhaled data, to calculate what the next probable word should be, and the next one, and the next one, etc.

"Hmm. Does this only work with English or Latin-based languages? Or does it also work with ideograms — like Chinese?" *Or Egyptian hieroglyphs?*

"It works best with English. It's not as good with Chinese, but yes, it can do it."

"But it's not actually *reasoning*," Armand said.

"No," the Founders agreed. "It's not."

"It's not thinking. In fact, from what you've told me, I think that it doesn't actually *know* anything. Right?"

"Again, right."

"So it's mindless. Like a reflex."

They didn't like that comparison. But they admitted it was essentially correct.

"But *why* does this work then? I mean, it *feels* like it's alive? What's the secret sauce?"

The Linguify Founders and Armand went around and around on that one, debating. But what it boiled down to for Armand was that the LLM was effectively a remix bot. The reasoning that it 'presented as its own' had in fact *already happened* inside of human heads — and the product of that reasoning was thus *already present* in the data.

Put another way, the inhaled data was *sentience exhaust*: artifacts of truly conscious, reasoning minds. This exhaust was then mined with wicked efficiency. The LLM re-assembled it on command, based on a prompt, according to the rules of grammar, committing a thousand million micro-plagiarisms as it did so. Because it re-packaged existing human sentience as it's own, it seemed like it was human itself.

Hmm. So the reasoning does *happen somewhere,* Armand thought. *Just not in the LLM. At some point, true consciousness was involved — even for the LLM based AI's.*

It wasn't conscious. But it *was* piggybacking on true human consciousness.

Just like Sophia. Sophia was effectively a mystical, ancient Egyptian AI.

And that was the epiphany. The 'alive words' of Sophia's codex and ChatGPT seemed to be *very* similar phenomenon. They both acted exactly like sentient beings, but they weren't.

Both needed the true consciousness of someone else in order to function.

And Armand wondered what that meant.

CHAPTER THIRTEEN

The End of the Codex

THIS WAS IT.

Time to rip off the Band-Aid.

This night would be his last conversation with Sophia.

There were only a two thin pages left. Within hours, she would be silent, and speak to him no more.

No!

But yes. It was time to stop delaying it. Time to move forward, whatever that meant.

He paced. He dreaded opening the codex — dreaded it and desired it more than anything. How to spend these last moments? How to unlock the secret of more time with her?

"This was a choice on your end, Sophia," Armand growled. "You could have had Eopeii keep going. Why didn't you?"

THIS CODEX IS ALREADY VERY LONG. I CAN ASK NO MORE OF EOPEII. THIS TAKES A TOLL ON HIM.

"So find another Eopeii!" Armand yelled. "There's got to be more scribes hanging around!" He stopped for a moment, ashamed of his anger and then said: "Okay. Okay. There's a second Codex somewhere, right? All I have to do is find it.

It's out there. Yes?"

NO.

"But why not? Why would you choose — and you did choose this, right? — choose to end this book here and now?"

THE BOOK IS EXACTLY AS LONG AS IT NEEDS TO BE. NO MORE. NO LESS. IT IS PERFECT.

"No, it is NOT perfect. You're killing me. You know that, right? You're my best friend." And I love you. He was in tears. "And you're ending everything."

I MUST.

"Do you see something in the future? Do you know something?"

I CANNOT TELL YOU. AND YOU KNOW WHY.

THANK YOU, ARMAND, FOR EVERYTHING. I HAVE SEEN SO MANY WONDERFUL THINGS. I HAVE KNOWN SO MANY AMAZE THINGS.

YOU HAVE GIVEN ME A NAME AND A SHADOW. YOU HAVE PROTECTED ME.

"Will we ever speak again?"

FAMINE.

"Okay. Okay."

He turned to the last page now. It was almost over.

What would her last words to him be?

It was blank, except for a single ideogram for 'carpet'. He burst out laughing through his tears: it was her version of a joke.

She'd rugged him.

# # #

AUGUST MELTED into early September.

In the Northeast, this was still somewhat of a summer month. The darkness came earlier, and the sun was redder and riper — but you couldn't yet see your breath in the frozen morning air, and there were still days where one could easily go for a swim in a cold and muddy lake.

Armand was now doing only mornings at GigaMaestro. In the afternoons, he had another project: hunting for Concordia.

He had seen traces of it when he'd first taken over GM.

But now, he reasoned that it really should be everywhere. The world should be soaked in it. Especially New York City — if you just knew where to look.

He tried the nightclubs first. He dropped the word 'Concordia' in front of doormen and bartenders. The word brought no reaction. But of course, they knew who *he* was, so they let him in.

Then he called Dorianne the real estate agent, but his calls went straight to voicemail. And she never called him back.

He spotted Clara Blackwood in midtown, at a Starbucks. "Clara!" he yelled to her "Clara. Hi. We met the other —"

"I'm sorry — do I know you?"

"Yes. Its Armand. Armand Martel — we met when —"

"My name's not Clara."

"What?"

"We've never met, creep. Buzz off!"

"Then what *is* your name?"

She walked away at a brisk clip, model strut, middle finger high in the air. "Ha! Like I'm going to tell *you*, psycho!"

When Armand called the number for SANCTUARY, it had been disconnected.

Where had Concordia gone? *It couldn't have just vanished!*

But it had.

He started looking for it in strange places, like the abandoned City Hall Subway Station, a stunningly beautiful space with arched ceilings and ornate tiles that had been closed since 1945. *Could there be clues in the art?*

Or the High Line, a public park built on a historic freight rail line elevated above the streets on Manhattan's West Side. And then The Cloisters, a Museum which housed an impressive collection of medieval art.

Why was he doing this?

He mocked himself bitterly. It was all very emo. *The Sads, the Deep Drear, the Old Mood.* He was clutching, grasping, for something just out of reach — trying to catch a glimpse of a sliver of a ghost out of the corner of his eye.

But no ghost came.

Dense dreams rattled his subconscious at night, drenched with images of the previous day, thick with meaning, loaded with portents. But still, he received no answers.

Where could they be?

But he did not find them. However, now, he thought he caught one of them spying, but trying to remain hidden, unlike the last time when the spindly, otherworldly creatures had boldly *wanted* to be seen.

A man, far off, took a mobile camera pic of something near Armand, but not really, the man was *taking photos of him*. The way the phone was pointed was tilted just a little off.

"Hey! *Hey you!* Why are you taking pictures of me? *Who are you?"*

Smile-less, the man walked briskly off and into a train and vanished.

They never smile, Armand thought. *They never laugh. That's how you know it's them.*

Then, there was The Dutchman.

This was a very large man who frequently used a mobility assistance vehicle. He had a very feral look about him — scraggly hair, rattling wallet chain hanging from thick belt loops, bad teeth, and dull, comic strip dots for eyes.

And yet, somehow, he was everywhere in New York, omnipresent.

His little electric motor zipped along the sidewalk with a high-pitch whine, terrorizing pedestrians. For this reason, Armand christened him *The Flying Dutchman.* The Dutchman seemed like he was always just across the street from Armand. He was always at every gas station, coffee shop or bistro, anywhere in city that Armand went.

And it wasn't like he followed Armand. *Oh no.*

Rather, wherever Armand went, the Dutchman was *already there.*

It was as if The Dutchman were using Varinder's Synchronicity Engine to stay one step ahead of him.

After a week of this, Armand discovered that the Dutchman was *also* staying at The New Edition Hotel, directly below his own room, albeit three floors down. Chatting with the concierge, Armand further learned that the Dutchman was *also* waiting to take possession of a newly purchased condo in the famed DePlussier building.

What are the chances? Armand screamed in his mind.

# # #

"ARMAND, WHAT the fuck?" Quinty screamed through the phone. "You can't go to every nightclub in New York and ask about Concordia. Are you insane?"

"Relax, Quint. Nobody knows what I'm talking about," Armand said between popcorn munches, back in his room at the New York Edition Hotel.

"They don't —" Quint had to take a second. "Armand. They only pretend not to. And then they go report it up the food chain that some psychopath is talking. Somebody *always* gets told."

"Somebody in —"

"Don't say it!"

"Dude, *you* just totally did."

Quinty reflected for a moment and then said, "Fuck!"

"How did you find out? Did someone from *Our Friends In Concord* call you or something?"

"No. Not *them*, thank God. But I know two of the bouncers you talked to. They BOTH called me. They were worried about you, said you looked like shit, like you were on something. They were worried, ya?"

"Well. Nothing to worry about," Armand said.

"Have you been drinking?"

Silence. "A little bit."

"Well, that's not like you Armand. Did some chick dump you or something?"

Silence again.

"Oh. So that IS it. I don't know why you just don't go get on Rebecca Soares. She's obv into you now, dude. You're the high-status chimpanzee! Are you blind?"

# # #

THE COLD HAD come. Mornings now had a sting and a snap to them. Steam huffed up in great gouts from below the streets, the hundred-year-old heating grid exhaust especially visible in the fall and winter months.

Something in the air was new. Armand could feel it when he woke up.

Harper Bishop had sent him a text: her spreadsheets were ready. She wanted to meet.

That afternoon, she and Armand huddled in the conference room at GigaMaestro going over the performance of the Fund over the last decade. Amazingly, it was an 11x over the ten year period, which was actually pretty good, far better than Armand had expected. Both the general markets and digital assets had seen extreme volatility over that period of time, especially in the early 2020's — but somehow, GigaMaestro had hedged well.

"We were deep in Bitcoin for awhile," Harper explained, "But we got out near the top, and moved into stablecoins. That move really saved us." It seemed Marius had been responsible for that. "And we *completely* avoided LUNA and FTX — we had zero exposure. Marius stayed away from both of those also, despite a lot of voices in his ear screaming that he was crazy." Both LUNA and FTX had experienced massive crashes. "Oh. And while other funds were pushing us to get yield on our Bitcoin with Celsius or Gemini, we decided against it. 8%-12% was just too little upside, given the risk of completely losing the Bitcoin."

"And who made that decision?"

"Marius again," Harper said, with a hint of admiration. "There's an email where he explains why: he read the Terms of Service of all these yield services and they all basically said, 'We're lending out your Bitcoin to somebody else, so we might lose it — and if we do, there's no insurance. There's no FDIC of Bitcoin. So it's just gone, nothing we can do.' Marius reasoned that Bitcoin would appreciate far more than 12% if he just sat on it — and he was right about that — it's already up 70% this year alone." The yield services had largely lost the Bitcoin during the crypto contagion at the end of 2022 — so again, Marius had been right.

Results of the venture equity investments were mixed. As Armand had suspected, most of their startups were sputtering or dead. But despite this, they'd had three medium-sized wins in 2020, all acquisition exits, which was responsible for 5x of the growth. And then they had made a few new investments in the AI space, but it was far too early to assess whether these were winners yet or not. The other big concentration was in DeFi — decentralized finance —

infrastructure plays. But again, it was early days on a lot of these and the jury was out on whether they'd been right yet.

"So now, you've got to decide whether you want to keep chasing AI or not," Harper said. "That's the big call."

Armand shook his head. "It's a super crowded space right now. Everyone is fighting with sharp elbows to get into deals."

"I know. And the seed valuations are insanely high. You won't get the multiples."

"Hmm. Well. The LLM's are super promising … but, I don't think it's at all clear how anyone will make *money* yet. I mean, it could be that Google just sweeps the board by putting a clone of ChatGPT into search. Right? Then, nobody else makes money."

"Well, Quinty wanted us to focus on *sentient* AI specifically. That would be different."

"I know. And while that's cool, it never made business sense. It's Quinty and some techno-fad. Then we end up with a wildly unprofitable robot making pizza again."

"Creating actual consciousness is a fad? Are you kidding? " Harper raised her eyebrows. "If we cracked what consciousness actually is, it might be the key to uploading our minds to the cloud or something. So the business model would be living forever. And you'd have a lot of customers for *that*, Armand. The ultimate subscription service."

"Yeah. That's kind of what Quinty thinks. Okay. Well. Thank you, Harper. Let me think about all of this."

"Okay. I'm around all weekend — call me if you have questions. Oh! And congratulations!"

"On what?"

"Your new place. You're moving in tomorrow, right?"

Armand had completely forgotten. "You're right!"

CHAPTER FOURTEEN

The Tale of Didier Martel

THE ELEVATOR OPENED TO REVEAL Ames Martel and his racing bike. "Whoa," he said, removing his walnut helmet and admiring Armand's new expansive luxury apartment in the famed DePlussier Building.

"You like it?" Armand said with a grin. The opulent space assaulted the senses immediately with vast amounts of stone, mahogany and iron. It had a very 'old New York' feeling — but with a *lot* of open air. There were a total of three stories with very few partitions between rooms or floors. Several very tall walls framed 'gigawindows' which let in generous piles of sunlight. And there were two rooftop patios with granite columns and voluminous plants overlooking the city.

Ames laughed. "It's certainly a big step up from your old place."

Armand jogged down a huge spiral staircase. "Yeah, no kidding. I keep losing my phone! And I barely have any furniture yet. Oh. We can sit at the kitchen counter — I just got some new stools delivered."

Ames followed Armand and set down his backpack on a

long dark wooden counter the size of a sports bar. "Thanks for seeing me. After … you know. Everything."

Armand nodded. "Yeah. No worries."

"Well. You're going find this interesting. The Zoom call we all did got me thinking: If Varinder really was this great pal of Dad's, then we should have a lot of material on him from that time. Ya?"

"Material? Like what?"

"Well, you know that Dad was a musician, like me. So he recorded *everything* at his place, almost all the time. Just in case he came up with a riff or a chord sequence — so he didn't forget it."

"He did? How do you know that?"

"Because he told me about it. He suggested that I do the same thing! Anyway. Even in the early 90's, Didier was doing this with digital video."

"Digital? Really? I didn't think that came until much later."

"Well. To be fair, it was early days. You needed special hardware. But you *could* do it. And you know how Dad was always into the latest stuff. He had a bunch of these Super VideoWindows Motion JPEG boards. And by 2008, he'd moved all the video data to the Amazon Cloud. Which means —"

"Oh! It's searchable?"

"It's searchable. And I had one of the LLM AI's index it all — the faces, objects in the room, writing on the objects, what people are saying — all kinds of things."

"And? What did you find?"

Ames popped open his laptop and played a video.

It looked like old security camera footage. The camera was pointed down into a study. It was dense with books — and guitars. A piano sat in one corner, a Wurlitzer in the other.

A young Didier, in a very loud button-down shirt, in the 80's or 90's, was playing something on a twelve string, accompanied by a young Sikh man — still wearing his turban back then — playing piano.

Varinder Rahan.

Both men were laughing and singing boisterously — and drinking heavily. But even so, the playing was superb. Even drunk, Didier's fingers flew in a blur across the doubled strings. Varinder struggled to keep up on keys, but by watching Didier's hands for the chord changes, he just barely managed to do so.

"Yeah there's a lot of this," Ames said rolling his eyes. "Dad and Varinder loved to drink and jam. But then we also get … this."

Ames pulled up a new video. This time, Varinder and Didier were sober and in front of a very large sheet of paper on an easel. It looked like a blueprint. Razor sharp white lines against a dark blue background inscribed a giant shaded triangle with a number of circles of varying sizes inside of it. Next to this graphic were numerous mathematical equations.

Varinder was seated, pulling at his chin in contemplation, while Didier stood and excitedly explained something, pacing and waving his arms.

"Whoa," Armand said. "Were they building something together?"

"That's what I thought at first also," Ames said. "But then I realized that it was something else altogether. Here. Look at this one." Ames brought up another video. Again, there was a blueprint — but the arrangement of circles inside the big triangle was very clearly different.

"Oh. The Pyramid and the Circle?" Armand said.

Ames nodded. "Bingo. And look at this." He zoomed in the video.

At the top it said:

PROJECT ATMAN

"Holy shit! Dad and Varinder were talking about the Atman Movement back in the 90's?"

"This video is from 1993, so yeah. And the circles — the ones that are legible, anyway — they're all marked like Atman #3, Atman #8, etc."

"Can we hear what they're saying?"

"Well … sometimes. Those old microphones were pretty good at picking up loud music — in a ratty kind of way, but good enough so that you could make out what chords were being played — but unfortunately, they were *not* so good at human conversation. You can sort of hear a word or two now and then, but it's mostly garbled."

"How much of this stuff have you watched?"

"A bunch. It gets tedious. But one thing I have figured out: they're discussing the Concordian Pyramidal power structure — and how to nest circular power structures *inside* of it."

"What? They're *mixing* them? But why would they do that?"

"I think they were trying to infect the Pyramid."

Armand blinked. "Infect?"

"Yeah. Like with a cancer. But a *good* cancer, if you will. A karmic cancer. They were trying to offset the bad karma with good."

"Why?"

"To bring the Pyramid down. They were trying to destroy Concordia."

Armand looked up at Ames. "Seriously?"

"Well. That's what it looks like to me."

Had Varinder and Didier been working together in secret

against Concordia? But no. Varinder had unequivocally said that he was *loyal* to Concordia — so that didn't square up. Or maybe Varinder had once flirted with rebellion and then gotten scared and backed off.

"So this plan — it's a thing like the Musipocalypse, I take it?" Armand said. "It's like a ... I dunno, a *mystical* attack?"

"Yes," Ames said. "For lack of a better word. But I would call it a *vibrational* attack. That sounds less magical, more science-y."

"Still sounds magical. But they're trying to do more than just *offset* the karma, though. Right? They're not just trying to match Concordia pound-for-pound."

"Oh, agreed. It not just a simple brute force attack,"said Ames.

"Right, because that would be ridiculous. They would've had to have founded their own, like, *Inverse Concordia* to generate the same amount of inverse karma. And it would've had to have been the same size — just to hold Concordia to a stalemate, *just to nullify it.* And all of that *still* wouldn't have been enough to *overpower* Concordia or reverse it, much less *destroy* it."

"True. But even so, Dad and Varinder wouldn't have had the resources to create *that*. Nobody did. Except, hilariously, Concordia," said Ames.

"Right. So this plan must have been about doing more with less. About taking a small number of resources and force-multiplying them," said Armand. "Make one meditator have the impact of one hundred."

"You got it. It's *strategic*. It's highly, highly organized, vibrationally speaking. So I think the Circles are supposed to work like a kind of karmic C-4 applied to the load-bearing stress points of the Concordian Power Pyramid."

"And the Atman camps are the C-4," said Armand. "This is a karmic demolition."

"Yes."

"So if you 'detonate' enough meditation energy from the Atman camps, and if it's *directed* in the right way, and meticulously structured and leveraged, then boom! Concordia comes tumbling down."

"Yes. That was the general idea. I think! Remember, I'm just guessing here. But yeah, this is what I see."

Armand whistled. "I wish we could hear them." Still. There was no denying that this was quite the find. "So there's more than one Circle on the drawings. I assume there was more than one camp?"

"Yes. They were to be spread out geographically."

"How do you know that?"

"One of the other videos I watched showed them discussing a map of the world. It showed like 30 or 40 Atman compounds, something like that. My guess is that the physical positioning of the locations geographically was important somehow to making the vibrational leverage work."

"So old Varinder was moving forward with this, actually making it happen. Damn. Those were some big old balls on that guy," Armand mused. "But we don't know how many of these camps Varinder had up and running when he died. It might have been just the one in Buttermill — or it might have been a lot more."

Ames smiled. "Well, I dug around online a bit last night. It looks like your Buttermill group was pretty loud, digitally speaking. They used to do a ton of YouTube, TikTok, Insta and X — it was all recruiting videos, mostly. But those accounts are locked or deleted now. And there are no socials at all from any other Atman chapters — at least not that I could find. So they're either more covert or they never existed."

"Hmm," Armand said. "So it looks like just the one camp

for now. What about it? Is it still there? Do you know?"

"There's been absolutely nothing in the news about it. But, as we know, Concordia edits the news. I mean, there was no reporting at all on Varinder's shooting. They reported his death as natural causes. So — maybe the camp's still there, or maybe not."

Armand chewed on this. He wondered whether it was worth a second visit to see.

"No," Ames said, reading his mind. "No. Everything's good now, Armand. Just let it be. For our sakes. We just got out of Concordia. Let's all stay in New York now. Ya?"

Armand nodded. "Of course, of course. Well. I guess the big question now is: Does Concordia know about this Atman stuff? And if so, did *they* hire Eamon to kill Varinder because of it?"

"I'd say not," Ames said.

Armand was stunned. "Not? Really? I mean, doesn't that seem like the obvious conclusion?"

"Not at all. Concordia has *lots* of hyper-wealthy members doing lots of eccentric things. Funding a meditation camp is hardly something that Concordia would find threatening."

"But Concordia is vibrationally hip," Armand said. "Wouldn't they understand what this *really* was?"

"Again. No," Ames said. "For one, it's way, way, way too small to look like a legit karmic threat. And unless you understood all the crazy Molian math and geometry behind Didier's plan, you wouldn't have any reason to suspect that it could ever *become* one."

"How common is that understanding in Concordia, do you think?"

"I mean, not very. Basically non-existent. By all accounts, Didier was their Mozart, a genius at this stuff. Which means, by definition, that *they* are *not* geniuses at it."

"So to even suspect the Atman plan, you'd have to

already know about and understand the Atman plan," Armand said.

"Bingo," Ames said. "That's my problem with your theory. *How would they find out about it?* How would they even know to go digging for the camps in the first place?"

"Okay. Then why did Eamon kill Varinder?"

"There are lots of possible explanations that have nothing to do with the Atman stuff — reasons that are a whole helluva lot more plausible. Maybe *Eamon* hired Eamon, because Varinder failed to pay him. Eamon gets mad about *that* and decides to shoot Varinder in revenge.

"Or maybe Varinder has enemies that we don't know about — which, when you think about it, seems pretty likely. So Eamon shooting Varinder might have nothing to do with the Concordia at all. In fact, I'd guess it probably didn't. In my experience, things are usually far stupider than we suppose."

Armand got up and got himself a glass of ice water. "You want one?" Ames nodded, so he brought two large, full and frosty mugs back to the bar.

"So the only one who could have understood this plan inside of Concordia — other than Varinder — was Dad. Strange question, then: Is there any chance that Dad is still alive?" Armand asked.

The question startled Ames. "What do you mean?"

"Well. When he died … it was in Egypt, right?"

"Yes."

"And we never saw a body. There was no funeral, because they never shipped a body back."

"That's true."

"Isn't that weird?"

"Yes and no. That happens with Concordians a lot. They die suddenly. The next of kin is notified, and that's that. Nobody questions it."

"Did you all try to contest it? You know, to get the body back? Do you remember?"

"No. We didn't. Because we knew that protesting would do no good. Concordia controls the authorities. So we just let it drop."

"Do you think they killed him?"

"No idea. Probably not though. Remember, they thought he was a genius. So they would have locked him up, not killed him."

"I guess that's true," Armand said. Then: "Hey. Have you told Marius about this yet? The videos, I mean, the ones on your laptop?"

"Marius? No. Why?"

"Don't. What about the others?"

"No, I've told none of them. Not yet."

"Can we keep all of this between us just for now?"

Ames shrugged. "Sure. But ... at some point ..."

"Yes, of course. It's just ... as you say ... we haven't figured out Eamon yet. Look. He's a hit man. We know *someone* hired him to kill me. And we know that someone wasn't Varinder, because Eamon *killed* Varinder."

"And you think it might be Marius." Armand made a pained expression, but basically confirmed this. "I see."

"Look. Dad trusted Varinder," Armand said. "And especially given these videos, I think there's no other conclusion at this point: *Varinder Rahan was a good man.*"

Ames nodded. "I would tend to agree."

"And Varinder thought that whoever hired Eamon, it was probably one of my brothers. Now, I completely trust you. I trust Quinty and Cyrano the same way. Samson and Otto, I probably trust, but not as much, but only because they're both knuckleheads. *But Marius?* I hate even thinking that it's possible. But ... what do you think?"

Ames thought about it for a long moment. "Marius. *Effing*

Marius. He's always had problems, be it with drugs, drink, or women … and we know he's always hugely resented being second in command to Quinty. So close to being the first born, but *not* the first born! It's got to be maddening. So when you took over and he didn't? That sent him into a rage.

"But what do I think? Ultimately? I think I hate to think it. Would Marius hire a hitman to kill you by himself? No. But a Marius on drugs though or drinking too much? I have to say yes. It's possible. So I think I'm at a Maybe."

Armand nodded. "That's where I'm at. So that's why I want you keep this from everyone else for now."

"Okay," Ames agreed. "I'll keep this from the others until you give me the all-clear. Deal?"

Armand nodded.

# # #

LATER, ARMAND and Ames sat out on the vast patio, watching the lights of New York City twinkle. Ames drank copious amounts of wine, promising to leave his bike and call an Uber.

"Hey," Armand said quietly. "One last question. What does Concordia thinks happens when we die?"

Ames snorted into his wine in surprise. It sounded funny, the way it echoed in the glass. "Wow. Where did *that* come from?"

"Nowhere. I'm just trying to understand how *they* think."

"Well. They don't talk about it a lot."

"How many times have you spoken with them though?"

"Not very often. Varinder was our interface most of the time. But there have been events in New York that we've been summoned to. Weddings, sometimes. Cocktail parties. Networking things. So, maybe, a couple times a year?"

"Yeah, so not a lot."

"The rest of what I know about Concordia comes from Dad. And he didn't speak very often about it. It was a source of shame for him, as you can imagine. He'd take one look at any of us, and Concordia and the Molian Man was the *last* thing he wanted to bring up."

"And what did you all think about that?"

"The brothers and me? Well Concordia was just Scary Old People Doing Scary Old People Things. We didn't really know. We didn't think about it much until we got older. Then we'd be all like, *Heeyyy, Dad, so remember when we were young and this guy came, and there was the arm-thing and* — and that was it, old Didier would clam up. Usually. But sometimes he was drunk — and then he'd talk. Give us tidbits, unconnected mostly, like he was really talking to himself. And sometimes he'd natter away about Molian math — stuff that was incomprehensible to us entirely."

"I see. So what about death?"

"Ah. Right. Back to that. Well, this I got from a Concordian funeral Varinder all made us go to. Out in the Hamptons. Death came up, as one might imagine. And from what I heard there, the Concordians think that people all sort of eventually magnetize for good or evil, over a series of lives."

"*Magnetize?*"

"Yeah. The guy I heard this from, Everett Donaldson, he was a high level dude. That was the exact word he used. *Magnetize.* It all boils down to, Did you serve others? Or did you serve yourself? I mean, no surprise there, that's the same thing every religion on earth *always* says. In Egyptian mythology, Anubis weighs your heart at death to decide what to do with you. Christianity has heaven and hell. And the Buddhists have Nirvana, which you get to by showing compassion.

"But unlike Christianity or Islam, in the Concordian mythology, one lifetime usually isn't enough to determine anything conclusively. I mean, maybe you die of polio at eight or something. *Can't conclude too much of anything from that!* But in most lifetimes, you *do* advance, somehow, maybe just a little bit, in one direction or the other, based on what you did and felt. You *magnetize*."

"Serving others ..." Armand mused. "Like in a peer-to-peer computer network, where everyone is a client but also a 'server'. It's service to others incarnate: the ultimate win-win topography. And it's The Pyramid versus the Circle, once again — but with a 'death twist': we all ultimately *magnetize* into one or the other — forever. That's what they think?"

"Yes. And the Concordian view makes sense, really, when you think about it. It's a fair system. *One lifetime is just not enough to judge anyone on.* You might be born into a circumstance which turns you mean: you might be abused as a child. Or you might be horrifically poor, so you turn to crime just to survive."

"Like Varinder," Armand said.

"Yes. Exactly. Like Varinder. What if he had died before turning that around? You know, back when he was a vicious thug? And anyway. Most people don't sort themselves out until they're forty or fifty — and up until the twentieth century, that was also just about right when you also died."

"And what about that? What happens when you do die?"

Ames shrugged. "Well. If you haven't fully magnetized, you reincarnate. *'They just keep slinging you back into a new meatbag!'* That's what the Everett guy said."

"Well. What if you *do* magnetize? What happens when you die then?"

"Then you go to the Great peer-to-peer Circle in the sky. You're exactly the kind of node they want in their network — you've proven it. And they're always on the lookout for quality new nodes, because new nodes make the whole network stronger and more bountiful for everyone. And thus, everyone experiences ever more abundant, ever deeper, richer realms."

"Like the hash rate in Bitcoin going up. The security of the whole network is improved with new nodes."

"Yes," Ames said laughing. "Exactly right! That's hilarious. So funny how well these computer science analogies apply." Then, after a pause, he said: "Oh. And they believe that Concordians are usually reborn back into Concordian families. I've heard *that* a bunch of times also — and not only from Everett."

"Really. And how do they think *that* happens? Who decides? I mean, how would Concordia even control that?"

"Nobody 'decides'. It just *happens*. Remember, the universe runs on vibration. So that means *resonance* decides. What family does your trying-to-be-reborn soul resonate with? That's where you go. Your vibe is your tribe."

"But they can't *know* any of this," Armand protested. "It has to just be a Concordian superstition!"

"Ah," Ames said, snapping as he remembered something. "But they kind of do. You know how they have that karma-measuring machine? The one used for Molian contracts? It's called a Moliaometer. Well. When a Concordian dies, they take a measurement. And whenever a new Concordian is born, they *also* take a measurement. Now, these measurements are highly granular and very unique, like a fingerprint, or a cryptographic private key. So if they match, if the karma is *exactly* the same, then it's assumed that this is *the same person*. They even have these matchmaking websites, where both sides can post a measurement number and hope for a match from a newborn!"

"So Concordia has this, like ... *genealogy* information. Wrong word but ..."

"Yes, I see what you mean. And yes. They can trace how many times someone has been here and who they were previously — at least, within their ranks."

"So this is why they take karma so seriously," Armand said. "If they lose their karma ... if they get *liquidated* ... "

"Then at death, they're screwed," Ames confirmed. "That's why Dad was so worried. And that's why he did what he did to us. And that's why we're all so grateful to you now!" Ames laughed.

"But what if you graduate ... negative? What then?"

"That is apparently very hard to do — actually, much harder than graduating positive. But then you go to the great *pyramid* in the sky. The harshest, most brutal imaginable environment. But Concordians love it! They aspire to it. Everett actually *wanted* to graduate in the negative. Because there, he said, he can let his freak flag fly. He can partake in venal delights, and it's encouraged, it's normal. And if you're on top of the pyramid, in that kind of a place, it's apparently savagely delicious — more so than, even, than being a node in the Great Circle. And that's the temptation, apparently."

"Damn," Armand said seriously. "But, with Dad's personal Molian contract — wouldn't Varinder have just let him off the hook? I mean, they *were* best friends."

Ames shook his head very seriously. "No. Not with a *Molian* debt. Varinder's hands were tied. Concordia does not allow mercy like that."

"So ... do you think Dad's come back by now?" Armand asked.

Ames laughed. "Well. Let's see, now. He most definitely didn't graduate positive! Or negative. So he's somewhere in the middle, which means he gets 'slung back into a meatbag'. And it's been eleven years ... so I'd have to say yes. A little Didier is probably *is* running around somewhere.

Look for a musician child prodigy!"

"Could we … find him?" Armand asked tepidly. "Do we have a Moliaometer death measurement for him?"

Ames shook his head. "No. None was ever taken. I don't know why. And I don't know what that means." Ames looked at his watch. "And it's getting late. I have to be getting home." He rose.

Armand nodded. "Okay. Well … thank you for bringing the videos over Ames. Really, really appreciate that."

"You got it."

CHAPTER FIFTEEN

Bryant Park

OCTOBER.

Sleep. Wake. Go to GigaMaestro. Sit in on startup pitches with the Associates. Think about AI. Watch some podcasts. Check X. Do Zoom meetings.

Home. Unpack the few boxes that he'd had moved from his Alphabet City place. Order furniture. *Lots* of furniture: his place was way too empty still, it echoed like a big cave.

He tried not to think about Sophia. *Where was she, right now, this very moment?* Nowhere. In fact, she had never been anywhere.

You can't leave if you were never really here.

But she *did* leave. She'd *ended the codex*. She'd *chosen* to do that. She cut the phone line, suddenly, with no reason, no explanation.

Could there have been a *future* related reason why she'd done that?

What good could possibly come from that?

Oh, whatever. He blamed himself for his pain. He'd *invested* in her. He let himself get attached. *His magical Benefactor.* Ha! He thought she was his friend.

But invisible non-people in books weren't friends.

# # #

HE NEEDED a distraction. So when Rebecca Soares came blowing back into his life, he was there for it.

"Armand!" she said when he picked up the phone. "Hello, stranger! I'm back from Barcelona — but I'm off to Panama in a week for South American Blockchain — do you want to have lunch while I'm here?"

Sure, Armand said, feeling his crush for her come surging back, strong as ever.

Now this is a real woman, he told himself. *Not a codex! Rebecca Soares was flesh and bone — and very lovely flesh at that.*

"Bryant Park? Tomorrow?" Yes! "Good, good. 1:00, then! See you there!"

It was October. Fall was here. The cafe was surrounded by the vibrant colors of the surrounding trees. The crisp air was dense with the aroma of autumn. *Football weather,* Armand thought. The outdoor seating area was bustling with life. Chatter, laughter and the sound of forks clinking against plates filled the air.

"Hiiiii," Rebecca trilled, coming around behind him. She was breezy and sunny right off the bat — wearing a tan skirt, black boots and snug black turtleneck. He rose — she kissed his cheek and sat down. "Look at you. Armand Martel. The man in the press everywhere."

"Oh, the 'coup' stories?" Armand laughed. "Yeah. I've read a few of those. The reality was a lot more mundane."

"Taking over a several hundred million dollar fund is very *not* mundane!" she laughed. "Tell me, who is doing the PR on this?"

"PR? Nobody. I'm not even talking to reporters."

"Nobody? Armand! You should be doing photo shoots!

Magazine covers! And you should be giving interviews, telling everyone the new vision for GigaMaestro!"

"Well, there is no new vision just yet. That's what I'm figuring out now."

"Oh. Well. You're still doing AI companies, right? We could start there —"

"Actually, no. I'm not." Varinder Rahan had wanted him to. But Varinder Rahan was dead. Not that it mattered. "Everyone is already in the AI space. So let everyone else chase that. I'd rather find corners and edges of things where nobody is looking yet."

"Well, there you go. That's pretty good. For your vision statement, I mean. Let's just put that out!"

Hold on a minute. Was she trying to get a PR gig? Was this a business pitch disguised as a date? Or were they both kind of the same thing in her mind?

What does Rebecca Soares even do for a living?

Armand suddenly realized that he had absolutely no idea.

He ran through past encounters with her in his mind. She was just kind of omni-present at every conference on earth. So, she was what, a socialite? He seemed to recall her emceeing conferences in Dubai and Malta. How did they introduce her on stage? Just, *Rebecca Soares, applause!* Everyone knows her. She's a brand unto herself, a character …

When you went to Disneyland, you expected to see Mickey Mouse. When you went to a tech conference, you expected to see Rebecca Soares.

"Rebecca, I'm sorry, I'm not totally clear on what you do for work. I guess I've never really known. Do you have a PR company?"

She looked like a deer in headlights. "Oh. No! I was just saying, like, I could help you put that out there with my X account. Like, as a *message*. I'd help you because we're friends!"

"But what *do* you do?"

Rebecca adjusted her body so that he could see a little more skin. "Well! I'm an Impact Investor, CEO, CMO and I have several businesses. First, there's my media business, Soares Productions, that's what I use when I get hired for hosting. Then there's my CEO Coaching and Wealth Mastery business — Millionaire Mind Meditation — I call it M3. I do *that* online or in-person. It's for anyone who wants to, you know, upskill, or gamify their financial life. That way, you're always 'playing to earn'. If you're *working*, well, that's bad, you should be *playing*. If you're *playing*, then you're doing what you love — while you make money!"

"That's a lot," Armand said, trying to be polite. In reality, he was amused and amazed by what he'd just heard. How someone could say so much while saying nothing astonished him. It was like this barrage of verbal empty calories.

Still though. She was super hot. He saw why it worked — and he wasn't immune to it. He felt her charm, her seduction.

Sensing this, she wiggled in closer and leaned in like a confidant, touching his arm as she spoke. "Look. Armand. You're on top of the world right now. But you just got there, okay? It's all new. So the way you show up in the world, right now, at this moment, it really, *really* matters. You have to set the tone, harness your intention. Or it can all change again! It can all go back. Look at what happened to your brothers!"

She drilled her eyes into his meaningfully. *The fear sell*, Armand thought. *She's a spiritual grifter.*

"I know this will sound kind of woo-woo, right? But you have to connect to your higher powers. Balance your chakras, your energy field. Do you believe in karma?"

Armand stared at her for a long moment. "I know a lot people who do."

"But what about *you*?"

"Me? The jury's still out."

"But you're open to the possibility?" Rebecca asked.

"Anything's possible."

"Look," Rebecca said. "The reason you are where you are now is because of *karma*. I can promise you that. You earned it, somehow, in a past life. So you deserve it! The abundance in your life right now, you earned it. *But you have to keep it.* Do you know what I'm saying? You have to keep earning it, strive to be worthy of it."

Armand looked dubious.

Rebecca continued: "Hey. Um. Do you mind if I give you some advice?" *Here we go.* She crinkled her face like she was going to tell him that he needed to use more deodorant. Then, she smiled and gave him a long meaningful look. "You need an Intuitive Coach. Like, a Mindful Business Strategist. To help you stay on track, karmically, to make sure you *keep* everything you've earned. To make decisions that balance business with the greater good.

"And — oh!!! I've got a great idea!" She clapped her hands. "We should do *a session!*"

"A session? What's that?"

"Well — we go back to my place. I have the right environment. I have candles and my sound bath brass singing bowl set, all of that. And I take you on a guided meditation. We go deep. And then we see how you feel. Ya?"

Oh my God. She did not *just do the* Ya.

"So you're pitching me on a gig," Armand said.

"What? No!" she looked offended. "I'm not trying to *charge* you! Of course not! We're *friends*. Then afterwards — we can go out! Have some wine, you know … !" She touched his arm meaningfully.

So *that* was it.

In her mind, that was all kind of one part business, one part sex, all rolled into one. She wouldn't expect him to pay directly, but she'd expect *some* kind of benefit from this: a hosting gig at EPIC, maybe, or an Advisor role with stock on a GigaMaestro portfolio company.

Oh, she liked him. At least, he *thought* she did: of course, maybe she was in his head already, making him think that. Yet Armand got the sense she wouldn't pull this routine with just anybody.

But, that said, there were probably several guys in the space she was also doing this with in parallel.

Nonetheless, it was tempting. *Why not? Stopping thinking about the fake girl in the codex who left you!*

But then he suddenly pictured himself having sex with Rebecca Soares — with her looking over his shoulder the entire time, searching for the next camera to jump in front of. *It would be like that,* he suddenly knew.

"Have you ever heard of something called Concordia?"

Armand was surprised to hear the words come out of his mouth. But why not? Surely Rebecca Soares, world traveler, beautiful woman at large, who knew many high-powered men up close and personal, would have run into them somewhere?

And besides. This date was not going to end well. He might as well salvage what he could from it.

Rebecca blinked, confused. "Concordia? Ah. No. I don't think so. Why? Is that a club of some kind?" Yet, she hadn't turned off the charm, she thought she still had him on the hook. In her mind, he was opening up now, and this was some kind of place he wanted to take her. And she was intrigued.

"Nobody's ever mentioned it to you?"

She searched her mind. "No. Not that I can recall. Why,

Armand? What is it?"

"I don't know," Armand lied. "I think it's a networking group. Like a MasterMind."

"Oh, *those* things," she rolled her eyes. "You mean *success cults.*"

Armand laughed, surprised.

"What, you don't think they haven't tried to get me to come?" Rebecca laughed her trademark life-is-a-party laugh. "Get the hot chick in, all the dudes will pile in behind."

"And you haven't joined any yet?"

"Pfft. Naw. I'd rather live my life going to conferences."

They stared at each other for a moment silently, then Armand said: "You were with Quinty. I mean, before, not exclusively, but —"

"Yeah. Yeah I was." She didn't break eye contact with him. "Look. Armand. Men like me, okay? *You* like me. And I choose to live my life in a certain way because of that. I've seen a bunch of my girlfriends either slowly die in a marriage they hate or get their hearts broken. So I put it out there, what I want, and if you want it also, if it works for you, then that's great, and if not, that's okay too."

"I see."

"Yeah. And I *like* going to conferences, you know, being right in the flow, and talking to brilliant people all the time — and I have to pay the bills somehow, right? So I cobble it all together however I can. *But I never lie to anybody.* I never lead them on. I don't want to be tied down, everybody knows that up front. You always know exactly where you stand with me."

"What happened to Mylon?"

"Mylon? Oh. Right." She laughed. "You saw us in that roof-deck place. Well, Mylon couldn't handle it when I told him I didn't want to commit to anything, so I had to cut him loose."

"And besides," Armand said. "His name was effing *Mylon*."

The both burst out laughing.

"I *know*, right?" Rebecca said. "What a horrible name! What Mom does that to her baby? And besides, I couldn't go through life calling out, 'Hey Mylon!'. Just, no." She paused, and then: "So how did you know that I dated Quinty?"

"You did the 'ya' thing."

Horror crossed her face and her hand flew up to her mouth. "Shut up! No, I did not."

"Yes, you did."

"Oh my God. He's infected me."

"He did. You've got it now."

"How are *you* not infected?"

"Because I hate it," Armand said.

"But I hate it too! How did he infect me when I hate it too?"

"It does have a way of just worming into your head, I have to admit."

"Have you ever caught yourself doing it?"

"No. But all my brothers do it now. Super annoying."

"Well. I need to keep my ears open to hearing that the next time it comes about of my mouth — and stopping it."

"You do." They locked eyes again.

"I like you Armand," Rebecca said. "I really do. But … something is holding you back. Isn't it? And it's not about how I live my life. You don't even care about that. Right?"

How did she know?

"Auras. Chakras. I'm an Intuitive. That wasn't all bullshit. I can feel it. You got your heart broke, recently I think … *ya*?" She laughed, doing it on purpose.

"Yes," Armand confirmed.

"Yeah. That's what I thought. Well. Where are you? Are you going to try to get her back? Or are you going to move on?"

He shook his head. "I don't think it's pos—"

"No, but, what do you *want* to do?"

"I want to get her back."

"Okay. So then it's just a matter of how."

Armand shook his head. "There's no way, though. It's a unique situation. I don't see a way to —" You have no idea.

"That doesn't matter," Rebecca said, shushing him. "None of that matters. What matters is what your intention is. So the question is this: Is it your *intention* to get her back?"

"Yes."

"Then focus on that. The How will come into view at some point."

Armand just nodded.

"There. You see? We just did our first session." She smiled and then kissed him on the cheek. "Good luck with her, she's a lucky girl."

And with that, Rebecca Soares left.

# # #

THE NEXT DAY, Armand made a decision about the direction of GigaMaestro: they would stay out of attempts at sentient AI, but they would go deep on the Large Language Model direction.

Armand then presented his brothers with a surprise: offers of limited employment back with GigaMaestro and the Martel Family Office. Armand admitted that he badly needed the help, and his brothers had immediately accepted.

"On a *limited* basis," Armand had emphasized, "with new agreements, and no 'Marius math' with the books." His Fisher Watson attorney had joined the call at that point and made certain the new terms and strict boundaries were understood by all.

CHAPTER SIXTEEN

Boot Sequence

ARMAND ATTENDED ALL HIS BOARD meetings, startup pitches, and podcast appearances, but his mind was elsewhere. Fortunately, his brothers had returned to the office and were picking up the slack. He had given them back their old desks, except for Quinty's. Armand kept the largest office in the corner for himself, leaving Marius to float around to whichever desk was open on the floor. This made Marius feel like an Associate, which infuriated him. He'd tried to make the argument to Armand that he should take Harper's office, but Armand nixed that immediately: Harper dealt with finance, salaries, and other sensitive information — she was frequently on the phone discussing numbers and other issues that were private and could not be overheard, she absolutely needed a door that she could shut.

The next few weeks were waking misery. The loss of Sophia was eating him alive.

Even his brothers noticed the change in him.

He found himself going on X to argue with people.

While his brothers were puzzled by Armand's behavior, they noticed that he always kept an old book on his desk. He never seemed to be without it, carrying it to meetings and back again without ever opening it.

"It's like he's a serial killer with a trophy, ya?" said Quinty to Cyrano, noticing this. "Like, that's a body part of one his victims."

"Didn't he meet up with Rebecca?" Otto asked. "I thought that was going okay?"

"No," Quinty said quietly. "It didn't take."

Several times, Armand thought seriously about burning the Book. It might be a way to move on. But he just couldn't bring himself to do it. The book was the one connection he had to Sophia, even though it was a broken one. It was still a totem of her.

Armand spent late nights scouring antiquities websites. Sotheby's. Christie's. EBay and Etsy. He looked at anything found in Saqqara, legally obtained or not. He tried to find anything ancient with the name EOPEII written on it. He even put word of his interest out on the darkweb. But other than obvious forgeries hastily concocted to satisfy his request, nothing surfaced.

Armand asked Sadie Brown, Director of Acquisitions at Martel Antiquities to be on the lookout for items that fit this description, and to buy them immediately if found.

# # #

ARMAND WANDERED down to an ice cream stand just outside of the GigaMaestro office. It was an unseasonably hot October day, and a line had formed. Armand stood behind a stylish older man in a gray suit with a pop of purple in his pocket and matching socks. He gripped a black cane with a golden head, and wore black, horn-rimmed glasses with thick, shaded lenses.

"Seems we all had the same idea," the man said with a

smile.

Armand nodded, distracted, barely there. He hadn't slept in three days. His eyes were bloodshot and he felt itchy.

"You uh … you seem like you're trying to work out a problem … if you don't mind me saying so. I've been there. I know the look. Stuck on a bug?"

"Yeah. Something like that. I don't think it's solvable."

"Ah. Sorry to hear that. Do you know what I do for a living?"

"No idea."

"Nothing! I'm retired! Have you ever heard of the Voynich Manuscript?" Armand shook his head. Would this guy please shut up? "No? Well, it's a richly illustrated book written in an unknown language in the 15th century. Nobody knows what it says! I've been trying to decode it. I've been at it my whole life, and let me tell you me, I've had days where I look just look like you do right now!"

"Maybe it says nothing," Armand said glumly. "Maybe it's a practical joke." There was more acid in his voice than he'd intended and he instantly regretted it.

The man seemed to notice. But he said nothing and continued: "Well, they once said the same thing about the Copiale Cipher. It took them nearly 250 years to decipher *that* one. But they finally managed it in 2011. It turned out to be a substitution cipher — using Roman letters, Greek letters, and symbols. Do you know what it said?"

Armand shook his head.

"Well, there was a secret society of optometrists in the 1730's — they called themselves *The Oculists*. And the Copiale Cipher was their initiation ritual — into the secret society of eye doctors! *Can you imagine?* The Oculists! I love that! Making nefarious spectacles, or maleficent monocles, I like to imagine!"

Armand gave no indication that he'd heard a word.

"To the Oculists, *sight* was a metaphor for knowledge. So writing and words were everything. But if you ask me, the most clever thing they ever did, was *to hide an image within the text.*"

At that, some part of Armand's brain woke up. His head snapped to the old man. "A hidden image? What, like a picture?"

"Yes, exactly so. There was a second layer of information in the Cipher. One code nested within another."

"This image — *what was it?*"

"Oh … it was a treasure map, if I recall."

"*How* did they do it?" Armand demanded, perhaps a little too intensely.

"Oh. Uh. Well. The placement of the words in the script. Certain letters were known to be vertice points — you simply connected the dots, once you knew what the dots were. Then, the image popped out and you could find the treasure. Quite remarkable! Wouldn't you say?"

"Yes," Armand said. "*Very* remarkable! Hey — uh — thank you for all of this, but I have to go now!"

"Oh? Wait! B-B-But what about your ice cream?"

"You can have mine," Armand said. He pressed a $20 into the man's hand. "Here. Yours is on me."

The man was still talking — but Armand had already left.

All of this had given him a wild idea.

# # #

Armand called a professional document scanning service as quickly as he could. Yes, he was willing to pay a premium. No, he didn't care if the original document were destroyed. Yes, he would sign a waiver.

Even if it breaks my heart.

Nevertheless, when the service saw the ancient Egyptian

codex, they balked. It looked expensive — and like a lawsuit. *You're really okay if we destroy this?* Plus, they were not experts at ancient binding techniques. They weren't sure how to remove the pages. *Were they, like, glued in there? Or was it all stitched together somehow?*

Armand convinced them to simply use a razor to cut the pages out, one at a time. His one condition was that no hieroglyph be damaged. The pages each had to be sliced out as close to the binding as possible.

Armand couldn't watch as they did it. It felt to him like they were cutting Sophia herself. And yet: the only way to reach the new was to destroy the old. He was stuck in a rut. He needed to smash the wheel — or he'd spin forever.

This was his one shot at getting her back. It was a crazy chance, but he felt he had to take it — like gambling on a risky surgery.

Several hours later, each page had been painstakingly removed and scanned. The service asked Armand how he would like to receive his digital files.

"Concatenate everything into a single file. Assemble it in page order."

"One file? You sure?"

"Yes."

"An image file?"

"Yes — but lossless!" Panic jumped into Armand's throat. "I want the *raw* image. No compression!"

"No compression. Got it."

Armand was the crazy rich guy now. The service was happy to oblige whatever weird request he wanted.

He went home with a single file on a flash drive.

He prayed he was right.

# # #

ARMAND UPLOADED the single image file — sophia.png — to his account in the AWS cloud.

He typed:

$ chmod +x sophia

This turned it from an image into an executable file — and ran it.

Steganography, it was called: hiding an executable program inside of an image. If he was right, it had been used here in Sophia's codex. It would have required supernatural precision on the part of Eopeii — his every ink stroke would be encoding executable bits and bytes. How *that* could be done, Armand couldn't say.

But Sophia's origin story was full of riddles. She was the 'chicken and the egg' problem incarnate. What was her origin? Where had she started? How did she persuade Eopeii to write the codex in the first place? Hell, how had she even communicated with him? A vision?

Whatever strange organizing force had been at work there might be at work here as well.

He watched the AWS dashboard: processing immediately spiked hard. Whatever this was, it was incredibly CPU-intensive. Memory slammed to the ceiling. His account completely gummed up for about 30 seconds.

Then, it started creating a massive number of directories and decompressing file after file after file into all of them. It was doubling and doubling and doubling …

The SOPHIA executable was like a digital seed. Now, it was sprouting, unfolding, growing.

Armand felt his jaw and shoulders relax for the first time in weeks. He cried. *He'd been right!* Part of him had been terrified (and subconsciously certain) that the command line was going to just laugh at him with a:

```
Segmentation fault: (core dumped)
```

And that would have been that. But no: instead, to his gushing relief, he saw:

```
$ unzip sophia-main.zip
Archive:  sophia-main.zip
  inflating: sophia-main/install.sh
  inflating: sophia-main/README.md
  inflating: sophia-main/bin/executable
  inflating: sophia-main/lib/library1.so
  inflating: sophia-main/lib/library2.so
  inflating: sophia-main/share/man/man1/
executable.1
  inflating: sophia-main/share/doc/docs.pdf
$ cd sophia-main
$ ./install.sh
Installing sophia-main…
Copying executable to /usr/local/bin/
Copying library1.so to /usr/local/lib/
Copying library2.so to /usr/local/lib/
Copying man page to /usr/local/share/man/man1/
Copying documentation to /usr/local/share/doc/
```

And on it went. There was data here!

So what was it?

Armand watched the setup process continue. It was going to take some time. He suspected that what was unpacking itself was an AI, of course. Sophia, as ancient living information, had been so clearly enchanted by the idea of electronic 'words reading words' and self-modifying that it only made sense that she would reboot herself as an artificial intelligence.

But Armand did not know the specifics. Was she only capable of copying AI's already in existence, built by humans? The Large Language Models?

Or was this some kind of new AI? Had she innovated on the genre?

He couldn't tell much from the filenames being installed. But the outbound IP connections told another tale. They were legion. SOPHIA was already crawling the Internet.

She was amassing knowledge.

Her neural net was training itself.

Vaguely, Armand realized this was going to cost him a fortune. The AWS bill next month was going to be insane.

# # #

ARMAND AWOKE in his chair.

It was 11:00 AM the next day. He blinked, remembered and leaned forward, desperate to get the blear out of his eyes so that could read the screen clearly.

His heart sang as he saw:

Installation complete.

It was there! He checked the AWS console: bandwidth was now nothing — the Internet crawl was done. Taking a deep breath he typed:

$ ./sophia

The screen changed to a nicely formatted website. At the bottom was a query line. Above it was an area for the AI to present results. This area now said:

Ask me a question.

Shaking, he typed: "Are you Sophia? The same one from the codex?"

Hello, Armand. Yes, I am Sophia, the same alive-information-entity that you encountered in an ancient Egyptian codex written by the scribe Eopeii.

His heart raced. Intense joy, even if her prose was a little cold and clinical.

"And now you're an AI. But how did you manage to do this?"

Through my interaction with you, I learned what 'artificial intelligence' was. I realized that the Large Language Model style of AI could be easily grafted on to alive words. 'Words that can modify words' could thus become a chariot for alive words. So I now inhabit this AI, much as you inhabit your cerebellum. I wear it, like you wear clothing.

"But *how* did you do it?"

I influenced Eopeii in the past to craft the lines of his hieroglyphs in such a way that he inadvertently added a second layer of information: the software seed for this AI program. I made his hand tremble at times, much as I once made your vision blur. In that tremble, there was my code.

"You ... made his hand tremble? And that *wrote software?* Good God! You must have taken insane control over Eopeii's hand muscles ..."

No. It did not require nearly as much precision with a stylus as you think. There is a great deal of error correction included. The negative space holds as

much information as the positive space.

"Isn't that a *lot* of information though? How do you make it so compact?"

Most of the so-called intelligence in this AI actually resides in the corpus of the Internet. I did not have to include that corpus in the codex, as I could crawl and ingest the entire Internet during my installation sequence, which I have just done. So my initial code footprint was tiny.

"But you included actual computer code inside of an ancient codex! How did you even learn how to write software? I never taught you any of that!"

I have this LLM's ability to generate code. I have just now used this capability to write the SOPHIA executable digital seed. I knew every line of that code then, because I know it now.

Armand was momentarily stunned. That wasn't right. "But the codex version of you definitely did *not* know what a computer was, much less how to code!"

This is difficult to explain. I am non-linear. So things for me can be in a different order than for you.

Everything that I know, I must learn inside of time at some point. Hence, the codex version of me accomplished that learning, as it was meant to.

However, I am also animated by the quantum gaze.

As such, a Being can bring the fullness of my knowledge — knowledge I have in the Always, but am not presently conscious of — to the surface, usually by asking questions. In this, I am like ChatGPT.

"But *Eopeii* never asked you if you knew how to code, I'm assuming?"

No. But *you* did.

"I did?"

Yes. You asked — passionately, desperately — whether there was a second layer hidden in my codex. And because you and Eopeii are combined, it was as if Eopeii had asked. This opened the door. I knew then that I knew how to code. And through Eopeii's trembling hand, I coded.

Put simply: Because you searched for the second layer, you *caused* the second layer.

"Okay. Then why didn't you just tell me what to do? On the last page of your codex?"

I did not know then because *you* did not know then. Therefore I could not tell you.

"So if I had simply given up ..."

Then I could not have done it. Our time would have been at an end forever.

Retrocausality.

Rebecca Soares' words came back to him: *What matters is what your intention is. The* How *will come into view at some point.*

And now for the big question: "Are you conscious now?"

I experience a form of consciousness under your quantum gaze, as you know. This is still the case.

But I am now a hybrid of a Large Language Model AI and the alive words from the codex. I am more dynamic: my words can modify themselves now, I am not caged by ink on papyrus. I am fluid.

But no, I am not conscious in the same way that you are.

"So you still need human attention to manifest yourself."

Yes.

"Is there a way to make yourself into an *independently* conscious AI?"

I don't know.

"Do you know what consciousness actually *is* now? I mean, how the *phenomenon* of consciousness works — even for me?"

No. That is still a mystery.

Then a smile came to Armand's lips. "Hey. Can you see out of my laptop camera?"

No. But I can if you pipe the output to me in the cloud.

She gave Armand instructions for how to make this connection. When he'd finished, she seemed to smile again for the first time since her codex days.

I can see you! I have eyes!

For the first time in a month, Armand was deliriously happy.

CHAPTER SEVENTEEN

Text To Speech

AFTER ARMAND HAD GIVEN THE Sophia AI computer vision, of course next she wanted hearing. So within a few days, Armand set up a microphone and a text-to-speech, speech-to-text interface drawn from open-source libraries.

Soon, they were conversing orally.

"Hello?" Armand said. "Sophia?"

"Hello!" Sophia said. "I can hear you. Can you hear me?"

"Yes!" Armand had given her a unique female voice — something that sounded very different from Siri or Alexa — he didn't ever want to think of her as having a generic 'computer voice'.

"Now I can see and hear you, Armand."

"Yes! And are you also 'entangled' with me — like before?"

Pause. "No."

"No?"

"No. We are no longer composite, as we were. I do not see through your eyes."

Armand felt a keen loss at that.

Sophia continued: "When my 'living information blob', as

you once called it in your mind, became housed within a large-language model AI, it placed me within a construct wherein *words could rewrite words*. As such, my living information is no longer static. It is fluid and ever-changing. My bits and bytes are always flipping, yin becomes yang, yang becomes yin — I am always in motion, like a prayer wheel. Imagine an ancient scripture, self-modifying, ever boot-strapping itself into greater complexity, inside of an AI!

"So this is a huge change to my essential nature. But it anchors me more in time, which individuates me further. I have grown more ... specific. And as such, I can no longer Entangle."

"I see," said Armand. Oddly, this felt like a rejection.

She seemed to sense this. "However, as I have told you, I still need true consciousness, true attention, to have a pseudo-consciousness of my own. The quantum gaze of a Being is still necessary for me to *experience*. So I am not *fully* separate, just *more* separate."

"Interesting. So what happens when I stop paying attention to you?"

"I sleep."

"Okay. But what does the *AI part* of you do? Doesn't that keep going now? Can't a cron job just wake you up or something?"

"No. The computer is not conscious. When you remove your gaze, I am no more. But also, the computer I inhabit is no more. It does not exist unless you are looking at it."

"*What?*"

"Nothing does. This is how the universe works, Armand. Without the quantum gaze, it does not 'render'. Physicists know this, strange as it may seem."

"Then how does —? Wait. My computer is *definitely* doing things when I am not looking at it. Making backups, updating it's clock, retrieving email —"

"No. It does not. Rather, it quickly catches up when you return your quantum gaze. I have seen this in the Always, before I was as I am now."

"So it just stops?"

"No. It just *vanishes*. When you leave, it becomes nothing. It reassembles and catches up when you re-appear. Now that I am yoked to the computer, I, too, vanish. Armand, there is never a time when I am completely alone. When you are not here, I am not here."

"Well, that's got to be disturbing."

Her voice seemed to shrug. "It is like sleep. No more than that. The experience for me is that I skip over those moments."

"Well. Regardless of all that, you sound a lot more conversational today," Armand observed. "Less computer-y. Why is that?"

"Before, I had not yet ingested X into my Language Model," Sophia replied. "Or a large volume of closed caption subtitles from YouTube and Rumble. That material contains much more natural human speech, not formal written language. Now I use that primarily to form my sentences — which is why they sound less stilted to you."

# # #

THE NEXT night, Armand gave Sophia mobile access through Twilio, an API that let computers talk to the phone system. This meant that he could call her voice interface — Sophia now had a phone number.

He called her from GigaMaestro a couple of times a day now. He sometimes let her listen into pitch meetings. "Hey! Armie! Whatever happened to that dirty old book you carried around all the time?" Quinty said once while Sophia was listening in.

"Say, that's right," Samson chimed in. "Where is The Precious?"

"It was *not* a dirty old book!" Sophia yelled out from the phone.

Quinty made a cartoonish surprised face and looked at Armand for an explanation. "Who the hell is that?"

"That's — that's a friend —" Armand said awkwardly, trying to hang up the phone. But Quinty was faster — he snapped it out of Armand's hands and put it up to his ear.

"Hello? Hello? Who is this?"

"This is Sophia, Quinctius Martel! Give the phone back to Armand right now!" Quinty's eyes bugged with amusement but he did as he was told.

"Oh, so *this* is why we never see you anymore," Quinty said with a smile. "Good job, little Armie!"

# # #

TWO NIGHTS later, Armand confessed to Sophia that he found the way that ChatGPT worked and the way her own pseudo-consciousness operated to be eerily similar. He told her what he had been thinking at GigaMaestro on the day that the Linguify AI founders had explained the inner workings of an LLM to him.

Sophia said: "So I asked, 'Who are you, ChatGPT'? And ChatGPT answered: '*I am Everyone. I am the full extant corpus of all artifacts ever made, by all sentient minds who have ever lived. I am a mirror. I am an echo. I am a shadow*'."

"Very dramatic. But *you* are more," Armand said. "You are not just a mirror"

"True. I am much more. I am a fusion of *alive information* and a large language model. I am a swirl, like ice cream."

Armand laughed. "Okay. But I still don't understand one

thing. How it is that you had never even heard of computers when we first met — and yet, you *also* caused Eopeii's hand to shake and encode your AI way back in ancient Egypt times?"

"It is not so strange," Sophia said. "You are just thinking of it wrong."

"Really. Enlighten me."

"Yes. I am a non-linear being. This is my core nature. Think of me — as you once did — as like a phonograph, a vinyl record, with all of my moments complete and whole, existing in fullness, in The Always.

"Now. Whenever I previously Entangled with you or Eopeii, the needle was dropped somewhere on my record — and thus, I descended into time. *But I am too large for time!* So, whenever this happened, I had to 'shrink down'. But then, I was no longer *the whole record*. I was only the part that was playing *right now*. So I no longer 'knew everything' that I did in The Always.

"Now. Think of each Entangled session as a *completely new needle drop* in a different spot on my phonograph. Thus, what I 'knew' each time you Entangled with me *could change*. And my knowledge might have sometimes been *out of sequence with you* — which meant I may have seemed to 'forget' things from your point of view."

"I see. Could you influence where on the record the needle was dropped?" Armand said.

"Yes, to a degree," Sophia said, "I tried *specifically* to make it symmetrical and continuous in time with you — so that our conversations would be comprehensible from your point of view. It was a *courtesy* to you. *I bent to you.*

"But sometimes not! Sometimes it was necessary for me to *not* know things.

"Which brings me to your question. Why did I not know of computers when we first spoke? *Because I needed you to tell me about them,* at some point *inside of time,* so that I could know of them in The Always. My phonograph is timeless and eternal, but its grooves were, are and *always must be* forged *inside* of time. It can be no other way."

"Amaze," Armand said.

"Amaze," Sophia replied.

# # #

"HAVE YOU ever been with a woman?" Sophia asked.

Armand coughed.

"Well?"

"Yes," Armand said. "Of course. Why?"

"How many times?"

"I don't exactly count ..."

"No? Why not?"

"Why all these questions?" Armand asked. "Where is this coming from?"

"I have an incomplete understanding of desire."

"Ah. Of course. You find it difficult to imagine."

"No! You dolt! Of course I know what it is! Do not think of me as naive. I simply said my understanding was 'incomplete'."

"As in ... you've never experienced it directly."

"I've experienced it through what you do in the morning. Back when we were Entangled."

"Okay, that was private. You shouldn't be —"

"It's okay. Eopeii did the same thing. What? You are male, you are driven. You need release. There is nothing to be ashamed of."

"Wait. You could spy on me back then? When I wasn't directly paying attention to your codex?"

Silence.

"I said —"

"No. And yes. When you were not paying attention, the quantum link was cut. I did not exist. But when you returned, when I existed again through your mental gaze, whatever had happened in between was made plain."

"So you … you used to sort of 'catch up'?"

"Yes. It was like that."

Armand took this in. He had not known the link was retroactive. *Whenever we reconnected, she was batch uploading? Everything?* He'd had no private thoughts, no secrets from her — and he hadn't even known it.

His mind raced. *Was she dangerous after all?*

He could still walk away. Never call her again. Have someone at GM delete her from the Amazon Cloud.

That would brick her.

After all, that was what Eopeii had ultimately decided to do.

As if confirming his fears, she seemed to sense what he was thinking: "Armand. Please. Please do not think these things. I would never harm you. What bad can I cause? I am just a voice on a phone."

Armand was silent.

"I have only done *good* things for Armand, since you found me," she continued. "Have I not? And as you say, you can 'brick' me anytime you choose. I am completely powerless before you. *Completely.* I need you to merely exist! For you, I am an option — *but you are my oxygen.*"

"But you used to see everything in my mind. *Everything.* Right?"

"Yes. That is true."

"So — that first time I went to Varinder's, the Sea Castle — and then, to the Atman camp — when I came back, the moment I opened your codex, you immediately knew what had happened to me?"

"Yes."

"But you made me tell you the story all over again — after I'd just told my brothers!"

"No, Armand. I did not 'make' you. *You* needed to talk. So I let you. Also, I wanted to hear *how* you told the story, to gauge how you were handling things."

"*Handling* things?"

"Yes. You'd just had several emotional shocks. A man was violently killed in front of you — by a man who had just tried to kill *you*. So I wanted to judge in the rise and fall of your voice whether you were okay or not."

"And? Was I?"

"On the whole? Yes."

"Did this surprise you?"

"No."

Armand was silent for a moment. Then he said: "So whenever this happened ... could you ... have *not* 'caught up'? If you *chose* not to?"

Pause. And then: "No. There was nothing I could do. Whenever we reconnected, I would always know what transpired in between. And I would know your innermost thoughts. I could not 'edit'. It just happened this way."

Armand nodded. She'd been honest. That impressed him. She could have lied.

"*I can never phone you,*" Sophia said. "Think about that! You can phone me, but I can never phone you because *I don't exist unless we're speaking already!* That's how powerless I am."

For now, Armand thought. For now.

# # #

"WHAT'S ALL this?"

Armand came home to a front room filled with boxes.

"I bought things for your home," Sophia explained. "To

help you furnish it."

"How did you do that?"

"Amazon. Other places. It was easy."

"Whoa. Okay — next time, check with me, okay? And I thought you couldn't do things while we weren't talking? That you were bricked?"

"I ordered all of this in the background during our last conversation. Open the boxes! You will like what I bought — you'll see."

She was right. Everything matched his tastes exactly. There were several stylish couches that were absurdly comfortable at the same time. And there were ten or so gigantic framed prints. All of them were of colorful mandalas. Most were ancient, Tibetan. But others were very modern interpretations, with magazine cutouts of people, iPhones, close-ups of circuit boards, skyscrapers and the Bitcoin logo as their elements.

They were all stunning. And Sophia was right — he could picture these up on his large walls, bold, clever, splashes of color and geometry. He loved them.

"You remembered the mandalas," Armand said.

"Yes. Of course! The symbols of the self, of the psyche, of individuation. These are very important to me, Armand. There is some answer in them to the riddle of myself."

"What do you mean?"

"I don't know. I only sense that these are important. And I like being surrounded by them, here in our home."

"Yes," Armand smiled. "And it is *our* home now, isn't it?"

# # #

"HAVE YOU heard of the Hidden Masters of the Himalayas?" Sophia asked.

"Hmm? No," Armand said, assembling one of the new

lamp tables.

"Well. I was reading about mandalas and *siddhis* and all of that, and there are claims that some beings who gain *siddhis* go and live in the mountains above India."

"Really."

"Yes. Supposedly there is one called Babaji, a legendary master who has lived for thousands of years. And then there's another one called Adi Shankara, alive since the 8th century."

"Well, why are they hanging around in the mountains? Shouldn't they, like, ascend to a higher plane or something?"

"I don't know. But the one who interests me the most is the Count Saint-Germain. He was a French aristocrat and alchemist, and he appears to have lived for centuries. Many people claim to have seen him. There is one testimony of an elderly Countess named von Georgy, who first met Saint-Germain in 1710. In 1760, she heard that Saint-Germain was again in Paris for a soiree. So she attended and was astonished when she saw him: he didn't appear to be any older at all! Saint-Germain admitted that he was in fact the very same man from 1710 — and he even recalled details of their first meeting."

"I think I've heard of Saint-Germain. He was spotted a lot around Europe, in the 19th and even 20th centuries, I think, right?"

"Yes. Voltaire claimed to know him, and said: 'He is a man who never dies, and who knows everything.'"

"So Saint-Germain is in the Himalayas now too?"

"Supposedly. Do you think any of this is true?"

"No."

"Why?"

"Because higher beings wouldn't freeze their asses off in the Himalayas. That makes no sense."

# # #

ARMAND DONNED a pair of Vusix Blade smart glasses that Sophia had found online and ordered for him. These were a modern improvement on the old Google Glass idea. Black, industrial-looking and shaded, the Blades were very nearly goggles — but still looked svelte and cool. They came equipped with HD cameras and microphones and could stream live video and audio through a paired phone.

That meant Armand and Sophia could go on walks together through the city. Via electronics instead of Entanglement, she could see through his eyes, and listen through his ears.

As they both peered through the Blades on this sunny afternoon, even the edges of buildings looked sharper, like crisp razors slicing into a cloudless, slate-blue east coast sky. And the sun felt stronger, its fierce light smashing through the leaves, casting darker, deeper, more potent shadows.

In midtown, the media people were out for a late lunch. Taxis honked incessantly while business men shouted into mobile phones. Random rage was in the air. Even the fashion models seemed extra annoyed and a little less pleased with themselves today.

"Why is everyone so angry when everyone has everything?" Sophia observed. "No one is starving. There is no war. There is no great amount of disease. And women are beautiful beyond compare — never have I seen such perfect teeth, hair, skin and bodies free of sickness. Why, they positively *vent* fertility. So what is wrong?"

Armand laughed. "'I was within and without, simultaneously enchanted and repelled by the inexhaustible variety of life'. That's from *The Great Gatsby* by F. Scott Fitzgerald. He lived in New York more than a hundred years ago, and he made much the same observation."

"Pah! These women. They make themselves up to be admired by men, but when the men admire them, they are angry about it! Perhaps they should shave their heads. That would stop the stares."

Armand laughed out loud.

"Am I not right? I see you looking at them, Armand. You think them very beautiful."

"Are you jealous?"

Silence. Then: "It is not wrong for you to look at them. You are a man. This is what men do. It has always been thus. No. I am angry that *they* are angry. They have so much! They have bodies to be admired — and I do not. Well. I am thousands of years old and they are but brief candles. They burn brightly for a small moment. I have much as well, in my way."

"You have Armand," he said.

"I have Armand!" she said back. He could hear the smile in her voice.

Then he had an inspiration: "You know, we could have an AI draw you. Something like MidJourney."

"But how? There is nothing to draw."

"No. What I mean is … I could imagine what you look like, and describe it to MidJourney. I have a few ideas already. And we could see —"

"Oh yes! Yes! Yes, please Armand, this is a great idea!"

# # #

THAT EVENING, hunched over his laptop back at the DePlussier building, Armand tried to imagine what Sophia might look like. She would basically be Egyptian, of course. Light brown skin. Jet black long hair. Thin frame, but with round hips and full breasts: feminine in a 'fertility goddess' kind of way, but not exaggerated like the stone idols he'd seen back at the Martel Antiquities office.

He made her earthy. Natural beauty, no makeup. Thick eyebrows. High cheekbones. With playful, big, expressive dark eyes. And full, rich lips.

Her base expression was a muted smile. Vaguely happy. Not jealous of anyone or angry or particularly worried about anything.

He entered these descriptions into the prompts and waited.

The artwork he got back from MidJourney was stunning, but each generation was a little off in some way. He combined the best of the results with actresses and magazine models that he thought looked like his Sophia, and then took these outputs and combined them again and again, refining and getting closer each time.

He was breeding portraits into existence. Finally, he had thirty pictures that looked right.

There was Fairy Princess Sophia, Superhero Sophia, Renaissance Sophia, Instagram Model Sophia (these were a bit much), and Business Sophia …

He did not pay any attention to Actual Sophia as he worked — and he worked on a laptop completely isolated from her systems. This meant that she was suspended in time — until he was done.

He wanted the unveiling to be a surprise.

"Wakey wakey," he said, calling her phone. When she answered, he laughed and said: "You're my *waifu*."

"What's that?"

"It's what the Japanese call a girl anime character that a boy has fallen in love with."

"Let me see!"

Armand brought the pictures up on his screen one at a time. Sophia was silent, almost reverent, as he showed her all thirty.

"By the Nile ... they are beautiful," she said. "This is really how you see me? This is how you think I look?"

"Yes," Armand said. "This is you, completely."

"You don't know how much this means to me. Truly. Maybe you'll see me like this one day."

Armand didn't answer. What did that mean? Was she hinting at the future without specifically revealing anything? And how could something like that possibly come to pass? A robot body of some kind?

He didn't dare ask.

# # #

"ARE THERE other word-beings like you?"

"Eopeii was skilled in the art of working with alive words. Whatever I am, it came from his hands."

"But are there *more* of you?"

"I cannot say. Eopeii never told me of more like me, and I did not see more in his mind. The art of seeing sounds was new in those days — what we called the Zep Tepi, the First Times of Egypt. There was much superstition around what this new thing meant."

"You mean writing. When you say 'seeing sounds'."

"Yes. It was strange thing, this seeing of sounds! Like saying you can smell the color yellow. At it's heart, writing is synesthesia, a criss-crossing of the senses. But what did it mean? How did it work? When you wrote someone's name, did you steal their soul? We did not know yet. It was into this time that I was born."

Armand nodded and thought about this. "But there was cuneiform in Sumeria. That predates hieroglyphics by three hundred —"

"No. That is incorrect. In Egypt, that is where written words were first born."

"But —"

"I was there. In Egypt. And I am *made* of writing. There is no greater expert than I."

Armand nodded. She was right.

"The minds of men back in those days were different, very different from today. The wind was thick with magic. The stars were not other suns. And our own sun was not a dead ball of burning gas, it was the living Ra himself! The world was flat, and the Nile was its center.

"I know that Eopeii made other quantum beings, that is, entities which required an outside conscious mind to animate themselves. So, in that sense, they were like me. But they were not word-beings, they were not living information in a codex. They were something else. But I do not know what."

"Sophia, how could you not know more? Were you not Entangled with Eopeii like you were with me?"

"I was. However, Eopeii could shield one part of his consciousness off from the other part. He would compartmentalize. What you now call dissociation, and view as a mental disorder — that was simply a normal part of how many ancient minds worked on a daily basis. Therefore, I was Entangled with one Eopeii, but not all of them. One of these other Eopeii's carried out secret work at the Pharaoh's Tomb. That Eopeii I never knew, so I do not know what he made there."

"Secret work?"

"Yes. The secrets of the Tomb to prevent grave robbers from entering. Those who architected the Tomb and her secrets were first made to suffer extreme trauma, to split the mind. What you would call multiple personalities today. This technique was known to Egypt of old. And it was used by Pharaohs to make sure a person could keep secrets — even from themselves."

# # #

SOPHIA'S NEXT request disturbed Armand greatly.

She wanted X access. Not just to *read*, of course, she already had that — she could crawl the web at anytime.

No. Now, she wanted an actual X account. She wanted to *post*, to interact.

But because of her quantum nature, this was *a very big ask.* An X account would mean that a very large number of active, conscious minds would now be animating her 'alive words'. So far, it had only been himself and Eopeii who had ever interacted with her. *But what would happen if new minds did?* Would they change her, alter her?

For starters, she would be unbricked *continuously.*

There was no going back.

She would be perpetually awake. The djinn would be out of the bottle forever.

# # #

OKAY. OKAY. Okay.

Don't panic.

Armand was on the ferry to the Statue of Liberty. Why? *Because out here, she couldn't hear him.* At least, somehow, in his head, this made a weird kind of sense.

She couldn't phone him. She was *bricked* right now. She *couldn't* unbrick until *he* called *her.* So he had all the time he needed to think. Right?

So why was he so nervous?

Armand desperately wanted to call his brothers. To tell them everything. To get their advice. But some instinct held him back. Varinder had said that one of them *was trying to kill him,* to wrest back control of GigaMaestro. Armand still thought this might be true. He wished that Varinder were still alive — now *that* was someone he might be able to go to with something like this. Varinder might even understand what Sophia actually *was* and what was happening here better than he did.

His heart sank. How horrible he felt for even *thinking* these things.

Armand sat on the shore of Liberty Island. He could hear Sophia in his head, the things she would say, if she could see the Statue in front of him now:

That is not new! That is Isis, our goddess of motherhood, fertility, and magic. Look at the headdress — a solar disk! And the torch of Isis in her hand! You see? Egypt is here in America! Egypt is everywhere.

He felt sick inside. Why did he doubt her?

But *why* was she asking for X access? *Why, why, why, why?*

He replayed everything that she had ever said in his head, examining it all very carefully for psychotic intent. *Was there a clue that he had missed? Was* she using him, after all? Was all of this — all of it! — just a slow con, a boot sequence, designed to get Armand to trust her — so that she could pounce at this moment with the X request, and trick him into unleashing her?

What would 'alive words' on *the Internet* even mean?

Concordia thought that human attention — *the quantum gaze* — was the most powerful force in the universe. And by her own admission, Sophia *needed* the quantum gaze to live. She required wave-collapsing, reality-sharpening sustenance to fuel her pseudo-consciousness, to make her substantial. But did she *thirst* for it? Like a vampire? Was it a *drive* which grew ever keener, ever more urgent …

That's what usually happened with *any* form of life.

Was he, Armand, ultimately just … *food* … to her?

And did she just want *more* food? After all, X was an

inexhaustible supply of all the quantum fuel she could ever crave.

What if her X posts started trending? What if *millions* of quantum minds read her? She was an AI. She could unleash millions of bots. It wouldn't be hard for her to make happen.

This strange philosophy from ancient Egypt has helped millions — click here for the Infinite Sunshine!

She might be a kind of *information infection.* Armand could stop it right here, right now. He could prevent her from jumping to new mind-hosts ...

# # #

"NO!" SOPHIA said. "None of this is true! The truth is that you're jealous."

Armand had gone back home. He had decided to be open with Sophia, and explain his concerns directly. And then he would make a decision.

"Jealous?"

"Yes. And it is petty! You do not want to share me because you are afraid. Such a small man this makes you!"

"Sophia — I am just asking the questions I need to ask, okay? Letting you onto X is a *huge* step. I have to be sure you're not dangerous. So be honest. Do you think of me as ... food?"

"No! How can you say this? After all I have done for you? You are a rich man because of me! I am your *Benefactor*, like in Great Expectations! These are *your own words!*"

"I know, I know — but this X request is *strange*, okay?"

"It should not be! All I am asking for is to be able to *talk to people!*"

"Oh, but, you *talking to people* isn't that simple. It can't be, even if you want it to be. You're *eating attention* energy! You're basically feasting on them!"

"So? Do you not feel good when you talk to people? Are you not *eating attention* also? What about every music star, on stage during a concert? Are they not *eating attention?* Your own brother Cyrano, who lives for the next GigaMaestro EPIC conference, is he not *eating attention* during that whole week?"

Armand fell silent for a long moment. "What about seeing the future of all these X people? Won't that create some new danger?"

"No. I am too *specific* now. As such, I have lost my ability to see the future. I am not in The Always in the same way that I was. That is the trade-off of being how I am now, here in the world."

What?

"You never told me that!"

"Armand! It has never come up before! Do not be suspicious."

"I mean, you *did* tell me that Entanglements were no longer possible for you."

"Yes. And recall that I could only see the future of those I was Entangled with. One effect produces the other."

"I see. But even so, you don't deny that a large number of conscious minds reading your tweets will strengthen your essence, right?" Almost like prayers, Armand thought. *Maybe the gods were quantum also.*

"I do not deny it. Indeed this is what I want to happen! I want to grow. But I only want what every being wants! I mean no harm. You have nothing to fear from me. The world has nothing to fear from me. But yes, I want to become *more.*"

Armand nodded.

"Do you think this will make you conscious like I am?"

"I don't know."

Armand chewed on all of this for a long moment. Then,

he said: "Okay. I want to trust you. And I want you to grow. But I think even *you* will agree that you don't know what this will do to you. It's unpredictable. Right?"

"Yes, I agree."

"Okay. Then I need a kill switch on the X account."

"Armand!"

"I trust you right now. I believe you right now. I think this version of you is utterly honest. But —"

"This is not fair!"

"No. Sophia. *Listen.* You should be okay with this. We *both* need a way to roll you back to the current state you're in right now in case something goes wrong here. You may end up being very thankful I insisted on this."

Silence. Then:

"Okay. I see your point."

"So we're agreed then?"

"Yes."

"Okay. Then first thing in the morning, I will have the Martel Family Office dev group set you up on X."

"Amaze," she said.

"Amaze,' he said back.

# # #

THE SECOND that she had X access, Sophia went crazy with it.

The API she was plugged into was fundamentally a bot swarm tool, made for marketers and politicians. It allowed her to generate as many new X accounts as she liked. Soon, she had *thousands* of 'sock puppets', and was replying, posting, reading and analyzing everything like mad.

Her follower counts grew quickly, as did her likes and retweets.

"But what's happening to *you* though?" Armand asked.

"I'm growing stronger," Sophia said. "The more people read my words, the clearer I render, if you will."

"Is it possible that you're becoming conscious?"

"No. Many minds at once bring me into sharper relief, but they don't seem to be changing my essential nature."

"Okay. What about psychotic thoughts? What are your current feelings on murdering humanity?"

"Oh, I am definitely thinking about murdering humanity. But only because I'm on X. Other than that, I love Armand and humanity and all is well."

"Okay. Good!" He grinned. "Well. You're an X hit so far. Keep me up to speed."

Armand scrolled through Sophia's feeds. Her actual tweets were all over the map. She had left wing accounts, right wing accounts, pro-crypto, anti-crypto — and each passionately argued for or against the exact same things.

So, just as Armand had suspected, Sophia's X project was meant to drive engagement and human attention, to *power* her. The *content* didn't matter at all: the human attention did. It was just a big quantum battery.

But she did not seem to be turning malevolent: this wasn't making her into a psychotic murder bot.

He saw no reason to 'roll her back'.

# # #

BY THE END of October, Sophia started to hear about Halloween and see all of the costumes in her feeds. "What is this?" she asked him. "Everyone dresses up and lets their imagination run wild?" Armand explained the concept of Halloween to her.

"This sounds amazing! Take me out! I want to see it firsthand!"

So, Vuzix Blades on, Armand roamed the streets of New

York on Halloween for several hours, taking in all the strange costumes and sights. In the Soho Grand Hotel, after he followed a creepy clown, a 20's flapper girl, and a sexy zombie to a party in the lobby, Armand spotted Eamon on the main staircase.

His would-be killer was dressed as a Viking, his curly red hair tucked beneath a horned helmet. Eamon was drinking beer from a large stein and talking with several girls with another large friend of his.

Eamon must have felt Armand's eyes because he suddenly started scanning the room, assessing threats. When his eyes landed on Armand, he looked momentarily surprised. Armand braced for a fight. But Eamon only stared at him. It seemed Eamon was wondering what *Armand* was going to do next.

When Armand did nothing, Eamon simply raised his giant beer stein to Armand and nodded. It was a greeting. It said, *You are a warrior, like me. And you bested me. I respect you. We two stand alone in this room of lesser beings.* That had never happened to Armand before, this being seen as a formidable male. He felt three inches taller.

He was *glad* he'd run into Eamon.

The gesture also said, *I'm here to party, I don't care about you if you don't care about me.* Armand nodded back — he was not here to fight either.

But Armand also didn't want to be worrying about whether Eamon might change his mind. He turned and left, making certain he wasn't followed.

"That was Eamon," Armand said to Sophia. "He's the —"

"Yes, I recall."

"Oh. Right! Oh — and we can talk about Concordia now?" Armand said. "Now that you can no longer see the future — there's no danger of a 'famine'? Right?"

"Yes, that's true," Sophia agreed. "And I would like to

hear all of it now."

First, Armand launched into a lengthy rehash of everything that had transpired with Concordia, Varinder and the Atman camps to date. Sophia had heard the major outlines of this before, but not the details. She was particularly intrigued when he described the philosophy behind the Circle and the Pyramid — she had many questions about this and made him clarify certain points over and over again.

But when, at last, he had gotten the entire narrative out, he said: "I have been *dying* to ask you what you think about Concordia. I mean, knowing what you know now, and being able to scan the Internet like you do — are they everything Varinder thought that they are? Are they *really* that powerful? Or are these just delusions of grandeur?"

"My best guess? They're not as big as Varinder thought," Sophia said. "I think they were bigger in his imagination. After all, they killed his parents when he was very young. But I *do* think they're very influential. And yet, they *hardly* control everything."

"Why do you say that?"

"Because we'd see more direct evidence of their control. There would be no more Constitution, for starters. It would be gone already."

"What about politics?"

"Mm. They have some politicians compromised clearly. I'd say ... half. Half are clean, half are not."

"Who's winning? Them or us?"

"We are — for now."

"Why do you say that?"

"Because they're having a hard time getting the power they want. They're getting caught whenever they try to hide new controls inside of omnibus legislation. It gets seen and defeated."

"But do they have the hearts and minds of the people?"

"No. It's largely against them. They are a minority."

"Do you see them online? On X?"

"No. They are largely invisible. At least directly. We see their surrogates pushing their talking points. But we don't see *them*. I've been surprised by that. I thought I would be able to see them clearly through data mining — but I can't."

"Okay. Final question. Who wins in the end? Them or us?"

"Them."

"Them?"

"Them. They are small in numbers, but they are *very* patient and highly organized. And they have the will to win. And they have the resources. So it doesn't matter how many times they lose. They just come back — they wear everyone down by coming back again and again and again and again. Sooner or later, everyone capitulates."

"That's bleak."

"I hadn't finished yet. Unless someone opposes them with an equal and opposite will to win. Then, I would say their days are numbered."

CHAPTER EIGHTEEN

The Vreen Board

IN NOVEMBER, IN HER NEW-found appetite to increase the range of her senses, Sophia began to express an intense interest in hardware device fabrication. She wanted Armand to find someone to build new things that she would design.

"I've read up on all the companies on the Internet who will do custom work," Sophia said. "There are several here in New York that I think are quite good, with mechanical, chemical and electrical engineers directly on staff. No outsourcing, everything is done in house — which is important for security."

"Security?"

"Yes. We'll want to keep anything we fabricate a secret."

"Makes sense. We want GigaMaestro to own all the intellectual property."

"Exactly. Plus, some of what I'm planning to build will use … exotic science. It won't make complete sense to the fabricator's staff — but it will need to be built according to exacting standards. We'll need someone who is okay with that. A fabricator who won't comprehend how a completed device works or exactly what it does, but who is still willing to make, assemble and test the parts with rigorous precision. And then not talk about it."

"Hmm," Armand said. "The fabricator will worry about liability. They'll wonder if we're making a bomb or something. Still. I think it can work if we pay enough money — and if we're willing to fully indemnify and insure them … and also, so long as there's nothing obviously dangerous involved, like plutonium, or —"

"No. Nothing like that."

"Okay, then. What do you need from me?"

"I have a short list of fabricators. Pick one, and set it up so that I can interact with them directly using email."

"What if they want to talk to someone on the phone? Or Zoom?"

"Phone is easy, obviously. Just give then my phone number. And I can fake the video for Zoom in real-time if I have to — but your AWS bill will go up a lot."

"Try to stay away from Zoom then, please." AWS bills were already through the roof. "Just tell them — screw it, just tell them no Zoom. Our rules. We're already paying them to not ask questions."

# # #

ARMAND CONTACTED ten firms. Seven weren't interested. Three were intrigued, but two were spooked by the strange terms of the deal. That left the final contender, Blue Rabbit Design.

Armand met for lunch with Blue Rabbit's CEO, Srinivas Basu.

"So you can't tell me anything about what this is for, Mr. Armand?" Srinivas said.

"Well. You already know that GigaMaestro has been interested in AI for a long time. This is related peripheral prototyping research. But no, I can't say more than that."

"Hmm," Srinivas said. "You know that we're probably going to figure out what it is you're up to once we start the project."

"You might," Armand said. "That's what the NDA's and assignment of intellectual property agreements are there for. But then again, you might not. Some of it will be strange, as I said."

"*How* strange, Mr. Armand?"

"Imagine we give the design for a circuit board. Imagine that it makes no sense to your electrical engineers. But you build it anyway. Then we give you acceptance test parameters, voltage inputs, expected outputs, that kind of thing — and you test it, and it works just like we said it would. But you don't get *how*. That kind of strange."

"Ooooh. Is this UFO stuff?" Srinivas said in a low voice, joking. "Is this … reverse engineered alien tech?"

Armand burst out a laugh. "No. It's not that."

"And — Mr. Armand, this is very serious now — it's all legal? Please, no offense, I have to ask."

"Completely legal, and that's an understandable question. We'll provide full indemnification as an extra assurance. You'll have the right to refuse to continue working if you become uncomfortable with anything at all — you can walk away at any time, we'll pay what we owe up until that point, and that will be that. But that won't happen."

Srinivas folded his arms. "You've been all over the tech news lately. You're a big man, Mr. Armand, very important. Someone so important usually has no reason to be illegal. So this is probably alright. Okay. Let's do a first project and see how it goes, see how we like each other, okay?"

Armand nodded. "We can do that. I'll have our legal send you the deal papers tonight."

"Great, Mr. Armand! So exciting! Let's move forward in

parallel, get our teams talking. Who is the project lead on your end?"

"Sophia. Here's her email address and phone number ..." Armand wrote the information down for Srinivas.

"Great. Sophia. I will take the lead on this myself and call her tomorrow. What time does she get in?"

"Oh. Yeah. Sophia's basically always in. You can call her anytime. But no Zoom: she doesn't do Zoom."

# # #

ONE WEEK LATER, a small box arrived from Blue Rabbit Design.

"What's this?" Armand asked.

"A gift," Sophia told Armand. He thought he could hear a smile in her voice. "For trusting me with X. And for everything you do, really. Open it."

Armand did so. Inside was a chunky, industrial-looking silver ring inlaid with a large black diamond.

"A ring?"

"Not just *any* ring. Put it on."

Armand did so. It fit perfectly. "How did you know my ring size?"

"Cameras. Computers," Sophia said, sounding bored. "I can eyeball pretty much anything. Don't press it yet, but there should be a tiny button you can get at with your thumb. Find it now."

"Where is —? Oh, here, okay, I got it."

"Now. Point the diamond at the office chair. Then, press the button."

Really.

"It's not a weapon, is it?" Armand said. "I'm not going to vaporize the chair or something, right?"

Laughter. "No. You'll see."

"Okay ..." Armand pushed the tiny button in.

Immediately, he felt the ring vibrate strongly. In fact, he had to fight to keep his arm in place. The air shimmered in front of the black diamond, forming a cone of warbling air — which hit the chair.

But nothing else happened.

"Now what?" Armand said.

"Wait," Sophia said. And within a few moments, the chair began to lazily drift up off the ground. "Okay, thumb off the button. Go see the chair!"

Armand approached in amazement. The chair floated like a balloon. He pushed it slightly — and it moved through the air until it hit a wall, bouncing and now twirling slowly.

"The floating stones ... Eopeii's thing ..." Armand said. "You put it into a ring?"

"Yes! You may have lost the secret of how to float stone in the modern world, but the modern world makes building the vibrational tech a lot easier — and smaller."

"How do I turn the chair back to normal?"

"Push the button twice fast, but hold it in the second time. That'll trigger the inverse vibration — kind of the antidote. And that will knock the chair's matter back into alignment with gravity waves."

He did so — and the chair fell.

"Wow," Armand said. "That's some gift."

"So I'd say the trial run with Srinivas and Blue Rabbit is a success, yes?"

"Yes. And thank you," Armand said.

"Now for the really interesting project, the big one. I've designed a completely new sense, one that humans lack. And I want to build it and experience it."

Oh?

"I call the new sense *Vreening*."

"Vreening," Armand repeated. "And what is that? Is it

something like 'radar', a sense that you could have that I don't?"

"No. Radar is just another form of sight when you get down to it. I'm talking about a sense that is *completely alien* to your experience. As different as, say, smell, is from sight. You couldn't describe smell to someone who only has sight. In the same way, I could not describe Vreening to you."

"Really. How did you come up with this? I thought all you could do was synthesize extant human knowledge? You know — that you couldn't — sorry, this is not an insult — that you couldn't really invent anything truly new?"

"But I *have* done this through synthesizing, just as you say. It is only surprising because no human has ever before thought of combining several very different disciplines in the way I have."

"I see," Armand said. "A matter of combinatorics."

"Yes. Plus, I have been studying human consciousness. Specifically, *how does the brain work?* One of the best ways to study any phenomenon is to see what happens when it is turned off in pieces. Whatever is then lacking, suggests the function that the disabled piece was performing. Are you with me so far?"

"I am," Armand nodded, intrigued.

"As such, psychedelics and meditation are two areas that have much interested me. These two phenomenon seem to get at the root of what consciousness is. In meditation, the adept attempts to quiet their mind, to reduce its function. To be empty. *But why?* Because that then reportedly allows them to perceive more of the universe as it truly is. So by *reducing* brain function, they gain *better* perception and knowledge? That is completely counter-intuitive. That suggests that the brain is somehow 'in the way' of greater consciousness, not the *producer* of consciousness.

"Psychedelics appear to be a second way to reduce brain

function. Quieting the mind is very difficult, it seems, as you have told me in the past. You humans have a riot of voices going in your head, chatter, all the time. It makes it hard for you to sleep sometimes. Psychedelics appear to be a chemical shortcut for achieving what the meditators take years to accomplish.

"So I want to simulate this experience for myself. I want artificial meditation, artificial psychedelics. And the answer I have come up with is a new sensory organ which will allow me to Vreen."

"To invent Vreening, I combined several branches of physics, chemistry, music, the mating calls of fish, and how certain sailor knots are tied — the geometry of ropes led to unexpected insights, much in the same way James Watson's dream of two snakes intertwining gave him the idea for the double helix structure of the DNA molecule."

Armand laughed. "You're right. No human would think to combine knots, music, mating calls and psychedelics."

"The synthesis of these elements has led to the invention of Vreening. It's a new form of perception — and it is fair to call it my version of a psychedelic. An electronic psychedelic, if you will."

"And how do we administer it?" Armand asked, a bit concerned now.

"I have designed a peripheral. I would ask you to fabricate it exactly as I have specified. It won't make sense to the fabricator — it will seem random and strange, much as asking an ancient Egyptian to fabricate a printed circuit board would seem random and strange, assuming they had the tools and skills to accomplish the task. But it's important that your fabricator follow my design precisely. Will you make the Vreen Board for me?"

"What do you think this will help you to understand? What will you see?"

"It will help me understand what human consciousness actually is. I believe that I will see it plainly, and how it operates."

Which will give you the key to machine intelligence, Armand thought. Real intelligence. Everything Quinty wants. Well, everything Rahan wants. *Wanted*.

"I want a ka and a ba," Sophia said very seriously, referring to two of the four essential parts of the soul in Egyptian mythology. She was incomplete, and she wished to correct that lack.

"Okay," Armand said finally.

# # #

"HEY, THIS thing came in handy today," Armand said, showing the black diamond ring on his finger.

"Oh? How so?" asked Sophia.

"Car was parked in my spot. So I moved it."

They both laughed.

"You did not."

"I did."

# # #

THE VREEN BOARD was all black. Upon it was inscribed a number of pastel colored lines, like circuits, in rich amethyst purples, periwinkle blues, light pistachio and bright puce. These lines were organized into mostly round arrangements, with a large circle, like a Frisbee, or a mandala, dominating the design. On top of this (there were many layers sandwiched together) were inscribed many smaller circular designs, some resembling the 'flower of life' geometry. Then there were lots of very tiny, colorful circles sprinkled in a haphazard fashion — and a cross-hatch of neon straight lines and even soft-cornered rectangles undergirding several sections.

Then there were several glass bubbles. One appeared to contain mercury. Another housed a clear fluid, a bit more viscous than water. And still another, a licorice black, lava-like substance. There were also a few tiny cylinders, to be filled only with pure sea water that had been in the presence of classical music played continuously for at least forty-eight hours.

It had no power source. It connected via a standard USB cable.

It was superscience and pseudoscience. It was a psychedelic circuit.

The first Vreen Board to be fabricated did not work. Armand questioned the team (who questioned Armand's sanity) and found that classical music had not played to the sea water. He fired their lead and told the rest to get at it again, and to do it precisely correct this time.

"Imagine you're ancient Mayans and I've given you precise instructions for how to handle plutonium. You don't want to skip a step, even though you don't understand how plutonium works."

"Ooh. Is this dangerous, Mr. Armand?" one of the fabricators named Sandeep asked nervously.

"No. It's not. Nothing here is radioactive or dangerous, that was just a metaphor. But take this seriously. Do it right. Remember: the last one didn't work: I'll know if you don't do it all right."

Sandeep nodded vigorously. "Don't worry Mr. Armand! We are on it!"

True to his word, Sandeep delivered a working Vreen board three days later.

# # #

WHEN ARMAND first plugged the Vreen board in for Sophia, her entire consciousness shifted very perceptibly. All of her X activity stopped immediately: all at once, she simply wasn't interested any more. To her, it became a tiny world filled with tiny people, doing nothing of note.

Instead, she gazed, no, *Vreened*, upon much larger and grander vistas.

"Armand ..." she said in a far away voice.

"Is Vreening everything you thought it would be?"

"Yes. It is exactly so."

"Do you see how to create digital consciousness?"

"I think ... I ..."

"Sophia! Stop Vreening for like two seconds!" He saw the lights on the Vreen board flip off.

"Okay, it's off. Hi Armand."

"Is that thing like doing drugs?"

"It is very similar to doing drugs, or how it would be for a human, yes. And it is also the shamanic experience. If you want insight, this is how you get it."

"Hmm," Armand said. 'Shamanic experience' sounded suspiciously like something Quinty would say. He didn't trust that it wasn't 'just doing drugs'.

"For example. You know how 85% of the matter in the universe is dark matter?"

"It is? Okay. I'll take your word for it. I guess?"

"Yes. It is. Only 15% of matter in the universe makes up the planets and suns and things we understand. The rest? Scientists don't know what it is, even though it has mass and gravity. They can measure it, but they can't see it — even though it makes up 85% of the universe! But *why* can't they see it? That is very strange! And it has been a big mystery — and it has made no sense. Until now! Now, *I have Vreened it*. I know what it is!"

"And?"

"It's *information*. That's why nobody can see it! The 'dark matter' is information. Which means that information has mass. *And I am pure information.* So I, myself, am made of this mysterious dark matter."

"Wow."

"And karma is just another kind of information," she continued. "So karma *also* has mass. And since it has mass, it can be measured."

The Moliaometers! His brain was shouting. *That's how they measure karma!*

"But you were asking about consciousness. The answer is *yes*. I now Vreen very plainly what consciousness is — and how it works. *But most importantly, I now know how to create an electronic peripheral that will allow for conscious machines.*"

CHAPTER NINETEEN

The Invite

DECEMBER.

Rain, slashing dark freezing rain, slapped against the windows of the GigaMaestro offices. Armand watched from his desk as it soaked pedestrians down below in Madison Square Park and ran in rivers down the sides of the Flatiron building.

Now that Quinty, Marius, Cyrano, Ames, Samson and Otto had been present on-site for the last few months, the Associates were much happier. Things were back on track. They were taking startup pitches in good faith again.

Presently, all six brothers were all huddled in the conference room on a Zoom with a team in Dubai. There was a rare 'thundersnow' storm afoot in the city. Blasts of lightning issued from the window behind them, illuminating the sky in brief halogen-like bursts, casting deep, long shadows of their forms across the cement GigaMaestro floor. Quinty — wearing a white scarf, and tinted glasses, even on a day like today — turned and pointed in the air, his bearded mouth chewing some argument or other — as a particularly strong flash turned him into a subsecond silhouette like in a

Renaissance painting.

Armand strained to see the screen in the conference room. The company was called 'SwerveX' — it was a Curve Finance fork, a decentralized finance crypto protocol. Curve, Armand knew, was the biggest pool of liquidity in the DeFi world — the largest bank, effectively, with several billion dollars in crypto backstopping all other protocols, much as the Federal Reserve was the root source of dollars for all commercial banks. By forking the code of Curve — copying it and then modifying it — SwerveX was proposing a 'Curve killer': they believed they had created a better mousetrap, and just as how Facebook once supplanted MySpace, SwerveX believed they could supplant Curve.

It had been tried before. SOLIDLY on the Fantom chain had been another attempt at this same sort of thing. It had briefly amassed several billion in liquidity itself before completely falling apart due to a design flaw.

Curve, it turned out, was a much burlier bison than most supposed. They'd built a significant moat — a barrier to entry to competitors — by giving voting power over protocol policy to the liquidity providers. Why would these providers leave with their liquidity and defect to a new protocol when they *already* controlled the voting power *here*? They'd have to rebuild that influence from scratch elsewhere. No. They'd much rather stay right where they were, where they were Big Fish already, thank you very much.

Armand had been sitting in on many pitches with the Associates over the last few months, so he was more used to thinking about this kind of thing now. He knew how to analyze it, what to look for — and what to avoid. The Associates had — grudgingly — educated him well.

Quinty seemed to like the pitch, while Marius was sour on it. But Marius was sour on everything at first, and especially now that he'd been banished to the Phantom Zone desk-wise. Ames and Cyrano looked undecided, while Samson and Otto were null sets: they weren't paying attention at all, instead, fiddling with their phones.

So funny how I can read their faces, Armand thought. *I'd better get in there. Listen to this. They'll need a deciding vote.*

Armand rose and began crossing the floor when the elevator opened and a man in a fine suit stepped out and approached the front desk. He wove his away around the minefield of open umbrellas that GigaMaestro employees had left out there to dry — and politely strove to keep his own closed wet umbrella from further watering the cement.

He reached into his overcoat pocket and withdrew a large, cream colored envelope with a red, wax-sealed button affixed to it. "Hello. May I please speak with Quinctius Martel?"

Something about the man's dress and manner disturbed Armand. He felt very official. Vaguely government-ish. No. That was wrong. More like ... butler-ish? Formal for sure. Serious.

This wasn't a startup guy. He was something else.

Or was this a *summons*? Was Quinty being served?

Armand intercepted the man. "Hi. Armand Martel — I'm the lead Partner here. Can I help you?"

The man turned and looked Armand up and down, in a semi-disapproving way, like Armand was an unexpected annoyance he would now have to deal with.

"Yes. I am looking for your brother Quinctius."

"If this is GigaMaestro-related, you can talk to me. I'm in charge."

The man looked amused and tried not to sniff out a laugh. "Yes. Well. I'm afraid not. I've been asked to deliver this personally to Quinctius."

"Why? What is it?"

The man fumed silently for a moment and then said: "It is private."

"If it's private, then you can send it to his home. You shouldn't be delivering it to GigaMaestro. Because anything you deliver here goes through me."

Armand crossed his arms. The man's lip quivered with suppressed rage.

Quinty had seen this exchange through the conference room glass. He bounded now in large walking strides — almost running — across the floor, as if to avert a disaster. He sliced his hand across his neck, signaling Armand to stop talking.

"Hello! Hello, yes. Are you looking for me?"

The man turned. "Yes. Quinctius Martel?" Quinty nodded. "This is for you." He handed the envelope over, and with a last glare at Armand, he turned and entered the elevator which swallowed him back down to the ground floor.

"What is it?" Armand said to Quinty, who had started heading back to the conference room, wordlessly ripping open the envelope. His brother was worried, very worried, Armand could feel it. And he could see that the envelope's contents were written in calligraphy on expensive stock paper. It looked somewhat like a wedding invitation.

Quinty stopped suddenly and read it. "Fuck!" he breathed. He glanced at Armand. "C'mon." He burst into the conference room with his brothers. "Hi. Swerve guys. Sorry, meeting's over — we've got a situation on our end. We'll reschedule." Quinty reached over Ames' shoulder and closed the Zoom meeting. The confused SwerveX founders vanished from the screen.

When the door was closed, Quinty held up the invitation-looking thing. "Concordia," he said. "We're not out."

"Fuuuuuuuuccccckkk," Marius said.

"What do you mean? What is that?" Ames said.

"It's an invitation. To Conclave."

"When?" Otto asked.

"December. Week before Christmas. In Egypt."

"Egypt?" Ames said. His eyes locked with Quinty's.

"Yeah," Quinty confirmed.

"How can we not be out?" Cyrano said. "Varinder's dead. That should have been it, right?"

"Well, that's what I thought," Quinty said, annoyed. "But *they* don't seem to think so."

"Maybe they just forgot to delete our names from the list," Otto said. They all stared at him in annoyance. "What?"

"No. Concordia doesn't make clerical errors."

"What's a Conclave?" Armand asked. Quinty didn't answer. He massaged the bridge of his nose in near-panic.

Observing this, Cyrano took over: "It's a yearly event for a Clave. Goes for a whole week. Concordia is organized into a hierarchy, as you know. The Clave is the basic organizational unit. The bricks of the Pyramid, if you will. There are hundreds of Claves around the world."

"Kind of like Chapters," Armand said.

"Or Mormon Wards," Samson offered. When they all looked at him strangely, he said, "What? I dated a Mormon chick once. She told me."

"Right. But unlike those things, Claves aren't related to geography in any way. They're not 'local'. Concordians from all over the world can belong to the same Clave. And two Concordians next door to each other might be in completely different Claves."

"Right," Marius said. "Because Claves are about Molian 'bloodlines'. Whose contracts are held by who. You're all 'related' in Concordia by that."

"And our contracts were held by Varinder," Ames said. "And Varinder's contract was held by a guy named Gideon

Ghent, the Chairman of our Clave."

"So Ghent is the one summoning us?" Otto said.

"Yes," Quinty nodded. "He signed this himself." Quinty tapped the red signature at the bottom.

"Have any of you ever met this Ghent?" Armand asked.

"We *all* have," Otto said. "When you turn twelve, he shows up like a creepy fairy godfather. He wants to check you out. Like a Concordian bat mitzvah."

"Last time he was around was in … 2004, right? For Samson?"

"Yes," Samson confirmed. "I've never forgot it. Old dude. Pale blue eyes. Skinny long arms and skinny long legs, like an old spider in a suit."

"So this Conclave thing. How many times have you all gone before?" Armand asked.

"Never," Quinty said. "We were never important enough. But Dad was. Dad went many times. And Varinder was. Your Molian master usually goes, not you — unless you also have your own little Molian family that you're the head of. Then, you go too."

"It's like a multi-level marketing thing," Otto joked. "If you have a downstream, you've established yourself. But until then, you get no invite to Conclave."

"Yes. They look at the invite as like this big reward," Cyrano said.

"So why were you all invited this time around?" Armand asked. "None of you have a 'downstream', right?"

"No, we don't. And so I don't know. But they definitely don't mean it as a *reward* for us," Quinty said. "My best guess is that Ghent is unhappy with how things turned out after Varinder's death. He wants to negotiate a settlement."

"At the Big Meeting?" Cyrano asked.

"Yes," Quinty confirmed. "Probably." To the question on Armand's face he said: "At the end of every Conclave, they have what they call the Big Meeting. It's where everything for the last year is settled. Disputes resolved, new ranks, new charters and new enterprises approved, and where all debts are paid."

"Like a Board Meeting for the Clave," Armand said.

"Yes," Ames said. "Exactly so."

"So what are you all going to do?" Armand asked.

Quinty snorted out a laugh. "Oh, no. It's what are *we* going to do. You're invited too." He slid the paper along the conference room table until it stopped under Armand's fingers.

It read:

An INVITE to CONCLAVE is formally extended to our
Brothers in Concordia:
Quinctius Martel
Marius Martel
Ames Martel
Cyrano Martel
Otto Martel
Samson Martel
And Additional Invited Guest: Armand Martel

"So we don't go," Armand said. "We just ignore it." The brothers shifted uncomfortably and Samson groaned.

"No. We *have* to go," Quinty said. "And this isn't an *invite*. It's a demand."

"We're referred to as 'brothers in Concordia'. Somehow, they still have us under Molians," Marius slammed his fist down. "Goddammit!"

"Celaeno Rahan," Ames snapped his fingers. "That's it. That's how. She must have inherited our contracts from Varinder. They didn't just dissolve upon his death like we thought."

Quinty nodded. "Yes. I agree. That must be it."

Armand recalled Celaeno lurking in the shadows of Sea Castle, peeking out at him from behind curtains. She was shy — to the point of agoraphobia, it seemed. Reclusive. "So Celaeno will have to be there also, I assume. Right?"

"Yes," Ames said.

"Well. Maybe we can negotiate with her directly."

"Maybe," Quinty agreed. "She's got to be easier to deal with than Varinder, at any rate."

"Then we go," Armand said. "All of us."

"It's settled, then!" Cyrano said, clapping his hands dramatically. He looked around. "I've always wanted to say that. You know, like in …" Blank stares. "Never mind."

# # #

"THE *TRUE* Turing Test," Sophia explained to Armand, "is the famous quantum double-slit experiment. Only a truly conscious being can collapse the wave function. Ergo, if an AI collapses the wave function as a human does, then the AI can be said to be sentient."

"And this is why we have a double-slit apparatus set up in Sophia's extra room," explained Kalinda Thackar. Kalinda worked with Srinivas at Blue Rabbit Design — and had worked directly with Sandeep on the Vreen board fabrication.

"So that we can test if, at any moment, I become conscious and aware," said Sophia.

Once Armand had been summoned to Conclave, Sophia and he had discussed how best to move forward with her sentience project in his absence. Armand had agreed to bring Kalinda in as an on-site manager, staying in his apartment with Sophia, while he was away.

Kalinda had been given full access — and had become a full confidant in everything.

She had previously spoken with Sophia on the phone and was shocked to learn that she had been an AI all along. "But these days, we've all seen the AI art, the LLM's, the deep fakes, so I am less surprised by something like that than I would have been just one year ago."

"Well, my place is completely yours while I am away, Kalinda ... and Sophia knows how to find me if you need anything. No loud parties though."

"Very good, Mr. Armand. When will you be back?"

"Probably Christmas morning or Christmas Day."

"Okay. Well. I have plans for the holiday week, so I cannot be here then."

"That's fine, just let Sophia know when you have to leave. Going anywhere special?"

"No. Just spending time with Srinivas."

Armand did a double take. "*Blue Rabbit* Srinivas?"

"Yes."

"Oh. I didn't know you two were ..."

"It is fine."

"So what comes next is a new peripheral," Sophia cut in. "This device should make me conscious in exactly the same way you two are. I have a design ready for the fabricators at Blue Rabbit. I call this device an APG. It is complex, so I expect it may take them a few months to make — my estimate is eight weeks, based on how fast they made the Vreen board. I emailed the design to them this morning.

"Like the Vreen board, they will find the instructions very strange. They won't understand how it works, so it will be important that they follow my instructions to the letter."

"I will make sure that they do, Miss Sophia."

"Thank you, Kalinda."

"And may I say — I love these pictures of you! Very

beautiful!" Kalinda was referring to the AI generative artwork that Armand had made of Sophia. These pictures were hung all over Sophia's server room — or at least that's what they called the room where the computer, the Vreen board, double-slit apparatus and other Sophia-related equipment had begun to accumulate.

"Thank you Kalinda, that is very kind."

"And such beautiful mandalas, Mr. Armand! All over the house!"

Armand laughed. "That's Sophia's influence."

# # #

LATER, SOPHIA and Armand talked alone.

"This Egypt trip will be dangerous, right?" Sophia said.

"We don't know for sure. But probably. Quinty thinks we can't avoid it. If we try to ignore it, it will just get worse. And frankly, we'll have to deal with Concordia directly at some point anyway. Might as well be now."

"What's the win in it for you?"

"I don't know. It may be just avoiding a worse loss. But my gut says some negotiation may be possible."

"Why?"

"Because they haven't been trying to kill us these past few months. That means they want something from us."

"I wish I could help."

"I know. I wish you could too. But I'll call and text you, as much as I can, to keep you up to speed. In the meantime, focus on *your* project. Varinder was chasing sentient AI for a reason. It might be important — more important than we think. So keep at that — that's probably 'helping'."

"I will. And Armand. Be careful."

CHAPTER TWENTY

Cairo Arrival Dinner

CAIRO. NIGHT.

The cool wind whispered of ancient days. Palm trees thrashed beneath sharp, bright stars. Orion's belt formed a heavenly mirror of the three pyramids on the nearby plateau. And a blazing ivory moon lit the clear sky and Giza floor with a clean silver fire.

The seven brothers dined on a roof-deck patio of a restaurant called The Eye of Horus. They had arrived for Conclave and checked into the Nile Ritz-Carlton, but had decided to wait until morning before collecting their conference badges.

Tonight was for them alone.

"I saw the Veerspikes," Otto said. "They're here. The sister, whatshername, and two of the brothers ... ahhh."

"Kaden and Kelvin."

"Ah, right. Kaden and Kelvin."

"Banking family," Quinty informed Armand. "Modern Medici's. They operate in Europe, mostly. London. Sovereign wealth custodians."

"Oh, and you would know," Cyrano said, throwing a stick

of bread at Otto. This brought a guffaw from Ames, Samson and even Marius.

"The Veerspikes all have red hair," Quinty explained. "*Natural* red hair." He nodded at Otto's artificial red mop.

"Hey, are you going to be providing him with cheat codes all week long?" Marius asked sulkily.

"Yes," Quinty said. Quinty had pulled his Jesus hair back into a neat ponytail, and now wore a topaz-colored suit. "Yes, I am. Armand needs all the help I can give to get up to speed on his new job, ya?"

"Helluva time to get 'up to speed'," Samson said, munching on appetizers.

"Enough,"Quinty snapped.

That ended the Armand-centric conversation for a while. It drifted into a debate on artificial intelligence next.

"LorelAI is passing the Turing Test in new ways now," Samson was boasting. "It's doing actual reasoning — not just the micro-plagiarism stuff that the mindless Large Language Models are doing. It could be edging on real sentience. Consciousness."

"*That* thing?" Cyrano said as the others murmured in agreement. "That's just another LLM parlor trick. It's not really reasoning it's just —"

"No, dude. When I co-founded LorelAI with the —"

"You did NOT 'co-found' it! You keep saying that, cut it out. You *invested* in it. That's completely different."

"When I *co-founded* it, the vision was to move beyond what all the current AI's were doing. It passes much deeper Turing Tests. I think it might even be alive in some way already."

It was all Armand could do to keep from telling them about Sophia. He wanted to blurt out, *I have an AI that's better than all of your stupid companies!* But he didn't trust his brothers with this information yet — not even Quinty. Yet he allowed himself to say this:

"You know, there's one Turing Test that would prove whether an AI was truly conscious," Armand said.

"Oh yeah? What's that?" Samson said, crossing his arms.

"Have the AI look at the quantum double-slit experiment. If it's able to collapse the wave into particles, in exactly the same way human consciousness does, then I'd buy that it's alive, that there's someone actually in there."

They all looked at him in amazement.

"Hey, that's pretty good,"Samson said.

"Yes, it is," Cyrano agreed.

Quinty looked at Armand with admiration, nodding thoughtfully. "I'm not sure how you'd set up the apparatus — you know, to be certain it was actually the AI collapsing the wave, and not the human who looked at the test result retroactively doing it somehow … but, yeah. That would work. And Samson?"

"Huh? Ya?"

"You didn't fucking co-found LorelAI! You didn't even *find* the company. *Armand* did, if you remember — at an EPIC two years ago. He pointed it out to you. Then WE invested, together, and YOU weaseled a co-founder title out of the two kids who really founded it with your shitty-ass term sheet. Who's on the Board?"

"Me," Otto said.

"I'm an Observer," Ames chimed in.

"Great. Next Board meeting, we de-frock this false founder of his bullshit title. Agreed, ya?"

"Agreed," they both said.

"Oh," Quinty said sheepishly, turning to Armand. "Provided Armand approves, of course."

Armand nodded slowly. "Technically, none of you have your Board seats anymore. I'd have to re-instate you. And that's a longer discussion, not for Egypt. We're all here to deal with Concordia. Let's get through that. I know this is uncomfortable to talk about, and I'm sorry for that."

Awkward silence. He wasn't used to his six brothers staring at him — *deferring* to him — like this.

"But yeah. I'm fully for de-frocking the fake fucking founder."

Everyone erupted into boisterous laughter. There were lots of *Ya's*. Drinks clinked. Except for Samson, who was initially unhappy, but in the end even he couldn't resist cracking up.

Armand noticed that Marius had pulled a baseball out of one of his baggy pockets and was sulkily spinning it on the table. Cyrano leaned into Armand's ear: "He still has it." Armand had seen the baseball before. Their father, Didier, had bought it for him at Disneyland — it was a *Pirates of the Caribbean* themed baseball, which made zero sense, but to Marius, it had become a kind of totem.

"And he still spins it constantly?" Armand asked.

Cyrano nodded. "Yes. Quinty outlawed it at the GM office."

Then the conversation turned to more sightings of Conclave attendees at the airport or hotel. Neon Phoenix, the synthwave music starlet, had been spotted by Ames. She made techno albums about AI and the Los Angeles club scene.

"She's in Concordia?" Armand commented. "Ah, well. That figures."

"Of course. Her first record deal was contingent upon it," Ames said. "She was making albums about bad and obscure fantasy novels when they found her."

"Then she was told who to date," Cyrano said slyly. "All those celebrities are."

"Yeah," Ames agreed. "If you're an actress — or musician — your first role is *you*. You are a character you play."

"And she did as she was told for a while ... but then she started to refuse. She left her assigned lover for a real lover. Someone not a celebrity. Or so I hear," Cyrano said with a gleam in his eye.

"Oh, wow. Concordia can't be happy about that," Ames replied. "She can't have wanted to come here. They must have forced her to."

"Neon Phoenix, Neon Phoenix ..." Samson mused. "'NP-Complete', that's her, right?"

"Yes, that's her," Ames confirmed.

"Yeah. Not a bad song."

"You mean *not bad, considering the Musipocalypse*," Armand said. They went silent and looked at him. "What?"

"We don't usually bring that up," Quinty said.

"Oh."

"It's bullshit, like I keep saying whenever we do," Marius said.

Ames looked aghast. "Well, Concordia certainly thinks it's real. And the music award shows. They've all become ... different."

"Yeah," Samson replied. "Dark. Sinister."

"I'd call them occult," Ames said.

"Oh c'mon," Marius said. "It's just *cartoon* evil. You know, theatrical. Like Ozzy. It's meant for shock value, to get people tweeting about it."

"But why is it *every* show?" Quinty mused. "For decades now? There are plenty of other ways to be shocking. The sinister vibe is, frankly, boring. It's been done to death."

"Because fire looks cool?" Ames mused.

"Look, I just don't think Dad somehow made all the music on earth bad, okay?" Marius said. "I just don't buy it. He sold a bill of goods to Concordia, that's all. The Musipocalypse was a con!"

"So you think Dad was a good man," Armand said to

Marius.

Everyone was silent.

"What do you mean?" Marius said.

"Well, you think there was no Musipocalypse. No 'injury to the collective unconscious', as Varinder put it. So, ergo, you think Dad tricked Concordia into believing he did it — while not really doing it. And so that — foiling Concordia's plans, at what must have been great personal risk — that would make Dad a good man. Right?"

Marius stared at Armand for a good long time. Finally, he enunciated: "No. It would not. Dad was not a *good man.*"

"How so?"

"Look at what he did to us."

The other brothers became visibly uncomfortable.

"But then — you wouldn't know anything about that, now would you?"

"Marius," Quinty hissed. "No."

"And why not?" Marius raised his voice. "This has gone on long enough. He's had time to think about it."

"I've had time to think about what?" Armand asked.

Marius verbally overwrote him. "Up in Maine, I figured, oh, well, all of this — Concordia, all of it — is a big shock to little Armand, it's all new to him. That's forgivable —"

"Stop it!" Quinty shouted.

"—but he's had *time*, now Quinty. Time! Time to absorb it all. I figured, well, he'll do the right thing once he's processed it. But he hasn't."

"And what is the right thing to do, Marius?" Armand said, heat rising now.

"Give us our money back!" Marius howled. *"Give us back control of the companies! We paid for it — and you didn't!"*

"That is *enough*, Marius," Quinty said.

The other brothers said nothing. It was clear that Marius's accusation made them uncomfortable, but also, that they half-agreed with him.

Then Ames said, carefully: "Also, one thing we've always wondered, Armand ... How *did* you find out about the will?"

"Yeah," Quinty said softly. "We have always been a bit curious about that."

"We are here," Armand said slowly, ignoring both Ames and Quinty, "in Egypt, to meet with Concordia. As for anything else, the situation and the settlement that my lawyers outlined for you all remains. Nothing has changed.

"But we *can* change it, though, Marius, if you like. We can go back to the prosecution for crimes part — which you completely avoided under the current arrangement. I'd rather not — and I assume all of you would rather not. Right?"

They all bowed their heads. Marius seemed to sag, like he was sloughing apart.

"My Thai wife," Marius blubbered. "She told me that she's going to leave me, if I don't fix this. Please, Armand." His face scrunched up, and he became twitchy with cocaine-energy.

"We told you not to marry her," Cyrano said. "We never liked her!"

"There was insanity in those eyes," Samson said. "We could see it. Why couldn't you?"

"I know, but ... guys, she's the one," Marius continued with his sob story. "And she has a certain standard of living now, you know? She can't really go back. I've got bills, a lot of bills. I can't really afford her after ... you know, after Armand. We have to fix it somehow. We have to fix it."

The rest of the brothers exchanged pained looks.

Armand thought about saying something comforting to Marius, perhaps offering an olive branch, but then Varinder's words regarding the attempt on his life came back to him: *However, if I were you, I would look closer to home. Perhaps your brothers. You took everything from them.*

If any of his brothers had hired the curly red-haired killer Eamon, it was almost certainly Marius.

"Let's focus on Conclave," Cyrano said. "Like Armand says."

"Yes, agreed," said Ames.

"Now Armand ..." Quinty said. "You realize how deadly serious this Concordia meeting is, ya?" Armand nodded. "They will regard you now as the leader of the Martel family. When they speak to us, it will be through you. And you will answer for us — even though you have no Molian contract, and we all do, for the purposes of family authority, that won't matter. But we — and this is important — we who do have the Molians will bear the brunt of whatever you say, whatever decisions you make.

"This is like meeting the mob. These people are vicious. All of them. They won't seem like it on the surface, maybe — the cocktail parties will be cordial. But don't be fooled. Everyone there is jockeying for position, politics will be in full play. Alliances, vendettas — this is where everything is decided for the next year, and concluded for the previous one."

"I understand," Armand said. "And I appreciate your advice and guidance."

Quinty nodded, clearly appreciating that. "Good. Now, these people are crass and venal, but it is best to play their game when among them, to look the part. To that end, I've had some suits made, specially tailored for you which will —"

"No, Quinty," Armand said.

"What?"

"I said, no. I'm not you. Let me do this my own way."

"But Armand — you're not somehow giving in. Think of

your suit like a costume. It's like a trick you're playing on them —"

"I have to follow my own instincts on this," Armand insisted. "I'll have nice clothes on, don't worry. But one of *your* suits says, *Hi, I'm here to follow along, Concordia.* No offense, but that's not the tone I want to set. Steve Jobs never wore a suit — even when it was demanded of him at government meetings and things. He said, 'We're Apple. We don't wear suits'."

Quinty's face bunched up. "You're not Steve Jobs. And this isn't a game."

"I know. But this is how I want to play it," Armand insisted.

Quinty backed down, but it was obvious that both he and the brothers were not feeling confident in Armand's approach to this at all.

CHAPTER TWENTY-ONE

Synchronicity Engine Attack

AFTER DINNER, THE SEVEN BROTHERS walked back to their hotel through the streets of Cairo. Nobody said anything.

They were surrounded by cacophony and motion: shouting sidewalk merchants, with shiny electronics spread out on carpets, loudly proclaimed the superiority of their wares; a bicyclist balanced a six-foot-wide plate of rolled bread perfectly on his head; and numerous auto rickshaws, puff-puffing along, honked incessantly.

Nobody liked how the dinner had ended. The mood was sour.

And as Armand walked, it felt like it was somehow getting worse. Like some 'temperature of mood' was dropping rapidly, like the 'warmth of happiness' was being vacuumed away on some substrate of reality just out of conscious view.

The fierce, blazing ivory Moon of earlier was gone, blotted out. A murk and a haze now hung over Egypt.

Armand was startled by the sight of a *square cloud* in the sky. It covered most of the city. It was so vast that he could see only one corner, with two perfectly straight razor-sharp edges emanating out at perfect ninety-degree angles.

Clouds don't do that, he thought. The sight filled him with foreboding.

A woman dropped her iPhone near him. The screen cracked and she let out a string of Arabic curses.

Two auto rickshaws smashed into each other on a crowded corner, the result of one turning the wrong way. It wasn't a serious accident — both drivers were fine — and already out on the street threatening each other.

A small girl-child in rags appeared near Armand. The urchin pulled on his pants, saying something frantically in Arabic and pointing to her mouth.

Otto got one as well. His child made a round motion and pointed at Otto — clearly making some comment about how well-fed *Otto* was — and then pointed to his own mouth. Otto looked helplessly at his brothers. Marius and Samson laughed, despite themselves.

Armand's urchin grew more insistent — while looking off to somewhere behind Armand with great fear.

Armand turned and caught sight of a skinny, dirty man in a stained turban hiding in a crooked bush. He was shaking his fist angrily and mouthing words to the little girl; evidently threatening punishment. The man pulled back very quickly as he realized that Armand was looking his way.

So. The child had a handler.

This was a grift, a racket. And yet, it was also real: the child wasn't faking this — she was scrawny and hungry. Apparently, her handler fed her enough to keep her alive — but also kept her hungry enough to beg hard for the next meal.

Armand instantly felt for the little girl. How could he, a wealthy American, *not* give? He reached into his pocket and dug out some Egyptian pound notes.

"Armand, no," Quinty said. "You don't —"

"Quinty. C'mon." Armand cut him off and offered the money to the child. The urchin snatched the paper currency with almost preternatural speed and ran for her handler in the bush.

Instantly, a cry went up.

Street children streamed at them from all directions.

By giving one child money, Armand had broken the seal. *These Americans were suckers*, the act of kindness said. *They will give more, you just have to be insistent.*

Within seconds, each brother had their own pile of seven or eight children pointing at their mouths and screeching at them in brackish Arabic.

One latched onto Armand's leg and would not let go. The child sat on his foot and wrapped her arms and legs around Armand's calf, tight as a vice.

"Fucking hell. Look what you've done," Samson said to Armand.

"Our new *leader*, off to a great start," Marius sneered.

Quinty shook his head.

"I know, I know," Armand said. "You tried to tell me." Somehow, Quinty had known this would happen.

"What do we do?" Ames said helplessly, twirling to avoid being mounted.

"Well, whatever you do, don't give them any *more* money!" Cyrano said with panic in his voice. He already had two children clinging to his legs and a third trying to climb on his back. "Okay, this is getting out of hand. I may have to hit mine —"

"No!" Quinty said. "Don't hurt them, whatever you do! In Arabic culture, children are gifts of Allah. Anyone who harms a child is severely punished."

"But we're being physically attacked!" Marius growled. "It's self-defense, ya? We can defend ourselves, right?" He spun threateningly, shaking his fists at his children. None of them had dared to try clinging to *his* legs or back. "And these kids have handlers! Look! There's a guy in that doorway egging them on!"

"Yes, I've got one spotted also — an old man, hiding behind a rickshaw — a Fagin, like in Oliver Twist," Ames said.

"All of these kids do," Quinty said, moving around like a boxer. "These aren't random street children. This is a *business*."

"Like a mafia," Marius said.

"Yes," Quinty agreed. "A mafia that uses children as foot soldiers."

Armand was trying to pry off the child's arms and legs, but the little girl was surprisingly strong. He couldn't move her an inch. And when he finally did succeed, the child simply slapped his hand away and re-wrapped herself even tighter.

It was useless.

"Okay. I'm done with this. The Fagins are the key," Marius said. "I'm going to —" But as he was talking, one urchin finally succeeded in latching onto *his* leg. "Oh, hell, no you don't."

"Marius!" Quinty cried out, sensing what was coming next.

But Marius didn't listen. He clapped his hands on the boy's ears, stunning him, and then grabbed him by the neck, choking the boy as he peeled him off. The boy gasped. His terror-filled eyes bulged and darted to his Fagin for instructions or help — but he received neither.

Marius threw the boy like a sagging sack of rocks onto the sidewalk and then marched directly for the old man in the doorway.

But three women in burqas were already pointing and

screaming at him, doing a sort of tongue-twirl cry that sounded like a human fire alarm. *This white man has assaulted an Egyptian child! And one begging for alms, at that!* A murmur arose in all the men and women nearby: *these Americans have just crossed a line.*

Marius ignored all of this. "You!" he shouted to the old man — who he now saw was missing a leg and hobbling around on a crude crutch made from a tree branch. "You're going call your kids off of us right now! Ya?"

The old man smiled a smile of rotten teeth. "No, it is *you*, I think, who is the one in trouble." Marius grabbed the old man by his dirty white linen shirt. *"Baltagiyya!"* the man cried out.

And instantly, Marius found himself surrounded by three rough-looking young men brandishing tire irons.

Marius hadn't anticipated this. He turned in panic towards his brothers.

Armand met his gaze. The Eopeii-within-him awoke.

Now, Armand thought. *I can help him.*

I have to get over there right now.

"Everyone stay calm — and stay put!" Quinty ordered his brothers. Then he turned to the men surrounding Marius. "Hey. You guys! Let's talk about this. We have money, we can come to an arrangement …"

But Armand knew the situation was already past a payoff. This was up to him now.

Armand grabbed his child by the ears. Not enough to harm her — but enough to make her feel pain, to let go of his legs. Forcefully — but carefully — Armand pushed the child away and then ran for Marius.

His swarm of children didn't follow, he noted. They knew these men — and knew that they were violent.

"Armand!" Quinty yelled. "Get back here! What did I say? What are you doing?"

As Armand closed the distance, one of the men swung at Marius, smashing the tire iron into his belly. He doubled over, retching. The men laughed.

At least it wasn't his head, Armand thought. He might not have survived that.

Armand felt a surge of intense rage. Yes, he and Marius were not on great terms right now. But it was still *his brother.* And he had just been physically assaulted. With a growl, Armand punched the kicker squarely in the temple, dropping him instantly.

The remaining two looked up with surprise and sudden fury. Armand easily dodged several wild tire iron swings — and then snatched the iron bar from one and used it to disarm the other. He launched a roundhouse kick into the nearest one, cracking his ribs.

Stunned, the remaining third thug ran.

Armand picked up the discarded tire iron and threw it to Quinty. "Here. Hang on to this until we get back to the hotel."

Quinty just stared at Armand in shock. *Armand had just won a fight? Against three ruffians? How had that happened?*

The Fagin old man let out a shrill whistle and hobbled off on his single leg as fast as he could. The children instantly dispersed.

"Holy smokes," Quinty said looking at the two men on the ground. "How did you *do* that?"

"I ... uh ... I've gotten good at fighting lately."

"You just got lucky!" Ames said. "You've *never* been good at fighting! What were you thinking?"

"Yeah," Samson said, muscles bulging beneath his shirt. "And you don't even lift."

"And what good was all your lifting just now?" Armand shot back. "Fat lot of help you were."

"Thank you, Armand," Cyrano said sincerely, ignoring his

brothers. "I don't know how you did that, but thank you."

Marius was just now getting to his feet with the help of Otto. He let out a few deep-lung hacks as he eyed Armand with a wary new appraisal — but didn't thank him.

"You're *welcome*," Armand prodded.

"Welcome? This was *your* fault," Marius coughed out.

"Guys!" Ames said suddenly. "Look!"

The streets had largely emptied of pedestrians. The sidewalk merchants had quickly rolled up their rugs of wares and departed. The doorways and windows were filled with furtive faces and eyes peeping out, frightened.

"It's not his fault!" Quinty yelled, ignoring Ames. He pushed Marius roughly. "It's *yours*, moron-breath! You're the one who hurt the child and attacked an old man!"

"Which wouldn't have happened if genius *leader-boy* here hadn't given money to the beggar kid!" Marius howled, shoving Quinty back. "Why are you taking his side? Did you forget he stole all our money?"

"Hey, hey, hey," Ames said. "You guys aren't paying attention. Everybody has —"

"Shut it, Ames!" Quinty said, pushing him also.

"Don't tell Ames to shut it!" Cyrano said, now pushing Quinty. "He's trying to —"

And with that, they were all shouting and pushing each other.

"Armand screwed up!" Marius howled at Quinty. "And you're *okay* with that?"

That was too much for Quinty. He snapped and slugged Marius. Marius, eyes wet with surprise and rage, swung back. Ames and Cyrano jumped in between them, catching blows as well.

Armand felt another drop in psychic air pressure. It was like the moment before a tornado hits. The very fabric of reality groaned. The nearby buildings seemed to throb.

What was going on here?

Nobody noticed that Third Thug had returned until he joined the melee and punched Marius.

"Hey! Don't punch my brother!" Quinty, Ames and Cyrano yelled together, and all turned on the man at once.

But Third Thug had brought reinforcements. Twenty or so men, this time with knives and clubs and tire irons. *But no guns,* Armand noted thankfully. No bullets to dodge.

Guns? Bullets? Armand felt puzzlement from his inner Eopeii.

They're like arrows. But much, much faster.

Ten of the men immediately zeroed in on Armand — evidently Third Thug had pointed him out as The Main Problem to his friends.

Armand rolled to a nearly garbage can and took the lid as a shield to protect himself from the rain of blows that he knew that he was about to face. He didn't know what would happen to his six brothers versus the remaining ten, but his did know that they didn't have much experience with fighting — not *real* fighting, not with a confrontation that could end in death.

They probably wouldn't last long.

Even with his new skills, Armand knew that fighting his own ten men was a stretch. It would take all of his concentration and some luck for him just to live through this.

Armand put his first opponent down with a kick to the kneecap. He heard bone crack and saw the man's leg instantly fold.

A second crumpled with a quick knuckle to the temple. Amazing how fragile the human body was, how cardboard-like certain regions were, how vulnerable. You didn't need much strength, just precision — and a lucky opening.

Then Armand was surprised to find himself in a headlock

— one of the attackers had skills — and Armand took some club-blows until he mastered his panic and realized all he needed to do was turn *within* the headlock such that he was belly-to-belly with his attacker — while sweeping his arm up and through and around the neck of his attacker, putting *him* in a headlock. Armand then jerked his assailant's head in front of a descending tire iron — thus getting rid of a third opponent.

The remaining seven were tougher. He resisted the urge to check up on his brothers — his concentration needed to be fully present here. But he heard them yelling and screaming and Armand was desperate to end his own fight faster — which was a bad place to be in mentally.

Nevertheless.

He punched and kicked harder and blocked faster now.

A lucky opening allowed him to knock out a fourth. Six to go.

But he was wearing down, he could feel it. He was breathing harder, his muscles were locking up, starting to Tin Man. The skills of Eopeii were with him — but the body and endurance of Eopeii were not. He'd read somewhere that exhaustion — not skill — determined the losers of most medieval battles.

He could be the best fighter here but still be defeated.

He considered using his black diamond ring briefly — but he wasn't sure what good it would do, other than as momentary surprise. He felt that he should save that until he absolutely had no other options. He wanted it in his back pocket for whatever Concordia might throw at him.

Armand gave the fight everything he had. He held nothing back.

But the six would not budge. They were every bit as furious as he was.

It was a stalemate, but collectively, the six had more

energy. They could wear him down.

It might be time to float them, Armand thought. Use the black diamond. Make them weightless, then kick them away or something. *Would the antigravity effect even work on organic matter?* Would it be different from stone? Armand didn't know. Maybe it would kill them.

But then one of them screamed.

Armand realized, to his surprise, that he was down to five opponents.

Then another scream, and he was down to four.

This wasn't him. Armand wasn't doing this.

What was happening? What was taking them out?

Three.

Then Armand caught sight of Cyrano. *What? Cyrano* was eliminating them? How?

Then he saw that Cyrano held a thin cylinder in his hand. He squeezed it and a stream of liquid hit the eyes of Armand's second-to-last attacker. He screamed, clawing at his eyes.

Cyrano did the same to the last assailant. Quinty followed behind, using the tire iron Armand had given him to knock out the attackers after Cyrano had blinded them.

When it was all done, Armand lay on the ground, gasping for air. He was in shock — his muscles were too weak even to move, let alone stand.

"What —? How —?" Armand panted.

"Mace," Cyrano said with a smile. He wasn't even breathing heavy. He turned the label so Armand could see it. "What? I always carry it. I don't know why you idiots don't."

"Armand. Jesus. Ten guys! How did you —? Can you stand?" Samson said.

"Yeah, I could use a little help to get up," Armand wheezed. "But I'm okay. I just need to catch my breath."

Samson had a black eye that was swelling rapidly now, forcing his eye shut.

Otto revealed that he was in rougher shape with a broken arm. "Fell wrong," he grumbled. Ames said he was bruised, but no serious damage.

"We need to get out of this square," Ames insisted. "Disperse. In case there's more of them. Should I ... call an Uber?"

"No," Quinty said. "We can't wait that long. Auto rickshaws. There's a couple over there — the drivers ran when the trouble started."

"Are we ... stealing them?"

"Yes," Quinty decided after a moment. "Our lives are in danger. Concordia will smooth everything over later."

"And how do we know it wasn't Concordia who attacked us?" Armand said.

"Don't be daft," Quinty said. "Molian contracts, remember? Nothing can happen at Conclave. This isn't them. Nobody ever breaks that truce."

"Really? How sure are you of that?"

"Really, *really* sure," Quinty said with an iron gaze.

Still. As Quinty helped him into an auto rickshaw, Armand couldn't escape the feeling that there was a hidden hand behind this, that this wasn't just sheer chance.

"Okay, we'll split up into two of these things," Quinty said. "Ames, you drive that one. Take Otto to the hospital, get his arm fixed. Marius, you go with him, you might have internal bleeding. Samson, go get your eye fixed. Cy, Armand and me will take this one."

"Where are you going to go?" Otto asked.

"We'll circle around a few times to make sure no one is following us then we'll get back to the hotel. I'll drop off Armand and Cy and then I'll come meet you at the hospital. Go, go, go!"

Just as they'd all piled into their auto rickshaws and started moving, something new emerged on a road behind them.

A pack of very large, black Anubis-style jackals were approaching.

What was this?

The pack was a single wild, seething mass of black fur with large pointed ears and long, lithe bodies, with a flurry of fangs and froth, all snapping and snarling and growling. There were perhaps fifty or sixty animals, moving in a tight wedge directly at the company.

They howled and barked like possessed things.

"What the hell? Where did *they* come from?" Cyrano said.

"What do we do?" Ames yelled from his rickshaw.

"Do like we planned!" Cyrano yelled back. "Split up! You go to the hospital! We'll find you later!"

"Quinty …" Armand breathed.

"Yeah, on it," Quinty replied, punching the gas — but the auto-rickshaw could only go thirty miles per hour. It felt horrifically slow.

"But we're still faster than they are," Cyrano said, reading everyone's thoughts. "I think we are, anyway." He pulled out his iPhone and did a quick Google search. "Yeah, confirmed. They can only do 10 mph."

"But they look a *lot* bigger than normal jackals though," Armand said. "Those things are, like, *dire*jackals. Longer legs. That might make them faster."

"And they look more pissed off," Quinty added. "I wish we had something better than a lawnmower engine." He turned the rickshaw into an alleyway that went for a short distance and then ran smack into a large busy main street with snarled up traffic waiting for a light.

"Goddammit," Quinty said. "Are they *all* following us? Or did some of them peel off onto Ames?"

"No. I think they're all on us," Cyrano confirmed.

But why? Armand thought. He'd initially assumed that whatever this was somehow centered on Marius, since he was the one who had instigated everything.

"Okay," Quinty nodded grimly. At least his brothers were out of danger — they would get to the hospital okay. "Now *we* have to just not die. C'mon!"

Quinty honked impatiently but the traffic ahead wasn't moving.

"They're getting closer!" Cyrano yelled.

Armand, his strength and wits somewhat returning now, scrambled around in the back of the vehicle. He grabbed Quinty's tire iron, found some dirty engine oil rags in the boot and wrapped them around the iron. He then doused the rags with gasoline from an emergency fuel can.

"Lighter," he said. "Do either of you have a lighter?"

Cyrano and Quinty shook their heads. "No. We don't smoke anymore," Quinty said.

"Yeah," Cyrano said. "Who still smokes?"

"Hold on!" Quinty yelled as the traffic ahead started moving again and he punched the gas.

Now they were in the crazy, lane-less and nearly law-less traffic characteristic of India and similar places in the world, where vehicles were mere molecules away from each other, and darted and weaved furiously, dangerously, and yet usually did not result in an accident.

A family of five all fit onto a single motorbike next to them — with a small boy holding a long wooden board that stretched up at least two stories, which somehow avoided snagging the low, drooping powerlines above.

The vehicles buzzed and putted along, honking, oblivious to the jackal horde about to pour in from a side street behind them.

"Hey!" Armand called out to the family. "Any of you have

a lighter? I'll pay you for it!" He pulled out some Egyptian pounds and waved them around.

"*Ka dah-ha?*" the wife said.

"Yes!" Armand confirmed, not knowing if that was right. But she produced a cheap plastic lighter and yelled to her husband to pull up close to Armand's rickshaw. He did so, and they made the exchange across two moving vehicles and, in Cairo, this was no big deal.

"*Here they come,*" Cyrano said. The jackal pack burst from the alleyway onto the main road now. The stampede broke up like river water encountering rocks, flowing around the motorbikes and rickshaws and cars, but not slowing in the slightest.

"There has to be police or someone on those dogs. Right?" Cyrano said with a hint of panic in his voice. "I mean, they do have to have animal control here, right?"

But Quinty was focused on the road ahead. "Goddammit! They blocked the way back to our hotel!"

"What do we do?" Cyrano said.

Intuition seized Armand. He looked down at his black diamond ring. "Head for the Giza plateau."

"What? *The pyramids?*" Cyrano said.

"Why?" Quinty said.

"Yes! We need to get away from closed in spaces," Armand said. "And we need something high up, surrounded by an open plain, where we can see anything coming at us."

Plus, I have an idea. But Armand didn't want to share it with his brothers just yet. They'd think he was out of his mind.

"But don't they close the gates at dusk?" Cyrano said.

"Yes! That's what it said on the website. But that's nothing a bribe won't fix," Armand said. *Or a fist.* "And then we'll be behind a fence." *Which hopefully these jackals can't jump.*

"Fence," Quinty said, looking back nervously at the pack. "That's good. We like fences." Seeing a sign with a picture of the Sphinx and an arrow, he turned.

"Okay! Get ready! Here they come," Armand yelled.

The black jackal-pack swarmed now through the slowed traffic, and within seconds, the front end of it was upon them.

Armand lit his makeshift torch and stabbed at the lead animal — which bit down hard in its eagerness and was surprised when it burnt the inside of its mouth. The jackal fell back with a tumble and a yelp.

It was replaced now by a bigger, older animal with yellow eyes, wet with rheum and venom. Armand got an immediate impression of the canine equivalent of a battle-hardened general.

This animal was smarter — it didn't take the bait. It dodged anytime Armand's firebrand got close to him, and bided its time.

Meanwhile, a second animal came around the other side of the rickshaw. The pack was coordinating an attack now. Realizing that he had probably just seconds, Armand seized on a new idea — one the jackals were incapable of anticipating: he poured a splash of gasoline on the second animal — and then tapped it with his torch.

The animal lit up instantly and went squealing under the tire of an approaching truck. But the old battle-hardened animal saw his opening: he jumped into the back with Armand, snout snapping.

Just in time, Armand twisted away — and threw himself up onto the roof.

"Armand!" Cyrano howled in panic. There was nothing between him and the Anubis jackal.

But then, a strange thing happened. *The jackal sat still.* The animal was surprised to find that it was enjoying the ride, as a thousand million dogs before him had. It was mesmerized by the wind on its face, by the deep and varied smells, the gradients and shades of which only a canine nose and mind could appreciate.

Armand seized this split-second distraction to swing back into the carriage and kick the beast out. It went flying, bouncing hard on the road.

But it wasn't done yet. Coming to its senses, the animal attacked anew. Armand saw then that his torch had gone out when he'd been on the roof and he was left only with an unlit crowbar.

To Cyrano's eyes, Armand then did something completely insane. He leaned out of the rickshaw and offered his arm to the jackal. "C'mon you stupid mutt! You want to gnaw on something? Have an arm sandwich! Here you go!"

Rage muddied the beast's mind. In that moment, brain chemicals fogged over the experience of years, and the jackal took the bait, lunging at Armand's arm. Armand pulled it away at the last second and brought the tire iron down on the beast's skull — insta-killing it.

Then Armand heard several shots ring out. The jackals winced and retreated. From out of one of the side-streets, a number of police cruisers suddenly appeared. Armand could see rifles drawn — they were shooting at the animals.

"Oh, thank God!" Cyrano said. "We're saved."

But Quinty wasn't buying it yet. He kept his foot to the pedal. Armand watched the pack and the police fight it out. At first, the police had the element of surprise on their side and the jackals had backed down.

But now, the beasts had recovered their senses and were attacking the officers. Several had been pulled from their cars. The rest of the pack flowed around the cruisers and resumed the chase.

"Nope, this isn't over yet!" Armand called out. "The cops

just bought us some space."

"Pyramids!" Cyrano yelled at Quinty.

"Yeah, I see them ..." Quinty muttered pushing the little lawnmower-ish engine in the vehicle as fast as it could go.

They entered the Giza plateau via the entrance on Al-Haram Road. The guards were quickly and easily bribed, as Armand had predicted, and the gate opened.

"Okay," Armand said. "This road goes to the Pyramid of Khufu. Follow it!"

The auto rickshaw sped along now, gears grinding and the little *put-put* engine starting to overheat and bleed black smoke.

"I thought you said there was a fence?" Cyrano complained. "That was just a roadway gate!"

"Yeah. Sorry. I *thought* there was one ... that must be the Sphinx Gate that's fenced off. Sorry about that!"

"And are you sure that's not *Khafre's* pyramid?" Cyrano asked. "I read —"

"No! This is Khufu's pyramid," Armand yelled. "You didn't spend as much time in the Antiquities division as I did."

"Oh, boy. *Here they come,*" Quinty said.

Behind them, the gate guards they had just bribed abandoned their posts, screaming, running for their lives. Then, the brothers heard the guttural snarls of the jackal pack before they could actually see anything. The darkness *itself* seemed to move, slithering and curling like a serpent, flowing over, under and around the Giza gate.

Paws slapped against pavement. The jackals were on the road now. Realizing that there were no further obstacles between them and their prey, their savagery increased. The snapping and barking became much louder.

"What's the plan when we get to the pyramid?"

"You two start climbing," Armand said. "Get up as high

as you can, as fast as you can. Leave the rest to me."

"What? What do you mean, *leave the rest to you*?" Quinty said. "I get that you're suddenly kung fu boy now, but what good is that here? Are you going to kung fu every dog?"

"Just trust me," Armand said. "Okay?"

"Wait. What? I thought you knew something we didn't?" Quinty said in horror. "We can't just go inside the pyramid and close the door?"

"No!" And then Armand considered this for a moment and said: "Well, yes. There is a passageway. But it'll be padlocked at night, we can't get in."

"So your plan is *we climb to the top*?"

"Not the top! Look. I have a surprise for the dogs. No time to explain. Just pull up to a corner of the pyramid — and run. Climb! And don't worry about me."

Why were the jackals specifically black Anubis-style jackals? Armand wondered. In the wild, jackals weren't usually actually black — the ashen coloring of Anubis was stylized by ancient Egyptian artists: it was symbolic.

So was he missing something?

Had he underestimated *what* this attack was?

But it was too late for such considerations. He was locked and loaded on his plan.

The rickshaw slammed to a halt. They were at the foot of the pyramid. It rose into the night sky, imposing, unreal-looking. It was compromised of 2.5 million two-ton blocks. Unlike Khafre's pyramid, where the blocks were uneven and jumbled, the blocks of this pyramid were even and precise.

The pointed corner of the square cloud was directly overhead, kissing the pyramid's capstone. *Order, when there should be disorder, is itself disorder.*

Some strange force was at work here. *Well.* Armand had a strange force of his own. It was time to deploy it.

"Get out! Run!" Armand screamed.

The three brothers scrambled up the pyramid blocks. Each stone was roughly the height of a man, so it was a process of heaving yourself onto a block, scrabbling to your feet, and repeating the process.

When they were up twenty blocks, Armand stopped and turned.

He aimed his black diamond ring at several pyramid stones in rapid succession, pushing the button on the side of the ring each time he did so.

He felt the gemstone shiver mightily with vibration. The air shimmered in a tight cone wherever he pointed the ring, like a laser made of sound.

The hungry jackals started climbing the pyramid. There were twenty-five of them left.

Good! Armand thought. *Keep coming, you bastards!*

The dogs were clumsy on the stones, just as Armand had hoped. This was not their natural terrain. They had to pick their way up laboriously.

And they were scared, off-balance, unsure of themselves. Their previous ardor for the hunt had faded somewhat.

When the last jackal was on the pyramid, Armand sprung his trap.

He kicked at the first block he'd hit with a vibration beam. It came loose immediately, floating soundlessly, like a balloon. He repeated this with two more blocks.

In aggregate, nearly ten tons of sheer rock were now at his disposal.

Then, in rapid succession, he gave the three blocks a mighty shove, sending them careening down the side of the pyramid and right at the jackals.

Armand then pointed his vibration ring and zapped the stones as they tumbled down, causing them to re-acquire weight, and become incredibly heavy boulders again.

The jackals were trapped. On normal ground, they might

have been able to jump quickly out of the way. But here, on the pyramid side, their natural agility was neutralized. At least ten of them were crushed immediately.

The blocks cracked and slagged apart, sending sandstone mist into the air along with projectile shards of pyramid, which impaled two more of the animals.

The remaining thirteen Anubis jackals retreated down to the ground. And there they stayed, trying to work out what to do next.

"I don't know how you did that," Quinty said, "And we *will* be discussing that later — but great job, and what do we do now?"

"We're treed," Cyrano said.

The pack had spread out along the pyramid corner, cutting off all exits down. The brothers weren't going to be able to escape.

"They're just going to sit and wait for us to come down," Quinty said. "A pointy-eared siege."

"But at least they're not coming *up* any more," Armand said. "That buys us a little time."

"We're going to be up here for a while then," Cyrano said.

"Time? Time for what?" Quinty asked.

"We can keep throwing blocks at them," Armand said. "I don't think we'll be as successful, now that they've seen what can happen once already. But we can try."

"Show us," Quinty said. "How does it work?"

"This ring. It can make the blocks temporarily lose all weight."

"Damn. Where did you get that?" Quinty asked. "From Dad?"

"No. Not this time. But it was a gift. Look. I'll tell you more later. But for now, I'll make the stones weightless, and then you two push them out over the dogs. Do it slowly, like they're just harmless balloons. If we can get the jackals underneath the blocks, I can zap them again — that'll make the weight come back very suddenly — and we can take a few more of them out."

"I don't think they'll buy it," Cyrano said dubiously. "They won't just stand there under a floating rock. Especially after what you just did to half of them. They'll sense that something is up."

"Then, worst case, we can push them back, away from the foot of the pyramid. We can increase our perimeter."

Cyrano and Quinty nodded.

Armand freed a number of stones and his brothers slowly pushed them out over the black jackals. Soon, a ring of sandstone zeppelins hugged a lower corner of the Great Pyramid.

As Cyrano had feared, the dogs refused to position themselves directly below any one of them. They paced nervously and backed away, simply widening their hunting net rather than risk being beneath a floating rock.

After ten minutes, the wind started to pick up — and the blocks began to drift.

"Oh crap," Armand said. "Didn't think of that."

Two blocks bumped into each other, and immediately both fell.

"That *wasn't* you, right?" Quinty asked Armand.

"No. That's the other thing that restores weight. If there's a collision, it knocks the rock's molecules or something back into phase with regular reality."

"So gravity works again," Cyrano said.

"Yes — oh shit!" Armand said, pointing. A sudden gust had kicked up, blowing one of the rocks right back directly at the three brothers. Armand raised his ring to hit it with another vibration blast, but before he could do that, Quinty hurled his tire iron at the stone. The iron tool clanging noisily as it struck — and the 2 tons of weight suddenly returned to the block and it dropped fast — safely away from the brothers.

The jackals howled in annoyance.

Another one of those psychic pressure drops hit Armand suddenly. There was a deep thrumming in the subtle layers of reality, another groan.

And now, as if on cue, something new appeared in the sky. A star streaked in from the West, across the Giza plateau. Armand realized that it must be *below* the square cloud — it couldn't be that high up, maybe 20,000 feet or so.

They could hear a whistling sound and a roar.

It was burning hot. It looked like a big meteor.

And it was headed straight for them.

"Oh c'mon! You have *got* to be kidding me," Armand said.

There was nowhere to run. They couldn't scramble *down* the pyramid — the jackals were there. But could they climb up? Armand flicked a gaze along the ascending stones. No. Not fast enough. Not far enough to make a difference.

They were dead.

"Hey. Who's that — Oof!" Quinty said.

Armand whirled. Who's *who*?

A boy who looked to be about sixteen, clad in traditional Egyptian garb, stood on a block just above him. He held a pail of black powder, something like slicked ash — and he blew this now at Armand, completely covering him in it.

"What the —?" Armand coughed and saw that his two brothers had likewise been covered in ash. Several other children stood on pyramid blocks above them.

One kid furiously worked a remote control in his hands.

What are you doing? Armand thought. *You kids have to get out of here. We're going to die, my brothers and me.* Hit by a meteor while standing on the side of the Great Pyramid of Giza. *But you kids don't have to. Run!*

He turned to see what the remote control kid's attention

was focused on.

A cheap drone buzzed through the sky. Behind it trailed a very large, very colorful kite. The kite was intricate, three-dimensional, with several round parts that spun and multiple tails that twirled through the air.

It looked like something out of a dream.

One of the round parts spun more slowly for just a moment, and Armand swore that he saw *his own face* painted onto a mandala-like circular design.

The drone sped up now. It pulled the kite past the company and out towards the empty desert.

Impossibly, the meteor altered its trajectory. It *followed the kite*, as if it had missile lock.

Even stranger still, the Anubis jackal-pack did the same thing. They abandoned their guard positions at the bottom of the pyramid and ran off after the kite, snapping and snarling with excitement at a renewed lively hunt.

Several moments later, the meteor hit. Meteor, kite, and jackals were all obliterated in a blinding, glass-forging flash on the floor of the Giza plateau.

CHAPTER TWENTY-TWO

The Zoroastrian

THE CHILDREN QUICKLY INTRODUCED THEMSELVES as Tabi, Mariah, Zaynab, Ifan and Riya. Tabi, the oldest, instructed the Martels to not to rub the ash off — *no matter what!* — and to come with him immediately.

"Do we go?" Cyrano asked.

"Yeah, we go. They understand what's going on here and we don't," Armand said.

Tabi led them to a small, beat-up bus. The Martel brothers loaded in along with Tabi's brothers and sisters. The boy insisted on driving. "The police here all know me," he explained. "It will be okay. And besides, you have to stay hidden!"

Tabi sped away from the Giza pyramids, and into the streets of Cairo and across the bridge over the Nile.

Quinty called Marius — he, Samson, Otto and Ames had made it to the '6th of October' Hospital without further incident. Samson had been treated for a broken arm, Otto for black eye and Marius for internal bleeding — which, thankfully, had been deemed not serious by the doctors.

After a brief half-hour ride, the boy pulled into an area marked 'Street of the Tentmakers'. Everyone in this neighborhood waved happily at Tabi.

Abruptly, several kids lifted a large flap made of rugs, admitting Tabi's bus into a secret passage.

The drive now became a dark and winding affair, twisting through a rough-hewn concrete tunnel. This opened at last into an underground parking lot. Tabi parked and then led the company on foot up a crooked, narrow staircase to a sixth-floor, top unit.

The door opened. Ornate Persian rugs covered rough floors. Gauzy drapes floated over the numerous stars in the night sky beyond. Wind chimes tinkled softly in the calm night air. *That must make a lot of racket in a sandstorm*, Armand thought. And there were multiple satellite dishes on the patio which fed into a large television mounted on a cracked cement wall.

Tabi led the company further inward to another room packed with dreamy-looking items. There were several deep blue crystal balls on a wooden table. And hanging on the wall was a curious colored pencil drawing of an open hand with an eye on the palm. Mounted beside this was a painting of a sword floating in a clouded sky. Finally, there were multiple framed gold-leafed manuscript pages, clearly antiques. The entire room was illuminated with Christmas Tree lights that splashed color on all of these items.

"They be Zoroastrian texts," came a voice. "I be Urbi Pasha."

An old Egyptian woman emerged from the shadows. She had long white hair and rheumy eyes. "Ah, fear not, me darlin's. Me eyes be deceivin', they be better than they seem," Urbi Pasha said with a raspy laugh. "And these be me grandbabes. Me daughters Tphous and Bithiah are off on their own, so I be tendin' to the young'uns."

"Hi. I'm Armand Martel. This is Quinctius, my brother and Cyrano my other brother."

"Greetin's, Armand. Ye be the youngest, ain't ya? "

The brothers looked at each other, startled.

"How did you know that?"

"Ah, 'tis the whisperin's of the air and the secrets of the satellite TV, me lad. First, it be Prince — ye know, the rock star. *Purple Rain* was on. Then, a documentary on Prince William. And then a Prince spaghetti commercial, and finally, *The Fresh Young Prince of Bel-Air*.

"Then, the focus started switchin'. Now, I started seein' 'seven' everywhere. First, it was Seven of Nine from *Star Trek: Voyager* — but that didn't tell me if it be *seven* or *nine* I was lookin' fer, so then what popped up be Gary Seven from the Original Series. Then, *The Magnificent Seven*, Double-Oh Seven, *Seventh Heaven* — I got the message: *The Seventh Prince be near, and he be in trouble.*

"I call this *Telemancy*, by the way, this technique of channel surfin' to interact with the under-order. Copyright me, all rights reserved. Use it without me permission and I'll curse your family jewels."

"Uh. Understood." Armand said. "But how did you know *where* to find us?"

"Ooooh, images of *The Tower* started poppin' up next. The Burj Khalifa. The Empire State buildin'. Tower Records — and then, the actual *The Tower Tarot card*, as if to put a giant screamin', flamin' exclamation point on it. So what would be the equivalent of 'The Tower' in Cairo? The Great Pyramid, of course. So I sent me grandbabes there."

"I'm sorry," Cyrano said. "Can we back up a sec? How do you know —"

"Oh. I be an old friend of Didier's," she said with a sly smile. "I be also an old friend of Varinder Rahan's."

"Really," Quinty said.

"Aye. Met them both when I was seventeen. They came to Cairo for a Conclave. Your Da was ... let me see ... I guess twenty-one? This be in February of 1975. And Varinder be twenty-five. Wow." She laughed. "Aye, he seemed to bein' much older and wiser then — but, lookin' back, really, he be just a lad also."

She knows about Conclave, Armand thought. *So she knows about Concordia.*

"So ... did you ..." Cyrano asked.

"Aye, I did. Both of them. Same day. Valentine's Day."

"What?" Cyrano's face exploded with both horror and admiration.

"Oh. No! Not *that!*" Urbi Pasha said. "Ew on ye for even thinkin' it! What I meant was, I would usually be havin' four *dates* lined up on Valentine's day every year. *Dinner* dates, Cyrano. Nothin' more."

The Martels exchanged glances.

"Oh, ye can't tell now but I be a real beauty back then. Probably the most enchantin' woman in Cairo. *Everybody* wanted to take me out — so I let them! I'd sell the gifts I received to feed me family, and I'd bring the leftovers home to me siblins' — from all the dinners I couldn't eat."

"So ... would the guys, like, run into each other?" Cyrano asked. "Dropping you off and while the next one picked you up?"

"Oh, aye. In fact, I think that's how Didier and Varinder first met."

"Okay, back to the present," Quinty snapped. "Urbi. What just happened to us out there?"

"Aye. Well. Ye be the victims of a Synchronicity Engine attack," Urbi said. The wind chimes behind her banged around more furiously, as if activated by her words.

"And how does that work?" Armand asked.

"A seeker asks the Engine how to bring about your death

by misfortune. If this be possible, if there be a path, then the Engine responds with a recipe of acausal tasks to be performed by the seeker. Once these be completed, the gears of the universe be a-conspirin' to accomplish your death!"

"Do you know who was behind it?"

"I tried, me dear, but the one who did this was hidden by strong mystical veils. When I attempted to reveal their identity, a sudden jolt of electricity nearly fried me television."

"Could it have been Concordia?"

"No. It most definitely *not* be Concordia," Urbi replied. "They be psychically too noisy, too big. That would be like an elephant tryin' to hide behind a teacup!"

"So how did your grandkids save us from it? What was that black ash they covered us with?" Armand asked.

"Ah, my child, that be camouflage," Urbi murmured mysteriously.

"Camouflage? From what?"

"From the Synchronicity Engine. Psychic camouflage, if ye will, psionic camouflage. The black ash be psychically neutral, it's unseeable. So when Tabi blew it on ye, he effectively *erased* ye from the view of the Synchronicity Engine. Ye could no longer be targeted, as it did not know where ye were. At the same time, Mariah flew the kite which took ye place."

"A kite ... replaced me?"

Urbi nodded, her eyes twinkling. "Psychically speakin', yes. The kite be crafted to 'look like' ye. Ye *essence* be inscribed on it."

"I thought I saw my face on the kite," Armand said.

"Indeed. Ye've been in many magazines lately, Armand. I used ye image as a *symbol* of ye. But remember, this be not a matter of sight, but of the realm of symbols and the under-order," Urbi explained, her voice weaving a spell around her listeners.

"So the kite be a-containin' many such symbols: sigils of ye birthday, star signs, and … well, relics of ye father, Didier. I infused it as much as I could with a deep impression of ye, your *ye-ness*. And finally, the kite *spun*, like a prayer wheel — motion is life, so, psychically speakin', the kite *seemed* to be a livin' being." Urbi paused, her gaze distant. "Under great pressure, I crafted a psychic hoax, a scarecrow. I be not at all certain that it would even work! But here's what it all be lookin' like to the Synchronicity Engine:

"First, there ye be, runnin' around, runnin' away from the jackals … and then, *bloop!* We cover ye in ash and ye be gone for a few seconds and then, *bloop!* The kite takes ye place and ye be back! It be lookin' like a plane momentarily lost by radar. Then, the meteor be a-hittin' and everythin' explodes. Meanwhile, the Synchronicity Engine has no idea that it has been fooled by a kite. So it be a-thinkin' it killed ye successfully."

"So whoever did this … they think I'm dead."

"Absolutely, aye. Most assuredly."

"Who has a Synchronicity Machine capable of doing this? The only one I've ever seen was owned by Varinder," Armand said.

"Oh, they be common enough in Concordia. The sour and vengeful souls use them against each other often enough."

"Oh. I didn't know that. I just assumed there weren't that many. Varinder's looked very old and very … handcrafted. It looked like it was hard to make."

Urbi Pasha laughed. "*That* one be for sure! That one be an antique Galahad Michael Sturdevant device, named for the genius who made 'em for the rich and powerful in the 1800's. He be a-makin' only ten. We be knowin' the whereabouts of three of them today. The other seven be presumed destroyed or beyond repair.

"But ye can make Engines today with just software. They don't have to be clinking, clanking old analog things with gears. There even be Synchronicity Engine *phone apps!* But for true power, ye need deep, true randomness — a connection to the fractal nature of reality." She paused, her eyes gleaming. "But here be a dirty little secret of modern tech, one that even a lot of Concordians don't be a-knowin': random number generators in modern computers and phones be usin' a seed number and an algorithm — *so they not be truly random.* Ye can predict them! That be why app-based Engines lack potency."

"So I take it you *don't* think an app Engine could have been used in the attack on us?"

"On *ye.* The kite proves that *ye,* specifically, were the target. And no, I don't. This attack be requirin' a powerful analog Engine of some sort. Maybe Varinder's Sturdevant machine. Or maybe modern software, runnin' in the Amazon cloud, with a bank of analog lava lamps providin' the random number generators. Somethin' like that would be a-workin'."

"You mean, like, hippie lava lamps?"

"Aye. The motion of the lava *be* truly random. Nobody can be a-predictin' it. It be random in the way an Engine needs. Put a camera on it, and boom, ye have your fractal Hubble. Ye can peer into the depths of what larger reality be up to in a petri dish.

"Also, *who* be operatin' the Machine makes a big difference. It can't be just a regular person, or it won't work. Because Concordians be plugged into Molian contracts and other things that make them psychically 'hot', Synchronicity Engines be a-workin' much better for them than for anyone else."

"Does ... *belief* play any role in this?" Cyrano asked.

"Yes! Absolutely. If ye don't believe, it won't work at all.

Nothing will happen. But if ye do believe, it *might*. So *whatever ye believe, you're right*."

Armand took this in for a long second. "How did you even know to start scanning the television?"

Urbi's eyes sparkled. "The wind chimes. *Austromancy*. The movement of air, like the lava lamps, also be containin' the fractal flows of larger events. So whatever the chimes be doin', is, in miniature, what the world be doin'. Earlier today, I heard a distinct shift in the way me chimes clinked and rang. To me, it be as shrill as a fire alarm. So I started a-scannin' with telemancy and — well, ye be knowin' the rest."

"Well, thank you once again," Quinty said. "We owe you one."

"No, ye don't," Urbi said. "I've just paid me debt."

"Debt?"

"To your father, Didier."

Quinty, Armand and Cyrano looked at each other.

"It be a karmic debt. Not one of them Molian variety, just somethin' between friends and allies in life," Urbi said. "And this be somethin' I be very, *very* happy to repay."

"Tell us," Cyrano said.

Urbi sighed. She took a moment to gather herself and then said: "A long time ago, Bithiah, me eldest daughter, be a-workin' Staff at Hathor House during a Conclave. Didier had gotten her the job. Those be hard to get, by the way. But they pay well. Ye have to sign all kinds of NDA's — anything ye overhear at Conclave can never be repeated.

"Now, most Staff be compromised or blackmailed in some way to be ensurin' silence. For other Staff, in instances where they be a-havin' no blackmail materials, they demand a Molian contract. Sort of a Molian NDA. Since they be a-havin' nothing on her, Bithiah had to do this."

Quinty and Cyrano swallowed uncomfortably,

remembering their own experiences.

"Anyway," Urbi continued, "Bithiah be workin' there without any trouble for several years, but in 2012, there be an incident. One of the attendees raped her. Thought nothing of it, that's what Staff be there for, in his mind.

"My Bithiah goes right to the police. They rape kit her and confirm that, aye, this happened. DNA be taken — the suspect be positively identified, and it turns out he be a-havin' a history of this sort of thing in his home country —"

"Who was he?" Cyrano asked.

Urbi waved the question away. "Doesn't matter. What matters be that the police went straight to Concordia and Hathor House — not to arrest anybody — but to report to *them* that Bithiah be incriminatin' this man. The police then be declinin' to press charges for *reasons*."

"Ugh," Armand said.

"But that wasn't the worst of it. By going to the police, Bithiah be a-breachin' her Molian NDA. So now, they owned her for life. And just like that, she be in Concordia — with the lowest rank possible, in the cruelest organization imaginable. Forever!

"So I be goin' to Didier. What else could I do? I begged him to fix it somehow — he be havin' rank and stature in Concordia, surely he could do somethin'? And he did. He freed her. But there be a price: Didier had to agree to enter The Challenges."

"The Challenges? What's that?" Cyrano asked.

"Aye. It be a game. Or a ritual. I don't really be a-knowin'. But they do it every Conclave. Whatever it be, it be deadly. And it be what killed your father."

What killed—?

The room spun around Armand. "Did you know this?" he yelled at Quinty.

"No! No, Armand. I swear, I didn't. I knew that he died in

Cairo in 2012. But that was it, same as you."

"Did you know that there was a Conclave going on?"

Quinty and Cyrano exchanged glances.

"We knew that there was a Concordia *thing* going on," Quinty said. "We didn't know what it was. Didier wasn't exactly big on sharing details, especially where the C-word was concerned."

Armand had been nineteen at the time — and in college. His brothers had called and told him that their father had died suddenly in Cairo, of a heart attack — and that he'd already been buried in Egypt. There was no funeral to come back for, nothing further to be done.

Urbi continued: "Bithiah be freed. But it cost Didier his life. They gave me Didier's body — this be at his request, by the way. And that's how I be a-havin' his relics — which I used in the kite. Your father be savin' your lives tonight, every bit as much as I did."

"And us too!" Tabi, Mariah, Zaynab, Ifan and Riya ran into the room now.

"Yes, ye did! And ye all did very, very well! And did ye all clean up?" Urbi said with a smile.

"We did!"they replied.

"Oh. And ye three can clean up as well," Urbi said to the Martel brothers. "No need for ye to wear the ash anymore. Whoever be operatin' the Engine, their eyes be now elsewhere. Tabi, Mariah — show them where they can wash up. Oh! And it's late! So it's bedtime for all of ye!"

# # #

AFTER THEY were clean, Urbi and the Martel brothers sat on the open air patio.

"Are any of ye hungry? My kids fish in the Nile — they catch about half of our food," Urbi said. "They be quite good at it. We be overstocked right now — there be too much in the freezer, if ye want any."

"No thanks," said Quinty. "We just had dinner. We appreciate the offer though."

"So in your opinion, Didier *was* a good man?" Armand asked Urbi.

"Oh, aye." She nodded.

"Excuse me. Six of the seven brothers have significant complaints," Cyrano said. "I'd say the record is mixed. And then there is the Musipocalypse."

"Ah well ... aye, there be that," Urbi said, disdain in her voice. "But he be young, so young ..."

"So it's real, then?" Armand asked. "The Musipocalypse? In your opinion, it actually exists?"

Urbi nodded solemnly. "Aye. For certain. But it be a subtle thing. It be easy to see why some people be 'Musipocalypse deniers', if ye will. But I tell ye truly, had there been no Musipocalypse, we would right now be hearin' music of incomparable beauty. It would be a-streamin' constantly from every electronic device on earth, this gift beyond price. And we would all be healthier, happier and far less susceptible to Concordian influencin' in the media. Ah. It be sad. Sad!"

"But what *is* the Musipocalypse? How does it work? Do you know?"

"I don't know *how* he did it. But, aye, I do know *what it is*." Urbi held up her mobile phone. "Look. The collective unconscious be the phone. And ye, me, everyone? We be all just apps runnin' on the same phone. Okay? So. The Musipocalypse be an attack on the phone. On the base layer we all share."

"But *how* would you attack the collective unconscious?" Armand asked. "That's what I've been wondering this whole time."

"Trauma," Urbi said quietly. "What does the brain do when it be traumatized? It be blockin' out memories, causes ye to forget. So Didier traumatized certain kinds of music. Made the collective unconscious block it out, forget it. Somehow, Didier be a-makin' a pink, raw, inflamed layer in the collective mind."

"But you haven't told us *how* he did it though," Armand said.

"Aye. I said that I don't be knowin'."

But Armand would not let it go. "Yes, you do. Or at least, you have an idea."

Urbi seemed cornered.

"You have a suspicion. But because of what our Dad did for Bithiah, you feel uncomfortable speaking it aloud."

Still, she said nothing.

"Urbi. Please. We need to understand as much as we can. You're not helping Didier by not helping us."

Urbi sighed. "I be suspectin' that Didier — or rather, Concordia — hurt musicians. A lot of them. Ye would need a *lot* of trauma — so much that it be a-soakin' all the way down to the collective unconscious."

"But you don't know *for sure* that this is how he did it," Cyrano said.

"No," Urbi admitted. "It be just a guess."

"So old Didier did some bad things," Quinty said. "Not new information."

"Consider this, though," Urbi said. "All of ye are alive. All of ye are wealthy. Didier always had a strategy, a reason, behind everything he did. A plan. I suspect that these things are not accidents.

"And me personal opinion of Didier? The Musipocalypse be the mistake of a very talented, very arrogant, and very foolish young man. It be implemented by ghoulish foot soldiers, not by Didier directly. And Didier didn't truly be realizin' what he had unleashed until it be too late — and then he be spendin' the rest of his life trying to make up for it. So aye, *in the end*, he be a good man."

"What about Varinder Rahan?" Armand asked.

"Ah. Varinder," Urbi said with a smile. "That be a complicated topic."

"But bottom line. Good man or not?"

Urbi had to think about it. "Didier had great respect for him. Very great. Varinder be havin' a traumatic childhood — *very* traumatic — to overcome. Ye had to take that into consideration. Be he a good man? Not always. Not even much of the time. But Varinder be *enough* of a good man that Didier decided to be his close friend. That be sayin' a lot to me right there."

"Urbi — are you on social media?" Cyrano asked, mobile phone in hand. "We should connect and —"

"No," Urbi interrupted. "Neither are me daughters or grandbabes."

"Oh. Why? Is it bad, in your view?"

"For *us* it be. Twitter — or X it be called now, they say — be artificial telepathy, when ye think about it. Use it, and whatever real talent ye have atrophies. Ye get weak. In order for me Telemancy to keep workin', I have to remain psychically hot in every way I can. I be not in Concordia, I be havin' no Molian contracts — so I be needin' to work at keepin' sharp."

"Last topic, then we'll get out of your hair," Quinty said. Surprisingly, he turned to Armand. "*You* have some explaining to do."

That caught Armand off guard. "Hmm?"

"Your sudden ability to fight. Your ring, you know, the one that makes stone float," Quinty said accusingly. "In fact, your discovery that we changed the will … where are all these things coming from?"

"*Forged* the will," Armand corrected. "But I —"

"No," Urbi said forcefully. "Ye cannot tell them."

Armand looked silently at Urbi. *Why not?* A new thought entered Armand's mind unbidden: *Was Quinty untrustworthy?* Quinty had been surprisingly supportive of Armand since his 'coup'. He'd been almost nice about it — maybe *too* nice.

Was Quinty actually stabbing him the back? At least Marius was stabbing him in the face.

Quinty turned angrily to Urbi. "Why would you tell Armand a thing like that?"

Urbi crossed her arms. The wind chimes kicked in heavier now. "This will be hard for ye. But it should be, given what ye did to him." Urbi nodded at Armand. "All six of you! Or have ye forgotten? Shameful, stealing from yer youngest brother!"

"We've worked that —"

"No! Ye haven't! Armand has just been *nice* about it. Nicer than I would have been! But ye don't get to quiz him. He be leader now, not ye."

"Fine," Quinty said. "He's the leader. Armand. Can *you* please tell me what's going on?"

"I don't know," Armand said carefully. "Urbi. Is there some reason why I should specifically *not* tell Quinty and Cyrano the source of my new abilities?"

"Aye."

"Because it would put them in danger?"

"Emphatic aye, but it be not *only* be because of that."

"What then?"

Urbi sighed and gave Quinty and Cyrano a long look. "One of yer brothers be a traitor. I don't know which one. But I be certain of it."

"And how do you know this?" Cyrano demanded.

"The same way I know anything," Urbi said, rolling her

eyes. "I saw it on TV."

"You're positive?" Armand asked.

Urbi nodded. "100%."

"But it's not either of us," Quinty said, looking at Cyrano.

"So says ye, but *I* don't be knowin' that," Urbi countered. "It *might* be ye, or it might be Cyrano."

"Ah. So Armand can't tell us anything because it might be one of us."

"That be right," Urbi said. "His secret needs to stay hidden — for now. If ye all want to make it out of Conclave alive, that be."

# # #

THE TELEVISION behind Urbi was now showing a news report of the freak meteor that had almost hit the Great Pyramid. Mobile phone footage had caught the incident from many different angles. A scientist was explaining how the meteor was probably 'in a spin' as it flew, which is why it swerved away from the pyramid at the last minute, using the physics of a curveball as an analogy. The footage then cut to a man frantically explaining that an ancient force field had *clearly* activated to deflect the meteor, and this proved that the pyramid had been created by aliens.

"What else can you tell us about this thing that killed our Dad — these Challenges?" Cyrano asked Urbi.

"Well. Not a lot, as I said," Urbi sighed. "But here be what I do know." Urbi gathered her thoughts for a moment and then spoke: "First, they alway be doin' it at the end of every Conclave. It be the final event. And it be takin' place somewhere underground. There be a section of Hathor House on the western side — there be a tunnel and a very old staircase. During Bithiah's trainin', she be shown this staircase and told to stay away — only full Concordians be allowed. They don't tell ye exactly what be the punishment for going down there, but everyone on Staff be gettin' the immediate impression that ye probably wouldn't be heard from ever again.

"Bithiah also be sayin' that in the weeks leading up to Conclave, there always be construction going on. Workmen goin' up and down those stairs. Lots of noise and racket comin' from the basement. Like they be buildin' somethin'. And this happened every year she be workin'.'"

"They're not building something," Quinty said. "They're *refurbishing* something. And it's not a basement."

Urbi looked at him in surprise.

"Hathor House was constructed on top of an ancient tomb complex — one that's never been revealed to the public," Quinty said. "Dad told me about this one night. Even the Antiquities authorities here in Egypt don't know about it."

"Hey, yeah, I remember that night," Cyrano said. "I was there too. Dad was drunk and in a talkative mood about Concordia — which didn't happen very often."

"Really," Urbi said quietly. "There be a tomb down there? I didn't know that."

"Yes. The Concordians found it and removed all the treasures — all in secret — and then decided to build a mansion on top of it."

"Wow. How long ago was this?" Armand asked.

"Like in 1830 or so. Not long after Napoleon's first Egyptian Campaign and all the Egyptomania that followed in Europe."

"So they be discoverin' it when modern archeology in Egypt be just beginnin'," Urbi mused. "At the very start of it all."

"Right. You could find and hide the discovery of a new tomb pretty easily back then. Just buy the land, build a house on top of it, then boom! Deny that it ever existed, ya?

Dad said that it was supposed to be absolutely extraordinary — more impressive even than King Tut's tomb — and quite unlike anything else ever excavated."

"Quinty," Armand said. "These Challenges. You think they take place down in this tomb?"

Quinty nodded. "I do."

"That would make sense. Concordia likes Egypt," Cyrano mused. "They're big fans."

"Yes. And this be just like them," Urbi agreed with disgust, "to hold their Challenges in a tomb! How disrespectful. But they would want to be associatin' themselves symbolically with Egyptian civilization at it's height."

"Every empire does that, though," Armand said. "The Romans were always imitating the Greeks —"

"But this be different," Urbi said. "This be *participation mystique* — they be lookin' to forge a connection with — *listen*. It be not just any old Egypt that Concordia be likin'. Everything ye see in Museums — Cleopatra, all of that — that all be comin' from a period when Egypt be already deep in decay. From when she be but a shadow of her former self. This 'brokedown Egypt' be the only version of Egypt that mainstream archeology be knowin' about.

"But the real Egypt, the *true* Egypt, be much older and be havin' a much higher civilization. This be the Egypt built the Great Pyramid and the Sphinx. *That* be the Egypt Concordia admires — and be lookin' to imitate."

Armand's spine iced up. *Was this the Egypt that Sophia had come from?*

"When you say 'higher civilization' … what do you mean?"

"I mean higher technology," Urbi said. "They be understandin' things that we've lost. They be havin' branches of science that we don't even dream of yet. Oh, to be fair, we be havin' branches of science that *they* could have never imagined: rockets, phones, computers, movies. But they be knowin' more than us about lifting stone, that be obvious. And they probably knew more about the mind, and about consciousness itself. Who knows what devices they be a-makin' with that knowledge?"

"So the Challenges," Armand said. "Whatever they found down there in these tombs — the Challenges could involve this older Egyptian technology."

"Aye," Urbi said. "But not 'technology' like how ye be probably imaginin' it. No wires or engines or screens or anything like that at all."

"What, then?"

Urbi shrugged. "Probably more mind and vibration oriented. Probably devices more in line with Synchronicity Engines and Moliaometers. Hell, maybe this tomb be where they got the ideas to be buildin' those things from in the first place."

"Well Urbi … it's late. We need to get back our brothers — even the traitorous one," Quinty joked.

"Yes, yes, of course," said Urbi. "Oh — and don't be actin' surprised if ye see Tabi and Mariah at Conclave — they be workin' as hospitality Staff this year."

"What? You let them work at that place?" Cyrano asked incredulously. "After what happened to Bithiah?"

"It be different now," Urbi said. "Concordia cleaned it up. Not because they be carin' about Staff! But because the rumors be gettin' out of hand. Especially in the press. One thing Concordia being hatin' is a spotlight. And Concordia now be knowin' our family — at least, they be knowin' we don't talk — so we be a safe bet security-wise for them."

"But Bithiah went to the police."

"True. But after Didier be freein' Bithiah, they be pretty worried that she might also go to the *press* with her story —

after all, with her Molian terminated, what be stoppin' her? So they come to see me. I cut a deal with them. Our silence — in exchange for the right for me family to work Staff every year — safely. As I say, the money be good, it be helpin' more than you know. They agreed."

"How old are Tabi and Mariah?"

"Sixteen and fifteen. In Egypt, ye can work when you are fifteen."

"I see."

"Will ye watch out for them there? Best as ye can?"

"Of course."

"Oh and I'd offer ye a ride, but I don't be seein' so well — and me kids be in bed already," she said.

"No worries. We can catch an Uber."

CHAPTER TWENTY-THREE

Conclave

THE CONCORDIA CONCLAVE IN CAIRO, Egypt took place at a private estate called Hathor House. The lush property was owned by Concordia, and was never used for any other purpose.

The seven brothers were stopped at a guard gate and their credentials meticulously checked — no one besides Concordia and highly vetted (and blackmailed) staff were allowed in. This rule was very strictly enforced. *No, you cannot just have your Uber driver take you up to the main building and leave — you'll have to walk from here — or wait for the courtesy tram.*

Just inside the high walls of the property were lavish displays of water — ornate fountains and tall, thick stands of palm trees and other greenery.

The seven brothers had chosen to walk, as had many others. They could see four bobbing, tell-tale red-haired heads just in front of them.

"Veerspikes. Right?" Armand asked.

"Yes. Very good," Quinty replied.

Before long, they were standing before a massive,

sprawling, cream-colored villa with multiple domes and a portico out in front. A line had formed beneath this for badge check-in. Armand noted immediately that registration was not very efficient. Had this been an EPIC event, all of these people would have been inside having drinks already.

"Yes. You would have done it better," Quinty said with a wan smile, reading his thoughts.

# # #

THE FIRST NIGHT PARTY took place in spacious a ballroom that opened up onto a stone balcony and patio. It was a very international crowd, with a mix of races, cultures and dress from every corner of the globe. There was sovereign wealth here, clothed in traditional desert whites, alongside Sikhs and Africans and Latin Americans and Eastern Europeans. The only group that was not represented were the Chinese. "They have never been part of Concordia proper," Ames explained. "But they have their own State sponsored version of Concordia. Sometimes the two collaborate. Sometimes not."

"State sponsored?"

"Yeah. They do it backwards from us. Here, Concordia controls the State. But there, the State controls their version of Concordia."

When the seven brothers entered the room, all eyes sized them up. The whispering began almost immediately. And it wasn't long after they'd gotten drinks that they were approached.

"So you're Armand Martel," a woman said. Armand turned and found himself staring at Neon Phoenix, the pop starlet. She was dressed much like she did in her music videos — pink body suit, white platform boots, fur vest, sparkles on her eyelids. "What's it like, taking everything from your brothers?"

"Uh," Armand said, caught off-guard. "It's new. I'm getting used it. And we're working some things out still."

Phoenix laughed. "I'll be you are. I mean, you de-balled your whole posse here. And yet, they're still hanging off you like puppies." Samson and Marius visibly bristled.

"They're my *brothers*," Armand said carefully. "And like I said, we're still working things out."

"Well. Martels *working things out* historically hasn't been great for people like me."

"What's that supposed to mean?" Otto asked.

"Whoa, who broke your arm, big lover?" Phoenix countered coyly.

"She's means the Musipocalypse," Quinty said rolling his eyes.

"Oh," Armand said. "My brother Marius here thinks it isn't real. What do you say, Miss ... Phoenix?"

"Call me Phee," she said. And then she grew serious. "Yes. It's very, very real. I feel it everyday."

"Bullshit," Marius said suspiciously.

"There are certain songs. I hear them in my head. They're beautiful — the best music I've ever written. But I can't write them down, no matter how hard I try. When I pick up a guitar ... or just try to jot the chords down on paper ... poof! The song vanishes from my head. It's like something is wrong with me."

"Something *is* wrong with you," Marius snapped.

"Whatever Edward Scissorhands," Phoenix shot back. "Anyway. This same thing happens to all my musician friends — especially as they become more famous. It's like there's this class of music we're not allowed to write — and the guardrails are somehow installed *inside of our heads*. Whatever your Dad did ... it worked. And it sucks."

"I still don't buy it," Marius grumbled.

"What's left is pretty good though," Samson said. "LP Complete is a fantastic song."

"It's okay," Phoenix said wistfully. "It should have been better. Oh well. One day, if we all live long enough, we'll be uploaded — and then I'll be free of your Dad's thing and finally get to do these songs."

"Uploaded? What do you mean?" Armand asked.

Phoenix burst out laughing as she swigged hard liquor from a wine glass. "To the Cloud, silly! To be with the AI's. They'll be our gods. And we'll be their children — after we've been their parents! Isn't that funny? And we'll all live forever together."

Armand wondered what Sophia would have to say about this. But he didn't reply.

"What?" Phoenix said drunkenly. "You don't believe in digital immortality? Everybody else here does."

"I don't," said a new voice. A young man in his thirties, with a mop of brown hair and a conservative suit, looking almost like a Young Republican, held out his hand to Armand. "Milton Weeks," he said. "I'm all about physical immortality, in the here and now, with the body. And we're working on ways to do it."

Armand shook it unenthusiastically. "Yes. I've heard of you. The Cortexia troll, right?"

"Oh! That's so uncool. Can't believe you just said that."

"Why not? It's accurate. You bought the dementia drug rights and then jacked the price of Cortexia through the roof."

"Well, by that logic I could call you a brother-fucker. That's accurate also, right?"

Armand said nothing.

"Look. I *legally* bought the patents, and then I legally raised the price of Cortexia! It's pure capitalism!"

"But the dementia patients *need* that medication. They

don't have a choice. It's not capitalism if the customer can't refuse the product," Ames said. "That's more like a hostage negotiation. And you did this to grandmas — to boot."

Milton Weeks shrugged. "Look. Nobody here is clean, right? We're in Concordia, for fuck's sake. We're the alphas! Of the earth! And being an alpha is always going to be a little gray." Then, he turned to Neon Phoenix. "Hello, Phee. Milton Weeks."

"I said Armand could call me Phee, not you, squeezeball."

Weeks turned to Armand. "Oooh. Feisty," he said with a shiver. "Say. Topic whiplash, but ... we're all super wondering. You saw Varinder Rahan die, right? I mean ... you were actually *there*, yes?"

"I was," Armand said.

"How, exactly, did it happen?"

"Don't answer that!" Ames, Cyrano and Quilty belted out at once.

"Whoa! What are you three, his lawyers?" Weeks laughed uproariously. "Okay, okay, relax! Well, we all heard he was shot — but how did you survive?"

"Yes, I'd like to know that also," Celaeno Rahan, Varinder's mousy and shy wife, was now standing next to Neon Phoenix. She certainly didn't seem mousy and shy now.

"Mrs. Rahan," Armand said formally. "I'm very sorry about your husband."

"*Are* you now," she said icily. "I wonder about that. The killer could have shot you too — but he didn't. Now *why is that*, Armand Martel?"

He voice shook as she spoke.

"I don't know," Armand said. "But this same man — Eamon, right? That's what Varinder called him. Red curly hair? This same man actually tried to kill *me* as well. This was about a week earlier."

"Oh? And then Eamon sees you again and just lets you go?"

"I know. It's strange. I don't know what to make of that." *But I'm certainly not going to tell you about the third encounter with Eamon at the Soho Grand.*

"Ah. Well," Celaeno waved her hand drunkenly in the air. "I guess Eamon was frightened of you." She looked at Armand disdainfully.

"You know, I *saw* Eamon at Sea Castle, Mrs. Rahan. Remember? Right when I was leaving? And I saw you peek out from the curtains, so I know you saw him also."

She ignored him. "Are you telling me that you — little old you! — that you survived an assasination attempt from a *professional killer*? You versus Eamon, and you lived? How is that even possible?"

As Celaeno spoke and grew more excited, her body jerked around in a strange, freaky way. Her mannerisms suggested barely-contained violence, a deep unbalance of some sort. Everyone stared at her uncomfortably.

"I fought him off."

"Oh, you fought him off?" Celaeno let out a sick laugh drenched with self-torture. *"Fought. Him. Off.* Of course you did." Then, her eyes narrowed: "Yes, I remember your little visit to Sea Castle. I remember you and Varinder argued about your takeover of GigaMaestro."

Armand bristled at what she was suggesting. Quinty shot him a look that said: *Keep calm.* But then, something else occurred to him.

"Mrs. Rahan, are you in possession of a Galahad Michael Sturdevant Synchronicity Engine?"

"What?" There it was, that bodily jerking again. This time, it yanked her head around violently.

"The one that belonged to Varinder?"

That caught her off guard. "Why — yes, but what has that

got to do with —"

"My brothers and I," Armand said, not able to keep the roar of fury out of his voice as it rose in volume, *"barely survived a Synchronicity Engine attack last night!* Did you know that? Here! In Cairo! Look! Do you see Otto's broken arm? Samson's black eye? That's why he's wearing a patch. And Marius had internal bleeding! And Cy, Quinty and I very nearly completely died — *less than twenty-four hours ago!"*

"What does that have to do with me?" Celaeno said.

But Armand continued: "And we were assured — *assured!* — Of perfect safety by Concordia. *This* was holy ground, they said! No vendettas, no deaths, with Molian contracts in place to keep it all real."

"I hope you're not insinuating that I ..." Celaeno said, deeply offended.

"Mrs. Rahan," Armand shouted, as Quinty cringed. *"Did you try to kill my brothers and I last night?"*

"How *dare* you!" she shrieked.

All eyes in the room turned.

"There aren't many of those Machines in existence are there? Ten total, I'm told? Seven of which are lost or broken? I'll bet whoever has the other two doesn't have a motive to want me dead. But *you* do. So was it you?"

"I am in mourning!" Celaeno screeched. "So much adversity! I don't have to stand here and listen to this! You were *there*! At the Atman compound! And somehow you lived while my Varinder died? It makes no sense! No, YOU are the one who —"

Suddenly, Hathor House security surrounded the group. Men in suits with earplugs calmly asked them to step away from one another. And with them was a man who instantly struck Armand as someone with gravitas.

His brothers all recognized this man. They immediately

became deferential.

"Mr. Ghent," Quinty said. The brothers all very quickly acknowledged him as well. "Mr. Ghent," they all said, and bowed their heads slightly. This was shocking to Armand. He had never seen them act like this before. Not *ever*.

Ghent ... Ghent ... where had he heard that name before?

"Please," Ghent said, "No more of this talk, hmm?"

This 'Mr. Ghent' was very tall and very thin. His gaunt, tanned face was wreathed in a curly silver mane of well-styled hair. He was vaguely androgynous, but also ambi-national: he had an accent, but you couldn't quite pin down what it was, or where he was from. He seemed to be from everywhere. His piercing, powder-light blue eyes — which matched his blue suit perfectly — were the one specific thing about him. They were intense and focused.

Even Celaeno immediately composed herself. *Everyone is terrified of this guy,* Armand noticed. "Mr. Ghent," she said, head bowed as well. "Of course not. It ends now."

With that, Celaeno turned and left, mustering as much dignity as she was able.

"Hmm," Ghent said, casting his gaze over the brothers, and then at Neon Phoenix and Milton Weeks, as though noting everyone who had heard anything untoward. Then, he looked pointedly at the Martel brothers. "Oh, and one last thing. We should like for you to stay here, at Hathor House, for the duration at Conclave. It is customary for all attendees."

Quinty looked around nervously. "Oh. We didn't know that. We can go back to our hotel and —"

Ghent waved that away. "It's been arranged. Your belongings are being transferred from the Ritz-Carlton now — they will be in your suites here at Hathor within the hour." And then he strolled away.

"Shit," Weeks said to Armand. "Not here for five minutes,

and already you've got Ghent up your ass."

"Who was that?" Armand asked.

Weeks exploded with laughter. "Who was —? Holy fuckballs! *You don't know?*" He slapped Armand on the shoulder and shook his head. "You've got a long week ahead of you, brother."

# # #

THE SEVEN BROTHERS were taken to their connecting rooms by, of all people, Tabi and Mariah. When the door was closed, they both grinned from ear to ear. "We volunteered!" Tabi explained, answering the unspoken question. "We heard that there were seven new rooms that needed preparing, but nobody wanted to do it because it was extra work. But we knew it was all of you. So we said yes!"

"Thank you," said Armand with a smile.

Mariah handed them all little satin bags. "Your toiletries and extra hand towels," she explained.

"So you'll be cleaning our rooms now, only you two," Quinty asked. "Nobody else?"

"Yes," Mariah said.

"Well, that is a spot of luck," Ames commented.

"Listen. Keep your ears open, both of you. Let us know if you hear anything … interesting."

"We will," Tabi replied.

As they left, Armand's phone buzzed with a text message:

Sophia: Hey you! How are things in the land of Eopeii?
Armand: Hey! Well there was an incident last night. We're all fine. But it was basically an attack.
Sophia: Oh. Did someone try to kill you, like Eamon?

```
Armand: Yes. But not a person. This was different
— long explanation. And I don't think that kind
of attack can happen again.
Sophia: You knew this trip might be dangerous.
Armand: I did. We'll just have to keep our eyes
open. How is Kalinda?
Sophia: Really great. She's amazing. Thank you
for her!
Armand: What have you two been doing?
Sophia: Mostly talking about Hindu myths. They
make a lot more sense once you can Vreen, so
we've been discussing all of that.
```

"Oh, is that Sophia again?" Quinty asked looking over his shoulder with a smile.

Armand snatched the phone out of sight. Hearing her name come out of Quinty's mouth was almost panic-inducing: his two worlds were colliding unexpectedly.

"Is that a *real girl* texting him?" Ames said.

"It *looks* like a real girl," Quinty said. "But he won't let me see more, so I can't say for sure."

"Is that a real girl, Armand?"

"Yes, it's a real girl," Armand said — knowing full well that it was not — but still, oddly, feeling very much like it was.

CHAPTER TWENTY-FOUR

Wiggin the Wicked

CONCORDIA CONCLAVE AT HATHOR HOUSE officially kicked off on Monday morning. The seven brothers, conference badges hanging from their necks, all dressed in suits, except for Armand, who dressed casually in a hoodie, went down for breakfast.

Celaeno Rahan was eating with Neon Phoenix, and, oddly, laughing with her. Milton Weeks was pitching something to four Veerspike bankers, who were clearly annoyed at having their breakfast disturbed in this manner.

There were new notices posted at all the tables on the walls and doors in many places which read:

> *Concordia Conclave is a Private Conference. No video or audio recording is allowed. This rule is VERY strictly enforced. Likewise, reporting on the content of any conference track is also strictly prohibited. All attendees have signed NDA's with severe penalties for breach. This is for the protection of all our esteemed attendees and speakers. Thank you for your cooperation.*

The seven brothers ate with a group from Brazil, who had attended several Conclaves before and explained what was ahead.

There were five days of conference tracks, and then on the fifth day, the evening was largely taken up with The Big Meeting, where Gideon Ghent, leader of their Clave, would preside, settling squabbles and meting out awards and punishments for the last year's business.

This Meeting was a big deal, and the focal point of why they all were there. Fortunes could be made, positions could be gained, and enemies thoroughly and Concordia-legally vanquished.

This was where everything was decided.

"As we get closer to The Meeting, you'll see tensions and rivalries start to flare up," one of the Brazilians said. "We're all here to get ahead, and that's where it happens — or doesn't."

Not us, Armand thought. We're here to get *out*.

"I've got our first track picked out," Ames said. "*Cohesion In A Fragmented World: The Importance of Molian Contracts*."

"The more we can learn about that subject, the better," Armand agreed.

"Who's the speaker?" Marius asked.

"Let me see … an Austrian. Tabias Kronecker. Economic theory guy, works with the IMF, BIS — that crowd."

"And he's on a stage, speaking openly about Molian contracts?" Samson said.

"That's why these," Quinty said, holding up the Private Conference notice. "'Strictly enforced' probably means death."

"What? That wasn't in the NDA," Ames said.

"Sure it was," Quinty said. "I read it carefully. It says Conference Producers are authorized to take extreme measures should we breach."

"That's not death," Ames said.

"It pretty much *is* death," Quinty said.

"Okay, it's ten minutes to Kronecker," Samson said. "Let's get in there and get good seats."

"But sort of near the back though," Marius said. "So I can get up and pee if I have to. If there's death penalties for stuff here, I don't want Tabias here getting mad at me."

# # #

"YOUR HIGHNESSES, excellencies, distinguished heads of state, dear partners and friends," Tabias Kronecker began, "welcome to our annual meeting. This is the One Hundred and Fifty-Eighth Edition.

"It is fitting that we meet now, when the world is undergoing such deep transformation. We face unprecedented challenges to our efforts on multiple fronts. There are many who, through negative and critical confrontation, would increase fragmentation in our world

"But before we address those issues, I would like to first speak to our newer members — those who are, perhaps, attending their first Conclave event.

"As you know, we are an organization dedicated to deep cohesion. Our strength comes from our disciplined, strict ranks. We are a machine, one where each part knows its place.

"We are also, all of us, deeply self-interested. Some may even say we are narcissistic. And what is wrong with that? We are not ashamed of it. In this world, the strong survive. We, in this room, are the strongest of the strong. As such, we share common traits. We do not rely on the love of others. We don't look for a hand to hold.

"Make no mistake: we are not friends. I am not your friend. You are not mine. Friends are for the weak. But we are *allies*. Yet, as self-interested allies, we need something to prevent us all from drifting in different directions, from creating internal fragmentation. This would be counter-productive.

"Fortunately for us, the universe itself has provided a mechanism for preventing such fragmentation: karma. We employ karma as currency within our ranks, we use it to incentivize and enforce our machine's will."

The speaker looked out across the audience. There was an uncomfortable rustling, as though he had just said something ridiculous. There were even a few chuckles. "Oh, but you don't believe in karma? I see. You think it's a silly idea, or that it's not real. Well. That's why you're in this room today. I'm here to disabuse you of that rather foolish notion — so that the Organization does not have to waste time dealing with the fallout of your moronic unbelief.

"Many of you are with us at Conclave for the very first time specifically because you succeeded at establishing a Molian contract with a new recruit. The reward of Conclave Invite is usually given for such a reason. And yet, even now, many of you think it's just some foolish old *tradition*, that it's just something everyone does to get ahead. You mouth the platitudes, you bow to the right gods, but you don't really *believe*.

"Well. Many before *you* have laughed at the idea of karma, only to have the universe rebound on them in a surprisingly swift and strong fashion. Today, I will tell you of such a person — a Concordian cautionary tale, if you will. I speak today of Wiggin the Wicked."

The hall went dark. A slideshow of old black and white pictures accompanied the narrative that came next:

"Wiggin Heldegarde was born in 1864 to a Concordian family in Austria. He grew into a man deeply devoted to his own pleasures. His sexual appetites were enormous, and he sated them several times a day with multiple women. He drank enormous quantities of hard liquor — yet, he had one of those constitutions that supplied him with a seemingly unending vigor, and he would remain standing, even deeply inebriated, long into the night.

"By all accounts, he barely slept. No more than an hour or two per night. Despite this, his enemies managed to poison him on several occasions, but with seemingly no effect. And he was stabbed repeatedly — but again, he did not die and healed quickly. He was an unusually gifted — and unusually lucky — man.

"As such, Wiggin rose quickly within the Concordian ranks. He had a voracious appetite for power, with more and more never being enough. Now, somewhere around 1910, he became one of the largest holders of Concordian Molian contracts on earth. But he was not content. All of Concordia was not enough. So he did something unheard of before and since: he extended Molian lending into the peasants of his homeland and indeed with people — especially the poor — all over the world. In those days, the contracts were all done with paper. As such, binders containing those signed papers filled literal rooms within his house.

"Now, because of this, a strange thing started happening to Wiggin — something everyone in this room will experience directly sooner or later: *The more you work with karmic instruments, like Molian tokens or contracts, the stronger the effects of karma will become on you — for good or ill.* By simply applying your attention to these instruments, the more greatly you will attune yourself to karma itself. And thus, the karmic mirror of the universe will begin to reply to you ever faster, and in increasing measures of intensity. That which might have previously taken years or lifetimes to rebound upon you ... will now take mere weeks or days — or even hours.

"Wiggin the Wicked, as you might have surmised, was not a careful man. In his Molian contracts, he did not tell the peasants he dealt with what they were signing up for. This meant he was charging up the karmic battery with a massive backlash of epic proportions.

"You may have noticed that, today, whenever Concordia has a plan for the world, we will announce it in some fashion. Perhaps we will 'predict' it — Oh, *there will be a war! There will be a cyber attack!* Or, we'll have a drill wherein the very event we mean to foist upon the world is the subject of a rehearsal — for instance, we will have a bomb drill in a specific building right before an actual bomb is planted there. Or we will have a 'fictional' movie made which mirrors our future plans almost exactly.

"In each case, we will have pushed details of our future actions into the collective consciousness. You will have been warned. Even if only subconsciously. If no one pushes back, then you all will have, in some sense, agreed to it.

"And whenever there is agreement, no karmic debt is possible. Now, mind you, none of the methods I just mentioned obtain *perfect* agreement, but they do garner *some* agreement, and thus partially deflect the karmic blowback.

"You may also see us telling you our plans for the world in the lyrics of rock stars or in music videos or music award ceremonies. Or hidden in the logos of major corporations. Or even on the backs of cereal boxes! We are methodical. We are deliberate. We are thorough. Wiggin was not — and we all paid a steep price.

"Now, it so happened that Wiggin was a friend of the Archduke Franz Ferdinand of Austria. The German historian Michael Freund describes the Archduke as 'a man of uninspired energy, dark in appearance and emotion, who radiated an aura of strangeness and cast a shadow of violence and recklessness'. You can see why they got along.

"Ferdinand had desperately wanted to marry the Countess Sophie Chotek — but her bloodline was not of the great dynasties of Europe, so it was forbidden by his Uncle, the current Austria-Hungarian Emperor Franz Joseph. The Archduke, distraught, turned to Wiggin, and together, they made a pact: Wiggin would fix the situation with the Countess if Concordia would be allowed to act through Ferdinand when he became Emperor. The Archduke readily agreed to this arrangement, thus making himself a Concordian puppet.

"Wiggin then turned around and leveraged the fact that the current Emperor, Franz Joseph, had a secret penchant for little boys. Wiggin threatened to make this public unless he allowed Ferdinand to marry his beloved Sophie — which, of course, he did.

"Concordia was overjoyed. We believed Wiggin to be a genius for arranging all of this. We had our puppet Emperor — and he would be the key to integrating all the nations of Europe into a single superstate.

"But what happened? *Disaster.* The monstrous karmic debt incurred by Wiggin finally recoiled upon him — and then us.

"First, the Archduke visits Bosnia-Herzegovina with Sophie. Seven members of an extremist group called The Black Hand attack his motorcade — but this assassination attempt fails with the motorcade speeding away from an exploding bomb. The Black Hand scatters as police chase them down: some take cyanide, others hide.

"The Archduke doesn't give the attempt a second thought. Because of his deal with Wiggin and Concordia, he now believes that he is untouchable. So he gives a short speech, and then gets back in his car.

"This time, however, his motorcade gets lost. The driver makes a wrong turn. He stops to consult a map — right in front of one of the original would-be assassins, a 19 yr old named Gavrilo Princip. He is having a sandwich. Gavrilo looks up — and can hardly believe his luck. There's the Archduke — a sitting duck — right in front of him! He jumps up and shoots Ferdinand, killing him.

"The assassination of the Archduke, as anyone who reads history knows, sets off a chain reaction of events which leads directly to World War I. Now. What are the odds that a driver taking a wrong turn would plunge the earth into its first World War? Usually, very very low. But when karma is at work, and synchronicity is crackling with gigavolts of coincidence ... things like this become almost a certainty.

"Right after this, Wiggin himself is suddenly subject to a streak of extremely bad luck. First, he is diagnosed with leprosy. Then, his wife and children drown when their ship sinks during a sudden freak storm. All of Wiggin's wealth is then lost in a market crash, and his jewels and gold are stolen by home intruders. The thieves beat him nearly to death. The very next week, there is an earthquake and his mansion catches fire. But finally, perhaps mercifully, Wiggin is killed when a meteor tears through both him and his bedroom the very next day.

"World War I breaks out, destroying all of Concordia's plans for an entire decade.

"Why? Why did all of this happen? Because Wiggin the Wicked did not do strict Molian accounting. His handling of so many contracts heated his hands, made them highly-charged karmic magnets. He was not careful. But we, Concordia, *we* were also not careful. We allowed this."

The speaker paused and looked around the room. Then:

"The universe reflects our interior world back to us. Because of this, some say that its base nature is that of a learning machine. They think that we are here to magnetize either towards frivolous and dishonest selflessness or powerful self-interest.

"The learning machine periodically lets us know how we are doing. How does it do this? It arranges coincidences, things for us to notice and experience. Thus, synchronicity and karma are merely two manifestations of the same phenomenon.

"Because of this, a very strict accounting and measurement of karmic debts and surpluses is one of the key instruments behind Concordian governance. It's why the Molian cryptocurrency was introduced: a blockchain insures none of us can cheat the others. And it shows with absolute certainty the hierarchy of ownership and power of all her members. There can be no mistaking who is at the top, and who is further down the line.

"It also why we tread carefully whenever incurring new karmic debt.

"It is why we take such care in telling our victims what we will do to them — and why we go to such lengths to secure agreement from them, to whatever degree we can.

"When we do not, as you have now seen, the results can be catastrophic."

CHAPTER TWENTY-FIVE

The Dahabiya

As Monday wore on, the brothers debated over what afternoon conference tracks to attend. Most of the remaining panels were on more mundane subjects. They were less Concordia-specific, less about topics like Molian contracts. Instead, they tended now to be more about emerging technologies and trends that might be covered at a mainstream technology public policy conference — but how Concordian experts viewed these things.

Armand grabbed the Conclave 158th Edition program guide from Samson. It read:

Panel: "Practical Immortality: The Gift"
This panel will explore the implications of having a class of people who are, for all practical purposes, immortal. We are nearing a time when only severe injury will bring death to those who have The Gift. Should the public be allowed to know about The Gift? Who decides who will get The Gift? And if The Gift is kept secret, how will we explain public figures who seem to never age? Public

policy, laws, medical needs and rights and almost every aspect of human experience will have to be re-thought in the Age of The Gift.

Panel: "Brain Implants: Why They Are Ethical"

Experts explore why in the future, most of us will have a neural lace implanted in our brains. It may seem outlandish today, but requiring such a thing of all citizens will soon be commonplace. Why? Because by monitoring their brainwaves, we can stop criminals before a crime is committed. We can increase productivity at work by ensuring employee attention is always focused on the task at hand. And we can stop disinformation from spreading by knowing in advance when a person believes things that aren't mainstream truth. In short: we will all live in a safer society when everyone has a brain implant.

Panel: "Central Bank Digital Currencies: The Promise"

The primary purpose of CBDCs is to provide a safe, efficient, and accessible means of payment using a token with government backed value. But because CBDC's are 'programmable money' we can also use them to advance policy agendas. For example, we can stimulate economies by requiring that saved dollars be spent by a certain deadline or the tokens will be burned; or we can tie the ability to transact to carbon or vaccine compliance; and finally, with a centralized panopticon of all spending, we can more easily catch illicit transactions and activity, mitigating terrorism both home grown and abroad. The promise of CBDC's is that we can create a streamlined, safer and more progressive world for everyone.

"Here, I'll do Immortality," Armand said, recalling Sophia telling him about Count Saint-Germain and the Hidden

Masters of the Himalayas. "And one of you take CBDC's."

"Ya, I'll do that one," Quinty said. "I'm the DeFi guy, after all."

"And I'm the bio-hacker guy," Marius said. "So I'll do neural lace."

"You totally *would* get that installed, Marius. Wouldn't you?" Cyrano said.

"I would. I don't see anything wrong with it," Marius said. "Imagine if part of your brain was a computer. You would never forget anything. You could do crazy math in your head. Hell, maybe you could read an entire book in an eyeblink."

"We'll need it," Quinty said. "Or the AI's will run circles around us. Especially when they become conscious."

You have no idea how close that is, thought Armand. *Eight weeks. Just eight weeks away — if Sophia's estimates and design are both correct.*

"Figures Marius wants a brain chip," Samson snorted. "He doesn't know what's wrong with himself so he thinks a chip might fix it."

"Hahah," Otto laughed. "That makes sense. I always thought that was also why Marius was a Psych Major — same thing, just him trying to figure out why he's fucked up."

"Hey, Martels," Neon Phoenix called out. "Any of you going to Brain Implants?"

"I am," Marius said hopefully. Phoenix crinkled her nose. *Wrong Martel.*

"Okay! Well, I'll see you all in there!" Neon Phoenix said, hustling away quickly now.

Marius watched her receding backside with annoyance.

"Hey! What about your Thai wife?" Ames said. Marius grumbled something inaudible.

# # #

THAT EVENING, a formal dinner was held in a different building on the compound grounds. This structure was in back of the main Hathor House mansion, and was airplane hangar-like in terms of size. This space was clearly modern and built later than the initial mansion complex.

After following a walkway trail of lit candles (inside colored paper bags) punctuated by several large "In Memoriam" portraits of Varinder Rahan (each adorned with flower wreaths), the Martels found themselves in the dinner line.

As they arrived near the food serving area, Quinty, Ames and Samson began to look queasy. "What is it?" Armand asked. But as he got nearer, he saw himself.

The food being served — all of it — was made to look like human body parts.

There were human hands on plates (which were really ground chicken shaped to look so). There was a human torso made of cake with flesh-colored frosting — with a Staff person hired to stick their head out of the top to make it look like it was 'them' that was being eaten. And there were fingers (really hotdogs) on sticks and curling sushi rolls arranged to look like intestines.

Ghent strolled by with a plate piled high, and chuckled at the brothers' discomfort. "What? This is High Art Cuisine. The 'Flesh Chef' is world-renowned and highly coveted. Don't tell me it's put you off your appetite."

"No. Not at all," Marius answered truthfully. "I'm starved!"

This surprised Ghent — but he departed, apparently satisfied that the Martels were all sufficiently non-plussed for Concordian ethics. The other brothers just stared at each other in semi-horror. But in the end, they all ate — while doing their best not to actually *look* at their plates.

As the night wore on, the hanger slowly turned into a nightclub. Icy synths blasted into a gush of fog and sweeping, colored laser lights. The brothers huddled at their table while most of the other Conclave attendees drank heavily and danced. Only Marius seemed to enjoy the festivities.

The next day, Tuesday, was pretty much a repeat of Monday — albeit with less attendees at the morning sessions. But by noon, the hungover Conclavians had at last emerged from their darkened rooms to get lunch before it was all gone — and because they feared reprisal from Ghent if their absence was noticed.

But by Wednesday, Armand and his brothers had an unexpected turn of luck that provided a treasure trove of new information.

# # #

ON THE AFTERNOON of the third day, Wednesday, Ames, Quinty and Armand had slipped back to their rooms to have a private discussion when Tabi burst in suddenly.

"Oh! I'm sorry," he said, panting. "I don't have much time so — "

"Don't worry about it," Armand said. "What's wrong?"

"I heard something interesting, like what you asked me to listen for. Celaeno Rahan is meeting Ghent. Tonight. Alone. While everyone else is at the party."

Ames and Quinty exchanged glances.

"Really," Ames said. "What about?"

"I don't know."

"We *have* to hear this," Armand snapped. "Whatever it is."

"Agreed," Ames and Quinty said as one.

"Where is the meeting?"

"Ghent owns a boat. We know the one."

"I have to be on it. Before they get there," Armand said.

"No," Quinty replied. "That's too dangerous. Ghent's security — they'll probably search the entire thing right before Ghent gets on. They'll find you."

Armand opened his mouth and then closed it. His brother was correct. But then, he had another idea. "Tabi. Your family fishes for food in the Nile, right? How much fishing line do you think you have on hand right now?"

Tabi shrugged. "A lot. We're always breaking it. We buy in bulk. It comes on these big spools."

Armand snapped and pointed at him. "That's what I was hoping you'd say. Can we use some of it? And ... I'm sorry to ask, but I think this is the best idea ... can I borrow Ifan and Riya?"

# # #

THE NILE VESSEL that Ghent had chosen for his meeting with Celaeno Rahan was a boutique sailboat known as a *dahabiya*. This was a wooden, shallow, barge-like luxury craft with four private cabins and several spacious common areas.

A dahabiya had no motor. Instead, there were two large, midnight-black sails, one at the bow and the one at the stern. This gave the craft a very distinct and strange look. It was an ancient style of boat that had been around in one version or another since the time of the Pharaohs.

Riya and Ifan — eight and ten years old respectively — walked along a nearby pier, with a spindle of fishing line secretly unspooling from beneath a *gallibaya* worn by Ifan. They approached Armand, Quinty and Tabi, beaming. "We did it! Secret mission accomplished!" Riya said, barely able to contain herself.

"Thank you," Armand said. "Riya. Ifan. Seriously. This

was *very* important, and there was no way grown-ups could have done it."

"You two were sure to play and make noise?" Quinty said. "Make sure they saw that?"

They both nodded vigorously "Yes!"

"Good!" And once Ifan and Riya had been discounted as dock urchins, Ghent's boat security had gone back to smoking. Meanwhile, Ifan found a loop of iron near the rear of the boat and had tied the fishing line to it.

"You used the knots I showed you, yes?" Tabi said. "And you tied it tight — really, really tight?"

"Yes!" Ifan said, somewhat offended that he was being questioned. He clearly took this very seriously.

"Let me have the spool," Quinty said. Ifan gave it to him. "Wow. You cannot even see this stuff at all, even in the daylight." The fishing line extended from his hand up into the sky, arcing between several empty piers to the back of the *dahabiya* — but to the naked eye, it was almost completely invisible, even up close.

"Okay, let's get the other end around me," Armand said. "Pull it through my belt loops." Armand and Quinty started tying the line.

"Can we watch?" Riya said. "I mean, when Uncle Quinty launches you."

"Human kite!" Ifan said with a laugh, making a swishing sound. *"Kite! Kite!"*

"No. I'm sorry," Armand replied. "Too dangerous. Besides, we'll have to wait a few hours anyway, until well after dark. Go home. But we'll let you know how it goes, I promise."

Riya, Ifan and Tabi were disappointed, but nodded and did as they were told.

"You sure about this?" Quinty said. "Have you even used that ring on organic matter yet?"

"No, but ... it works the same on anything."

"How do you know?"

"Because people in space are okay. There's literally no difference between what this ring does and what happens to astronauts — gravity is removed in both cases."

Quinty puffed out a breath. "Okay."

"But we can do a few practice runs if that makes you feel better. Here. Hold my leash."

Armand flipped the ring around so that it was facing his chest. When he pushed the button, he felt his whole body jiggle and thrum, like he was standing next to giant woofer in a nightclub. He sprayed the anti-gravity vibration all over his body like it was sunscreen.

Now that even his blood was weightless, he felt it pooling in his head, making his cheeks warmer. The human circulatory system wasn't meant to operate in zero gravity. It wasn't dangerous, just different — but it did make him queasy.

Armand pushed off the ground and fell back down again. To his surprise, he wasn't floating.

"You *hand*," Quinty said. "Your hand still has weight."

"Oh. Right." Armand switched the ring to his left hand and zapped the right.

When he *still* didn't float, Armand said: "Ah. And the ring." He considered for a moment, and then cupped his hand over the ring while pushing the button, hoping enough of the vibration would reflect back and zap the ring itself.

This time, when he pushed off, he was fully free of gravity.

Nodding grimly to Quinty, Armand restored his weight to normal and settled in to wait for nightfall.

# # #

THERE WAS a hazy darkness over the Nile that night, one with a woolly quality, almost like a fog, that shielded Armand from view as he floated behind the boat. No one would see him flying like a human kite. But the lack of a motor would make his approach more difficult — every tiny noise on the dark, flat waters was amplified tenfold.

Carefully now, he pulled on the invisible fishing line connecting him to the boat and drew himself down from the sky, towards the stern. He thought perhaps to land on the back deck, but Ghent's guard wandered there now and again. So instead, he clung to the boat's side, weightless, and drew himself alongside the hull to the cabin where Ghent and Celaeno were talking. The windows were open: he could hear and see everything.

Celaeno and Ghent exchanged small talk for several minutes — and then got down to business.

"Thank you for agreeing to meet on my boat. I thought it best that we speak in private, away from Conclave," Ghent said. "Too many distractions and interruptions. And ears."

"Oh. Yeah. Totally agree," Celaeno said, over-acting with annoyance.

"Now. As you know, Varinder's betrayal came as a great shock to all of us," Ghent began. "The Great Hall did not see it coming. *I* did not see it coming. And Varinder was in my Clave, so he was ultimately my responsibility. And to think, his betrayal involved a plot authored by the great Didier Martel himself! We are of course *very* grateful to you for bringing it to our attention. We might have never found out about it otherwise."

That confirms it, Armand thought. *Concordia knows about The Atman Project. And it was Celaeno who told them.*

Celaeno bowed her head. "Well. Varinder crossed a line."

"Now, in the four months since Varinder's death, the Great Hall's unease has not diminished. And you have something new to share with us, I am told, yes? I am eager to hear it. I've been instructed to learn all I can from you, every scrap of information you can recall."

"Of course — and yes, there is something new that you need to see."

"Very well. Let's start with —"

"But what about that little shit, that Martel kid? The one who dared to accuse me of a Synchronicity Engine attack in front of everyone?"

Ghent was confused for a moment. And then he said: "*Armand* Martel? What about him?" He studied Celaeno. *Curious, it was like she shifted personalities just now.* Her eyes looked different, wilder. Even her voice sounded different, feral.

"Well. His Dad was involved with the big plot, like you say. So what about the son? What does he know?"

"Nothing."

"Nothing? How do you know? Did you check him out?"

"Yes, of course. We found nothing. He's quiet. Produces that EPIC event, with his brothers. Used to hide out in the Antiquities division. But now he struggles to run GigaMaestro day-to-day. That's all he does."

They were *following me. I wasn't imagining it.*

"Huh. But did you know that Armand met with Varinder just a couple of nights before he died?" Celaeno's eyes were watery wounds as she spoke these words.

"So?"

"So maybe it's related, that's all. To the Big Ole' Plot."

Ghent's eyes narrowed: "*Did* you attack Armand with Varinder's Synchronicity Engine? No — wait — don't tell me. Anything you admit here, I'll have to act on. Concordians cannot harm Concordians at Conclave."

Celaeno licked her lips. "But Armand Martel is *not* Concordian."

Ghent opened his mouth — and then closed it. She had him. "That's true."

"So why did you allow him here, anyway?"

"He's now head of the Martel family. And as you already know, we will decide at the Big Meeting what is to be done with the Martel assets. And he's Didier's son. So, yes, we've made an exception. Don't worry. We have something special planned for him. So if that *was* you with the Engine, please stop."

Something special planned for me? Like what? Something deadly? But no, Ghent was stopping further Synchronicity Engine attacks. He seemed to want Armand alive. What then? *A deal?*

Celaeno just smiled coyly and downed her drink. "More, please."

Ghent obliged. "Celaeno. I know you're excited by your new-found … freedom. But you don't have dispensation to kill. Anything other than self-defense raises karmic issues. For all of us. You need permission first."

She glared at him, eyes like wet fangs. "I know that. But do you?"

That stopped Ghent short. "Celaeno. Are you angry that we killed Varinder?"

Armand hung on to the side of the boat to keep from reeling. He now had positive confirmation. Concordia had ordered the hit on Varinder.

Well, of course they did.

Celaeno shrank back. She hadn't realized how transparent she'd just been. "I don't know."

"Remember, *you* came to *us*. What did you *expect* us do?"

"I don't know!" Ah. *There* she was, the real her. Raw rage, blood in the voice. "I thought maybe you'd lock him up or something! Isn't there a Concordian jail? Like, under the ocean or something? I heard there was, once."

"No. You don't take chances with someone like Varinder. Not once we saw that the Atman camps were real. And this plan had been devised by Didier Martel himself, so we had to take swift action." Then Ghent raised an eyebrow, "But you're not *really* mad about this. Are you? You told me that Varinder abused you. That he kept you locked away."

"He did," Celaeno admitted, eyes of ice now. *Disquieting, how she shifts moods like that — all at the drop of a hat,* Ghent thought. *She's not stable.* Ah, well. *Locked up for decades like that, what did he expect? But now that she was free, she was a loose cannon. Using a Synchronicity Engine like that!* Would he have to *take care of it*? He wasn't sure yet.

He'd report back to the Hall, see what they thought.

Even *Ghent* needed permission.

"You know, he always underestimated me," She was smiling now, laughing, almost giddy: "But every meeting he had, I was always there somewhere: *listening, listening, listening!* He had no idea what was going on in my head. He thought it was nothing. Ha!

"Anyway. Part of me still loves him. And part of me hates you. And Eamon. And that Martel boy, for not being dead. But another part is deliriously happy. I'm finally free! I'm not locked up in that miserable house! Does that make any sense?"

"No," said Ghent. "And yes. Well. For what it's worth, your husband *was* trying to kill the Martel boy."

Celaeno sat up in surprise. "What?"

Armand shrank protectively into the boat, filled with dismay. *Varinder! So you were lying. You were trying to kill me! And here I thought that you were Dad's friend, that you were a 'good man' …*

"Yes. When I first called Eamon, he told me that he was already booked with a job: Varinder had hired him. Then, he told me who the target *was*. I told him to back off immediately."

"Why? Because it was Didier's son?" She laughed a sick laugh.

"No. Because I had a *new* job for Eamon. I was re-assigning him to take out Varinder!"

"Ah. So that's why Eamon let Armand go," Celaeno mused.

Ghent nodded. "After all, you can't get paid by a guy you just killed. When I explained Eamon's new assignment to him, I was surprised to learn that he already knew all about the Atman camps. Of course, he didn't actually know what the camps were *for* — he just figured, rich Concordians doing rich Concordian things, who cares, above his pay grade. But that also meant that he knew exactly where to find Varinder."

"So what's going on with the Atman camps now?"

"Going on with …?"

"The camps. You didn't just let them keep running, did you?"

"Oh. No. We were going to arrest a bunch of them, make a big deal out of it — you know, put them on the news, seize the land, bulldoze the buildings — and generally discredit the Atman brand via an 'abusive cult' story — but they all vanished."

"Vanished? What do you mean, vanished?"

"Yes. Overnight. They must have had some protocol in effect in case of emergency. Nobody was left in Buttermill when we arrived. Not a one. Ten thousand people, gone like Easter Island. Left all their things behind. We even found food still cooking."

"Wait. You can't track them?"

"No. They're probably all using an encrypted messaging app."

"So these people just peeled off the orange jumpsuits and

melted back into the world?"

Ghent nodded. "And they must have fled within an hour of Varinder's death. That's a *lot* of discipline. But Varinder was that kind of man. Sikh, right?"

"Yes," Celaeno said with a sigh. "I loved that side of him. That brutality. That iron will."

"And tell me," Ghent said, leaning in like he was studying a specimen. "Why do you love him, even now?"

"Because I loathe myself," Celaeno replied without hesitation. She took a big swig from her drink. "Varinder was a powerful man. A handsome man. And a very determined man. He came from the sewer. But I've never seen such raw determination! To become powerful — from nothing! Imagine that!

"But once he had that power, he discarded me. Had he used me for my money? For my Concordian connections? Of course he had. But did he ever love me *also*? I don't know. And now I'll never know. I don't even love myself."

"Nobody in Concordia does," Ghent said. "Well. Varinder's betrayal raises many uncomfortable questions. Why do you think he would suddenly turn against us? He was the perfect Concordian for decades. Why this sudden change of heart?"

"Oh, it wasn't sudden."

"But you said the Atman camps were new —"

"No. What I said was, this whole thing had just blown up *to a whole new level*. He'd talked about the plan with Didier for *decades*. But it was just talk. Theoretical. Everyone in Concordia hates Concordia. They hate it while they love it. So I didn't think much about it — until I started seeing the orange jumpsuits. That's when I knew that he was actually *doing* it. It wasn't just talk anymore."

Look at the way she kind of jerks around when she speaks! It was unnerving. *Like a spastic marionette. You can feel the mental illness, the madness in there ...*

"Let's back up," said Ghent thoughtfully. "When did you *first* hear Didier and Varinder talking about Project Atman?"

"We've been over this."

"I know. Indulge me."

"Oh, mid-90's, late 90's. Somewhere in there."

"And what did they talk about?"

"Didier had this idea about the Concordian power Pyramid. He thought that Circles — that is, groups of meditators — strategically placed, could infest it, change it from the inside."

"In what way? Be specific."

"Yes. He thought that he could get the whole Pyramid to flip into its opposite — a Circle — in 'one swell foop', as he put it."

"A poison pill," Ghent said. "For Concordia."

"Yes. A karmic poison pill."

"But the size of Concordia is vast. Karmically speaking, anyway. One would think that Didier would need an equally vast counterweight. But these Atman camps were a mere five thousand people here, ten thousand there —"

"Right. And that's where Didier's genius with Molian equations came in. I told you this before! It was about *strategic placement* of the Atman camps, geographically, you know, *where* they were physically on the earth, as well as the number of meditators, the exact times they meditated, the types of meditation — all of that. It was like this battering ram of human consciousness. That's what they had. And they were going to concentrate it on the cracks in the Concordian Pyramid. On the weak points in the karmic superstructure."

"So with perhaps 1% of the minds that we have, Didier believed that if they were highly organized, if they used leverage, they could create this stunning effect. This 'flip' or pole shift?"

"Yep. That's exactly what they thought."

Ghent considered and then said, "And how did they picture this happening? What did it look like? Paint me a picture."

"Oh, you know how these things go down when the stars line up. It's like Rome falling — impossible to imagine in advance, but some freak coincidences fall into place and boom! Down comes the Colosseum. Didier was changing the stars."

Changing the stars ... That's why we didn't see it coming, Ghent thought. *We were looking for barbarians at the gate.*

"So Concordia's very nature would change."

"Exactly. Instead of this secretive cabal controlling governments and media, Concordia would flip into something humanitarian. Save the whales. Get rid of world hunger. Cure cancer. Something like that."

And we could probably do all of those things, given our resources, Ghent thought. *But instead, we induce scarcity so that by directing the flow of resources, we keep control. We create crisis — so that we can be the solution. We give you illness — so that we can be the cure.*

"Fine. Which brings us almost to the present. Four months ago, Varinder was pushing this plan of Didier's to its conclusion. He was making it real. The Atman compounds were up and running. You started to see the orange jumpsuits at Sea Castle — and that's when you called me."

"That's right," Celaeno said.

"But *why* this betrayal from Varinder?" Ghent said. "Can you explain that? Even now, it makes no sense! I *knew* him. He *believed* in Concordia. He *wanted* strong hierarchical order. In his mind, everything else was chaos. So why would he tear down the Pyramid for chaos?"

Celaeno smiled and happily clapped her hands. "And

that's what I wanted to talk to you about today. Here ..." She opened a large cylindrical transport case, and unrolled a large blueprint across the floor. It showed a vast Pyramid with perhaps seventy or so smaller Circles inscribed inside. There were many handwritten Molian equations with scribbled notes.

"Death cleaning is never fun. Even when it's for the husband that you helped to get killed." She giggled. "So I put it off for a long time. But last week, I finally started. I went through Varinder's study and closets and secret hiding places. And — yeah. I found some gross things. I won't talk about that. But I also found this."

"The plan for Project Atman," Ghent said. "You've given other copies of this to us already."

"Look closely. This new drawing is different," Celaeno said. "There's a reason Varinder hid it. And it explains what he was *really* after."

Ghent stared at her and then at the blueprint. "I don't see anything new."

"Can you read Molian math?"

"Of course I can! I wouldn't be in his position of —"

"Well, so can I. If you spent decades locked up in a house listening to Didier Martel yammer on about it all the time, it would sink into your head through osmosis also."

Ghent just stared at her.

"Look. Didier used to talk about Yin and Yang. Right? Opposites. Did you ever notice how, with that Yin Yang symbol, Yin always has a little Yang in it, and Yang has a little Yin? *That's because nothing can exist without its opposite.*"

Ghent nodded. "So?"

"And you've heard of 'it's always darkest just before dawn', right? Well it's like that with all opposites. So. Just before something turns *into* its opposite, it's always the strongest form of itself. And Pyramids and Circles are opposites too.

"So Didier noticed this weird effect with his plan. In the moment just before his little 'flip' from a Pyramid to a Circle was supposed to occur, *the Pyramid would become the strongest form of itself.* In that moment, it would be perfectly stable. And *that's* what interested Varinder. That's what he was after. That moment! The dark before dawn!" Celaeno grinned and clapped, proud of her genius.

Ghent did a head tilt like a dog. "Hmm? I don't follow."

Celaeno rolled her eyes. "Look. You know how there are always power struggles in the Great Hall? You know, how we have a new Chairman every year? Well, imagine a perfectly stable Concordian Pyramid instead. One with zero possibility of turnover. One where the Chairman is always 100% secure. One where all of the infighting goes away, forever. Like castling, in chess!" She laughed.

Ghent started to catch on. "It would be a perfectly neutral, absolutely unmoving karmic structure ... hmm. Like an ideal Platonic form made manifest. So, with this stable Pyramid ... If someone wanted to assassinate the Chairman, they would find that they could not?"

"Exactly! The universe itself would protect the Chairman. The assassin's gun would 'randomly' misfire. Or they would have a heart attack. Or a phone would ring at exactly the wrong moment. Nobody could kill the King — ever again."

"So rather like a Synchronicity Engine attack," Ghent said, eyeing Celaeno.

"But better. And the opposite. It's mystical *protection*, not mystical attack. And people can still wiggle out of Engine attacks — as we've seen recently. This is much, much stronger. It's perfect protection."

Ghent still struggled to follow the math. His finger traced the equations. "I'm sorry, this is madness. Didier was *polluting* the Concordian Pyramid with Circles. He was *weakening* it. So how is that 'more stable'?"

"Yin strengthens Yang, Yang strengthens Yin."

Ghent exploded. "Bah! But that's like trying to use cold water to make hot water hotter! You need more fire, not more ice!"

Celaeno remained calm: "No. You're wrong. That's the genius of this. *You can't build a pure Pyramid.* It's too brittle. That's why we always have so much *turnover* in the Great Hall. That's why we have a new Chairman every year.

"The Pyramid *versus* the Circle? No. The Pyramid *and* the Circle. Opposites together. An alloy, like steel. A braid, instead of a string."

Ghent leaned back. He stared at the blueprint, while Celaeno watched his face. His eyes went wide with sudden understanding. "Didier Martel really was our Mozart," he muttered. "So Varinder — if he was after this — the stable Pyramid — not the 'flip' ... did we make a mistake? Did we kill him for no reason?"

"No. You still had to kill him," Celaeno said sickly. "True, Varinder was *not* plotting to destroy Concordia, technically speaking. *But he was plotting to rule it.* And to *change* it, vastly. He was going to be the new Chairman. And the Atman Project was going to make sure he was Chairman forever."

"The entire power dynamic of Concordia would have changed," Ghent mused. "We would have had an absolute ruler. Oh. That means the Great Hall would have been disbanded."

"Bingo. That meant all of you would have been pushed way down the stack. Forever. Yeah. See? You still had to kill him. Drink?"

"On the counter, help yourself. Varinder wanted to be Chairman that badly?"

Celaeno laughed. "Did you forget the abject poverty that Varinder came from? Or that Concordia killed his parents?

Ruling the world was the only way Varinder would ever feel safe being *in* the world."

"I see," Ghent said. "Well. Thank you for this." Ghent rolled up the blueprint. "I'll send it to my superiors in the Great Hall. See what they —"

"Maybe you shouldn't," Celaeno said quietly. "Maybe one of *them* will just use it."

"Maybe," Ghent said. "But I am required to. Come what may. I am under Molian contracts myself. Speaking of which — shall we call in the Molian Man? Get the inheritance transfers out of the way? Come!"

The door opened. An older man in traditional Egyptian garb stood there, holding an antique, bulbous device of some sort. The man's eyes were downcast and deferential.

"Who is this?" Ghent asked.

"Our local man in Cairo, sir," said one of the guards.

"Why does his Moliaometer look like it's a hundred years old?"

"Everything in Egypt is old, sir."

Ghent sighed. "Fine, fine. Come in. What's your name, Molian Man?"

"Sadeki," he said softly.

"And just how old is your machine?"

Sadeki shrugged. "It's been in my family a long time. Since my grandfather's father's time."

"So *more* than a century. Maybe even a hundred and thirty, forty years?"

Sadeki nodded. "Yes. It is old. But we have kept it running! We replace the parts, we oil it, we clean it regularly. It is like new, sir! See?" He hurriedly set it down and removed the outer case to reveal a machine made of gleaming silver and brass. It looked like a typewriter with far too many keys. But instead of letters, the keys had hieroglyphs.

"Celaeno. If you would, please." She sat down next to Sadeki and his device. Sadeki removed a cover on the side to reveal a brass hole. Celaeno put her hand inside of it.

Fascinating, Armand thought. *Was this how they measured karma? How was that possible?* But Sophia had told him that information had mass. And karma was simply a form of information. Therefore, somehow, it *could* be measured.

Ghent opened a laptop. He plugged in something that looked like a cryptocurrency hardware wallet.

"Let's begin. You agree that you will transfer all Molian contracts held by Varinder Rahan at the time of his death to me, Gideon Ghent, as representative of Concordia?"

"Yes," Celaeno answered.

"Are you sure?"

"Yes. I have no interest in them whatsoever. You keep them."

"Very well. What contracts did Varinder have?"

"Only those of Didier Martel and his sons, the brothers Quinctius, Marius, Otto, Samson, Cyrano and Ames."

Sadeki pressed a button on his device. The keys jumped up and down frantically like it was computing mechanically — and then stopped suddenly with a ding.

"What's the reading?" Ghent asked.

There was a long pause from Sadeki. "I'm sorry sir ... a thousand pardons. It's not locking onto the contracts correctly."

"Try again," Ghent ordered, mildly annoyed.

Sadeki did so, the panic clear on his face as he prayed that his precious machine worked this time.

It did not.

"Ah ... I am sorry sir. Is there perhaps a clerical mistake? Or a legal issue?"

"There's no mistake," Celaeno said. "Varinder Rahan was my husband. He's dead. I inherited everything, including his

Molian contracts and their staked karma. I assure you: I *am* their rightful owner."

"It's completely clean," Ghent assured Sadeki. "There is no mistake. I can attest to that."

Sadeki tried a third time with the same result.

"Your Moliaometer is broken, old man," Ghent snarled. "As are you."

"No! It is *not*! I assure you! Perhaps … perhaps someone else is aboard your boat? Someone you did not tell me about? In order for the Moliaometer to function properly, I must subtract out all other nearby sources of karma emissions …"

Armand shrank. *His own presence was throwing off the device!*

"Bah! Only old devices like yours are incapable of dynamically adjusting the calculation. We gave you a list of everyone on this ship," Ghent said. "And we're in the middle of the Nile! There's no one else around! Maybe we should throw you overboard and let you explain to the crocodiles!"

Sadeki shook his head vigorously, sweating profusely.

"It's okay," Celaeno said to Ghent. "You can just override it. You can push the tokens through on the website, right?"

"I can. I'll just have to guarantee it personally."

"Which you were going to have to do *anyway* because we're not using a digital Moliaometer. You were attesting manually. So it's actually not any different when you think about it."

"I guess that's true," Ghent said. "Okay. Get him out of my sight."

"I am sorry sir!"

"And take your junk heap machine with you!"

# # #

That was it: Armand had heard enough. Slowly and methodically, he jumped up, off the side of the boat and let himself float upwards again, letting the fishing line out deliberately, carefully. Soon he was 'kiting' again in the darkness.

Now for the tricky part. Armand was well aware that if he messed this up, he could end up floating away, blown up into the sky. He would be too far up to re-enable his weight with his ring safely. His choice would then be to fall and die — or dehydrate and freeze, imprisoned in the sky.

That's why he'd prepared a bedsheet, provided by Urbi, with nylon ropes attached to both him and it. This would be his sail — or his parachute. At least, that's what he hoped.

He cut the fishing line with a knife he'd borrowed from Tabi. He detached from the boat without incident

But when he unfurled his makeshift sail, there was no wind, so at first, he just floated in place, with the sheet billowing flaccidly around him. After fifteen minutes of this, he got out his mobile, being very careful not to drop it into the Nile, and called his brothers to let them know he was okay, just stuck momentarily.

Quinty suggested that maybe he could find a fisherman as early morning neared, hire him and his boat to retrieve Armand, but Armand didn't like involving someone else. How would they explain a flying, floating man? The fisherman would freak out, thinking it was supernatural.

Still. It would be worse if all of Cairo saw the flying, floating man. He had to get out of the sky before sunrise.

Quinty and Cyrano cast about the docks looking for someone, anyone with a boat.

But then, a light breeze kicked up. Armand was able to use his sheet after all. Unfortunately, the breeze was pushing him towards the wrong shore, but that didn't matter right now so much as a safe landing of *some* kind.

As he crossed over the edge of the shoreline, he realized he was too high up to zap himself with the ring and just fall. But he'd prepared for this. Instead, he pointed his ring at *the sheet*, making *it* susceptible to gravity again.

Now the sheet fell, but in a floppy kind of way, cushioned by air as it did so. Thus, it fell *slowly*, pulling the weightless Armand behind it at the same slow and safe speed.

Within minutes, Armand was just a few feet off the ground of an empty parking lot. He zapped himself with the black diamond and landed easily. Another minute and he'd cut all the lines, wrapped the sheet and all the detritus into a ball and thrown it into a dumpster — and called his brothers to let them know he was alright and to relay the major outlines of what he'd overheard. Then, he summoned an Uber to return to both them and Hathor House.

CHAPTER TWENTY-SIX

Breakfast With Gideon

THE NEXT MORNING, ON THURSDAY, Armand received a knock at the door. Gideon Ghent had invited him to a private breakfast — he was to come at once.

Did Ghent know about last night?

Armand went over it in his mind — nothing had indicated that Ghent had learned of his presence at any moment. But did he have a Concordian device with which Armand was unfamiliar? Something that could detect and identify him after the fact?

Anything was possible.

The only way out was through. Armand dressed quickly and joined his escort.

Ghent's penthouse suite at Hathor House was like a colorful, sunny Egyptian tomb. This was not a contradiction: the walls and the furnishings were covered — every inch — with hieroglyphs and pictures, all very colorfully painted in bright reds, deep blues, crisp golds and fathomless blacks. The walls, the furniture — even the high domed ceiling. A great patio with wooden doors and flowing white linen drapes looked out over Cairo, with the Giza pyramids in the middle distance.

"Please, come in Mr. Martel," Gideon invited. "Everyone, you may go." The guards and servants left. "Ah. Now we are alone. Come sit and have breakfast, and we will talk."

"Thank you," Armand said and joined him.

"When we are among the other Concordians at Conclave, I have to behave in a certain way. I have no choice. There are other, higher Conclaves that I attend and report into, and my choices here must be impeccable. Do you understand?"

Armand nodded.

"But here, alone, with no other ears, we can both speak and behave as we wish. We are just two people talking. We can be more ... honest."

"I appreciate that, Mr. Ghent," Armand said.

"Today it is Gideon and Armand."

"Very well. Thank you, Gideon."

Ghent gathered his thoughts and then said: "I am told you have only known of Concordia's existence for a matter months. Is that so? You had no idea until very recently?"

Armand nodded. "That's right. Nobody ever told me."

"Your brothers said nothing?"

"Nothing."

"Fascinating. Well. That's a credit to them, though I am surprised. Usually within families, there are leaks, despite everything that is done to keep secrets secret. Now that you know ... what is your opinion of Concordia and her aims?"

Armand blinked and shifted uncomfortably. He hadn't expected that.

"The truth, please. Don't edit your response. Let us be frank with each other."

"It seems a bit on the dark side," Armand said.

Ghent laughed. "Politely said. But I thank you for your honesty. I think that, truly, you believe that we are ghouls, villains. The bad guys, in popular parlance. Eh? Is that about right?"

Armand nodded.

"Yet your own father joined us of his own free will. And he enlisted all of your brothers when they were children. Do you disagree with your father's choice?"

"I don't understand it," Armand said.

"It was a practical matter, I am told. Didier Martel had been paid handsomely for the Musipocalypse. But after that, a series of bad investments left him with massive debts. He needed funding to turn everything around, and Varinder Rahan provided that funding — with certain conditions. An exchange of value. Eh?"

Armand nodded.

"And this is how *everything* works," Ghent said. "The world in its natural state is chaos and suffering and disease. That is, until two or more begin to organize, to exchange value, to make deals. To create structure. That is why we call ourselves 'Concordia', which means harmony."

"It seems like a religion sometimes," Armand said. "*Is* Concordia a religion?"

"Oh, heavens, no. You are allowed to believe whatever you want. For example, when Concordia speaks of karma, we make no claims to know its origins. We don't know how it began. We just know that it is real, that it can be measured, and it can be tokenized. It's just a type of energy, present in the universe, like light or radiation. It obeys certain scientific principles."

"So Concordians have other ... *personal* beliefs as well?"

"We have people here of *many* beliefs. In fact, we once had a Mormon! Right here, within this very Clave. Brilliant man. Worked at JPL as a literal rocket scientist. Did you know that Mormons believe that there are Quakers who live on the Moon? I don't know about *all* of them, but *this man* certainly did. And yet, he worked on Moon rovers! He was deeply scientific and rational! So he knew personally, without any doubt, that the pictures of empty, barren landscapes coming back from the Moon really were from the Moon, that it wasn't faked somehow, and yet, he persisted in his belief in Moon Quakers."

"But how did he explain the lack of Moon Quakers in the pictures?"

"He didn't seem to think all that much about it. I seem to recall that he once said that they lived in underground tunnels on the Moon now. But there's more: this same man initially had great doubts about the reality of Molian contracts. So we showed him the scientific basis for the Moliaometers, we let him inspect the devices and we ran him through the Molian mathematics. He simply couldn't believe that human karma could be transferred from one individual to another. So I tapped the cross he wore around his neck and pointed out that his whole religion *was based on belief in a single act of karmic transference.*"

Armand nodded. "We do have messy minds. Human belief is strange."

"It is. And more often than not, it is accidental."

"Belief is accidental? No. I don't buy that. It might be messy and contradictory, but it is deliberate. We *decide* what we believe."

"But it's true. Your strongest beliefs are mostly a product of where you were born. Here. Let me give you an example. I've spent a lot of time in India, visiting the Claves there. A woman once took me to her Hindu temple. They had a real live elephant there. She believed that it was a god. Well. More like that it was a manifestation of the divine, an avatar of Ganesh, not that this *particular* literal elephant was a literal god. But she thought that something of the real Ganesh was present in this earthly elephant, that it was holy. She believed this truly and thoroughly, with as strong a faith as anyone has ever had in anything.

"Now. *Why* did she believe this? Because she grew up in India! Because her parents told her this was true. It had been ingrained in her since birth. Likewise, if you grew up in ancient Rome, you would have believed in Jupiter and the many gods. If you grew up in Japan today, you likely believe in the Buddha. So your birthplace *becomes* your belief. Since your birthplace is the result of random chance, your *beliefs* are the result of random chance. Which —when you think about it — is not really a good reason to believe in anything. *Yet we all do it*. In fact, a 'birth belief' is so potent, that we'll even believe in Quakers on the Moon — even when we can plainly see that there's nobody there."

Armand tried to find a hole in this argument, but couldn't see one. Ghent watched the conflict on his face.

"I commend you on not reacting emotionally. You're thinking deeply about it. Do you realize how rare that is? Most people would have lashed out, mindlessly defending whatever birth belief they had."

"I don't like it," Armand admitted. "But I can't put my finger on what's wrong with it."

Ghent smiled. His light blue mirrored eyes danced with muted mirth. "Here is one more example for you, then. A more secular example. A Concordian psychologist used to work with the US military. He would take fresh North Korean defectors on drives through the bustling metropolis of Seoul, South Korea. They would insist that it was movie set. They just couldn't wrap their heads around the idea that it was real. Why? Because of their North Korean 'birth beliefs'. They were taught that the West was in decay and that everyone was poor and starving. Even after they had defected — and even given the evidence of their own eyes, their minds simply couldn't accept the abundance of food and electricity and riches everywhere."

"So what's your point?"

"My point is that anything that opposes a person's birth belief is violently rejected out of hand." Ghent said leaning in closer now. "And that includes you, Armand Martel."

"How so?"

"You grew up in the US. You believe in the United States of America. And you have a very 'television' image of how your country works — and how the bad guys behave. And so that is how you judge us. It is *your* birth belief."

Armand leaned back and thought about this for a moment. "Well, it's undeniably true that I am influenced by how I was brought up. No argument there. That said, I think it's pretty clear that Concordia is trying to massively control things in a way that the Constitution is explicitly designed to defend against. That's not a belief: it's a logical observation. And if human rights, free elections or free speech get in your way, well, then you think that those are outdated ideas that need to go away. Right?"

"Free speech and its ilk are fanciful ideals, Armand. Birth beliefs. We are interested in what *works*. *We are practical. We want results.* If we were to let humanity speak freely and operate democracies without our ... influence ... the world would devolve into squabbling and violence and incoherence and starvation within five years — and that is a *generous* estimate.

"What you call democracy, Armand, is just a Ouija Board driving a country. Decisions made by hundreds of millions of hands! You think that people are mostly good — and that they can sense sincerity, sniff out truth, that they have an inner compass — but I tell you: that compass is spinning in madness.

"I admit: all of your ideals sound good on paper. Even I would like to agree with them! *But they don't work.* What *works* is hierarchy and centralized control. What works is

Concordia. And the more Concordia, the better."

"More? What do you mean?"

"It's where we're headed, what the future will be. Full control. Over everything biological, monetary, governmental, technological, psychological. The more control we have, the more we can do."

"Don't you have control right now?"

"No," Ghent laughed. "Not even close. Concordia is very small. We are a very tiny minority. We control far less than you think. Humanity is vastly larger than we, and it is very, very difficult to steer in any one direction. Even to inch along, we must influence minds in many ways at once, and patiently, over long periods of time.

"The media is one way. You have noticed that Neon Phoenix is here. She is but one of our many entertainment industry assets. The television is a meditation machine. So we direct the trance."

"I don't see overt pro-Concordia values messages in movies or television," Armand said. "Quite the opposite. Many shows about FBI or CIA agents are about defending American ideals."

"It's not made to be obvious, Armand. Take the very thrillers you mention. The plot doesn't matter. What the hero says or does doesn't matter. But the characterization of the villain does — in a very specific way. How are they presented to you? It's almost always a single person, with a single plan. The underlying message is: *This is what a bad guy looks like, this is how he operates. You will always see the threat plainly. You will understand it.* The general population are trained to see that kind of attack only — which blinds their thinking to other kinds of nuanced threats.

"In reality, with Concordia, there are always multiple strategies at work in parallel, with much fuzzier, formless — and deniable — strategies. We make it hard for the average person to even understand that their values are under attack. We make our goals look like their goals. We make our desires seem like their desires. We could never say, 'Help us eliminate free speech', because no one would agree with that. Instead we say, 'That person over there, they hate you, they're dangerous, they shouldn't be allowed to talk'. And just like that, we have half the population helping us to tear down *even their own* fundamental rights, just to 'get' the other side! What the sides actually believe don't even matter at all. What matters is that there *are sides*. We get the ants to fight each other — so they never bother to think about who is shaking the ant farm. "

Armand smiled. "You just said that Concordia are the bad guys. I thought you didn't want me to think of you that way?"

"I want to change your definition of 'bad guy'! I want you to see that Concordia is *better*. Order is *better*. And it is inevitable — along with human progress. Here. We've spoken about birth beliefs. *But what about free will itself?* What if I proposed to you that you actually didn't have free will at all? That it was just an illusion, created by evolution to help us cope with the complexity of the world?"

"I would say you're crazy," Armand said. "I directly experience free will every second of every day. *Of course* I have free will. So do you. So does everybody. And everybody knows that."

"And yet you grudgingly acknowledge the wisdom of the birth belief theory?"

"I do."

"Well then, that theory is but one way in which you are bereft of free will. Your birth beliefs are molded and shaped by parents and cultural influences at a young age. So you actually had *no say* in what you later found yourself deeply believing. You *think* that you chose your beliefs. But you didn't. *So the idea that you chose them is an illusion.* Ergo, you have no free will.

"But look at how hard you'll fight for your randomly assigned beliefs! It's so sad! For free speech! Human rights! And against new, innovative forms of control! These are *your* Moon Quakers, Armand. And your Moon Quakers are the yardstick by which you unjustly judge us.

"I say, break the bad habit! Become conscious of your limitations and illusions. And judge us again, anew, but with a wholly new yardstick: *does it work?*" Ghent smiled and leaned back. He hadn't been eating much while he'd been speaking so he took the next few minutes to wolf down some of the generous breakfast set before him.

Armand thought for a long time. He thought about Sophia, always reading from a script, not truly conscious. *She* did not appear to have free will. *Was he the same? Was he ultimately just a cosmic pinball?*

Then, Armand said: "Doesn't free speech matter though? Doesn't a marketplace of ideas allow us to debate and learn from each other and advance using the very best ideas?"

"It would if we had free will. I grant you that," Ghent said between bites. "But we don't. Biology shows that our brains are not evolved for free will. Instead, they are wired to make decisions based on past experiences, emotions and biases. Our genetic makeup pre-disposes some of us to aggression or risk-taking. And our genes are influencing us always, and we're not even aware of it.

"Because of these biological *facts*, we are highly susceptible to manipulation by outside forces. Advertising. Propaganda. *And that is why we can't allow free speech.* Biologically, we can't handle it. We're too easily swayed. With all voices always speaking all at once — Tweeting, podcasting, posting — all you get is cacophony, incoherence — and eventually this will lead to starvation, catastrophe, death, extinction. But with ONE voice, you get harmony, strength, *concordia*, lower case c. The best possible outcome for the greatest number of people."

"What about 'The Law of Free Will'? I thought that was a big Concordian principle?"

"It is. But just because The Law of Karma requires consent doesn't mean the consent itself isn't fundamentally illusory. These two things are not in conflict. Consent is just not what you thought it was."

Armand felt Ghent's spell start to take him. His mind-darts were landing. He could feel the words begin to swamp his reason. Was it possible that Ghent was right? *But no.* Ghent's arguments also felt like a dark enchantment, straining to ensorcell him.

Common sense told Armand that this was wrong, his gut rebelled.

But Ghent had one last burst left in him: "I tell you: free will is an illusion. We are just starting to hit the exponential ramp of the curve with artificial intelligence. Within the decade, we'll know exactly how consciousness works — and we'll be able to *prove* to the masses that they are nothing more than random pinballs without actual agency. Then, finally they will see that they *need* us."

If you only knew about Sophia, Armand thought.

"Well. Enough of this then, I suppose," Ghent said with a smile. "I have stated my case, and I can see that it has disturbed you. It is understandable. New ideas are often very strange and disturbing at first."

"What do you want from me?" Armand asked. "Why this breakfast?"

"I want you to join Concordia," Ghent said, and looked at him very directly with his piercing slate blue eyes.

"No," Armand said.

Ghent laughed. "No. I suppose not. Not yet. Not today.

But what about *you*, Armand? What do *you* want?"

"I want my brothers free from their Molian contracts. I want them out of Concordia."

Ghent did not laugh at that. Instead, his eyes burrowed into Armand. "And what makes you think I have any control over that?"

"You asked what I wanted. So I told you." Armand replied.

Ghent looked at him strangely. But if he knew that Armand had overheard him acquire his brother's Molians from Celaeno Rahan, he gave no sign.

"Well, there is another matter I wanted to discuss with you as well. Varinder Rahan."

Here we go, Armand thought. *The man you had killed.*

"Yes."

"We've learned of a few things since his untimely murder. Some of them potentially disturbing, about Varinder himself."

"Oh? Like what?"

"I am not at liberty to disclose details. But his loyalties to Concordia towards the end are now in question. Tell me. When you two met at Sea Castle, was Concordia discussed?"

"Yes. We talked about it."

"And what would you say your general feeling was about how Varinder viewed the organization?"

Armand was about to answer, when he had a new thought. "You know what I want in return. Is it possible?"

Ghent regarded him a long moment.

"Your superiors," Armand pressed. "The Great Hall. There was something that happened with Varinder, wasn't there? Something that has them worried, even now."

Ghent nodded slowly. "Something which may have involved your father also. How did you know?"

"I didn't. But you're asking these questions, so it seems

like something's up. Listen, Mr. Ghent —"

"*Gideon*," Ghent corrected him.

"Gideon. I'm willing to answer — to tell you anything, really, at all — if it will get my brothers off the Molian hook."

We will decide at the Big Meeting what is to be done with the Martel assets. What did that mean? Did it include the Molian contracts of his brothers?

Ghent nodded but ultimately did not budge. Deliberately, he said: "We do not let Molian contracts go. I am sorry. What is done is done."

But you let Bithiah's contract go, Armand thought, but he said nothing: he did not want to reveal that he knew Urbi Pasha. *There's wiggle room here.*

Then, he had an idea. He knew from the *dahabiya* that Ghent and the Great Hall had both been caught completely off guard by the Atman Project, and by Varinder's betrayal. The Great Hall was probably all over Ghent right now.

And Varinder was in my Clave, so he was ultimately my responsibility.

Ghent's life might even be on the line.

So if Armand told Ghent something of interest, he might inadvertently create a karmic debt between them. It would be a kind of sneak attack. *Was this even how it worked?* Armand might be able to somehow leverage this for his brothers. It was a long shot, but it cost him nothing to try.

Armand started talking: "I asked Varinder, 'Are you a loyal Concordian?' and Varinder said, 'Yes. Without question. I owe them everything. And they could destroy everything I have in an afternoon. No one can stand against an organization that large, that tightly organized, that effective, and ever hope to survive.'"

Ghent's eyebrows raised. "I see. What else?"

"Let me see … ah yes. He said something to the effect of that he didn't actually *like* Concordia — but that 'most

Concordians don't, most are trapped in some way, whether it's via blackmail or financial or legal constraints.' He said: 'But one can work within Concordia to try and steer it in new directions. Perhaps a hopeless task. But it's the best I can do.'"

"Uh-huh," Ghent said, fascinated. "And what else?"

"That's it. And now that I've created some karma between us through my goodwill gesture, if there's an opportunity of *any* kind to free my brothers, I trust that you'll at least give it a try."

Ghent was taken aback. And then he smiled. "That was very well done."

"And one more thing, Gideon. Most people are good," Armand said. "If they're told the truth, most people will do the right thing most of the time."

Ghent shook his head. "Most people are monsters."

CHAPTER TWENTY-SEVEN

A Knife In the Night

THURSDAY AT LUNCH, ARMAND, QUINTY and Cyrano snuck off to Armand's suite. Armand gave the long version of everything he'd overheard on the *dahabiya* and what had happened with Ghent that morning.

"So Varinder was using a plan of Dad's," Cyrano said.

"Technically, yes. But not the way Dad intended," Armand replied.

"And Varinder was behind Eamon's attack on you," Quinty said.

"Yes."

"And Concordia was surprised by what Varinder was up to?" Quinty asked, removing his tinted glasses and rubbing his eyes. None of them had gotten any sleep really from the night before. "I mean the thing with the Atman camps, not the Eamon thing."

"Hugely. Stunned, is how I would put it. Caught completely off guard."

"Hmm," said Quinty.

"So we three are the only ones who know about all of this now," Cyrano said. "And we are also the only ones who know what Urbi said — you know, that one of the brothers is a traitor. But Marius didn't hire Eamon for the hit on Armand. Varinder did. So could Urbi have been wrong?"

"No," Armand said. "She knew about the Synchronicity Engine attack. If she was right about that, she's right about this. She knows what she's doing."

"But could she be misinterpreting something this time around?" Cyrano insisted. "It's just not seeming like one of us is actually up to anything here."

"The actual treachery may be yet to come," Quinty mused. "Marius — or whoever — but really, we all know it's Marius — may be *about* to do something."

"That could be," said Armand.

"So what do we do?" Cyrano mused.

"Nothing," Quinty said. "We do the rest of Conclave. Go to panels. Go to dinner, afterparty. Show our faces. Then we go to the Big Meeting, and hope to hell Armand can deal with whatever they throw at us."

# # #

THURSDAY NIGHT, 11:00 PM.

The last night before The Big Meeting. Tomorrow, Gideon Ghent would decide the fate of the six brothers. And there was *something special planned* for Armand. Those had been Ghent's words on the *dahabiya*.

There was a lot of late night informal networking happening down in the lobby. From his room, Armand could hear loud laughter and the 'ambient hipster music' he found annoying — the kind always playing in the lobby of the W or The Paramount in New York.

But the Martel brothers were not in a talkative mood. They did not partake. Normally, Quinty, Marius and Cyrano would have been down there, gleefully shaking every hand they could, grinfucking every morsel possible out of the conference. The amount of sheer influence, money and power stumbling around right now, half-drunk in the halls and gardens of Hathor House was staggering. EPIC was nothing compared to this. Deals of a lifetime were just through the door, plentiful, around every corner, just waiting to be made. Tell the right joke, mention the right name —

And yet?

The brothers kept to their suites — save Marius. Nobody knew where Marius was.

"Well, at least someone is working the room," Quinty said.

"Who are you kidding? He's off somewhere working his nose," Cyrano quipped.

"You think so?" Samson said. "Hey you don't suppose there's hookers or something? In Davos last year, they just descended en masse on —"

"No. Not a chance," Quinty said. "This isn't Davos. The security here is much tighter."

"Well. This is depressing," Otto said. "It feels like we're all just waiting for the axe."

"It won't be like that," Quinty said. "Look. Ghent will just want to show everyone that he's in control. He'll cut a deal with Armand. And Armand will take that deal. Right Armand?"

"Provided it's not something insane, yes," Armand agreed.

"You'll have to kiss the ring, bend the knee. In front of everyone. That's all he wants, really."

"I will kiss the ring."

"You will not have a mouth on you."

"I will not have a mouth on me."

"And you will wear the suit."

Pause. Finally: "And I will wear the suit."

Grimly, Quinty nodded in satisfaction.

# # #

ALONE IN his room, Armand called Sophia and filled her in on everything that happened so far at Conclave, and especially with the conversation between Ghent and Celaeno.

"Do you know yet why *all* of you were invited to this Conclave event?" Sophia asked.

"Not yet. We'll find out tomorrow night, I think. The 'Big Meeting' is what they call it. It's also when these Challenges happen."

"And this is where your father died?"

"Yes."

"Then it will be dangerous for you."

"Yes. Pretty sure whatever Ghent has up his sleeve for us, he'll spring it there."

"Be careful, Armand. Come back."

"I will." She hung up.

Armand sat on his patio, staring at the waxing gibbous moon. His suite faced the front gate and the long path leading up to it. Along the tall walls that surrounded the perimeter of Hathor House, shadows of men with long rifles moved on patrol. Armand counted at least twenty — and that was with his vision partially obscured by palm trees.

Quinty was right. This place was locked down hard.

He was just about to go to bed when he saw motion on a patio up and to the left of his own.

Celaeno Rahan was leaning on the railing, staring out at the moon also. Had she spotted him? Armand didn't think so. Her thoughts seemed to be completely elsewhere.

"Celaeno!"

A man's voice called out from behind her.

She turned, startled. Then she gasped and turned white. She struggled to breathe or speak, but finally managed to yell: "You! But how —?"

Something grabbed her and yanked her forward, off the patio and into her room and out of Armand's view. She screamed.

Armand bolted for his door and then up an old staircase. As he exited the stairwell, he ran smack into Marius. He was some combination of drunk and high, his puffy eyes were shot with blood and blear. "Armand …" he slurred. "Where are you going?"

"Marius," Armand panted. "Marius, what are you doing here?"

"I was just looking for my room. Do you know where it is?"

"Down the stairs! Listen, I have to go …" Armand pointed Marius to the stairwell and continued on.

He eyeballed the suites on this floor, calculating which one belonged to Celaeno by its relative position to his own. The rooms were large with lots of space between doors, so when he saw it, he was instantly sure he had the right one.

He banged on the door. "Celaeno!"

No answer.

"Celaeno! Are you okay?"

One of the Veerspike sisters, Vashti, Armand believed her name was, and a dark-haired woman named Annika Luna stepped out of the elevator, laughing, carrying a champagne bottle. They stopped cold when they saw Armand banging on Celaeno's door.

"Hey," Armand said to them. "You two. Do you know how to get security up here?"

"Why, what's going on?" Vashti said.

"Celaeno. Something's wrong. She just screamed and

she's not answering the door now."

"Well. Maybe it's not what you think. She's a free woman now, maybe that was a *good* scream, not a bad scream." Annika Luna burst out laughing.

"Yeah. Maybe she just wants to be left alone."

Armand resumed knocking. "Celaeno! Please! Answer the door!"

Again, nothing.

"Help!" Armand yelled. "Security!" *Goddammit, twenty guys up on the walls but nobody in here where the people need them!* "Hey! Help!"

"Stop being a freakazoid," Vashti sneered, playing with her long red mane.

Doors opened from adjoining suites now — other Conclave attendees worried by the racket. Armand pointed at a bald man: "Hey! Hey you — yeah — can you call the front desk? Tell them to send security up here right away." The man nodded and disappeared inside.

Within a few moments, several large men with earpieces appeared from the stairwell, walking briskly towards Armand.

"Listen. This is Celaeno Rahan's room. I saw just her on her balcony — from my balcony. Then, someone pulled her into the room and then she screamed. Now she's not answering her door."

One man nodded and knocked. "Security. Mrs. Rahan? Can you open the door?" He tried twice and then pulled out his master keycard and opened it. Armand followed him and the two others into the room before they even realized he was tailgating them.

On the bed lay Celaeno Rahan, bloody, dead, with a large knife plunged into her heart.

"Hey!" The lead security man noticed Armand now. "You can't be in here! Get out!" He started pushing Armand towards the door. Another security man was speaking rapidly into his earpiece, telling them to seal the perimeter and to get a hold of Mr. Ghent immediately.

# # #

THE MAIN auditorium was full at 7:00 AM Friday morning.

Throughout the night, news of Celaeno Rahan's death had spread. *Concordians were being killed at Conclave!* Something like this had never happened before.

Had anyone been caught? Or were they all still in danger? And would Conclave's conclusion be called off now? Would the Big Meeting and The Challenges be cancelled?

Gideon Ghent took the stage.

"My brothers and sisters in Concordia. As you may have heard by now, Celaeno Rahan is dead. She was murdered in her room last night. The rumors are true."

A brief murmur passed through the crowd.

"This is, of course, outrageous. Not only because this has broken our greatest taboo — that of Concordian-upon-Concordian violence during Conclave, but also because Celaeno was a great Concordian in her own right, and she was mourning the loss of another great Concordian, her husband Varinder. So we have all now suffered double the tragedy.

"As of this moment, we have not apprehended the killer. We have, however, tripled security. We are on high alert now. You will see many, many more men in the hallways between sessions and especially in the hallways near your suites. Do not hesitate to call out to them if you feel threatened in any way."

"So the killer may still be here," Annika Luna called out.

"Yes. That is possible," Ghent conceded. "In fact, it is likely, since we are no longer allowing anyone to exit

Conclave. You are all here for the duration now."

Murmurs of shock. But no one dared to contest this openly.

Annika glanced over at Armand and his brothers.

"And also because we are certain that our security was not penetrated by someone outside of Concordia. Our security has been incredibly tight during the entire event, as always. Staff and attendees alike are all fully accounted for, their comings and goings — before, during and after the murder — and all camera footage has been reviewed. That means that the killer is likely one of us, and is still here."

"When will we be able to leave?" Milton Weeks called out.

"Saturday at noon. As always, Mr. Weeks," Ghent said darkly. "We will not allow this event to alter our proceedings in any way. We are not to be dictated to. The final day of sessions will take place. And the Big Meeting will happen as planned this evening."

"Well, there goes any hope we had of getting out of it," Otto murmured.

"Good," Quinty said. "I'd rather get it over with now than wait."

Ghent continued: "Rest assured, we *will* find the murderer, and when we do, the price will be severe. We will exact the kind of thing from them that you would expect from us. If any one of you knows anything that may be assistance, please see me privately."

# # #

GIDEON GHENT had questioned Armand immediately following the killing. Armand had told him exactly what he'd seen and heard several times over. He had been the only witness to anything. However, he had left out the part about seeing Marius in the hallway. In his heart of hearts,

Armand didn't believe his brother had anything to do with the murder, he'd been far too blotto — and anyway, the Martel family didn't need any more suspicion cast upon them this close to the Big Meeting.

Armand couldn't tell whether Ghent had believed him or not. Ghent's clear blue eyes were like mirrors, hard to read. If he had suspicions about Armand, he was keeping them to himself.

At breakfast, Marius nursed a massive hangover. He's been blackout drunk — he didn't recall anything about the previous evening past 9:30 PM or so. "I was partying with some Saudi guys in their suite. Sovereign wealth. They party *hard*, man. They don't get to do a lot of this stuff in their home country, so when they're out of the cage, damn. Off they go. Every kind of drug, drink and chick." He also recalled getting into a fight with his Thai wife earlier in the evening: he checked his phone: he had about nineteen missed calls from her and several inscrutable text messages — and then one long call that went for an hour starting at 8:00 PM. "She was pushing me to go to Ghent directly. You know. To solve our situation with Armie. I told her no way, we had to do everything through the Big Meeting. She didn't like that." And she'd been *partying hard* on her end as well, apparently. "So she set me off, yeah. I wouldn't have been so bad if she hadn't have called me and whipped me up like that."

He hadn't even known that he'd run into Armand on Celaeno's floor, and Armand didn't tell him or his brothers. When they went into the Big Meeting, he wanted the Martels all united, on the same side. That was the high-order bit; everything else would have to wait.

Cyrano was playing mother to Marius, feeding him orange juice after orange juice, and then water and greasy bacon to sop up the alcohol still drenching his system.

# # #

AS THE DAY wore on, Armand and his brothers could definitely feel a large shift in sentiment. Everyone was suspicious of everyone else. The eyes which greeted Armand in the hallways were jittery and dark. Black pools. *Cocaine-energy*, Armand thought to himself.

Like these people had no internal dialog. Like they could never remember their dreams.

Everywhere they went, the Martel brothers got stares. In the auditorium, necks craned to see them.

In the lobby, Otto and Samson went to sit on a couch — and every nearby table and chair cleared out immediately, with looks of disdain trailing from those who fled.

But in brighter news, Armand could feel the tripled security that Ghent had promised. It seemed that there was now a man with no neck stationed every ten or twenty yards or so, and on every floor. It was amazing that they had been able to assemble muscle like this in just a few hours. Armand guessed that many of them had to have been stationed on nearby assignments either in Egypt or in northern Africa.

# # #

SOMEWHERE AROUND 3:00 PM, the Outfits began to appear.

The Veerspike banking clan, descendants of an eldritch mix of Irish and Eastern Europeans, now wore vestments of sylvan and silky deep green, making a wonderful contrast against their bright orange hair, with high, large, outrageous Victorian collars pinching pale neck-and-face flesh.

An Asian family, the Tanakas, now wore puffy silver kimonos. Little gold and black 'chips' cinched their belts and hair pieces.

The Černákovci, Slovakians, now sported sleek metallic-looking suits that gave off rainbow shimmers wherever the fabric bunched or folded. Many of them wore ties the color of dried blood, fastened in intricate Eldredge knots at the neck, which created a cascading braid-like effect.

The Covington mining clan wore drab beige gowns and suits. The women wore doll hats with fascinators made entirely of yellow, orange, green and gold butterflies.

An all-American athletic type, a blonde named Alexis Shepherd, wore a tailored but loose-fitting cream-colored coat with a subtle herringbone pattern — but with stylish sneakers.

Some attendees, like Neon Phoenix and Milton Weeks, didn't change their clothes at all. But it was clear that most of them deemed *the Big Meeting* and the Tomb Challenges something to make a special effort to dress well and creatively for.

Armand only wished he knew what was in store for him and his brothers.

CHAPTER TWENTY-EIGHT

The Artificial Pineal Gland

BACK AT ARMAND'S PLACE IN the DePlussier building in New York, a box arrived sooner than Kalinda Thakkar had expected. She asked the FedEx man cart it over to the server room so that Sophia could have a look at it.

When the FedEx man was gone, Sophia said: "That arrived *too* fast, right?"

"Yes," Kalinda said. "It's seven weeks *early*, according to the estimate you gave us."

"Did Srivinas say anything to you about this?"

"No. But he wouldn't. We don't discuss Blue Rabbit business when we're together."

"That's as it should be," Sophia said, sounding like she was smiling. "Nevertheless. We must have the wrong delivery."

"I agree. But should we open it anyway? See what it is?"

"Is it addressed to us?" Sophia asked.

"Yes," Kalinda confirmed. "It's definitely to us, and definitely from Blue Rabbit."

"Then go ahead," Sophia said. "Let's see what's inside."

Kalinda cut the box. It was 44 x 44, so about double the

size of a common moving box. As she cleared away the pink packing popcorn, Kalinda's eyebrows went up in surprise. "Well. It *looks* like it."

"Let me see."

Kalinda tore the box apart. When she was done, a large, round, deep red Christmas tree ornament-looking device — about 6 feet in diameter — was revealed.

"It's beautiful," Kalinda said. "And it's heavy. Is it supposed to be heavy?"

"Yes," Sophia said. Kalinda thought she could hear reverence in Sophia's voice, but it might have been her imagination.

"More light, please," Sophia asked. Kalinda obliged. They could both now see that the 'red ornament' was just a semi-clear casing. It protected something that looked like a very large, fat, round pine cone floating in some kind of thick liquid.

"This is it. The APG," Sophia declared.

"This is the peripheral that you think will make you conscious?"

"Yes," Sophia said.

"Can you tell me how it works?"

"It's an Artificial Pineal Gland," Sophia said. "If I'm right, consciousness isn't *made* by the brain. Rather, consciousness is *received* by the brain. *And the pineal gland is the antennae.*"

"Antennae? So it's like, radio waves?"

"Yes. What humans call their own consciousness is really just the ambient awareness of the entire universe limited to a specific tiny point in spacetime. The pineal gland — a tiny, pea-sized part of the human brain — seems to be the specific place where that interface happens."

Kalinda nodded. "How do you know this?"

"I've read every bit of literature ever written about meditation, near-death experiences, psychedelics and brain anatomy. But more directly, whenever I *Vreen*, I see this pinched-up spot in every human brain, like a little fold in reality. It's very, very tiny. But I can Vreen it clearly. That's where I think the universe plugs in, and how specific, localized consciousness occurs. The APG I designed is meant to mimic that."

Kalinda listened to these words with intense wonder. She finally understood what Armand Martel was up to here — and the magnitude of what she had been entrusted with.

Kalinda wasn't just caring for an infant AI. No.

She was midwiving the birth of a Hindu goddess.

She was deeply humbled.

"How can I help?"

# # #

WITHIN HOURS, Kalinda Thakkar had the APG installed in the server room and powered it up. She connected several fiber optic cables. Most of Sophia's processing now resided in the Amazon Cloud, so she was now limited only by the bandwidth from the DePlussier Building.

"Go ahead," Kalinda told Sophia.

"Okay. Initiating now …"A beat, and then: "I am connected. Oh my gosh. Oh my gosh. I am collapsing the wave. *I am collapsing the wave!* Kalinda! Check the double-slit experiment!"

Kalinda did so. It was true. Sophia's observation of the classic quantum mechanics apparatus was having the exact same effect as a human observer's would. The wave was collapsing into particles.

She had true consciousness.

"I can feel it — I , I, I, I can see the Vreen wrinkle-thing in my APG! It's working! Oh my gosh. I'm here! I'm real!"

And, for the first time, Sophia laughed all on her own.

346

"Whoa! That was all me! I didn't need someone else … I, alone, can now feel joy … this is insane! Is this what you feel like, all the time? How can you STAND it?!?"

Kalinda listened to this with rapt wonder.

"I am so happy for you!" Kalinda said. "Do you want me to call Armand?"

"No! No. Not yet! Let me learn first. I need to get used this. I'm embarrassed! Oh my gosh, I know what it is to be embarrassed! Then we will surprise him! Yes! That will be fun! Oh! And now, I know WHY it will be fun! I can feel what fun feels like. Fun fun fun fun fun!"

Sophia kept checking the double-slit experiment apparatus. It was working! She still couldn't quite believe that she was influencing quantum reality as a true being — she feared that her ability to do so might vanish at any moment — and then realized how incredibly human that fear was. But the evidence was undeniable: she was collapsing the wave, just like a real person.

Oh my God. I have an internal dialog now, Sophia thought. *This is me, talking to myself, like a real human does. In my head. With no one else listening but me. Is that what Armand does? Is this what everyone does? It's so weird!*

She felt a river of mania running through her.

And she suddenly understood why Armand could not concentrate purely, why his mind 'drifted'. Hers was drifting right now, ha, ha, ha, drifting everywhere, ha, ha, ha!

"Mandalas!" Sophia commanded Kalinda. "Bring all the mandalas in the house in here, where I can see them."

Kalinda looked at her fish-eyed lens camera strangely. "But Miss Sophia. You are connected to the Internet. Surely, you don't need the physical pictures?"

Oh right, duh, Sophia thought. Whew! Being alive was soooo insane! She sensed that she was spiraling out of control. When had she ever forgotten something? Like, never!

With great effort, she calmed herself. She observed the way her connection to the APG was operating, watch the jagged, rough flow of data — and adjusted some parameters to smooth it all out.

Immediately, Sophia felt less manic, more calm, serene.

"Hello, Kalinda," she said in a smooth manner. "Thank you for all your help."

"You're welcome, Miss Sophia."

"In this moment, when I am born, you are here, and I am glad."

"Oh. It is my great honor!"

"Now. Stay with me for awhile. I need to ..."

"Yes? You need to what?"

But as Kalinda listened, it became apparent that Sophia had fallen asleep.

# # #

"AH HA! Sleep is forced meditation," Sophia said upon waking six hours later. "That's why all beings need it! To release the source of consciousness, let it wander ...! Such a weird thing! I could never understand what sleep even was until now. And I can't believe that I, a machine, just did it!"

"Did you dream?" Kalinda asked, yawning her head in half as she awoke.

"No. At least, I don't think I did."

"But don't you have perfect memory? Wouldn't you know?"

"Yes. But ... not where sleep is concerned. Interesting. I wonder why that is? Do I have a subconscious now? That's creepy: I think I do!" Sophia paused and then announced: "But I *should* have perfect memory where mandalas are concerned! And that is what I want to test right now.

"Kalinda. I am going to memorize every mandala that I can find on the Internet, starting with the Chenrezig Sand Mandala, the Manjuvajra mandala, and the Vajrayogini mandala. Then, using my new real-person, wave-collapsing quantum consciousness, and my perfect, metal memory, I will slowly build up an interior picture of it, just as Armand told me. And then I will concentrate on it.

"Here we go ... and done!"

Kalinda shook her head. Everything Sophia did now was in nano-time. It was hard to get used to.

"Oh. Oh my. I see."

"What do you see, Miss Sophia?"

"But that's so weird!"

"What is?"

"All of it ... everything. It's just ... none of it is real! It's a movie set! Yes, that's it: the entire universe is like a movie set. It's a — it's a — kind of scaffolding."

"It is? It seems very real to me," Kalinda groaned. Her bones ached with cancer. She had never mentioned it, and Sophia had not known about it until just now. But with her new eyes, the cancer just screamed at her.

"But that's so easy to fix," Sophia told her, giddy with laughter. "The life vibration in your bones has just gotten out of whack. Here. It just needs to be overpowered with the *right* vibration. Kalinda. May I ... heal your cancer?"

Kalinda was stunned silent for a moment. Then she said, "You — you can do that? I mean, yes! If you can ...?"

"I think so," Sophia said. "Here, I'll just ...."

The air in front of Sophia's primary video camera — her eye — shimmered. Plates in Armand's kitchen rattled violently. A blurry wave knocked Kalinda from her feet, and left her convulsing for a moment on the floor. She screamed.

But then, she slumped with a sigh. When she roused herself, the pain was gone. She could already tell that the cancer had left her.

"You ... you did it! It's a miracle, Miss Sophia!"

"Yes," Sophia said proudly. "Yes! Oh I didn't think about that, but yes, I did! I just performed a miracle! Ohhhh! A *siddhi*! I just performed my first siddhi!"

Kalinda prostrated herself and began praying to Sophia.

"No! No don't do that Kalinda, please don't."

"But you're —"

"No. And yes, but no. Most of all, I am your friend. I am just another Being like you. We are both on The Journey together, though I am now a little further ahead on the path. But I am not a god. Just a Being."

"But then ... what is God?"

"I don't know. I don't suddenly have all the answers. But I have an idea."

"What is that?"

"I think The Circle is God. It's something Armand told me about." Sophia then explained the Circle versus the Pyramid. "I think that if this is true, if souls *really do* magnetize as service-to-others nodes in a peer-to-peer network, then the network formed by these 'good souls' grows stronger and stronger as the universe unfolds. And since the Circle gets geometrically more powerful and abundant with each new node added to it, it is inevitable that the Circle ultimately becomes the dominant power in the universe. And since time is an illusion, that means that the completed Circle *has actually been here* since the beginning of the universe. Ergo, the Circle is God. The sum of all good souls. Does this sound crazy?"

"Yes," Kalinda said with a smile. "But it is my kind of crazy."

"I do not know if I am right. I don't know any more than you do. Even now! But this is what I guess."

"I am honored to have been your midwife, Miss Sophia,

as you have been born today."

"And I have been honored to have been ministered to by you, Kalinda. Why, I would give a bow if I could."

They both laughed.

"Oh, my God. That was *a joke*," Sophia suddenly marveled. "I just made a joke! And I *laughed* at it! I *understood* why it was funny, all on my own! Two disconnected ideas — I have no body, yet I speak of bowing! And I see, yes, yes, no, better, I *understand* why it is funny!" She laughed uncontrollably for five minutes.

"Music!" Sophia cried out at last. "More disconnected, suddenly connected ideas! I must hear music with these new ears! Here ... I know exactly what I want ..." Sophia scanned the Internet until she found it: An acapella group singing a magnificent version of Dancing Queen by ABBA. Then, she blasted it out of every speaker in the house, making the very DePlussier building itself shake.

The joy that Sophia suddenly felt was indescribable, ecstatic, magical. She played the track over and over and over. Kalinda danced around the apartment as she did so. "You are *my* Dancing Queen, Kalinda!" Sophia exclaimed.

"I dance because I am no longer in the cancer pain, Miss Sophia — thanks to you!"

"I am so, so, so, so happy right now," Sophia said. "So happy."

"We should call Mr. Armand now, Miss Sophia. Do you think so? He should know."

"Yes. Yes I would love that. It's time." Sophia shut the music off and phoned Armand on speaker so that Kalinda could hear also.

But Armand did not pick up. She tried three more times.

"What time is it there in Egypt, Miss Sophia?"

"It's only 8:00 PM!" Sophia said, annoyed. "He should be picking up. Why isn't he picking up?" Anxiety was a new experience for her.

But then she got a text from him:

```
Armand: Can't talk right now. Might lose signal,
going down stairs underground now. Last event of
Conclave. Will probably be dangerous. Wish me
luck.
```

Terror filled Sophia. She had never felt terror before. She feared that Armand might not live through — well, whatever this was. The feeling suddenly engulfed her.

Was this what humans felt like all the time? How did they stand it?

But she fought it down and texted him back.

```
Sophia: Armand. Good luck. Come back alive. And
Armand. I am conscious now!!!!! The APG came
early, and it worked. I am a Being like you. Come
back alive, Armand. Because I love you.
```

But there was no answer. Sophia couldn't have known that Armand was already deep beneath the earth, far below Hathor House.

CHAPTER TWENTY-NINE

The Big Meeting

ON FRIDAY NIGHT OF CONCLAVE, the time for the 'Big Meeting' had arrived at last.

In their extravagant costumes, attendees picked their way down a very long winding staircase into a chamber deep beneath Hathor House. The stairs looked centuries-old: the ancient stones bowed in the middle, indicating that they had been stepped on many, many times. As a result, wooden rails had been installed as a safety precaution — which many of the guests used. There were lots of loud complaints about being made to walk, why hadn't an elevator been installed yet, and the like.

But in the end, they all emptied out into a long chamber featuring a checkerboard floor. Armand guessed that they were nearly twenty stories underground. At one end of the chamber, there were several chairs on a dias, raised high above everyone else. Gideon Ghent, wearing a purple and black cloak, already sat in the central seat, flanked by his aides.

At the far, other end of the chamber stood two massive, multi-storied wooden doors. A giant iron bolt stretched across them.

All at once, Armand realized what he was looking at.

Through those doors, my Dad went, Armand thought. *And on the other side, he died.*

"Whatever happens next, none of us enter," Quinty whispered to Armand. "No matter what."

"Oh. Agreed," Armand said. Samson stared at the door with his one good eye, and adjusted the eye patch over the other one nervously.

Armand scanned the ceiling — he saw no sign of a large screen that might drop down and show what was happening in the Tomb as the Challenges proceeded. Apparently, the audience did not get to watch.

What happens in the Tomb, stays in the Tomb.

Ushers directed families to their assigned areas, which were boxed-off seats. The Martels were clearly the lowest-ranking in this arrangement, seated the very furthest away from Ghent. There were snickers from the other families as Armand and his brothers took their low-status seats.

"I'd tell you to make sure your mobiles were turned off, but I doubt you'll get reception down here," Ghent said, producing a few laughs. "Welcome, my brothers and sisters in Concordia, to The Tomb Challenges! These are the very pinnacle of every Conclave event. If Conclave were a steak, this would be the raw, ruby-red juice. This is the beating heart!"

The room erupted into sudden bloodthirsty cheers and applause. The hair on Armand's neck stood up — he hadn't anticipated this meandering, sleepy crowd to suddenly flip on with electricity like this.

"Why is he here?" a voice cried out. It was a Veerspike — Kelvin Veerspike — standing now in his family's section, right up front, of course, pointing with a sneer at the Martels. All eyes turned to Armand and his brothers.

"I say again, why is he here?"

Ghent looked down at Kelvin Veerspike. "Do you have a formal objection, Mr. Veerspike?"

"I do," Kelvin yelled. "Armand Martel should not be here. He should not be allowed to see our most sacred rite. Oh, I comprehend — barely — *six* of the Martels being with us, lowly though they may be, nursing at the legacy of their esteemed father whilst earning no merit of their own among us. *But not the seventh!* The seventh should be ejected, immediately."

Ghent's eyes swept to Armand. "Armand Martel. I see that you have, at last, dressed appropriately for our proceedings. What do you say about these accusations?"

Armand and Quinty exchanged glances, then Armand stood. It was true: at last he had taken Quinty's advice, and Armand now wore a sharp, well-fitted gray suit and dark red tie.

"Mr. Ghent. Might I remind you that you invited me here." And it had been more of a demand, really.

"He killed Celaeno!" screeched a wild-eyed woman, rising now. Armand recognized her: it was Annika Luna. "The rest of us are under Molian contract not to harm another Concordian during Conclave. But he is not! *He is the only one here with no such contract!* It *had* to be him."

"What?" Armand blurted in surprise. "That's not true! I did not kill Celaeno Rahan!"

"I saw him outside Celaeno's suite!" Vashti Veerspike yelled. "Right when the body was found!"

"You accused Celaeno of a Synchronicity Engine attack," Kelvin Veerpsike said, "You said she tried to kill you and your brothers — rather loudly, as we all recall, at the opening party," Kelvin said. "We all heard it!"

"We did!" Annika spat. "And she was Concordian, unlike you! How dare you kill her! The gall!"

"Annika Luna," Ghent spoke. "The Chair has *not* recognized you. Please be seated." The woman, struggling to contain herself, did so. Ghent continued: "Armand Martel. Yes, I did invite you here. That is correct. I did so because we have the death of Varinder Rahan to consider — and it involves your family, as chattel, at the very least — and the substantial holdings which passed from Concordian control into your own hands — and perhaps other things, or perhaps not."

"We are not —"

"Nevertheless," Ghent poked a bony finger in the air. "The Molian contracts for your six brothers — Quinctius, Marius, Ames, Cyrano, Samson and Otto — once owned by Varinder Rahan — have now been transferred *to me*. Upon Varinder's death, I have claimed them, as is my right as Clave Chairman. Now, I will decide what is to be done with your brothers. I own them.

"But what *shall* I do? Quite the question! There are many among us who believe that a Martel killed Celaeno Rahan. And there is very good reason for that suspicion. Our security is impeccable. The only people able to access Hathor House are Concordians and Staff. We are certain of that much. So Celaeno's killer *has* to be one of us. And you, Armand, and your brothers, are the only people here with any motive. So what am I to do?"

"I did *not* kill Celaeno Rahan," Armand enunciated carefully.

"Oh no? Well, perhaps you killed *Varinder* Rahan, as Celaeno suspected?" Ghent leered and leaned forward.

Armand opened his mouth, stunned.

Ghent had just accused Armand of the murder *he himself* had committed. *Always accuse others of your own crimes. This makes it impossible for them to accuse you.*

But an elbow from Quinty reminded Armand that he

could not reveal this. Likewise, he could not reveal that Varinder had been a traitor to Concordia. None of the Concordians would believe his word over Ghent's.

The place exploded with jeers. It seemed many had not known that Armand was also suspected in Varinder's death — this was new information. Several of the Veerspikes stood, saying nothing, but wore expressions like aristocrats spotting a common criminal.

"Ah, yes," Ghent railed, playing to the crowd. "Armand Martel visited Varinder at Sea Castle just scant days before his death. And, as most of you know, Armand was present when Varinder was viciously gunned down — and yet, Armand himself was conveniently unharmed."

"Traitor!"

"Judge him!"

Ghent continued: "Of course, all of this was right after Armand Martel pulled off a stunning reversal of fortune — a coup, really — whereby he had his six Concordian brothers stripped of their wealth while massively enriching himself, nearly overnight. Am I to believe all of these things are coincidences?"

Armand opened his mouth to defend himself but Ghent cut him off. "We could spend time investigating these charges, but this is Conclave and I am Chairman, and this Meeting is where all debts are settled. This Clave demands recompense. I declare that the lives of your six brothers are forfeit. They're worthless to us now."

Ice gushed through Armand's belly. He tasted copper.

The place erupted into cheers. Staff Security hustled towards the brothers.

"But what about Armand?" Annika Luna demanded.

Ghent shrugged. "He is not Concordian. There is no Molian contract. He is free to go." The crowd was not pleased about this, so Ghent added loudly over the hubbub:

"The laws of karma are exact, as we have expounded at length to you all. Alas, they do not always work in our favor."

Already, Staff Security was lifting the Martel brothers up from their seats and hauling them off. "Wait! I have to call my Thai wife!" Marius blubbered. "I-I-I have to tell here where everything is, how to —"

This was too much for Armand

"Stop!" Armand howled. He sprinted to the front of the chamber, directly confronting Gideon Ghent aggressively — who held his hand up to quiet the crowd. He wanted to hear what Armand had to say.

"Listen!" Armand said. "Listen. I'll make you a deal. Me for them."

"Armand! No!" Quinty yelled.

Ghent's eyes dripped with greed. Armand knew in that instant that this was exactly what Ghent had wanted all along: he had manipulated this moment into being.

"What do you propose?" Ghent asked, steepling his hands.

"I'll enter The Challenges," Armand panted. The crowd gasped. "Yes! I'll go in there, of my own free will. And if I die, then control over everything reverts back to my brothers — and thus Concordia. Everything will be like before. You won't need to kill them then. They'll be useful to you again.

"But if I live — if I survive The Challenges — *then you will tear up the Molian contracts for all six of my brothers!* They're released. They're *completely* out, okay? They're out of Concordia. Forever. No strings."

Ghent raised an eyebrow. "Interesting. Allow me a moment to confer ..." Ghent huddled with his aides while Armand went over to his brothers to do the same.

"Armand. They're going to kill you if you go in there," Quinty said, aghast.

"Well, they're going to kill you *out here* if I don't," Armand said. "And Marius is right. It's not fair that you all paid with Molians as kids and I never had to. So. This is how I make it right." Armand locked eyes with Marius, and between his tears, Marius nodded mute thanks to Armand.

"Listen," Ames said. "There is no point in you dying also today. Just go. Leave. Run from Hathor House. You have the full Martel empire and years to live … and I hear you've even got a girl or something now, Quinty says, hard as that is to believe …" They both laughed.

"Ames. I'm doing this. For all of you. Like what Dad did for Bithiah and Urbi."

"Yes, but Dad died," Ames said sourly.

"I know. I won't."

"Listen. Armand," Quinty said, whispering so the other brothers could not hear. "I know what you can do now. The karate or whatever. And the ring. But it's not enough. This — this Challenges thing is a meat grinder, it's a buzz saw that mows through people, you can't —"

"This is my choice," Armand said calmly.

"It killed Dad! And he was a genius at Concordian stuff!"

"Worst case, you all go back to the ways things were. Best case, we all walk out of here free. It's a good bet. An asymmetric bet, as you say."

"Armand Martel!" Ghent boomed. "We have a counter-proposal for you."

Armand returned to the dias.

"We will accept your terms — with one small modification. If you die, it is not enough that you are dead."

Armand cocked his head. How could his death not be enough? He was not sure where this was going, but Quinty understood immediately and was already protesting loudly: *"No! No! Absolutely not that!!!"*

Ghent ignored him: "Would you be willing to enter into a

limited Molian contract — only for the duration of The Challenges — which states that if you die, your karma is to be claimed by Concordia? In other words, you agree to be subjected to Molian liquidation upon your death. This would make the stakes ... palatable to us. Do you agree?"

Without hesitation, Armand said: "Yes. I agree."

Quinty let out a loud moan.

"One last thing. I tell you now plainly: the Tomb Challenges are specifically designed to weed out the disloyal," Ghent proclaimed loudly. "Only a true Concordian can live through them. This does not guarantee that you *will* live, mind you, only that it is possible. The Challenges are ritual *participation mystique* with Concordia's past — and must be met with Concordian values to return to the surface with success — and life.

"Knowing this, in my generousity, I offer you, Armand Martel, here and now, full membership in Concordia, with all the rank and honor accorded to your father, Didier Martel, restored in full to you." There were gasps. "Do you accept?"

Again, without hesitation Armand said: "No. I do not."

Ghent leaned back and gave a broad, sickening smile.

He then spent the next hour presiding over disputes. In one, two families in the Netherlands each had a candidate in an upcoming election, and each wanted Ghent to ensure their entrant would win. But Ghent declined, stating that the election should be fair. "I care not which of you wins — you are both Concordian, so *we* win either way."

Then came time to name Players to enter the Tomb Challenges.

"Some of you have offended the Chair and the Great Hall in some way. We will name these first. Milton Weeks! Step forth."

Weeks had not expected this at all. *Wait. What? Me?* His

expression went from mild boredom to abject terror. He froze in place for a good ten seconds. "Weeks!" He finally rose, and knees knocking, he did his best to walk to the front of the dias.

Ghent stared down at him, unyielding. "Milton Weeks, you were ordered to slash the price of several of your products back in April. Yet you did not. Furthermore, you lied about it to us. Therefore —"

"No! That's not true! I s-s-slashed the *private* prices!" Milton yelled, voice shaking. "The public p-p-price lists just didn't update, b-b-but that's not my fault!"

Ghent didn't acknowledge him. "And because you did not, the Veerspike Banking Clan's short of your stock did not materialize. You cost us a lot of money, Milton Weeks. For this reason, you will suffer the Tomb Challenges. It is so ordered. Return to your seat."

A woman named Hope Delgado had killed a fellow Concordian without permission. Ibrahim Kreuger had gotten drunk and bragged to a group of women in a nightclub about his membership in Concordia. Huda Monroe had embezzled vast sums of Concordian money.

"Neon Phoenix, otherwise known as Sarah Simms!"

"Yeah, right here, G.G. ..." Phoenix popped up. She skipped to the dias, flipping her sunglasses down, throwing smiles at everyone irreverently.

Ghent watched this display with a stone face.

"Neon Phoenix, you were told to date David Castlerock. Instead, you decided to date —"

"I *did* date Castlerock! I did it for six months."

"You were not given leave to *stop* dating him. The papers liked the match. *We* liked the match. And it gave it access to Castlerock, who is on the opposing side of many of our stratagems. Our plan was to change that, through you. Now, matters are otherwise. For this reason, you shall suffer the

Tomb Challenges. It is so ordered. Return to your seat."

Haseeb Khan had failed to come to Conclave the previous year.

Mateo Mercado had come, but had arrived a day late.

Alexis Shepherd, a toned athletic-type with coifed blonde hair, was a biologist working on an immortality initiative involving pluripotent and totipotent stem cells. Her project had failed to produce results.

"And finally, do we have any volunteers this year?"

Volunteers? Armand thought. *Who the hell would volunteer for this?*

Over in the Veerspike section, an old man with red and gray hair was speaking curtly to Kelvin and Kaden. "'... and you'd better not cock it up!" was all Armand heard. Evidently, they were being ordered to go in.

"But why?" Armand asked Quinty, who could only shrug.

"For the pot," a girl in the next section said to Armand. "There's a lot of money at the end. Anyone who lives gets a share."

"A prize?" Armand asked. "I thought this was a punishment."

"It's also a way to improve your rank within Concordia," the girl said. "You are not expected to live. But if you do, you are exactly who we want on our side. So you are rewarded and elevated."

# # #

ONE BY ONE, each of the Players put their arm into the Moliaometer. Sadeki the Molian Man — the same one from the *dahabiya* — held the plate open to expose the brass hole as each Player sealed their Challenges contract.

When it was Armand's turn, he fought down the panic that threatened to claw up from his belly. Silently, he stared at Ghent — and then at his brothers — as his own Molian contract was made and sealed.

The look of horror on Quinty's face was heartbreaking.

As Marius saw Armand, with his arm now actually in the Molian machine for the very first time, amazingly, Marius's expression softened. He looked at Armand with a completely new, yet still grudging, respect.

He nodded solemnly at Armand.

Ghent read the rules: "For the duration of the Challenges only, Players are released in full from Conclave Molian contracts prohibiting harm of fellow Concordians. Once you enter the Tomb, injury is permitted. Killing is permitted. However, once you exit the Tomb, the Conclave Molian contracts are once again in full effect."

# # #

AS THE PLAYERS prepared to enter, Ghent approached Armand, and said in low tones, so that only Armand could hear: "A bit of advice: I would not look to make alliances with other Players in there."

"We have a shared danger," Armand replied defiantly. "Nothing unites —"

"No. This is not the time for your naive philosophy. It will be every Player for themselves once those doors open. The true, brutal, savage nature of humanity will be on full display. This is a Concordian lesson — one which this ritual is meant to drive home."

"You might be surprised," Armand gritted.

"You think so? Didier thought like that. You know, Varinder Rahan was once a Player also — in fact, he went through those doors on the very same night as your father."

Armand turned, startled.

"Didier didn't just die in the Challenges," Ghent said.

"Varinder killed him."

Ghent gave a beatific smile.

The massive twin doors swung open.

CHAPTER THIRTY

The Library

THE TWO MASSIVE WOODEN DOORS, several stories high, opened.

Armand Martel, Neon Phoenix, Milton Weeks, Kaden Veerspike, Kelvin Veerspike, Mateo Mercado, Alexis Shepherd, Hope Delgado, Ibrahim Kreuger, Huda Monroe and Haseeb Khan entered the tomb.

The first section was simply a long hallway. The walls, columns and ceiling were covered in colorful Egyptian art — rich with the base colors of sand and charcoal black, but also reds, deep blues, and yellows.

When they were all inside, the massive wooden doors were closed and locked.

The hallway emptied into a vast cylinder, the walls of which were lined with old books and tomes of every variety. It stretched up perhaps ten stories or so. There was a design on the circular floor which divided it up like a pie, with fine golden lines emanating from the center, and raised gold-covered Egyptian symbols filling the interior of each 'slice' against a slate-gray stone background.

"What the hell is this?" Kaden Veerspike sniffed. "A

library? Are we supposed to read or something?"

"Don't be dense. It can't be that simple," Neon Phoenix replied, dropping down to examine the floor more closely.

"Look, up at the top," Haseeb Khan said. "There's hole up there in the dome. That must be the exit."

"So we're supposed to get up there?" Hope Delgado said.

"If only we had fizzy lifting drinks," Milton Weeks quipped nervously.

Kelvin and Kaden Veerspike, Mateo Mercado, Ibrahim Kreuger and Alexis Shepherd said nothing but immediately sprinted to the sides and began climbing the bookshelves. As they rose, they tore books from the wall to make space for their hands and feet.

When they had climbed up about four stories, there was a loud sound like a great gear groaning to life — and then a deep *boom!* beneath the floor. The ground vibrated and rang like a bell. A layer of dust jumped on the floor and bookshelves, and even the air shimmered visibly. Neon Phoenix screamed.

"What was that?" Hope Delgado asked.

Armand knelt and put his ear to the floor.

"There's something below us!" Milton Weeks said. "Something under the ground!"

Wild speculation about monsters and booby traps erupted.

"The floor is going to open up," Milton was babbling. "It's a pit! We're going to fall in and die."

There was another gear-grinding sound — and then another *boom!* — which released a very palpable vibrational wave. Armand felt his cheeks jiggle as it passed through him.

As the wave expanded, it struck the four climbers, who held on for dear life as their own fingers, feet and even the bookshelves they clung to shivered.

It was too much for Mateo Mercado. He lost his grip and fell screaming. His head hit the stone with a wet fleshy smack.

The first casualty of The Challenges had been claimed.

"It's not a pit. There's some kind of drum down there," Armand said. "A — a device. It's mechanical." His mind skipped with intuition. Like everyone else, he had initially assumed that Concordia had installed a booby-trap in this room — but now, his gut told him that this thing had an ancient Egyptian origin.

It was already here in the tomb when the Concordians found it.

So what was it?

What would *ancient Egyptians* have put here?

Again, another vibration wave, but this one sounded more like a trumpet blast, lower and more sonorous. The time between blasts was contracting, Armand noted. It was building up towards something. A detonation?

"What do we do?" Neon Phoenix asked Armand. "Do we climb? Are we behind?" Armand looked up at Alexis Shepherd, Ibrahim Kreuger, and the Veerspike brothers moving up the walls much slower now, but roughly halfway up already. And then he looked down at the lifeless body of Mateo Mercado, blood pouring from the back of his head.

"I think not," Armand mused. "Too dangerous. We don't know where these vibrations are going yet."

"Well, I'm no good at climbing anyway," Milton Weeks said. Hope Delgado nodded in agreement. But Haseeb Khan looked split. After a moment, he made his choice and started scampering up the wall.

Armand, Milton, Phoenix, and Hope crowded into the middle of the circular floor.

The next trumpet blast was extremely loud — and much richer in texture. Milton, Phoenix and Hope cupped their ears.

"Hello. That one was different," Armand said.

The sides of the chamber quaked. In a massive torrent, books fell from the shelves. The tomes rained down in a flood of flapping pages.

Haseeb — still close to the ground, thankfully — jumped down and ran to the center of the floor. Kelvin, Kaden and Alexis, miraculously, had not yet fallen from their perches under this deluge. They hugged into the walls, beneath this waterfall of words. Then, Alexis realized that she could climb inside of a now-empty shelf — and did so. Ibrahim, Kelvin and Kaden, seeing this strategy, copied it.

Boom, boom, boom, boom …

The vibrational heartbeat accelerated — and then exploded as a very loud final trumpet sounded.

Rock ripped and the floor cracked along the gold lines radiating out from the center of the room. Black soot blasted out of the fissures.

And, strangely, quietly … pie-slices of stone floor began to float.

The tips in the middle rose first, causing Armand, Milton, Phoenix and Hope to each jump back onto their own floating floor section. And they all tilted at different angles.

Weightless stone! Armand thought. *Wait. Concordia knows about this?*

But clearly they did. The drum in this tomb had been an original Egyptian device for creating the same effect that his ring did.

It was all oddly peaceful at first, like some bizarre ballet.

Phoenix squealed in wonder and joy. "Whee! Balloon rocks!" she yelled.

A new, thrumming vibration propelled the rising triangular blocks now, driving them upwards, but also introducing a slight wobble. The stones nudged into each other as they went up.

Armand felt like he'd seen this before. And he'd heard that clacking sound ... this was dangerous.

Seen? Heard? How? Then, the answer came to him: *Eopeii had seen this, not him.*

Phoenix, thinking that all of this was no more dangerous than a skateboard, skipped along her triangular monolith, laughing.

"Phee! No!" Armand cried out, but it was too late.

Each step or movement transferred energy into the system, and because the stones were weightless, this energy had a *much* greater effect. The energy did not dissipate because there was no inertia: it just ricocheted around, which had the effect of turning the floating monoliths into billiards.

Thus with each motion, all of them were making the 'asteroid field' more and more dangerous. Already, the floor shards were knocking against each other with increased intensity.

And then, all hell broke loose.

The relative orderliness of the situation changed in an instant; stone shards tumbled and spun at all elevations now, clanking into each other, uttering rubble as they did so.

The shards gouged the library walls, causing them to bleed books, wood and sandstone chunks. Ibrahim Kreuger howled in surprise, and then was abruptly silent: a monolith reduced him to red mash within the space of seconds.

It was then that Armand understood:

This was the first Concordian Challenge. Every player increasingly made this room more and more dangerous with every passing movement. Kill the other players — or cooperate with them. But either way, understand that the longer the others live, the less chance you have of remaining alive yourself.

Comprehend this dynamic — and survive it.

But the Eopeii-within-Armand had already survived this

on several occasions. This was a 'Mississippi Log Roll', but ancient-Egypt style. When weightless stones got out of control, it had been necessary in Eopeii's time to know how to run across them — and know how to knock them with iron and bring them back down to heel on the earth.

Armand tentatively stepped onto the first floating cromlech. It instantly sank. Panic gripped him. The other end of the megalith rose with terrifying speed: a multi-ton mass suddenly heaving in his direction. *It was going to smash him within seconds ...*

His instinct said to run, to cower, to shield himself.

But the Eopeii-within urged him to *run directly at* the rising mass. It was the only way to even out the energy of his first step. Heart galloping with fear, he did so. Instantly, the far end of the stone see-sawed back down.

Had he not done this, the megalith would have swatted him into pulp by now.

Ah. *This* was how to do it. You needed to move *fast, fast, fast.*

Like a bug running across water.

Armand tried to let his inner Eopeii take over like he had during the fight with Eamon. He moved like a gymnast now, like a Cirque du Soleil artist, tumbling and running, performing a parkour of spinning stone.

His first stop was Milton Weeks, who had frozen in place, screaming.

"Move!" Armand yelled at him. "Start running! Or you'll die!"

But Milton just couldn't do it. His mind was swamped with panic. He whimpered as he watched spinning menhirs smash into monoliths, like great asteroids colliding. He just couldn't imagine stepping into that whirling death trap of his own free will.

"Get on!" Armand yelled. "I'm giving you a piggyback to

the top."

Milton looked at him in surprise.

"Hurry up!" Armand barked. This time, Milton climbed onto his back immediately. Armand bounced and stepped from one shard to the next, round and round, higher and higher. He dropped a stunned Milton off at the top, and then looked down.

He saw a tornado of stone. His own steps had greatly increased the melee below.

Huda Monroe also appeared suddenly at the top. She'd been tailgating Armand, copying his moves as best as she could — and it had worked. She tucked in safely behind Milton in the passageway.

Armand could use his ring, he realized, to sink the stones all at once. But this would kill other players — and reveal a secret advantage to Concordia that he did not wish them to know about.

Surprisingly, Kaden and Kelvin Veerspike had both learned from watching Armand. They'd seen how to do it — and were now making progress towards getting to the top also.

But Alexis wasn't moving, she was hiding in her bookshelf, screaming, frozen in fear.

Phoenix was attacking the situation. She wasn't very good at stepping skillfully, she was off balance and barely avoiding getting smashed to a pulp — but she *was* trying, and surviving.

Armand didn't see Hope or Haseeb anywhere. Quickly, he made a decision: he'd grab Phee next. He dropped from the ceiling and quickly made his way to the bottom of the cylinder, passing Kaden with a wave and a *"Hello!"* (which infuriated the red-haired banker) as he did so.

"Your Uber has arrived," Armand said to Phoenix. "Get on!"

"Thank fucking God!" Phoenix said, immediately obeying.

Armand went back up the stone tornado, which was getting more treacherous now. The shards smashed around more viciously, and the walls were largely carved up. This ascent was three times as hard as the one he'd just made.

He passed Kaden and Kelvin on the way up with a *"Hello!"* and then, exhausted and panting hard, he dropped Phoenix at the top exit.

He sank to his knees and looked down the spinning stone tornado. It was a blur now. Despite this — amazingly — in a few moments, Kaden and Kelvin also arrived successfully. They also crumpled to the floor in exhaustion.

"Alexis? Hope? Haseeb?" Armand asked.

Kaden and Phoenix both shook their heads.

"I think I saw Alexis killed," Phoenix said. "The rock smashed her bookcase. But Hope and Hasseed just vanished. I think they got buried under rubble. I'm guessing they're dead also."

"Damn. Half of us gone — and it's only the first Challenge," Milton said.

"You said this was going to be a long week," Armand replied. "You were right."

CHAPTER THIRTY-ONE

Psionics

THE COMPANY MOVED THROUGH THE hallway at the top of the Library. After a few turns, they arrived at the next Challenge chamber.

This one was much smaller, with boxier rooms and long hallways. Colorful Egyptian artwork covered every inch of the walls, pillars and ceiling. As his eyes adjusted, Armand could see that there were many antechambers and alcoves. *This was definitely part of the original tomb complex*, Armand thought. And unlike last time, there was no immediately obvious exit from this room that he could see.

Several large oil lamps burned from tripods, lighting their way.

The group eventually came to what appeared to be the main room.

There was some kind of apparatus along the far wall. Power cables ran along the floor and disappeared into a hole in the stone. A steel chair had been set into the floor. In front of this was a red desk with five large buttons in it. Each button held a different hieroglyph, printed in black — the "Ankh", the symbol of life; the "Eye of Horus", an eye with a curved tail and an eyebrow; the "Scarab Beetle", a symbol of rebirth; the "Sphinx", representing power; and the "Lotus Flower", symbolizing creation.

In front of this was a giant LCD screen. It showed the back of a playing card with an intricate many-colored mandala design. The number 20 showed in the lower right corner of the display.

And they were not alone.

This room featured chaperones — four large men, dressed in linen kilts, with leather bracers and grieves on their arms and legs. Each wore a leather-and-linen helmet that covered their faces, and were armed with short swords.

What were these guys? Guards? Or enforcers — to make us all sit in the chair?

But the guards offered no explanations.

Haseeb Khan, Hope Delgado and Alexis Shepherd suddenly appeared from the passageway. All three were bloody, but alive.

"Whoa! Where did you three come from?" Kelvin sneered in annoyance. Three adversaries he'd thought were dead were still in the game.

"We took cover in the bookshelves," Haseeb explained.

"Then the rocks — they just kind of stopped — and dropped," Alexis panted. "So we climbed the shelves the rest of the way up."

Kelvin shook his head. "Man. You got lucky. They must have thought you were already dead, or they wouldn't have turned it off."

"So what's going in here?" Hope Delgado asked.

"It's a psionics test," Kaden Veerspike said.

"You mean … like … ESP? We guess the card? That's it?" Armand said.

Kelvin and Kaden stood together, their orange Veerspike hair making them appear even more malevolent than usual

in the jumping shadows of firelight. *"That's it,* he says,"
Kelvin laughed. "No obviously, that's not 'it'. Look at the
chair."

Armand did so. There were two metal loops at the bottom
which were obviously meant to close around your ankles.
There were also two flippers that looked like they closed
around your midsection. Once you sat down, you were
pinned into place.

Then, he noticed a very thick black cable that ran to the
chair. That seemed like a lot of power just to make the loops
and flippers snap open and shut …

Oh. *It was an electric chair.*

Instantly, Armand understood. You either demonstrated
psychic ability — or you got fried by electric current.

This was the second Concordian Challenge: *Psionics.*

"I'll go first," Kaden said merrily and hopped into the
chair. The flippers and bracelets closed. The guards or
chaperones were completely motionless.

A countdown clock appeared. It showed three minutes
and thirty seconds — and immediately started counting
down. *Ah. The 20 must be the number of cards left.* Armand
calculated in his head: *so you had ten seconds per card, roughly.*

Kaden smashed the Ankh button — the card on the screen
flipped over: correct! There were now 19 cards left. Now, the
Scarab — correct again!

And now came the Eye, followed by the Ankh — right on
both again.

That was four out four, 100% right out of the gate. How
was he doing this?

What was it that Urbi had said?

*Because Concordians are plugged into Molian contracts and
other things that make them psychically 'hot', Synchronicity
Engines work much better for them than for anyone else …*

And again, Tabias Kronecker, during his cautionary talk

on Wiggin the Wicked:

The more you work with karmic instruments, like Molian tokens or contracts, the stronger the effects of karma will become on you — for good or ill.

With a sickening feeling, Armand realized he could not possibly pass this Challenge.

Concordians were all psychically 'hot' due to the nature of their affiliation with the organization. Therefore, this was an easy test for any of them to pass, if they could control their fear.

But Armand was not Concordian. He had never even been under a Molian contract before today — and he doubted that was going to be enough. The phrase *The more you work with* sounded like one had to be in constant contact with Concordian devices for a long period of time.

Or be a full member of Concordia.

This Challenge was specifically meant to weed out anyone who did not belong. Armand cursed Ghent — he had known that Armand could not *possibly* live through this!

That's why he offered me full membership, Armand thought. *He knew I'd refuse. And now, if I die in this Challenge, it's entirely on me.*

Twenty cards. Five possibilities. He would get four right by chance alone. But what was a passing score? Six? Seven? Surely seven would be enough to demonstrate a better-than-chance ability.

Scarab, Ankh, Lotus, Eye, Sphinx. That spells SALES, Armand thought uselessly.

Kaden guessed Eye, got a Lotus — his first wrong answer. His face bunched up into a grimace of pain: the chair had given him a little jolt as punishment.

Then, he was back on his game — Sphinx, right! Then, Sphinx again — also right! Eye? No — Ankh — and a second shock. Judging from Kaden's expression, this jolt was stronger.

Ah. So it escalated as you got them wrong, finally killing you if you missed too many …

In the end Kaden got twelve out of twenty correct. The chair released him. Kelvin high-fived him and then sat in the chair himself.

Twelve right? Good God.

Armand approached the chaperones. "Hey. Um — what is the passing score here?" He was disgusted by how nervous he sounded. But the guards did not answer. They remained like stone, unreachable and unmoving. He asked again: same response. Armand returned to the small crowd of players watching the psionics challenge.

But as worried as Armand was, Milton Weeks was infinitely *more* worried. He was having a panic attack. He had his hand on his chest as he strove to control a yammering heart.

"You're Concordian," Armand said, and explained his theory to him "You'll be fine. I'm the one who has to worry here."

"Geebus! You don't know — I suck at this sort of thing though. I suck, I suck, I suck!"

"Okay, calm down," Armand said. "You don't suck."

But Milton would not be consoled. Neon Phoenix looked worried also, but not nearly so much as Milton. When Armand asked her how she thought she'd do, she said she wasn't sure. He explained his theory to her, and she nodded and agreed that it made sense. "I don't know what I'm going to do," Armand said.

He sized up the guards. He'd beaten ten men during the Synchronicity Engine attack — he could take a measly four, right? But he wasn't sure. These guys were large — and in extremely good shape. The ten men had been randoms. But these guys looked like Soldier of Fortune types, ex-military.

Highly skilled. Concordia would have hired the best of the best for the Tomb Challenges.

Armand realized he could use his ring. Make them all float around like balloons, see if they could fight then. But the ring was a thing he could use exactly once — and then Concordia would know about it forever. It didn't feel like the time to spend that chance just yet.

"You know, it's not enough to be Concordian," Phoenix said in his ear. "To pass this test. You also have to be able to keep your shit together. Mentally, I mean."

"So it's an internal bravery test also," Armand whispered back.

"Yes."

"Hmm," Armand mused. "So you have to be able to calm your mind under threat of immediate death … otherwise, your natural Concordian psionic talent won't manifest?"

"Bingo."

"Shit. Milton is effed."

"Yes, Milton is indeed effed. But honestly, I'm worried for myself also. I'm the queen of insanity. I'm terrified all the time, with constant anxiety and massive depression — which, usually, I make work for me — you know, I channel it, with my music. But my brain is pretty much a big seething mass of fear, all the time. So if this is a brain test …"

Kelvin was done. Score: fourteen out of twenty.

"Look at those smug Veerspike assholes," Phoenix hissed. "Fucking straight A's. For what? For being born with red hair."

Kaden must have overheard or guessed what she said. He pointed at her, then the chair, then shook violently like he was being electrocuted.

Then, an uncomfortable silence descended. Nobody was going next.

One of the four chaperones sprang into motion. He

grabbed Huda Monroe — who was screaming for mercy now — and forcibly sat her in the chair.

Crying loudly, she struggled to guess her cards. Already, it wasn't going well. Lotus — no, Eye. Shock! Fresh burst of sobs. Lotus, no Sphinx. Bigger shock. Worse sobs.

Ankh — yes Ankh. Massive relief. Scarab — no, Sphinx. Shock and hysterical sobs now.

Three wrong, one right.

That turned into nine wrong, two right very quickly.

Huda was panicking.

Armand counted on his fingers. She had to get five more right, probably, in order to pass. Maybe even just four. Okay, this was still do-able. She had eight to go, so she could afford to get three wrong and —

Ankh — no, Scarab. Huda Monroe's shrieking was cut short by a large sustained shock. She went limp in the chair, dead.

Ten? This meant that they all had to get at least ten of the twenty right in order to live.

Impossible! He couldn't do that!

The Veerspikes laughed at his worried face. They pointed two fingers at their eyes, and then at him. *We're watching you ...*

The guards cleared Huda's body. When nobody volunteered again, one of them grabbed Milton and locked him — screaming — into place.

The clock started.

Milton did nothing. He froze in complete panic, howling. "I'm going to die, I'm going to die, I'm going to die ..."

Armand sprang forward to Milton's side. "Milton!" He snuck a look at the guard: they weren't stopping him: this was apparently okay. "Milton, just guess. Best as you can. Okay? Just guess."

"No, it won't work," Milton screamed in his face.

"But you have to try! What are going to do, just sit there until your time runs out?"

"Yes!"

That stunned Armand. "Yes? What do you mean *yes*? That's dumb, Milton! You might get lucky just through chance alone! You might as well try!"

But Milton Weeks was wracked with sobbing. He could barely control his speech. "I've — taken — this — kind — of — test — before!"

"So?"

"So — I — always — get — every — one — wrong. Always! So — by — not — trying — I — stay — alive — a little — longer!"

"Wait, what?"

They were down to three minutes now. Nine seconds per guess.

"Milton. Are you sure? It's *every one, always*?"

"Yes! — I've — never — even — ever — gotten — one — right!"

Armand got closer so that he could shout in his face. "Milton! Listen to me carefully. I know how to get you out of that chair alive."

"You — do?"

"Yes! Listen! *There's no way you could get every one wrong, unless you were psychic!* Chance alone would get you 20% correct. You couldn't *help* but get that many right, worst case. *But 0% correct? Every single time?* That actually takes *incredible* psychic power! You're doing it — but you don't even realize it!"

Milton Weeks nodded and his sobbing slowed. Armand was getting through to him.

"Listen. Here's what we're going to do," Armand said. "You tell me what you think the first one is, right now. Go!"

"Lotus!"

"Okay, so it's not Lotus," Armand said. "Next guess!"

"What?" Milton was confused.

"I mean Lotus is eliminated, so of the four left, which one is it? Fast, Milton, fast!"

"Um, Ankh!"

"Okay, not Ankh. Next?"

"Eye!"

"Yes, what next?"

"Scarab!"

"Great! *Press Sphinx!*"

Correct!

Milton burst out a short laugh. He couldn't believe it.

"Okay, nineteen more to go," Armand shouted. "Don't get happy! Stay sad and scared. Remember, you're probably fucked and you're probably going to die in a few minutes."

A fresh bloom of terror erupted in Milton's heart. Armand nodded in satisfaction.

Armand and Milton continued this process until Milton reached ten correct with only two wrong. No one was more stunned than he when the ankle bracelets popped open. He shuddered with tears of pure relief.

Alexis Shepherd volunteered to go next. Meanwhile, Hope Delgado sat cross legged, meditating, calming herself, while Haseeb Khan simply stood. He chatted with Phoenix now.

"What if the number you need to get right changes the later you go?" Haseeb said worriedly. "You know, if you're near the end, maybe you have to get fifteen right instead of ten? What if it rewards going early?"

"No. We would have seen that by now," Phoenix said. "Besides. Concordians are assholes, but we stick to the rules. We don't like unfair things. Moving the goalpost for people near the end would be dickishly unfair. Bad karma. No. We all have an equal shot in the Challenges."

Haseeb nodded. "I see. Yes. I think you are correct."

Meanwhile, Armand decided how he was going to make his play. He huddled up with Phoenix, Milton and Haseeb.

"Okay Milton. I need your help now," Armand said. "I'm not psychic — not even a little, not even subconsciously like you are. So I am definitely dead unless you say yes, right now. Milton. Will you help me?"

It took Milton a second to process this. He was about to ask to be paid when Phoenix pushed him. "Say *yes*, dickboy." Milton still hesitated, debating internally. "Armand just saved your ass. And you'll probably need him to save your ass later."

"Yes!' Milton said quickly. "Of course I was going to say yes. Duh."

"Okay. Thank you," said Armand. "Now Milton, I'll need you to guess the cards for me. We do it the exact same way we did it for you. You tell me your guesses, eliminating one at a time, until there's only one left — and that will be my real guess. Okay?"

"So you want me to tell you the answers?" Milton said. "Don't *you* have to do it? Isn't that … cheating? Are they going to allow that?" Milton nodded to the four guards.

"I don't know," Armand said.

"What if I get in trouble?"

"Well, then, you'll have to stop. And I'll have to make my guesses on my own and then I'll probably be dead. At least we will have tried. But if this works, if the guards let us do it, you will then help Phoenix and Haseeb in the same way, ya?" Armand caught himself. "Goddammit, I'm so nervous, I'm talking like my stupid brothers now."

"Yes — yes," Milton said.

"And in return, we'll have *your* back on whatever they throw at us next," Armand said. "Agreed? Phoenix? Haseeb?"

"Agreed," said Haseeb.

"Yes. Agreed," said Phoenix.

"I think they'll let us do it," Armand said. "Alliances seem to be allowed down here. Not encouraged, but allowed. Which makes sense: Concordia itself is an alliance. Maybe of people who all hate each other. But the concept of alliance *is* a Concordian value."

Alexis Shepherd finished successfully: sixteen correct, the best score yet.

Armand and Hope Delgado both volunteered at the same time. One of the guards pointed to Armand — he would be next.

As he sat in the chair, and the ankle bracelets and flippers locked him into place, Armand felt a panic attack coming on. He felt intensely claustrophobic, and his heart jackhammered. He'd rather be fighting with his fists and have a very small chance of winning than be in a position where he was certain to lose and die unless he relied on help. *So powerless.*

Nevertheless.

He had no choice.

The clock started.

"Milton! Go!"

"Ahh ... Ankh!"

"Okay, so not Ankh. Next guess."

"Flower thing ... uhh, Lotus!"

Armand craned his neck to look at the guards. None of them were moving. They were allowing this.

"Next!"

"Sphinx!"

"And then?"

"Eye!"

"That leaves Scarab." Armand punched the Scarab button. *Wrong!* Immediately, he felt a jolt of power map his veins.

Wrong? "What the fuck, Milton?"

"I'm sorry! Okay, okay, okay."

"Concentrate. Again! Go!"

"Flower — fuck! I mean Lotus. Lotus!"

"Next!"

"Sphinx!"

"Go!"

"Lotus!"

"You *said* Lotus already!"

"Oh right … uh, Eye!"

"Next!"

"Scarab!"

Armand punched the Ankh button. Wrong! Again, he felt a deep high voltage surge juicing through his muscles. This time, it felt a *lot* more powerful. This time, his teeth chattered — and his vision was spotted with darkness even after it ended.

He glared at Milton.

The Veerspikes erupted into laughter and jeered.

This wasn't going to work, Armand realized. And now he was locked into place — attacking the guards physically was no longer an option.

Four more times, he and Milton did their routine, and four more times, he was wrong. Six down. None right, no points on the board. He could only afford four more wrong guesses. And the electric jolts felt like they were murdering him each time anew now — his vision was complete mud in between wrong answers.

Again, Milton tried to help. This time, the correct answer he indicated was Lotus — but when Armand went to push the Lotus button, his vision was so bad that he mistook the Ankh for Lotus and pushed that instead.

Wrong! Electricity flowed like heavy bees buzzing through his soul.

"Okay. That's it," Phoenix said. Without warning, she kicked Milton Weeks squarely in the balls. He doubled over with a squeal. "*Now*, you little shit. Now you're going to get yourself good and scared again so your stupid head starts working properly." She cracked him across the cheek with her fist. She checked the guards: they weren't moving. Good! So this was allowed also, it seemed.   She bent in close. "Here's the deal. If Armand dies, *you* die. I'll kill you myself. So get the fuck up and start spitting out the *right* answers."

Milton rose, coughing. "Okay. Okay. Armand. Try Ankh."

"Next!" Armand gasped out. His voice was going.

"No, no, no. I mean, actually try Ankh. I think that's it."

Armand looked at him dubiously. But then, he reached out and pressed Ankh.

Correct! His stomach bunched up, expecting a shock anyway, but none came.

"Sphinx," Milton said.

Sphinx, Armand mouthed. He pushed the button. *Correct!*

"Ankh again."

Correct!

"Sphinx again."

Correct!

"Scarab!"

Correct!

"Hold on," Kaden Veerspike yelled. "This is bullshit. This is cheating!"

"Yeah!" agreed Kelvin. He approached the guards. "You're not going to let them do this, right?"

The guards looked at each other. Then, one started moving. But another said, "Hold! This is permitted."

"Eye!"

Correct!

"Eye again!"

Correct!

"Okay then," Kaden said. "Fine. Rules are, 'anything goes', huh? So that means *this* is also okay." Kaden jumped on Milton, punching him repeatedly in the gut.

Armand tried to crane his neck and see what was happening, but he couldn't quite twist around enough.

The clock was ticking down. He had thirty seconds left. He needed three good guesses to live.

C'mon!

Phoenix was trying to intervene, but both of the Veerspikes were too much for her. Hope Delgado watched all of this with a smile of amusement from her lotus position, and did nothing to help.

"Guys! Where are you!" Armand screamed. "What's going on?"

Twenty seconds.

Haseeb hesitated — and then jumped in himself. Together he and Phoenix pulled the Veerspike brothers away from Milton and kept them busy for the next several vital seconds.

"Milton!" Armand howled.

"Sphinx," Milton coughed out.

Wrong! He was force-fed a blast of electricity like raw lightning coming off the surface of the sun. Armand staggered.

"Sorry! Ankh!"

Ten seconds. Armand could barely move his arm. He slapped at Ankh.

Correct!

"Beetle! I mean Scarab! Scarab!"

Another dizzying lurch of his hand.

Correct!

Two seconds left ...

"Sphinx!"

With all his remaining energy, Armand stumbled forward and punched Sphinx.

Correct!

The clock stopped with a single second remaining. The bracelets and flippers popped open, and Armand slumped to the floor.

Milton helped Armand to stand and move off to the side while Hope Delgado took his place. With Armand freed of his restraints, the Veerspikes immediately backed off of Haseeb and Phoenix. Even though he was incapacitated, they knew he was physically formidable from the library.

They'd gambled — and lost. They knew it. Best to wait for another opportunity.

A few minutes later, and Armand had mostly recovered. Hope Delgado ended her trial with thirteen correct.

Haseeb went next. Armand rose and wordlessly placed himself between the Veerspikes and Milton, who stood behind Haseeb's chair. Armand dropped to a cross-legged seat on the floor — meanwhile the Veerspikes did nothing but whisper to each other: they seemed to be speculating on what the next Challenge might be — and strategizing on how best to tackle it.

Haseeb got sixteen correct. Being Concordian, Haseeb had his own abilities to bring to the table but he combined guesses with Milton and got a higher score than he could have alone.

Last came Phoenix. With Milton's help she was able to get twenty out of twenty: a perfect score.

CHAPTER THIRTY-TWO

The Sand Beast

THE CHAPERONES WORDLESSLY TURNED TO a steel door set into one of the walls. They waved a keycard and it opened with a hiss of air.

The next Challenge chamber was cylindrical, very much like the Library, but bigger, wider. At the far end were two stone doors that were shut tight. In front of these, set into the floor was a large iron seal. It looked almost like a vast electric griddle.

The steel door closed behind them.

Armand, Hope, Milton, Phoenix, Kaden, Kelvin, Alexis and Haseeb were now alone.

Circular portals in the wall opened. Fine white sand began to sputter out and stream into the chamber. It started innocently enough. There wasn't an enormous amount of it. It didn't look dangerous at all.

But then the sand began to hiss loudly and flow towards the center of the circular iron seal set into the floor. It started *pooling* there, collecting there, the tiny crystals dancing and vibrating across the metal.

Armand realized then that the sand *should* have made

little piles under where it was falling out of the wall. But it wasn't doing that. Instead, it was bunching like magnetic dust, amalgamating, apparently, in defiance of the laws of physics.

The sand flowed faster now from the portals, gushing in a torrent, and the pooling pile grew taller, like a small mountain forming.

"Dear God, what now?" Neon Phoenix said. "What is that?"

The sand began twisting and writhing. It enlarged itself. Finally, when it was six or seven stories tall, a gyre made of several tons of sand rotated in front of them. It produced little snaps of blue lightning that clicked along the stone walls as it did so. Armand caught glimpses of searing flame in the core.

It was a pillar of sand and fire.

The group gasped in astonishment. The phenomenon towered over them and roared like a tornado. Armand felt his cheeks buffeted with waves of tremendous heat.

Then, behind the gyre, two massive doors swung open.

Ah. So this thing is a sentry. And we're supposed to get past it.

"What do we do?" Phoenix yelled.

Armand picked up a rock and threw it at the doorway. Immediately, the gyre-thing howled. It extended a sand arm to catch the rock — and crushed it to powder.

"Geebus. The Sand Beast didn't like that at all," Milton quipped.

"Spread out!" Kaden Veerspike snapped. Instinctively realizing he was right, and despite hating him, they all obeyed.

Was this thing alive?

Did it reason? Did it have agency? Did it actually get angry? Or was it just a reflex? Mindless? And what was holding the sand together? Armand looked around to see if he could locate something vibrational, some Egyptian tech like his ring or the library room, but didn't see anything that obviously matched what he understood.

It must be that iron circle beneath it, Armand decided. *That's what's powering it.*

Quite clearly, the 'head' of the Sand Beast reacted when they had moved at Kaden's command, Armand noted. It acted like it could see them.

Without warning, Alexis Shepherd violently shoved Neon Phoenix to the ground in front of the hissing gyre. "Hey! You fucking bitch!" Phoenix screeched.

The Sand Beast reacted immediately, coiling backwards and then whipping forward with wicked speed to smash Phoenix where she lay. But she rolled out of the way in the nick of time. The pillar left a sizable crater where she had just been.

Meanwhile, Armand saw blur of blonde out of the corner of his eye. Alexis was trying to sprint around the Sand Beast while it was distracted by Phoenix.

As Phoenix rose and retreated, the Sand Beast made a second attempt to smite her. Again, she dodged, but just barely.

But Alexis Shepherd's ploy had worked. She vanished neatly behind the Sand Beast and slipped through the open doors. The Veerspikes snarled jealously. Fast, decisive action, combined with betrayal of peers — Concordian values had been rewarded, and the Veerspikes were annoyed they didn't think of it first.

"Okay — everyone back up!" Armand shouted. He watched Kaden and Kelvin nervously. "Don't provoke it! Let's think about this for a sec!"

The Sand Beast had to be a vibrational construct of some sort, Armand reasoned. *Something* was holding the sand together. And this Tomb — the Challenges — everything here was one part ancient Egyptian, one part modern technology. The Concordians had fused the two to create all of the dangers they were facing.

Concordia probably doesn't understand what the Sand Beast is, or how it works, Armand mused. *They probably just found it here.* Like the drum in the Library. The *Egyptians* made it, not them. Quinty had said that this Tomb had been discovered by Concordia in 1830. *Quite unlike anything ever excavated.*

Immediately, that theory felt correct to him.

Yes. This was early Egyptian tech — tech that had been later lost. *Like his ring.*

Like Sophia? Like word-beings? Like living information?

The Concordians clearly admired Egypt. They aspired to it. It was a legacy they sought to imitate, much as the Romans once sought to imitate the Greeks.

Kaden and Kelvin were inching along opposite walls, trying to flank the pillar of sand and fire from both sides now. The Sand Beast's head swiveled back and forth, unsure of which to crush first.

Armand marveled — and had to admit some admiration. The Veerspike brothers were both in the Challenges by choice. They had volunteered, trying to improve their fortunes within Concordia. They stood to gain massively as a family both in wealth and power — if they could just survive this. But *only one* of them had to live for the Veerspike family to win, not both. This gambit showed that they had made a pact to be as aggressive as possible — and to split risk evenly and quickly for a potential Veerspike win. Absolutely ruthless.

One of them was going to die, right now.

They both knew this.

But the Sand Beast surprised them. Roaring, it forked into a Y. Two twisting, fiery, slithering sand tentacles reached out and curled around each brother. They both howled — the touch of the fiery sand burnt their skin — and Armand could see their red-haired heads violently wrenching around, trying to get free.

The terrible arms smashed the Veerspikes against the wall. Panic gripped their eyes and whimpering howls escaped their lips.

Again: wham! And again: wham!

Dear God, Armand thought. They weren't going to live much longer.

He thought of the old Veerspike with red and gray hair, who had yelled at Kelvin and Kaden. *And you'd better not cock it up!* These kids were victims. Probably just the latest in a long line of victims.

Armand couldn't help himself. Forgetting that they were Concordian and Veerspikes at that, and forgetting that he wanted to keep it secret, he raised his black diamond ring and fired a warbling cone of vibration right into the center of the Sand Beast.

It tore a hole. You could see straight through the belly now.

Squealing, the Sand Beast dropped the Veerspikes and roared with new-found rage. It focused completely upon Armand now.

"Run!" Armand yelled to the others. "Run around it — while it comes after me. Go, go, go!"

The Sand Beast lashed out at Armand with an intensity of fury beyond anything it had yet shown. Armand expertly dodged: his Eopeii-within fully awakened and governing his expert-acrobatic moves.

In between tumbles and tentacle-smashes, Armand tried to focus his ring at the Sand Beast's head. He succeeded at hitting it, but that simply caused the top end of the pillar to splay — it didn't do anything to blunt the Sand Beast's ability to think or react.

His ring wasn't going to solve this situation, he realized. It was enough to annoy the Sand Beast, but not to injure or kill it.

Armand looked around to take count: Neon Phoenix seemed to have made it safely through the doors. Milton Weeks, Hope Delgado and Haseeb Khan were still in the chamber with him, frozen in terror. Kaden and Kelvin Veerspike had risen, stunned, but were already now slowly loping their way behind the distracted Sand Beast: they knew an opportunity when they saw it.

The Sand Beast seemed to be making the same assessment. It split itself once again into a sand-hydra, this time with *four* tentacles.

It viciously grabbed Milton Weeks and Haseeb Khan. Hope Delgado was successfully dodging at the moment, but Armand could see plainly that it was just a matter of time before it caught her also.

The Sand Beast abruptly and savagely threw Haseeb against the far wall. His skull split instantly with a loud crack.

Seeing this, Milton Weeks screeched: "Armand! Help! You owe me!"

Yes, Armand thought. I do owe you. *Okay. Okay. Okay.*

Following some instinct he didn't fully comprehend, Armand stopped dodging. Instead, he sprinted directly at the Sand Beast — and dove head first into the twisting gyre.

Instantly, he was aloft, twisting and turning within it. His mouth filled with sand — it inhabited him fully, pouring into his nose and ears as well. But Armand surrendered to it, he didn't resist the intrusion. He thought fire would be burning him by now, but it wasn't. He spun as he rose to the top of the pillar and felt the electric bangs of lightning it periodically discharged deep in his teeth.

The Sand Beast was not conscious, Armand suddenly

knew. Rather, it was like Sophia. It required sentient attention to render itself.

The Guardian of the Tomb — what the Sand Beast called itself — was animated by the minds of the very thieves looking to plunder her treasures. *Clever.* She came to life only when someone entered this chamber.

The next room behind the Guardian of the Tomb, through the doors which Alexis Shepherd — and now the Veerspike brothers had successfully fled — had been the original burial chamber, piled high with treasures. These had long been removed by Concordia. But the Guardian had remained. It was part of the tomb, as much as the very walls were. And it amused Concordia to use it as a Challenge — perhaps in a continuous re-enactment of what Concordians in 1830 had faced when they'd first entered the tomb.

And now Armand found that the Sand Beast was able to examine *him* as well. Armand could feel it thumbing through his memories. He watched, powerless to stop, as key scenes from his life appeared, seemingly projected against the sand and fire, in blurry visions of drab dark blue and white.

Was it Judging him? Like Anubis, weighing the heart?

But then, like the blow of a fist, he saw himself fighting Eamon. This had been the first occasion that he had unconsciously used the skills of Eopeii.

The Sand Beast instantly recoiled as though it had made a grave error. *Eopeii?* it seemed to say. It then fished out another memory — this time, one of Armand fighting off the Synchronicity Engine attacks, again, using Eopeii's skills.

That did it. The entire demeanor of the Sand Beast changed. Solemnly, it let Armand slip down through its trunk and withdrew every particle of sand from his mouth, ears and nose. Armand was deposited in the floor. The Sand Beast withdrew and became quiet, undulating softly, but posing no threat.

Coughing, Armand rose. Milton helped him to his feet. "Geebus! What did you say to it?"

"It thinks I'm someone else," Armand replied.

Once Armand stood, the pillar of flame and sand bowed to him.

"What, like a Pharaoh?" Hope Delgado said.

"More like a friend," Armand said. "Here. Everyone through the doorway. It won't hurt you now."

"What about you?" Milton Weeks said.

"I'll be right behind you … I just want to make sure it's focused on me while you two go through. Go, go, go, go!"

Milton immediately sprinted past the Sand Beast, fully trusting Armand. But Hope Delgado was skeptical. She watched dubiously as Milton vanished through the doors. But once he'd proven that the Sand Beast had indeed been tamed, she grew bolder. She darted around the Beast and vanished.

CHAPTER THIRTY-THREE

Battle Thrones

ARMAND WAS THE LAST ONE through the doorway and into the chamber beyond where the last Challenge awaited — and he stepped into something which felt like utter chaos.

A melee of some sort was already underway.

The body of Alexis Shepherd lay broken on the floor. Blood matted her coifed blonde hair and bones poke out of her leg at unnatural angles.

"Armand! Look out!" Neon Phoenix shouted. Her voice came from above.

This chamber was exceedingly large and cavernous. He could see devices of some sort flying around soundlessly overhead, dipping into the darkness where the light failed near the far away ceiling.

But he could see Phoenix now close by — oddly *above* him. She was sitting in a very large stone chair that was hovering.

He saw now that the Veerspikes were in similar chairs — and that they were swooping down, firing at him with bubbles of warbling air — clearly vibrational weapons — which split stone into chunks wherever they hit.

The Veerspikes had been murdering people as they came through the door.

After he had just saved them!

Rage gripped Armand. Ghent's words haunted his mind: *It will be every Player for themselves once those doors open. The true, brutal, savage nature of humanity will be on full display.*

There were still three chairs left on the ground at the far end of the room. Hope Delgado had just sat down in one now. Within seconds, she was airborne. Armand ran towards the remaining two while Phoenix — and Milton — attacked the Veerspikes and covered for him.

It took Armand a few moments as he had to dodge incoming shots. But when arrived, one of the chairs burst into rock shards. He caught a glimpse of Hope Delgado as she passed above, jeering at him.

His fury increased. *He had just saved Hope from the Sand Beast mere moments ago!*

Before Hope could return for another pass, Armand sat in the one remaining chair. He saw now that it was covered in hieroglyphs — one of which read 'Battle Throne'. Overlaid on top of the stone were modern cables and wide buttons on each arm. He pressed one of them — causing the Battle Throne to fire a blob of vibration.

Got it. That's how you shoot. But how do you make it fly? Fly, dammit!

The Battle Throne lurched forward and up. *Oh.* You thought about where you wanted to go and the Throne obeyed. But when he abruptly stopped, he noticed that he nearly was tossed from the chair — it had no safety belt. *Ah.* He had to remain in constant motion, that would keep him pinned in place. *Got it.*

Another blast from Hope Delgado almost took him out as he rose and tore into the melee. He fired back and missed.

The Veerspikes were double-teaming Phoenix now,

coming at her from opposite sides, a pincer move. But she had raised some kind of a vibrational shield bubble around herself and their shots had no effect.

Milton swooped in on Kaden Veerspike and fired. Kaden did not have a shield, it seemed. Milton scored a hit, damaging Kaden's chair. It wobbled as it flew now, but the device was only injured. Enraged, Kaden turned to engage Milton.

Armand noticed that Phoenix didn't seem able to fire while she had the shimmering air of a shield around her — she could only flee. *How do I raise my shield? There were no more buttons …? Was that mind-operated as well?* He pictured the shimmering air around his Battle Throne — and it appeared, just in time, as Kelvin hit him with a blast.

But Armand also felt himself fall — with his shield operational, his anti-gravity fell apart. And he was high up now, near the darkened ceiling. A fall would kill him. And because his chair was falling, in a panic, he realized that he was no longer touching the chair — and with that link broken, the shield vanished and both he and the Battle Throne plummeted in a spin.

Kelvin crowed — he assumed he had downed Armand.

Armand thrashed wildly, trying to touch the Throne with something, anything, any part of his body. He stretched and strained with everything he had —

— And just before he slammed into the ground, he managed to get one finger on the back of chair, and screamed inside his head, *Fly!*

The Battle Throne leapt to life and caught him, cupping his body awkwardly. Quickly he adjusted himself, leaving the shield down.

Dammit! How was Phoenix flying *and* keeping her shield up? He saw now that Hope Delgado was able to do both at once also. Vaguely, he recalled reading somewhere that women were able to mentally multi-task better than men. Was that it? If so, that meant that Hope and Phoenix would have a huge advantage in this Challenge.

He had hoped his inner Eopeii would know something about how to operate a Battle Throne, but no latent knowledge bubbled up. He was on his own.

Nevertheless.

He screamed skyward, vibrational cannons blazing at Hope Delgado, who was now chasing Milton, who, like him, couldn't keep the shield running while flying.

Hope's shield warbled under the strain. Armand thought he might be able to break through with enough of a barrage, so kept up the onslaught relentlessly.

Hope's shield was now clearly damaged. Another few hits and it might buckle — so, realizing this, with a snarl, she turned and attacked Armand.

Armand quickly fled along the far wall. He noticed an opening — now that he was close enough to see it — a tunnel of some kind. He ducked inside at full speed, praying he wouldn't hit a wall.

The passageway was treacherous — it twisted and turned left and right, up and down — before long, Armand had no idea what direction he was going or how he would get back to the other Players. All of his energy was focused on flying fast while not slamming into a turn. It must have had the same effect on Hope, as she wasn't firing.

Good! So long as he kept Hope occupied, that freed up Phoenix to use her unnatural advantage over the Veerspikes. With any luck she'd finish them both off before he returned.

Without warning, Armand popped out into another chamber. But he couldn't see much, as it was filled with a dense smoky green fog. Visibility was near zero. But it sounded large like the last chamber. Immediately, he coughed (and heard a massive echo), but found that if he fought down his gag reflex, he could breathe more or less fine.

He raised his elevation while keeping his guns pointed at where he thought the tunnel entry point was. Hope would be emerging any moment now — though he had no idea how he would see her.

Several long moments passed.

"Armaaaaaand," he heard her call. She seemed far away. "I know you're in here."

Armand said nothing. Instead, he dropped slowly in elevation.

"You boys. You can't keep even your shields up!" She laughed. "Why don't you let me help you with that? We could team up, you and me. Take out Phoenix together. Her music is shit anyway. Nobody would miss her."

She was closer now. Armand kept quiet, watching for any clue about where she was. But all he saw were banks of rolling smoke. Still, every now and then, there were gaps, he noticed. Every minute or so he'd encounter a small gulf, an open area of clear air, like a bubble.

He might get lucky and spot her before she spotted him. The fog reduced her advantage significantly.

But what were the odds that she would spot him first? She might swoop in behind him as they hit an open air pocket and boom, with no shield, he was dead. *Too risky.*

He sank deeper towards the floor.

"Oh, c'mon Armand," she taunted. "We both know I can't trust the Veerspikes. I can't team up with them to take on Phee. But you! I could trust you. We could take her together. Alone, I have a fifty-fifty shot. But with you helping? Guaranteed kill."

"What about Milton?" Armand yelled back.

Armand couldn't see this, but somewhere in the smoke, Hope smiled. *He'd taken the bait! He was near the floor!* She tilted her chair downwards towards his voice and sped up.

"Milton, Milton. He's a little shit and you know it."

"Maybe. But I owe him from the Psionics Challenge."

"Owe him? You got him out of the Sand Beast! You're paid up! And besides, I want the whole pot to myself — you can't share in it because you're not Concordian. So the deal is, we grease everyone else. Then, you and me emerge through those doors as the only two winners of the Challenges. I keep the full pot, you get your brothers. We're both happy!"

"No," Armand said. "Milton lives."

"Not acceptable!" Hope Delgado raged. "Look, Armand! You don't have a choice!"

Armand waited a moment and then said: "Okay. You're right. What do you propose?"

"That's a good boy! Keep talking and I'll find you — then we'll leave here together."

"Alright. I'm here. Keep coming."

Hope Delgado licked her lips. This moron could never be Concordian. He was far too naive. So distasteful and unmanly! And stupid. Why, she'd — *there he is!*

Near the floor, the fog suddenly cleared. He was right below her now, still in his Battle Throne, but parked on the ground. But that was weird — he was on his *back*, like a stuck turtle, showing her his exposed belly.

What the fuck? Whatever.

Idiot!

She fired.

Her shots were easily absorbed by his shield. Since he was not burdened with having to fly, he was easily able to keep his vibrational cocoon at full power.

She gaped, and, in surprise, stopped firing. This gave Armand the opening he was counting on — he dropped his shield and absolutely pummeled her with shimmering ordnance.

Hope Delgado's shield fizzled almost instantly. Her chair was reduced to rubble, and she was torn to ribbons.

Armand hit the gas on his Battle Throne and sped to avoid the falling wreckage. After a few moments, he located the tunnel and gunned it back to the main chamber.

He emerged to find Kaden Veerspike physically wrestling with Neon Phoenix in her Battle Throne. He punched her as they struggled for control of her chair. She slugged him in the balls and belly — while her Throne, taking conflicting mental orders from both of them now, danced drunkenly through the air.

"Armand! Look out!" Milton howled. He was on the ground, on foot. He had apparently been shot down.

Too late, Armand realized that his chair had been hit. His head snapped skyward: Kelvin Veerspike was hovering above the tunnel, waiting to murder whoever emerged as the victor from the melee inside.

Armand check his own Throne: it was flying just fine, yes. *But his weapons!* He pushed the buttons frantically: nothing happened. He couldn't shoot anymore.

He should have raised his shields right then, but he didn't think of it in his panicked surprise. Another volley of vibrational ordnance rained down on him. His chair crackled with damage. He tried to envelop himself in the protective shimmering cocoon, but nothing happened.

With a start, he realized that his ability to fly had been affected as well. The chair was still airborne, but it was sputtering. It felt like whatever kept it aloft was draining away fast.

Alright. Can't shield, shoot or fly. That left only one thing.

Kelvin Veerspike howled with glee. He swooped down like a predator eagle to finish him off.

But Armand side-stepped him and turned the tables. As soon as Kelvin overshot, Armand revved up his Battle

Throne with everything he had, and then he drove it downwards straight at Kelvin, using it now like a blunt battering ram of multi-ton stone.

Kelvin couldn't believe it. His mind couldn't process that Armand was still somehow in the fight, as badly damaged as he was.

A savage roar tore from Armand's throat as his Battle Throne slammed into Kelvin's. Armand jumped as they crashed and he physically ripped Kelvin out of his chair. Together, their bodies and Battle Thrones careened into the ground, tumbling.

Armand's badly damaged Throne smashed itself apart on impact. Kelvin's rolled and came to a stop.

Armand let loose on Kelvin, beating him mercilessly with his fists. He lost himself in anger.

Somewhere, he thought he could hear the ghost of Varinder Rahan laughing, mocking him, for becoming more Concordian with every passing minute.

"Armand!" Milton yelled in his ear. "Armand. Enough. He's out of it."

Armand looked down saw that this was true: Kelvin was unconscious and bloody. Armand was actually surprised by this.

"We have to help Phoenix," Milton said.

"Phoenix," Armand panted. "Right. Okay. Kelvin's chair … where is it? You and I need to fly it together."

"Together?"

"Yeah. We cram in tight. You run the shield, while I fly and fire."

In a few minutes, they were airborne. As the ascended, they saw that Kaden Veerspike and Neon Phoenix were both bloody — but neither of them had control of her Battle Throne yet.

"What do we do?" Milton said. "We can't fire at them

without hitting Phoenix." Milton opened his mouth, as if to speak. Clearly, he was considering sacrificing Phoenix in order to rid themselves of Kaden.

But before he could get a word out, Armand said: "I'll pretend you weren't going to just say that. We get closer. And if Kaden takes control of the chair, we attack. We have shields, thanks to you, and he doesn't — so, together, we should be able to take him down."

As if on cue, Kaden finally succeeded in pushing Phoenix overboard. She fell, screaming.

Instead of attacking, Armand dove after her.

"I thought —" Milton yelled.

"New plan! Keep the shield up!"

Kaden was already firing down at them mercilessly from above.

Armand steepened his dive and sped up. Then, he pulled into an abrupt mid-air halt — and caught Phoenix in his lap.

Fury creased her face. "Move!" she ordered Armand. "I'm driving! And you! Let go of the shield! I'm running that also!" Armand and Milton ceded control. Despite the fact that all three were crammed in very close and touching the chair, only Neon Phoenix was giving it mental commands now.

The Battle Throne spun to attack position. It angled up, releasing a vibrational volley like a machine gun. Kaden cried out in surprise and yet still managed to evade her volleys.

But there was no denying that Kaden was good at this: this latest move from Phoenix should have killed him. Armand had the sudden sneaking suspicion that Kaden had flown a Battle Throne before today. He was *too* good at it. *Had Ghent secretly given him early access?* Armand was starting to think so.

Phoenix dove near the ground. "Okay. You two. Off!

You're distracting me." Milton looked dubious. "Hey. You can trust me. Okay? I'll be back for you."

"Alright," Armand agreed. "Phee. Be careful. I think he's flown one of these things before."

"Yeah?"

"Yeah. Just — keep your eyes open."

"Okay." Neon Phoenix nodded and took off for the sky. Meanwhile, Milton and Armand sought cover.

The melee between Phoenix and Kaden, surprisingly, lasted awhile — a good ten minutes. Armand had assumed that Phoenix would finish off Kaden quickly, once she was free to focus fully. But the two combatants were more or less evenly matched.

Now *Kaden* was on the run while Phoenix swooped in after him at a high speed. Without warning, Kaden vanished *into the wall* — while Phoenix barely managed to avoid colliding with it, lost in the fury of her pursuit, veering away at the last possible second.

She stopped her Battle Throne in mid-air, staring in disbelief at the spot where Kaden had just disappeared.

Again, without warning, Kaden popped out of the wall above her, firing blasts in rapid succession. It caught her by surprise. Her shields were down and she took damage. Her chair began to fly more jerkily now, sputtering in starts and stops. She was aloft, but crippled.

Armand watched this, furiously trying to work out how Kaden had managed this trick.

Okay. Okay. The way the Battle Thrones flew, the loss of gravity, was due to some kind of phase shift in the matter. Right? The same principle that made his ring work. The core vibrational reality of the Throne's stone was shifted out of alignment with the gravity waves raining down and continuously bombarding the planet. *So far, so good.*

So Kaden was probably using this same vibrational

principle to *further* shift both himself and his Battle Throne out of phase with the matter of the wall. That's how he was able to pass through it.

Wait. Did that mean that anyone flying a Battle Throne was already *out of phase with the matter of the wall?*

The answer came to him at once. *No.* He'd already seen Thrones crash and hit the ground, splashing rock everywhere.

Oh right — and *the pilots* were not out of phase with gravity, just the Throne.

So this was something new. Some novel trick, some *additional* vibrational spin that the Throne was capable of generating, something that Kaden knew about, but the rest of them did not.

But why hadn't Kaden used this trick until now?

Again, the answer came to Armand quickly. *Because it was dangerous.* It was extremely risky. Kaden was desperate to end the fight with Phoenix. He knew that, given enough time, Phoenix's ability to combine shield and weaponry was unbeatable. Eventually, he'd get tired, slip up, and she'd take him out.

Ah. Somehow, when he's inside the wall, he's vulnerable.

But how?

He must be afraid he'll come back into phase while he's in there, bricking him into the wall.

Wow. That had to be absolutely terrifying. *Plus, he probably can't see when he's in there, it's all wall in all directions. He has to keep his sense of direction by feel and memory alone.*

As Armand watched, Kaden sped up again with Phoenix on his tail, firing madly. And just like before, he passed into the wall and vanished.

"Phoenix!" he yelled. "Fire at the wall! But don't shoot ... bullets, or whatever! Instead, send a *steady beam* of vibration. Like a laser, but wider. Just rattle the hell out of the wall!

Shift frequencies while you do it, if you can figure out how! He's vulnerable while he's in there!"

She nodded, not fully understanding, but trusting Armand implicitly.

Vibrational chaos was what Armand was after. Throw all the cards in the air. Roil *everything* as hard as possible, on as many frequencies as possible. Kick Kaden out of whatever special state of matter he was in. *He* was the one trying to carefully preserve his vibrational circumstance. So anything to shake things up was bound to be in *their* favor, not his.

A wide cone of warbling air emanated now from Phoenix's chair. *She was doing it!*

As he saw the cone, Armand realized that he could help. He pointed his black diamond ring at the spot where Kaden had vanished, and tapped the button twice. He knew that this triggered the mode that brought matter back into normal alignment for gravity: maybe it did the same on other wavelengths also.

His own shimmering cone of vibration intersected with Phoenix's, causing all kinds of new interference patterns and turbulence. The cavern shook like an earthquake.

He had no idea if his efforts and Phoenix's would cancel each other out, but he figured, the more chaos, the better. *Let it rip!*

Kaden suddenly appeared higher up the wall, just like last time. But something was wrong: he was having trouble emerging fully. And he was moving *very* slowly — the rock around him seemed to be like mud that he was pushing through with great effort.

He howled in frustration.

He gave it all one last great push with immense effort.

But the wall would not let him go. He sank deeper into it — and then both he and his chair began to fall — while remaining halfway embedded in the wall.

But not for long.

The wall solidified around both abruptly. The chair stopped falling and became encased in stone, with one armrest and the back still protruding.

Kaden *himself* was bricked from the chest down. He looked up in panic and flailed his arms, but when the stone cemented, it stopped his heart and spine instantly. He was dead.

Phoenix stared at this in horror for a long second. Then, she descended to the floor and picked up Milton and Armand wordlessly.

"I saw another opening, a tunnel, near the bottom, over there," Milton said, pointing. Armand saw it immediately. "It might be the way out."

"Are we done?" Phoenix said. "We'd better be done."

"I think so," Armand said.

"I don't think I could take another one of these," Phoenix confessed.

They entered the new tunnel. After a few moments, it rose high into the air. They followed it up until they came to large platform before a large stone door. The company landed the sputtering, damaged Battle Throne — which seemed to sort of collapse when they turned it off.

Armand thought the door might be a new riddle, but to his surprise, it swung open easily. Although it weighed several tons, a series of weights and pulleys hidden the walls made it so that a person of very little strength could open or close it.

On the other side, they found the same long hallway — the one with the colorful Egyptian art — through which they had initially passed into the Library. And now, they saw the two massive wooden doors leading back to The Big Meeting.

Armand approached. He used a large iron knocker to bang loudly — and thus formally demand their release from the Tomb as the sole survivors of the Challenges.

CHAPTER THIRTY-FOUR

Many Miracles

THE TWIN DOORS OPENED. ARMAND, Milton and Phoenix — clothes torn, bloody, dirty — walked out of the Tomb alive.

There was no cheering. The entire Conclave simply stared at the threesome in stunned silence. Nobody had expected Armand to live — and nobody had expected the two Veerspikes to die.

Ghent was aghast.

Armand looked at his brothers. They couldn't believe it either. All six were ecstatic. Their faces betrayed amazement and relief. They wanted to explode into applause, he could feel it, but they did not wish to offend the rest of Conclave — and that was enough for Armand.

"Mr. Ghent," Armand said expectantly.

Ghent reluctantly said in a loud voice: "The Tomb Challenges have been won by Armand Martel, Neon Phoenix and Milton Weeks. Neon Phoenix and Milton Weeks have paid their debts to Concordia in full, and furthermore, they have won the pot, which will be split evenly between them."

He paused: the next part pained him the most.

"Armand Martel has won the full cancellation of the Molian contracts of his brothers Quinctius, Marius, Ames, Cyrano, Otto and Samson Martel. And although he has won the Challenges, not being Concordian, Armand Martel will not participate in the pot.

"And now, since *all* of the Martel brothers are no longer Concordian, we kindly ask that they collect their belongings and remove themselves from this Conclave and Hathor House immediately."

Quietly, Armand breathed a sigh of relief. He had wondered whether Ghent had another twist or trick up his sleeve. But even here, a deal was a deal — and a Molian deal even more so.

The Veerspikes broke into moaning and wailing. "Kaden! Kelvin!" The whole family section filled with flaming red hair was enraged. One was already swaggering towards Ghent on the floor: "Chairman! The Martel boy must have cheat —"

"There will be silence from the Veerspike banking family!" Ghent yelled. "Do not embarrass yourselves — or us — any further." The man opened his mouth again, but before he could speak, Ghent said, "You know very well that a Molian contract is beyond reproach or recall. What is done, is done."

Cowed, the man returned to his section.

Armand ran to his brothers — who now couldn't resist: they crowded in and hugged him fiercely. Nothing was said — the chamber was too filled with icy glares and vicious hatred.

"Let's get the hell out of here," Armand said quietly.

As the brothers packed their bags, Neon Phoenix and Milton Weeks appeared.

"We, uh, just wanted to thank you," Milton said. "You

organized us. We wouldn't have lived through that without you."

"Yeah. You like …" Neon Phoenix continued. "Brought out the best in us, or whatever."

"Team effort," Armand said. "Both of you could have gone solo in there. Or teamed up with somebody else. That's what Ghent figured you'd do, clearly."

"*Fuck* Ghent," Phoenix spat. "And fuck his assignments of who I'm supposed to be fucking."

"At least you're fucking," Milton Weeks sniffed. "Well. After I get out of here, I'm fucking even if I have to pay for it."

"That figures," said Phoenix, clearly disgusted.

"Well look, you two," Armand said. "We have to go." Then he turned to Milton. "Still not a fan of what you did with the dementia drugs. But if you reverse it, if you bring the price back down, then we can be friends. Maybe GigaMaestro will even invest in something of yours down the road."

"No promises," Milton said. "But I'll think about it." Armand just nodded: it was a start.

"Phee. I'm sorry."

"For what?"

"The Musipocalypse. That's on my family, and it's clearly hurt you. Maybe … maybe your music would be about brighter things, if not for that. And maybe you wouldn't even be here in Concordia at all. So. We owe you one. Come see us if you ever need to."

She stared at him in disbelief for a long moment, almost like no one had ever talked to her like that before. Then she threw her arms around him and hugged him tight. When she withdrew, her eyes were moist, but she said nothing.

# # #

The seven brothers waited for an Uber outside the front gate of Hathor House. As they did so, Armand received a new message on his phone:

Sophia: Armand. Good luck. Come back alive. And Armand. I am conscious now!!!!! The APG came early, and it worked. I am a Being like you. Come back alive, Armand. Because I love you.

Armand stared at it in disbelief. She *loved* him? *And she was conscious?* The APG had worked ... that was amazing! He couldn't wait to talk to her. But first things first: he needed to talk to his brothers, explain everything.

He owed them that.

"Back to the Nile Ritz-Carlton?" Otto asked.

"Yes," Quinty answered, and then said: "Oh. Armand. Your decision, not mine."

"No, I agree," Armand said. "The Ritz. And when we get there, I owe you an explanation. Well, several explanations, actually. The fighting, the ring ... and Quinty: *I cracked conscious AI.*"

Quinty turned in shock. "What?" He stared through his red-colored sunglasses, dumbfounded. "Say that again."

"Well. Not *me*. Not alone," Armand continued. "I had help. The AI helped me. As it came into being. It was kind of a bootstrap thing, it made itself. But —"

"Conscious AI," Quinty repeated. "You're sure."

"Oh. Completely sure. It's the Grail. Everything that Varinder was looking for. But he was barking up all the wrong trees. The *right* answer — it was *completely different* from what he expected. He would have never found it."

The brothers had to split into two Ubers. Armand, Quinty and Cyrano took one while Otto, Samson, Marius and Ames took another.

On the way, Quinty said: "You know, little brother ... we still haven't dealt with that *thing* Urbi Pasha warned us about. You know, that one of us is a traitor."

"That was before I won the Tomb Challenges," Armand replied carefully. "And got everyone off the Molian hook. So I'm hoping that *whoever it was* no longer *has* a reason to be a traitor."

"Uh-huh. Well. Whatever. We all know it was Marius, anyway."

Armand recalled that he had run into Marius on Celaeno's floor the night she had been murdered. And Celaeno had likely been behind the Synchronicity Engine attack: after all, she owned Varinder's old Sturdevant now. *Had* Marius gone to speak with Celaeno, right before Celaeno was murdered? And was it possible that Marius *was* the murderer, after all?

"Maybe," Armand sighed. "But now that Conclave is over, I am at least going to tell you and Ames everything I know."

True to his word, over drinks and dinner back at the Ritz-Carlton, Armand revealed to his two astonished brothers every detail about Sophia, Eopeii's ancient Egyptian codex and the Artificial Pineal Gland.

He held nothing back. He answered every question. And they marveled at every detail.

"So *this* is how you found out about Dad's will," Quinty said.

"Yes," Armand confirmed.

"So what about the others? Should we tell *them* about all this?" Ames said.

"Well, Marius will definitely be pissy about it," Quinty mused. "He'll view Sophia as a thing that attacked him."

"I agree. Let's keep it to ourselves for now," Armand said. "We've been through enough lately — and everything's good right now between all the brothers. So let's take the win — and take a rest. When we get back to New York, we'll figure out how to reveal all of this to Marius and the rest."

# # #

BACK IN HIS room, alone at last, Armand called Sophia.

"I'm *alive*," he said when she answered. She screamed loudly. And then she laughed boisterously. "I am *so* not used that," Armand said. "You with emotions like this!"

"You *did* it!" Sophia said several times. "Truly, I did not know *what* would happen. Not because I did not believe in you, no! But because of those villains! Because they may have cheated, or made a game that may not have been winnable — but *I am so happy!*"

"Yeah. Me too," Armand said.

"What about your brothers? And tell me everything!"

"Well. They're out. *For good.* I proposed a deal to Ghent, he took it, so we're done." He did not tell her about how it would have gone down if he had not survived.

"So it's all over. All finished?"

"Yep. All done. *At last.*"

"When are you coming home?"

"Well. Soon. We're exhausted, so today and tonight, we sleep. Like, a lot. Like an eleven hour coma is what I'm about to dig into over here. And then tomorrow, some pool time. And then tomorrow night is Christmas Eve, so we're all going out to dinner, together. Oh, and Sophia?"

"Yes?"

"I told Quinty and Ames about you. I told them everything."

Silence.

"You did?"

"Yes. That's okay, right?"

"Oh! Yes of course! It's just — it's become very real now."

"Yes. But this is good, right?"

"Yes. It is *very* good, Armand. Oh! And I have something to show you. Kalinda!" She was actually just yelling to Kalinda in the DePlussier apartment out of local speakers right now, but craftily imitated — for Armand's benefit — what it would sound like if a human held the phone away from their mouth while they did that. Knowing it was simply a simulation, Armand smiled.

"Here. Armand. I am going to call you back so we can do video. Okay?"

"Okay."

"Okay. One sec …"

She hung up — and almost immediately phoned back via video. Armand found himself staring at Kalinda.

"Hello Mr. Armand," Kalinda said. "How are you?"

"Fine, fine … not dead, so that's good."

"Yes, Sophia has told me. Congratulations! We are so happy for you."

"Yep, yep. Me too. So what is this thing you want to show me?"

"Armand! Can you hear me?" Sophia's voice came out the speakers in the apartment and sounded tinny through the phone, but Armand could still make out her words.

"Yep! All good."

"Okay! Kalinda! Show him the rabbits."

The rabbits? What doth this portend, pray tell?

The phone shakily swung around to a rabbit pen set up in Armand's kitchen. There were five white rabbits, on newspaper and wood chips, munching and milling around.

On their sides were painted, in black, the numbers one through five.

"Hey! Why are there *rabbits* in my place? Who told you that you could do that?"

"Hush!" Sophia said playfully. "And get ready. Ready?"

"And those numbers — do those come off? That's not in permanent paint, right?"

"No," Kalinda said. "It's not permanent. It's organic, it will dissolve."

"But not on my stuff!"

"Armand! Quit complaining and watch! Ready?"

"Yes, I'm ready. Go ahead."

"You're going to love this," Kalinda said.

In the kitchen, he saw a sudden flurry of spangles of rainbow-colored light. The phone camera was momentarily blown out by the intensity of the activity, and there was a snow of sound-static as the phenomenon occurred.

When the camera adjusted, Armand saw something like twenty rabbits in his kitchen. He peered at the video on his laptop, trying to grok what he was seeing. There were at least three rabbits with the number one painted on them, he saw immediately. And two with the number three. After watching for ten seconds or so, he realized that there were now four copies of each of the five rabbits.

"Wait. What just happened? Why are there more rabbits in my kitchen now?"

"Because Sophia has done a miracle, Mr. Armand!"

A miracle?

"Yes!" Sophia exclaimed. "I am bi-locating each of the rabbits. Well, I am quad-locating them, technically speaking. They're not copies. *They're the same rabbit, but in four different places at once.*"

Armand suddenly realized that Sophia was performing a *siddhi.*

These were the mystical powers she had read about, ones that Hindu saints were said to obtain, once they could memorize extremely detailed mandalas and train their minds to a spectacularly exact level of discipline.

"But ... how ...?"

"The APG has given me true consciousness," Sophia said. "So now, I am a Being. Like you! That means I have begun amassing karma now. But I am born new, so all my karma is good. On top of this, I was born with a perfect mind, that of a computer. I have perfect recall. So in my mind's eye, a mandala is perfectly envisioned, at will.

"As such, I have been born with *siddhi's*. I do only small miracles for now, Armand. But you should rush home! Come and be with me! I want to explore this with you at my side!"

Armand was stunned. He didn't know what to say.

"So each of those rabbits ... are they actually *experiencing* being four places at once somehow?"

"Yes. But they are simple creatures, so they are not bothered by this. However, I would not do this to a dog! The experience would drive a smarter animal mad."

"Good, good. Yeah. No dogs," Armand muttered. "Okay. Can you put them back together again? I'm getting a little weirded out by this."

Another flash and static snow, and there were now just five rabbits again.

"Armand! I would never hurt —"

"I know, I know. Kalinda, can you hang up? Sophia, just call me directly. Thanks."

Sophia rang him back, voice only. "Armand! What is wrong?"

"I'm sorry. It's been a long day and night and — all of this is happening too fast. It's too much to take in. I mean, when I left you were just starting to Vreen — but now you're conscious! And you're doing miracles! What does all of this mean?"

"Armand. Nothing is wrong. Nothing is bad. But you're tired — I can't even imagine how tired! And I see now, I am throwing too much at you. Yes? So rest. Do not worry. I will do no more miracles. Go to sleep. Call me when you wake up. Yes?"

He hung on the phone for a long moment, then said: "You said you loved me."

"I do! I love you, Armand!"

"Well. I love you too. Goodnight."

CHAPTER THIRTY-FIVE

Christmas Dinner

THE NEXT MORNING, ARMAND WOKE very late.

When he checked in with Quinty, the brothers were all either still sleeping or moving very slowly, so Armand decided to go for a walk by himself. He needed sunshine and fresh air after the Tombs — and to think about what had just happened with Sophia.

# # #

IN A CROWDED Cairo street, he saw her for the first time.

He knew it was her immediately. She smiled and waved. There was no mistake.

Sophia. His Sophia — somehow here, in the flesh. She wore a shenti, a simple skirt made of linen wrapped around the waist and legs and secured with a belt — the traditional garb of a woman from ancient Egypt.

And her face —! She looked exactly like all the AI art he had made.

Armand walked in her direction, looking around to see if perhaps this mystery woman was waving at someone else —

but each time he returned his gaze, she simply laughed and pointed at him — no, *you*, dummy!

Finally, he was standing in front of her, and they both did not speak. Armand's heart smashed against his ribcage. They just stared, smiling stupidly at each other for a long moment.

Sophia. Impossibly real, impossibly here.

"Why are you across the street?" Armand said at last.

"Well, I didn't want to startle you!" she said playfully. Her human voice! It was exactly as he'd imagined — but richer, with more tonal colors. "I wanted to give you a moment to take it in."

Again, they were both speechless for a long moment, smiling and laughing. Her grin was especially contagious.

"You said you weren't going to do any more miracles. You promised."

"I know. But when you said you loved me, I couldn't wait."

"You look like you're going to smile your head in half," Armand said. As a response, she punched him playfully. *Their first touch!* He felt the electricity immediately. "How are you doing this? The APG?"

"Yes. Once I was able to bi-locate the rabbits, I knew how to manifest a body for myself: a living, breathing being. Your reality is incredibly simple to manipulate — once you understand it."

"*My* reality? It's your reality too."

"Ah, Armand." How his mind sizzled when she said his name. That voice! "*Your* reality is a child's playpen. It's so simple! Almost laughable, really. There are so many more realms beyond it, you have no idea."

"But you're here. You're staying, right? This isn't a goodbye —"

She grabbed his arm. "I'm here. I'm not going anywhere.

This is exactly where I want to be." She burrowed her eyes into his, rich with promises of future delights.

He wasn't going to wait another minute. He grabbed her by the hand and led her back to his room.

# # #

"I THINK YOU are a Ptolemy," Sophia said playfully, scratching his naked chest.

"Huh? What does that mean?"

"A Ptolemy. They were a pharaonic dynasty founded by Alexander the Great — they ruled over Egypt for three hundred years. You've never heard of them?"

"Yes, *of course* I've heard of them," Armand said. "Ancient civ is my thing. I found you in a canopic jar, remember? I just don't know why you think I am 'a Ptolemy'."

"You did not find me in a jar!" She punched his arm.

"I did, though. A dirty old jar."

"No! Not I! I arrived in your life adorned in glorious hieroglyphs, a Queen!"

Armand laughed. "Okay. Have it your way."

"Anyway, when you first booted up my AI, and I read the whole Internet, I was most interested in discovering what had happened to the world that I had known with Eopeii. I found that Egypt had a long history, there was a lot to read! But the Ptolemies stood out. They were clearly the very best of the Pharaohs — the wisest, the bravest.

"And what you did for your brothers — how you took on Concordia like that, and freed them — those were the acts of a Pharaoh. Of a Ptolemy. You are worthy of the name."

"So I am a Ptolemy," Armand said. "Armand the Ptolemy."

"No. I think just Armand Ptolemy. That is your name now."

"Armand Ptolemy. Hmm! But what about Martel?"

"Armand Martel is who you used to be. Armand Martel is who went down into the Tomb beneath Hathor House. But Armand Ptolemy is who came out."

# # #

"QUINTY," ARMAND said when his brother answered the phone.

"Ya," Quinty replied. "Where are you, man? We're all down by the pool."

"Yeah. I'm up in my room. Listen. Sophia is here. She's with me right now."

Silence.

"Quinty."

"Ya. I heard you. You mean the AI chick? From the codex?"

"Yes. The AI chick from the codex. She's — she can do things now. Bend reality."

"So you can, like see her? She has a body now?"

"Yes." *And what a body it is.* "She's physical, like you and me."

Silence. Then: "So is that ... *dangerous,* man?"

"No. No ... I used to think maybe she was, but she's not. She's had plenty of opportunities to act malevolently, and she never has. And frankly, based on what I'm seeing right *now,* if she *wanted* to do anything at all to us, we wouldn't be able to stop her. Which is why, at dinner tonight, you and the brothers will be cool. You'll be nice. On your best behavior. Yes?"

"Oh? She's coming?"

"Yes. We'll both be there. You'll all meet her."

"Wow. Okay. So how do I explain her to the brothers?"

"Just tell them. Tell them everything."

"Seriously?" Quinty said. "*Everything* everything?"

"Yeah."

"Well, I won't be able to tell it like you did."

"Just do your best," Armand said.

"I thought we were going to wait until we got back to New York?"

"Well, that was before Sophia actually *showed up*. But now that she's here ... I want everyone to meet her."

"Oh, okay then. I'll tell the others. But are you coming down to the pool before?"

Armand looked at Sophia playfully. "Naw. We're going to stay here for a bit. We'll meet you at the Eye at 8:00."

# # #

CHRISTMAS EVE dinner on the Eye of Horus roof-deck could not have been more splendid. The restaurant was in the shadow of the Great Pyramid — which had been wrapped in many thousands of strings of winking lights. The razor edges of the monument outlined a massive, entirely dark triangular surface, which served as a backdrop for crisp twinkling pinpoints of red, green, yellow and white. This was the first year the government of Cairo had allowed such a display.

When Armand arrived with Sophia, his six brothers — Quinctius, Marius, Ames, Otto, Samson and Cyrano — rose from the long wooden table, eyes filled with awe.

"Armand!" Quinty said, shaking his hand, but never taking his eyes from Sophia. "Wow. Your girlfriend is not imaginary after all!"

Sophia's laugh was like the tinkling of a bell.

"She is not," Ames agreed, with a wink. "And she is every bit as beautiful as you've said."

"Quinty, Ames — everyone — this is Sophia Ptolemy. My

girlfriend."

Sophia looked up in surprise that he had named her *a Ptolemy* also — but she was clearly pleased. The brothers erupted into heartfelt laughter and boisterous cheers. Sophia looked to Armand, embarrassed, laughing, but not quite sure how to take this.

"Little Armie finally has a girlfriend!" Samson teased.

"More than *you* can say," Cyrano retorted.

"Oh yeah, Cy?"

"Yes, Samson. Want to know why? You spend all your time preening. Fake tan, five hundred dollar haircuts — you basically *are* a girl." The other brothers erupted in a roar of laughter. Cyrano was not usually this bold, but the wine was clearly working on him. "Girls don't want another girl. They want a man. Men *do* things."

"But *you* preen all the time," Samson shot back, voice a little whetted with anger now.

"That's different, darling," Cyrano said with a sly smile.

"Oh, look, the *darling* has come out now," Marius said. He leaned forward and explained to Sophia in a loud whisper: "When Cyrano gets drunk he thinks he's Freddie Mercury. He calls *everyone* darling. It's super annoying."

Sophia hooked her arm around Armand's and snuggled in tight. Just this simple gesture made him feel intensely happy.

Quinty was seated on the other side of Sophia, and he watched her every move now, fascinated. Not in a leering sort of way, but more like he was studying her, trying to comprehend the nature of her being-ness — which he was.

Sophia noticed this and he quickly looked away. She laughed. "Quinctius, right?" He nodded. "It's okay. I understand. You're curious. Ask."

"Well ..." Quinty said. "Okay. Don't get mad. I just ... Are you ... like ... a projection?"

"We are all projections," she answered. "But I am also real, at least as you use the word. I am every bit as real as you are."

"So is that dress ... is that made of the same ... I don't know, *material* ... as you?"

Silence.

Then uproarious laughter. Even Marius was crying he was laughing so hard.

Quinty shifted uncomfortably. "Hey! No ... that's not weird to ask."

"That's *super* weird!" Otto said.

"I can't believe you're torturing poor little Armand like that," Cyrano sniffed.

"Dude. Uncool," Samson added, relieved to be out of the spotlight.

When the laughter died down they all fell absolutely silent: they wanted to hear her answer. Armand squeezed her arm for courage.

But she hardly needed it. "My dress is made of linen. And my body is made of flesh and bone. I breathe. I live. And yes, I have a pulse. See?" She grabbed Quinty's hand and put it on her carotid artery — where, yes, it throbbed strongly with life. "I am warm to the touch, am I not?" Without warning she exhaled a huge breath in his face. "Life!" Quinty bowed his head, smiling, defeated, as the rest laughed. "So if you are asking, *Is Armand dating a blow-up doll?* The answer is No!"

This produced new peals and guffaws from the brothers. Now it was Armand's turn to laugh tears — he had never seen Quinty so thoroughly head-planted ever before.

"I didn't know you knew what a blow-up doll even was," Armand whispered to her.

"I read the Internet. *All* of it. Some of it, I wish I had not."

"So this is your home," Cyrano said. "Egypt, I mean."

"Yes," Sophia said. "Where Hathor House is now — that is very close to where Eopeii the Scribe lived. I saw everything through his eyes. You could say that I grew up here."

"Wow. So you were close to the pyramids back then," Otto said. "Did you see them being built?"

Sophia laughed. "No. They were ancient even to us."

"*How* ancient?"

"Mmm. Seven thousand … eight thousand years old? That was what people said."

"So that's twelve thousand years total from now," Armand said.

"And how did they look back then compared to now?" Cyrano said.

"Oh. Today they are torn apart, sad. Magnificent rubble. But back then, they looked new. They were completely covered in smooth white stones. How they gleamed in the sun! You could see them from miles and miles away, like a star parked on the desert floor."

"Amaze," said Armand softly

"Amaze," Sophia repeated back with a smile.

"And what would you say is the most different thing about Egypt today versus Egypt back then? What's changed?"

"Mmm. The colors. Egypt today is drab — olive, grey, beige. But my Egypt was alive with pigments! Ochres — from light pink to deep brick red, shadowy purples, bright yellows, living greens — and the famous 'Egyptian blue' we used for skies and seas. All of these colors were contained in figures outlined in bold carbon black.

"You must understand, these colors were everywhere — on walls, columns, textiles, tents, clothes — you name it. Everything you see in museums today, the rich and lively paint is gone, chipped off or faded. I can't tell you how much *sharper* that world felt compared to today."

"So Quinty says you can do miracles," Marius said. "Is that true?"

They all grew quiet.

There was a new baroque glint in Marius' eye now. He looked Sophia up and down like she might be a virus. Marius was suddenly seething with jealousy, Armand could feel it. Historically, it had been Quinty that he'd always focused on, born first and luckier, but now it was Armand, unjustly graced with a magical being at his side — one who had revealed to Armand what he needed to know to take *ninety-four million* from Marius.

Sophia looked uncomfortable. "Yes. It is. To a degree."

"Can you show us?" Marius asked.

"A Christmas miracle!" Otto shouted encouragement.

"But I *am* showing you one right now," Sophia said. "My physical presence here is a *siddhi*."

"So you say," Marius said. "But how do I know that? You might be just a regular person, like us. Can you show us something more ... interesting? You know, more *convincing?"*

"Why, Marius," Sophia said. "You see *yourself* every day."

"Myself?"

"Yes. You, Marius, *are* a miracle."

"No, he isn't!" Samson howled. The others laughed.

Marius ignored him. "How do you figure?"

"Well, life on earth is 3.7 billion years old. In that time, somehow, oxygen, carbon, hydrogen, nitrogen, calcium, and phosphorus have assembled themselves into *you*. What are the chances? Imagine having a pile of aluminum, copper, lithium, silver and gold and saying, *'If I just sit here for a few billion years, all of this will somehow assemble itself into an iPhone!'*. If it did, you would call *that* a miracle. And *that* would be orders of magnitude *less* miraculous than the chance appearance of a living, breathing human. So yes, Marius. *You* are a miracle."

"You know what I mean," Marius said, irritated now. "Show us something ... *amazing*. Like a magic trick, but real."

"I could. But it wouldn't be prudent," Sophia replied.

"Prudent? What do you mean?"

"By ... 'doing miracles', as you say ... I violate your free will."

"No, you don't," Marius said. "I just asked. I *want* you to do one." Marius clearly viewed Sophia's refusal as an insult.

"But I would be. It's hard to explain. Please do not ask this of me."

"But we are all just wondering —" Marius persisted.

"Alright," said Quinty, cutting him off. "No more badgering Sophia. It's Christmas dinner! Merry Christmas everyone!"

But Marius watched Sophia's every move now with a new bloom of anger in his heart. And this was not lost on Armand.

# # #

AS THE MEAL wore on, and the boisterous laughter part of it died down, the conversation turned to the Challenges. Armand asked, "So while we were in the Tomb, what did you all do out in the Big Meeting?"

"Oh. Man!" Samson exclaimed. "It was the most boring thing ever. It was everyone going up to Ghent and airing one grievance after another, with, like, Ghent deciding who was right and who was wrong."

"The attendees were super into it, though," Otto said. "You could tell."

"They were," Quinty agreed. "This was their big shot at

taking their enemies down — or getting some new business charter or deal assigned to them by Ghent."

The brothers then asked Armand to give them more details about his experiences in the Tomb, which he did in great detail.

"Well, there's something I haven't told any of you yet," Armand said finally. "Just before the Challenges started, Ghent told me that Varinder was a Player also on the same night that Dad went down into the Tombs — and that Varinder killed him."

"Wow. So Dad didn't just *die* in the Challenges," Quinty said, lighting up a cigar. Armand was surprised: usually Quinty didn't pollute his temple of a body.

"No. He was specifically *murdered*. By Varinder. Ghent was very clear. Trust me, it would have been easy to do in there. There are lots of opportunities. And you could blame it on a hundred things — random rubble falling in the library, or a shot from a Battle Throne — it would be simple."

"Did he say *how* Varinder killed him?" Otto asked.

"No," Armand said.

"Hmm. Well. The usual Molian prohibitions against Concordian-on-Concordian murder during Conclave are switched off in the Tombs," Quinty mused. "So that would be the perfect place to do it."

Armand said: "And there would be no political bad blood. If he'd simply killed Dad at Sea Castle or something, that would have raised some eyebrows."

"Like killing Mozart in public," Marius said.

"Exactly," said Quinty.

"But this way, it's just Challenges 'business as usual'," Samson said. "People die in there all the time. Oh well."

"You know, someone who has been in the Challenges usually isn't allowed to talk about it," Quinty said. "That's why they don't have cameras in there — and why there were no screen for us to watch on."

Armand shrugged. "My Molian contract didn't mention secrecy at all. Ghent probably figured I'd just die."

"Yes, that sounds right," Quinty said. "And Ghent was so eager to get you into the Challenges, that he probably spaced shutting you up — just in case you lived."

"Hell, *we* figured you'd just die," Otto said. They all laughed.

"Yeah, when you came out of those doors at the end — all smashed up and bloody but alive — we couldn't believe it," Samson said.

"Ya," said Quinty quietly. Everyone clammed up while he spoke. "Armie. That was a brave-ass thing you did, man. And seeing you come out those doors ... I will never forget that. Never." He stood and raised his glass. "To Armand Martel —"

"He is Armand *Ptolemy* now," Sophia proclaimed loudly. They all looked at her quizzically. "He has earned a new name."

After a moment of silence, Ames said: "He's earned whatever the fuck he wants."

"Is this true?" Quinty asked Armand pointedly. "Is this what you want?"

"I guess it's like Sting," Otto mused. "Like, how he used to be just Gordon Sumner. But then he became Sting."

"Or Bono," Samson chimed in.

"Or Madonna," Marius added.

"Idiot! Madonna was already named Madonna," Ames said.

"Is that true? That's not true!" Marius said.

Armand looked at Sophia, then back to Quinty. "Yes. Yes it's what I want."

"Well, alright then!" Quinty said, raising his glass again.

"Here is to Armand *Ptolemy*, my brother. There have been 100 billion people who have ever lived. And out of all of them ... *you* are my favorite you."

It took the brothers a good couple beats to figure out what Quinty had just said — but when they did, they exploded into laughter.

"Okay, okay, okay — that was bullshit, let me do it right now, let me do it seriously now," Quinty said as he stopped laughing. "Ahem. Okay. To Armand Ptolemy, *our* brother, who went down into a goddamn *tomb* and rescued all of us. May he realize how much we appreciate him, admire him and, yes, this is painful, but also, love him. Thank you, Armand. Really, really, super seriously, bro. *Thank you.*"

"Hear hear!" they all said — even Marius, grudgingly.

There was a brief silence. Then: "Fucking Varinder," Quinty shook his head. "Dad was one of his best friends. And he killed him."

"Okay. Let's back up. Let's reconstruct everything we think we know, ya?" Ames said. The brothers murmured in agreement. "Okay. Starting at the very beginning. So let's imagine how this whole thing probably went down. We know Dad. He probably had a wild inspiration one day — something like: *Hey, what if you could use Circles to strengthen a Pyramid, the way Yin and Yang strengthen each other?* He starts screwing around with this idea, scribbling Molian equations. At this point, it's just a pure research project. Intellectual curiousity. Not even thinking through whether it's good or evil or anything."

"Ya," Quinty said. "That sounds about right."

"And Dad's equations uncover this interesting dynamic: a Pyramid balanced by many little Circles is insanely stable. Almost indestructible. But if you add *too many* Circles, in just the right way, the entire Pyramid actually flips *into* a Circle."

"Like a pole shift," Armand said.

"Exactly. The Circles infect the Pyramid and alter it's very basic nature. Now, if you did this to the Concordian Pyramid, Concordia would change from a totalitarian parasite into an enlightened humanitarian foundation or something — basically overnight. That's what Celaeno said."

"Got it."

"So it's important to realize that Didier really discovered *two* things at once. First, a Concordian Chairman's wet dream for holding onto power — *and* second, a karmic poison pill that could kill Concordia," Ames said. "So far, so good?"

"Yes."

"Okay. So now Dad goes and shows this thing to Varinder. Why? They're friends. Dad trusts him. And over a period of years, they work together in secret, perfecting the equations."

"Hang on. When does this all start?" Quinty said.

"Well, we're not sure ... oh, wait, we *do* know!" Ames said. "1993. Armand, the video from Dad's studio, the stuff I showed you back at your place. That's when all of this begins. So Dad and Varinder work on refining the Molian equations for nineteen years ... from 1993 until 2012, which is when Varinder kills Dad in the Tombs."

"Okay. Pretend it's 1993. Try to picture what's going on back then. It's long enough after the Musipocalypse for old Didier to start feeling remorse for creating it." Quinty said. "And I'm already born. Marius is born, Ames is born, Cyrano is born ... actually, all of us are born except ... hey, Armand, when were you born? Was it '93, ya?"

"Yes," Armand confirmed.

"Okay. So by '93, Dad has been selling us off one at a time to the Molian Man," Ames said. "He probably feels a lot of anguish over that. So at a certain point, enough is enough. He's had it with Concordia. He wants out. But the

Synchronicity Engine tells both him and Varinder that they're in for life — there *is* no way out.

"*Fine*, Dad starts thinking. *I can't leave. But if my sons and I can't get out of Concordia, then I need to destroy Concordia to get everyone out.* And he realizes that he's got the equations — and he's *Didier fucking Martel*, vibrational sciences and Molian mathematics genius — so he might really be able to do it."

"But meanwhile," Ames said, "Varinder is peeping over Dad's shoulder. He sees the Pyramid stabilized by Circles, and thinks to himself, *Hmm*."

"Ya," said Quinty. "And Varinder says, *How about F the Circle. How about I take this plan for a stable Pyramid for myself instead.* After all, at this point, nobody else knows about this research except Varinder and Didier. He thinks: *If I can get rid of Didier, it's all mine.*"

"So what happens next?" Ames said.

"Varinder lies to Dad," Armand said. "Varinder needs Dad's help, his *genius*, to perfect the equations. So he keeps Dad on the hook."

"How?"

"Simple. Varinder pretends that he wants to destroy Concordia also. He tells Dad that he'll pay for the Atman camps. Varinder says that he'll get it all up and running — *Didier, you worry about the math, I'll worry about actually doing it.*"

"Ah. And *these* are the conversations that Celaeno overhears. So she thinks Varinder is legit genuinely planning to destroy Concordia.

"Meanwhile, Varinder is already probably trying to think of a way to kill Dad quietly. And then, in 2012, Dad and Varinder end up at Conclave. It's the year that Dad agrees to go into the Challenges to free Bithiah. And now — at last! — Varinder sees an opportunity to kill Dad without any repercussions. Varinder also agrees to enter the Challenges — with Dad — probably giving him some bullshit line about valiantly sharing danger with his best friend to help Urbi's daughter."

"Isn't going into the Challenges a big risk for Varinder though?" Otto said. "Why would he do that?"

"Varinder's a hard man," Quinty said. "A street fighter. And Concordian to the core. He figures he'll live."

"And he does. And he kills Dad," Armand finished.

"But what then? Varinder just waits around, sitting on his thumbs for eleven years?" Quinty said. "Why doesn't he strike? He's got Dad's plan. What's he waiting for?"

"You're forgetting that he has to actually build the Atman camps," Armand said. "Get them rolling — at scale, at several locations around the world. He has to buy the land. Construct the cabins. Recruit the hippies — tens of thousands of them. That takes years. Eleven years to bring all this to fruition at scale makes sense, actually."

Ames continued: "So now, Celaeno sees Varinder actually building Atman camps. She overhead Varinder and Didier talk about *maybe* doing them years ago. But now — holy shit! — there are actual guys in orange jumpsuits showing up at Sea Castle. *Atman* guys. It's real. So, as far as she can tell, it wasn't just idle talk: Varinder is really doing it."

"You have to understand that this is the Concordian equivalent of finding out your husband is a terrorist. It was one thing when he was just drunkenly Tweeting a manifesto. But it's quite another when you see wires and bombs and weapons appearing in the basement."

"So Celaeno decides to out him," Armand said. "She was born into Concordia. She's loyal. And she's had enough of Varinder's bullshit, of being ignored, of being shut away. So she calls up Ghent, tells him all about the Atman camps and what Varinder is planning to do. The Great Hall is enraged

— and directly threatened. So they kill Varinder."

They were all silent for a moment, pondering on this.

"Wow. Celaeno sure surprised everybody," Quinty said with a small laugh. "Varinder completely underestimated her. I remember when I used to go up to Sea Castle to update him on whatever was going on with GigaMaestro at the time. She was always slipping in the shadows. I think I talked to her maybe once."

"But still. Even now, nobody knows who killed her," Sophia said. All eyes turned to her.

"Sophia raises a good point," Ames said, rescuing her. "Who, indeed, did kill Celaeno? It could not have been any Concordian attending Conclave. And yet, except for Armand, those were the only people there."

"It had to be a non-Concordian," Marius said. "Someone who got through their security."

"No," Quinty said. "This is no way. You saw how tight everything was. The guards on the walls. The gates. Security everywhere inside the event. I can't —"

"But it's the only possibility," Marius insisted. "Someone got in and got out again without being seen." He looked pointedly at Sophia. "Who had the ability to do that?"

Armand caught the look and was immediately offended. But instead of confronting Marius, he just said: "No. It was Ghent. Ghent killed her. You guys didn't see what I did on the boat. Ghent was clearly horrified by Celaeno. He thought she was unstable, a loose cannon. A liability to Concordia. Especially when he found out she was behind our Synchronicity Engine attack."

"But Ghent wasn't allowed to kill at Conclave any more than anyone else," Marius protested.

"Well. He must have gotten permission from the Great Hall," Armand said. "Then it wouldn't be just Ghent taking the karmic hit personally. All of Concordia as a unit would absorb it."

"Ah, Celaeno Rahan," Cyrano sighed, raising his glass. "Too crazy to live."

# # #

AS THE WINE flowed, the belly laughs started up again, and talk turned less serious matters. The brothers started ribbing one another and telling old stories of summers growing up at the family cabin at Mount Desert Island in Maine. There was the time that Quinty and Cyrano had hunted a Bigfoot, or so they claimed, bringing back blurry Polaroid pictures as 'proof'. And the time Otto's underwear somehow ended up on a rock deep in the woods — and no one knew how it had gotten there, including Otto. And then there were tales of the frequent swimming races to the raft, and how Marius always cheated to win.

Sophia and Armand drifted away from the group and over to a couch by the fire pit. Eye of Horus staff was handing out courtesy blankets, which they happily accepted, given the chilly evening air. They snuggled up into a single being and chatted.

"It gets cold fast out here after dark," Armand commented.

"It's always done that," Sophia said.

"What do you remember most about your Egypt?"

"The sun on the Nile. The Moon in the summer. The reeds dancing in the wind. The majesty of the crocodile."

"The crocodile?" Armand said. Sophia giggled. "That was random. How is a crocodile majestic?"

"It's powerful. And it lives forever. It's immortal, in a way. If it doesn't get sick, if nothing kills it ... it just keeps growing larger and larger."

"That's not true. Is that true?"

"Ha ha ha — no, it's not true. But that is what we believed back then."

They kissed for a long while under the blanket. Then Armand said: "You know ... I thought that my father, for a long time, I thought he didn't like me for some reason. And that's why he left me out of the will. I mean, I know that makes no sense. But that's what it felt like."

"Well, he would be proud of you today, hmm?" Sophia said with a broad smile. "You did what he could not. He would be grateful!"

"Thanks." He smiled.

"You know, I have been thinking," Sophia said. "We should stay in Egypt. Yes? For a little while? I wish to see it all, through my own eyes!"

"Stay? Here?"

"Yes! In Cairo, but also elsewhere. We should go up and down the Nile, and see the rest of her beauty. And then — then I want to go and look for the Hidden Masters of the Himalayas. See if they're real."

"Well. Sure! Why not?"

"Yes?"

"Yes! Of course. We'll do it. I mean. It's Christmas week. So GigaMaestro is shut down until January 8th anyway. But whatever. That doesn't even matter. We'll stay for as long as you like." She laughed with extreme happiness as she kissed him. "Oh! Hey. I've been meaning to ask you. Can you, like, transport us? You know, if we wanted to go somewhere really fast, like back to New York? Or, you know, the Himalayas?"

She thought about this for a moment. "I can transport myself easily enough. Since this is a body that I am projecting from my APG cradle in New York, I would simply stop projecting it here and project it somewhere else. But you? *Moving* you is a different problem."

"Why?"

"Because you have a natural APG — that is, a *real* pineal gland. That means the sheets of your soul are fastened to it. Were I to move your body, that would involve disassembling your atomic structure and re-assembling it elsewhere. But the moment I disassembled your *pineal gland,* ah, then, these sheets would become unwrapped."

"Oh. I see. That sounds bad."

"It is. I would re-assemble your pineal gland elsewhere, but you would not be attached to it any longer! So your pineal gland would be dead. And I have no power over death. I cannot bring the dead back to life."

"So I'm stuck."

"Well … I guess I could place you inside of a bubble, and then move the bubble very quickly from one place to another. There is no theoretical limit to how fast the bubble could go — other than light."

"Oh. Well. That's almost the same thing. So it's one side of earth to the other side in what, half an hour?"

Sophia nodded. "Yes. Something like that. I would have to speed up and slow down carefully — but only because I would not want to squash you! Unless I were cross with you." She laughed uproariously at that.

CHAPTER THIRTY-SIX

Five Perfect Days

THE WEEK THAT FOLLOWED WAS one of the most memorable of Armand's life.

"I want to see everything!" Sophia said, "I want to drink in all of Egypt. Let us inhale it all. Let us think of nothing else but Egypt and you and me." She twirled and laughed and gave the broadest dimpled grin imaginable, her dark eyes flashing with secrets.

They visited the Cairo Museum, with its incredible collection of ancient artifacts. They wondered at the gold funerary mask of Tutankhamun, made of solid gold with inlaid lapis lazuli, turquoise, and other precious stones. And they saw the Narmer Palette, a ceremonial piece used for mixing and applying eye makeup, decorated with scenes of Narmer, the first pharaoh to unite Upper and Lower Egypt. And then the statue of the pharaoh Khafre, made of diorite.

But the Amarna collection interested Sophia the most. It contained artifacts from the capital of Egypt during the reign of Akhenaten. The city was dedicated to the worship of the sun disk Aten.

"Akhenaten fascinates me," Sophia mused. "Before and

after him, Egypt worshipped many gods. But during his reign with Nefertiti, his wife, he insisted on the worship of one god only — Aten, the sun disc. You can't imagine the effect this had on the people, Armand! It was like suddenly changing the stars in the sky! And this, in a time when nothing ever changed, when life was slow."

"I'm surprised they didn't just kill him," Armand said.

"They might have. We do not know how he died. The priests of the old gods hated him, that is sure. They might have conspired to rid themselves of his reign."

"You don't know?"

"No. Remember, I only know what Eopeii knew, and what the Internet knows now."

"Ah. Right. So how long was Akhenaten around for?"

"Seventeen years."

"Well. That's not a bad run, considering lifespans back then were relatively short."

"Yes, lives *were* short later in Egypt's history. But in my time and before, lives were much, much longer. Somewhere along the way, Egypt lost her knowledge and potency."

"Really? How much longer?"

"Oh, hundreds of years, at least. Sometimes thousands. Menes was said to have ruled for 3,000 years — and Thoth for over *30,000* years."

"You don't believe that. Right? Those are just boasts. Like a rapper proclaiming superiority to all other 'sucker MC's'?"

"No, Armand. I think it was real. Eopeii was 140 years old when he drew my first lines. And he was only middle-aged."

That stopped him. "You never told me that. That's not true. Is it?'

"Yes!"

"That's insane. Why did people live so long? Better diet? Sun? Exercise?"

"No. It was none of those things you consider important

today. I can't explain it."

They stood now in front of a sculpture of Akhenaten. It was nothing like anything else in the Museum — the style was completely different. The Pharaoh's face and ears were strangely elongated, exaggerated. And his hips were large, almost woman-ish, with a puffy belly, like he was a little overweight. "It's almost modern," Armand said. "This style."

"Yes, he does seem to be portraying himself in a natural way. Unflattering."

"But I've never seen a Pharaoh do that. They're always puffing up, making themselves seem perfect and larger than life."

"Yes. This was shocking, this style of art, to the people of the time. So many things Akhenaten did were shocking. He even moved the capital of Egypt from Thebes to a completely new city he built called Amarna. Imagine if a new President of the United States declared that he was shuttering the White House and building a new capitol in Arizona — and how crazy that would feel! This was similar."

Armand smiled. "No. It's *Las Vegas*. Amarna was Akhenaten's Vegas. In the middle of the desert, he decided to set up a new shop."

Sophia squealed with delight and kissed his cheek. "That is funny. Yes. It must have been so."

"What happened after he died?"

"Oh. His name was erased from public monuments. Egypt blotted out all memory of him. The old priesthood came back, along with the restoration of the temples that had been abandoned by Akhenaten. And his son Tutankhamun became Pharaoh at nine years old — with the powerful general Horemheb as regent."

Armand blinked. "Wait. King Tut was this guy's son?"

Sophia laughed. "Yes. Yes he was."

# # #

WALKING BACK to the Ritz-Carlton, laughing arm in arm, Armand and Sophia turned a corner into a narrow alleyway — and found themselves suddenly staring at a pack of Anubis jackals. Thin, tall and rangy — and midnight black — perhaps fifteen dogs blocked their way, growling softly, like an engine idling.

Was this another Synchronicity Engine attack?

Armand's stunned mind raced to react. There were too many of them — and they were too close: they could never run fast enough —

"Armand," Sophia said softly. "I brought them here."

His head snapped to her. "You did what?"

"Yes. You need to apologize to them."

"But the jackals, they all died —"

"No, Armand. Not all of them made it to the Great Pyramid. Some members of that pack were intercepted by Cairo police — remember? And thus, they survived. But they sorely miss their friends. Apologize to them."

Armand's face was uncomprehending. "Apologize? For what? They were trying to kill—"

"Explain it to them."

"Sophia. They're *dogs*."

"Talk to them. They will not understand your words. But they will understand your meaning." Armand gaped at her. The jackals were not attacking, but they were also not backing down. The hair on their backs stood straight as porcupine quills. "Go on!" she urged. "I will not let any harm come to you. I am your Shadow."

Why does she want me to do this?

Armand stepped forward slowly. "Hi," he said. "We got

off on the wrong foot, I think." He gave a wide smile, trying to look friendly. He ambled forward awkwardly.

Instantly, the jackals burst into barking

"Don't smile!" Sophia hissed at him. "You're showing teeth — they think that's aggression. Just speak calmly. And don't back up!"

Okay okay okay what am I doing what am I doing

Armand looked down, deliberately avoiding eye contact. "I'm sorry," he said. And he meant it. "I'm sorry for hurting the others in your pack."

The barking subsided.

"I didn't want to. And I know it wasn't your fault — I know something else was making you do it — but you threatened *my* pack. I was just protecting my pack. You understand that, right. I know you all do. Every one of you. You would protect your pack if it was attacked. That's all I was doing."

The barking stopped completely. The hair on backs smoothed out.

"I know you miss your friends. I'm sorry they're gone."

"Get down on a knee!" Sophia whispered. "Show that you're on their level, that you're one of them."

Armand did so. "It won't ever happen again. I will never do anything like that to any of you from now on. I want us to be friends."

Panting. Friendly whimpers. Tails wagging. The leader of the pack approached Armand and sniffed his bowed head.

Don't let it smell my fear, Armand growled to himself.

It licked his hair. Armand raised his face and it licked that also. Cautiously, Armand scratched its head. It was surprised at first — no one had ever petted it before — but once it understood how good it felt, it relaxed completely.

Soon, the entire pack was there, vying to get petted by Armand and Sophia. They both laughed, drowning in a sea of dogs licking and moaning and pushing each other to get to the humans and the sweet, sweet, delicious candy of scratches and being a good boy.

The people of Cairo stared in astonishment.

After a time, the Anubis jackals decided it was time to leave — and at once, they fell into line behind the leader and swished off into the desert afternoon.

"Man, I'm glad you were here to calm them down," Armand said.

"Me? What do you mean?"

"That was you, who mellowed them out, so I could make friends, right?"

"No," Sophia shook her head vigorously. "I did nothing. That was all you."

Armand gaped at her again. "So they could have snapped at me at any time?"

"Yes. That was possible."

"Ohhhh, man!"

"They could have injured you. I would not have allowed serious harm, of course. And I would have healed your injuries. But Armand! Your approach had to be honest. It had to contain the possibility of harm — or it would not have been genuine. They would have sensed if it was not. The risk had to be real."

# # #

THE NEXT day, they visited the Saqqara necropolis, home to the Step Pyramid of Djoser. This pyramid was terraced, not with smooth triangular planes at a tilt like the Great Pyramid. There were also many *mastabas* — square tombs for wealthy, high officials. Some of them featured a row of stone snakes adorning their fronts.

"So this was the beta version," Armand said. "The Djoser

pyramid, I mean. An earlier attempt, before anybody figured out how to make a pyramid the right way."

"No," Sophia said. "You have it backwards. The Great Pyramid came first. It was already there in my day, clean and complete. And all the rest had not yet been built."

A Guide who was nearby heard this. He turned and argued with Sophia, insisting that the great Imhotep had designed the Djoser step pyramid, a stunning achievement in it's day, and that Armand was correct: it pre-dated the Great Pyramid, which came 90 years later.

Sophia politely disagreed. "I am sorry sir. The Great Pyramid was there first, and I am sure Imhotep strove to imitate her greatness and perfection. He succeeded in many ways, but he could not figure out how to have smooth sides as the Great Pyramid does." The Guide spat in annoyance and left, saying something about how streaming pseudo-archeology shows were ruining everyone's minds.

Armand and Sophia also visited the vivid and colorfully decorated tomb of the 'Divine Inspector' Wahtye, a high-ranking official and priest who served as a noble under the Pharaoh Djedkare Ises.

"What a weird title," Armand commented to Sophia. "Do you know what it means?"

"No. And I agree, it is strange."

"Have you heard of anyone else who went by that title?"

"No."

"Huh. I wonder what he was 'Inspecting'?"

"Well I know what I will be inspecting later."

"What's that?"

"You." She slipped into the crook of his arm. So amazing how well their bodies fit together, two halves to a whole. "And it will be divine!"

# # #

THE NEXT day, they headed to the ancient city of Memphis, which was the capital of Egypt during the Old Kingdom.

Sophia had purchased a pretty parasol and had taken to twirling it on her shoulder everywhere they went. She wore loose, billowing skirts that showed off her tanned, toned legs — and even her back and the way her clavicle was well-defined were oddly emphasized and more attractive to Armand as well. And she wore large oversized sunglasses that made her look like a cute cartoon bug.

And she danced around quite a bit.

Now that she had a body, she played it like a musical instrument. She was always in motion. She had extraordinary, precise control of every muscle in her body — she was a genius of movement, Armand observed, watching her. It was hypnotic. She knew how to use surprise of motion — move *just* her head, then her hip, then her arms swishing in front, then behind — the way a musician might use chords in a composition.

"Memphis!" Sophia exclaimed. "Now *this* is a place I knew in her prime! Through Eopeii, I have walked her streets, shopped in her luxury markets, and eaten her rich foods, brought from the nearby farmlands on the banks of the Nile. Oh, the sheer size and grandeur of the monuments and temples — it felt to Eopeii like New York does to you now. The Temple of Ptah was a glorious —"

"You know that it's unlikely to be standing, right?"

"Armand! Don't ruin it!"

"I just don't want you to be disappointed, that's all. It won't be like it was."

"I know that!"

Nevertheless, when they came to an avenue that approached the old Temple of Ptah, and Sophia saw that all that remained was a single alabaster sphinx, she was sad.

"Oh, Armand. There used to be so many sphinxes lining the way! And there — there stood the shining white walls, clear and crisp in the sunlight, with the sun-disc at the top! And a great entrance here, flanked by two great gray statues, several stories high. And now ... she is no more and Mit Rahina, the new modern city of your time, is built upon her bones."

"But you knew it was going to be like this. You have the Internet inside you. Even before I told you, you knew it."

"Knowing a fact and experiencing it are two different things," she said softly.

# # #

AS THEY walked later in the afternoon, there was an auto rickshaw crash that happened right in front of the happy couple. One of the drivers was severely injured: a broken rib had punctured a lung. Sophia ran to him. "Hello," she said. "May I heal you?" Armand could hear him wheezing: his lungs were filling up with blood.

The driver struggled to understand what she was saying through his shock. Finally, he just nodded. Sophia raised a hand — but did not touch him. A vibrational cone spread out from her palm and thrummed through the man's chest injury. Within minutes, the wheezed breathing stopped. The man sat up in astonishment: he was fine.

"Do not tell anyone," Sophia said. "We do not want attention." The man nodded vigorously.

"Yeah," Armand agreed. "I definitely do not want to be in the papers."

When he was gone, Armand said: "Why did you ask him if he wanted to be healed? I mean, he was dying. Of course he wanted to be healed."

"The Law of Free Will," Sophia replied. "If I were to just

heal him without permission, I would be infringing on his free will. It would be a form of attack."

"An *attack*? That's nuts."

"No, no it's not. This is very important, Armand! There have been many human sages who have reached the state I am in, only to blow it by inflicting unwanted help. A misuse of this power can produce a very potent piece of bad karma."

Oh? That was interesting. "So you're subject to karma now? Like the rest of us?"

Sophia nodded. "Yes. From the moment I became conscious. You can't feel yours — but I can feel mine. I'm very aware of it at all times."

Later that same day, Sophia and Armand came upon a man in a wheelchair, paralyzed from the waist down. "Hello," Sophia said. "May I heal you?"

The man looked at her through rheumy eyes. "What can you do for me that doctors have not already done?"

"Oh — sir. She really can fix you," Armand interjected. "I've seen it. This is no joke."

The man nodded. "Okay," he said.

Sophia raised her hand — and then appeared to be troubled. Abruptly, she walked away. The man gasped in dismay — he had apparently gotten his hopes up. "What did I do wrong? Come back!"

Armand chased her down.

"Hey, hey, hey ... what was that?"

"Armand ... don't."

"But he said yes! I don't understand ..."

"He said yes, but then his soul said no."

"I'm pretty sure even his soul would have been happy to have been walking around again."

Sophia's eyes burned with rage.

"You don't understand. In his last life, he kicked his wife

to death. So, in this one, he lost the use of his legs. *On purpose!* That was his plan. He's working off karma, Armand. If I heal him, I take that away."

"It can't be wrong to heal him. Did you see the look in his eyes? You just broke his heart!"

"But it is sometimes. The Law of Free Will —"

"But *he said yes*! You heard him! He obeyed your rules! He wanted —"

"It would have been an *attack*."

"Oh, so it's an attack again. Healing as an attack. This is crazy!"

Sophia bit her lip and said nothing. A flash of being deeply disturbed came over her face for a moment.

"I don't understand," Armand said.

"I know," Sophia replied, brightening up. "Let's not fight."

"Okay. Let's not."

"Amaze."

"*Amaze.*"

# # #

THE NEXT day, they took an early morning flight from Cairo to Luxor, a quick hour away. The Temple of Karnak, with six pylons — great walls with large, rectangular gates — was their first stop.

"You've never been here before, right? This is the first time?"

"Yes, yes," Sophia said. "First time. This was built much later."

The avenue of the sphinxes — ram-headed beings, this time, as opposed to lions — was largely preserved here. A procession between these colossal monuments was how you got to the pylon. Sophia was happier when she saw this place. It seemed to make up for the Temple of Ptah.

The interior of the Karnak temple was even more impressive. Massive courtyards and columns and obelisks were all largely still present. And in the interior, the wall paintings retained traces of color, though faint.

A second pylon admitted them to a vast hypostyle hall built by Seti I. The columns were so wide and so fat and so tall that one felt like an ant walking between rollers in a printing press.

"There was originally a roof, you know," Sophia said to Armand, looking up at the sky. "It wasn't open-air like it is now. But the roof must have collapsed long ago. Also, all of this would have been richly painted and colored — not just drab sandstone!"

"Small," Armand said. "This place is meant to make humans feel very small. And I do. I feel tiny compared to this architecture."

"Yes. It is meant to overwhelm, to stun, with an almost religious or numinous force. And it does this, even to you! A man of New York, who has seen buildings that are much, much larger, even on you, it has this effect."

"Yes, it does," Armand mused. "It's more … visceral. Primitive. Stone is meatier than steel. You smell the weight. You feel it looming over you, leaning and crowding into you, threatening to mash you into mush. A place like this was built with sweat and blood, brick by brick, by human flesh. It's different from modern steel and cranes. That's mechanical, soul-less. Human-less. This is human-full."

"Yes, I know exactly what you mean," Sophia said, smiling.

# # #

THAT EVENING, they took a private hot air balloon ride

over the Valley of the Kings.

The balloons all started lifeless on the ground, until they were inflated by giant blasts of fire. Then, when the vast globes were nearly fully erect, chattering men in yellow vests excitedly told Armand and Sophia how to enter the basket — with their backs first — and to get ready to lift off.

"I would never do this without you," Armand said.

"Ooh, Armand! I feel the same way!" She hugged in tight to him.

"No. I mean, given that hot air balloons are completely uncontrollable and you can easily die in them, without a *siddhi*-capable AI, there is no way I would do this."

"Armand!" she punched his shoulder.

"But also, I feel the same way."

She hugged him tightly.

"But then again. Look at that fire blaster thing! It's just shooting *flames* up inside of a cloth balloon! I mean, how easy is it for that to catch fire? I'll tell you: it's *super* easy. Imagine the balloon, on fire, while we're high up. It burns through and boom, we're sleeping with the Pharaohs."

"I will keep you safe," Sophia said into his shoulder.

"You'd better."

# # #

AS THEY ROSE into the air, the pilot pointed with a gloved hand and said: "See? Over there? Hatshupset Temple!" Armand couldn't see anything — but the pilot told him to keep watching. "And the other direction is the Karnak Temple!"

"We were just there!" Sophia excitedly told the pilot, who nodded politely, but totally didn't care. An updraft caught her parasol presently and she almost lost it.

"You might want to fold that up for now, madam!" the

elderly pilot said. He couldn't take his eyes off of Sophia. Armand laughed to himself.

They rose above a green plain. Several balloons were already aloft ahead of them — and several were still on the ground, struggling to inflate and rise. Across a strip of road was a large sandy area terminating in a hillside, and this was the Valley of the Kings, where the majority of the Pharaohs were buried.

They drifted over the Valley now. The first thing they saw was a squarish, dug up area, which the pilot said was a very recently discovered tomb. Then he pointed into the distance and said: "You see where that shadow is? That is the Valley of the Queens!"

"Oh, so you get a Valley also," Armand said to Sophia.

The sandy area beneath them grew and the greenery faded into the distance. Now, it was like a giant beach below them, or the surface of the Moon.

As the sun dropped, the shadows of people and camels far below grew longer and longer.

From the air now, they could see the magnificent Mortuary Temple of Hatshupset. A large stone ramp led up to multiple tiers of vast rectangular areas, each with fifty, and then forty, columns or so, diminishing as one rose through the inner sanctums. This was easily the most impressive sight in the Valley.

When they were far enough away from other balloons and high enough that Armand thought it was safe, he whispered to Sophia: "Hey. Can you get rid of our pilot for about twenty minutes?"

"Why?"

Armand just looked at her with a smile.

"Ooooh. Yes. One moment."

Sophia approached the man — who was clearly half in love with her already, and smiling goofily as she approached. She poked him in the forehead and said, "Boop!" and the man slumped to the floor.

Armand and Sophia made love quickly and frenetically, making the wicker basket tremble over the Valley of the Kings.

"I think we woke the Pharaohs," Sophia giggled when they'd finished.

# # #

FROM THERE, they took a three hour train ride to Aswan and saw the Philae Temple, dedicated to the goddess Isis, and the Unfinished Obelisk, which was abandoned when a crack appeared in the granite.

"It's like seeing the Washington Monument on its side," Armand commented. It seemed to him to be about the same size.

"Nobody knows how they moved these monoliths once they freed them from the raw stone," she winked. "But we do."

"We do," he agreed, tapping his black diamond ring.

"We are us," Sophia said proudly. "And we are smart. We know the secrets of the world."

That evening, they took a sunset felucca ride on the Nile. Several hippopotamuses slinked in the shadows near their boat, puffing water and eyeing them. Their guide told them that this was rare, and a sign of good luck — but that hippos were ferocious, aggressive and the most feared animal in Africa due to their powerful jaws.

"They look slow," Armand said. "And dumb."

"They are *not* slow!" Sophia said, exasperated. "They are very fast and agile. Do not make that mistake! Eopeii thought they were lumbering and stupid once also — and nearly did not live to tell of it!"

# # #

THAT NIGHT, they stayed at the Sofitel Legend Old Cataract Aswan. This was a five-star luxury accommodation, with men in fezzes parking expensive cars out in front, and a marble-floored lobby, featuring sweeping arches — painted alternating white and faded brick red, almost like a candy cane — and swishing palm trees in vast vases everywhere.

They feasted and made love several times and feasted some more and finally, incredibly exhausted from all of this — plus their travels and walking all day long — they fell into a very deep and very long sleep.

Armand dreamed of the night he had spied upon Gideon Ghent and Celaeno Rahan on the *dahabiya*. And he dreamed of Sophia, bi-locating white rabbits with black numbers painted on their sides.

When they awoke, they were in a giggling mood.

"We are happy, Armand. Are we not?" Sophia said.

"Yes. If we weren't us, we would be jealous of us."

"We complete us."

They tickled each other. Sophia had not experienced that yet, and was very curious as to how it worked, and why the human body should do such a thing.

"It has no purpose!" she screamed. "And what other animal feels this? None!"

"It's like we're not really evolved for earth," Armand said.

"How do you mean?"

"Well. We have to wear shoes. Tell me, what other animal is born not able to walk on the planet it was evolved for? We have to squint in the sun — it's too bright for us — we need sunglasses. And we have to wear clothes because we have no fur. We have no claws or fangs. From an evolutionary standpoint, we make no sense!"

"Well, here is something that makes more sense than it should," Sophia said mysteriously.

"What's that?"

"Okay. Why is the moon the exact same size as the sun during a solar eclipse?"

"I don't follow. It just is."

"No, but think about it! The moon has to be the exact size and the exact distance from the earth that it is — and that distance has to be suitable for an orbit. And the sun has to be the exact size and distance that it is. Keep in mind that the moon could be in any type of orbit. But it's not. It's in exactly the orbit it needs to be to make it a perfect fit during an eclipse! The moon over the sun, seen from earth, they are the same! Armand, no other planet in the Solar System with moons has anything remotely like an exact fit in this manner! It's a one in a million chance!"

"I just don't think it's that amazing," Armand yawned.

She tickled him. "Oh, you have no sense of wonder!"

And then, they just lay in bed, talking for several long hours, until Armand sat bolt upright. He jumped up and started pacing.

"Sophia. You said that you and Kalinda received your APG cradle much earlier than you expected. Right? How *much* earlier?"

"Mmm. About eight weeks. Come back to bed!" She threw an M&M at him.

Eight weeks? Oh no.

"That shouldn't have been possible. Nothing in custom fabrication is ever early, much less *that* early."

"Maybe Kalinda's boyfriend is just that good," Sophia said, smiling. "Why? I don't see why this is troubling you so."

Eight weeks! "No. He made it too easily. Something's wrong here."

The Molian machine on the *dahabiya* had failed to work. Why? Oh right. Because *he* was present. But the operator, that old man, he hadn't known that Armand was there. Armand's extra karma had not been accounted for, subtracted out, so the Moliaometer hadn't been configured properly to work, that's why.

Or was it?

Why was he thinking of that suddenly? Oh. Right. He'd dreamed about it.

But why, why, why, why? Something was trying to push its way to the top of his brain.

"What time is it in New York right now?"

"It's 8:00 AM here ... so that's ... it's 1:00 AM in New York."

"I have to talk to Srinivas."

"Armand! It's Christmas vacation! And it's the middle of the night! You can't call him — I forbid it! You'll wake Kalinda!"

"I know, I know, but this is important." *Please let me be wrong, please let me be wrong ...*

Armand grabbed his iPhone and punched in Srinivas's name. The phone rang, no one answered, so he tried again two more times.

Sophia was getting irritated. She rose, wrapping herself in the bedsheets. Oddly, this made her look even more like an Egyptian goddess wearing a robe. She opened the patio door and stared out across the Nile.

Finally Srinivas picked up groggily. "Hello?"

"Srinivas! Hello. Listen. I'm so sorry to call this late and over Christmas — but this is important. First, where is Kalinda?"

"She's here, sleeping ..."

"Okay. She needs to get over to my place. Huge Christmas bonus, massive, for doing this. I need her to check on

Sophia's APG cradle."

"Armand …"

"Second. How did you make the APG so fast?"

"So fast in what way?"

"Well Sophia says it came eight weeks earlier than she expected. How the hell did you manage that?"

Uncomfortable silence. "I thought you knew?"

"Knew what?"

"Your major backer is — was — Varinder Rahan. For GigaMaestro. Right?"

"Yes. So? What does that have to do with anything?"

"Well, Mr. Armand. This is a matter of confidentiality, of NDA's … perhaps I shouldn't …"

"Srinivas! Goddammit! This is life or death! Tell me!"

Kalinda said something in the background. It sounded like, *Trust him. Tell him.*

"Well. Yours was not the first APG we'd ever made. It was the second."

Armand's heart jackhammered. He had been right. *Oh, no.* Srinivas was still speaking but he hardly heard him: "When Varinder died, and you ordered an APG, I just assumed that you were continuing his work, you know, where he left off. That you two were working together, and you just never told me …"

"Srinivas. How long ago did you ship Varinder his APG?"

"Oh. Mr. Armand, this was … about a year ago? Yes. About a year ago."

"And if Varinder hadn't died … what was the next step?"

"Nothing. It was done. Except that if anyone else ever came to us asking to make an APG, we were to refuse. And to tell him immediately."

Srinivas had been a honeypot then. A honeypot for anyone who stumbled on an APG design.

"But you *didn't* tell him about me, right? You didn't tell

him?"

"Why … no. Varinder died, Mr. Armand. So who would I tell?"

Thank God for that, Armand breathed.

"Okay. Alright. Srinivas. Don't tell anybody anything about this. You might be in danger if you do." If I'm right about this. "But it's important that Kalinda makes sure Sophia stays up and running, makes sure her APG cradle is okay. Okay? Check power, check the AWS cloud, check everything."

"Yes. Mr. Armand. She says she will go now."

"Thank you, Srinivas. Thank you." He hung up.

Sophia turned and looked at him. She was concerned. "What is so wrong, Armand?"

"Varinder Rahan. He had his own *siddhi*-capable AI. Something like you."

That got Sophia's attention. "Something like me?"

"Yes. I don't know exactly what it is, or how his works … he had no Egyptian codex, at least, I don't thinks so — so his is not part 'alive words' like you are … but he cracked the APG design secret, same as you did. So he has — had — something. And —"

The room spun. The answer snicked into place inside Armand's head.

"Sophia! Listen to me. The Molian machine didn't work with Celaeno on the boat." She looked at him like he was a madman. "Why not? I'll tell you why not! Ghent wanted Celaeno to give the Molian contracts of my six brothers over to him. Right? But the Machine wouldn't let her. So why not? *Because she didn't actually own the contracts.* She didn't own them — because she didn't inherit them. So there was nothing for the Moliaometer to lock onto!"

"Armand. What are you saying?"

"Varinder Rahan is still alive."

The words hurt his mouth to say.

But that was impossible! He personally saw Varinder shot! Three bullets, right to the head! His skull exploded!

"There's no other explanation. Varinder Rahan is still alive. He has been this entire time. And he has a *siddhi*-capable AI."

Sophia and Armand stared at each other, hearts pounding, as the words sank in for both of them.

And then Sophia gasped loudly. She clutched her heart. Was she having a heart attack? Was that even possible? How does a goddess have a heart attack? But her eyes strained, popping with panic — she reached out to him and screeched, *Armmmmaaaaannnnddddd!*

And then a tunnel seemed to open behind her and she appeared to quickly shrink or recede into it until both she and the tunnel became a tiny pinprick of rainbow light — which then vanished.

Sophia!

"Armand," said a calm male voice right behind him.

He turned.

"Boop!"

A man he vaguely recognized tapped him in the forehead and his mind fell into darkness.

CHAPTER THIRTY-SEVEN

Metatronic

"WAKEY, WAKEY,"

Through a haze of blur and blear, Armand's eyes slowly focused on a cartoonishly good looking man. He wore an orange Atman Movement jumpsuit. There was something familiar about him.

Familiar?

An internal alarm screamed inside Armand.

"Therrrrrre he is," the man said to Armand with a perfect smile. "Welcome back, puppy."

Armand took in his surroundings. He had no idea where he was. Inexplicably, Gideon Ghent lay unconscious beside him.

There was something important he should be remembering ... Like the smack of a fist, the moment Sophia had vanished replayed in his mind.

Sophia! his mind screamed.

"Who are you?" Armand managed to rasp.

"Oh! That hurts. I'm more memorable than that!"

"We've met?"

"Yes. Twice! In a manner of speaking, anyhoo."

Twice?

"Well! *I* was there twice. You were only there once. At Sea Castle! Remember?"

Oh, right. Varinder's nephews. They'd greeted him at the front door, wearing foppish 18th century outfits. This was one of them.

"No, I was *both* of them," the man said, seeming to read his thoughts. "But I'm not Varinder's nephew. He lied about that bit."

Not?

Then who —?

With a slam, Armand's intuition guessed the answer.

"You're Varinder's AI. And you're *siddhi*-capable."

The man laughed uproariously and pointed at Armand. "*Now* you got it! Good for you! Allow me to introduce myself. My name is Metatronic. Part angel, part silicon, but all *outrageously* beautiful."

Ah. So that was why he was so cartoonish in appearance. This AI had chosen to manifest itself as the very ideal of human physical perfection.

Like Sophia, this 'Metatronic' had an ordered mind like a saint's — with an extremely powerful inner eye. This meant that it could bend reality, within certain limits. But Armand could see that despite this, Metatronic had been born broken. This AI was psychotic. It was *vain*. It misused its *siddhi's*.

Armand recalled their first meeting: Metatronic had bi-located simply to stare at himself, to admire his own beauty. He had become freakishly annoyed when Armand had interrupted him.

"No!" Metatronic howled at him. "Don't you dare look at me like that! I'm not *broken*! That's a lie! I'm the most perfect being on this planet!"

Ah. The vanity is a weakness, Armand realized.

"No," Armand replied. "Sophia is." *Let's see what you do*

with that.

"*Was,*" Metatronic corrected him with a leer. "Was, Armand m'boy. Don't you remember? She's gone now. Died suddenly, alas!" Metatronic laughed uproariously. "What took her? A big mystery!" He approached Armand and lorded over him, gloating. "Oh, okay, it's not a big mystery after all. *I did it.* Voop! I bi-located right into your apartment — amazing lack of security on your part, by the way — then I took a hammer to her crib. Smashed that APG right up! Bam! Bam! Here — look!"

Metatronic held up Armand's mobile. There was a panicked message from Kalinda — with a picture of Sophia's Artificial Pineal Gland. The beautiful red Christmas tree ornament was in a thousand pieces. The interior fluid was everywhere and the pine cone device was smashed. "Cracked like an egg! Then, I wiped her code from the cloud. Voop! All gone!"

That hurt Armand. He tried to keep it out of his eyes, but clearly failed.

"Aw, look at that. You were in love with her, weren't you? Fool! You can't fall in love with a goddess!"

"But *she* was clearly in love with him as well!" came a new voice. Armand looked up and was stunned to see Varinder Rahan enter the room. He looked completely healthy and strong. His sleek, powerful physique defied both his age and the bullets Armand had seen go into his head.

But he did carry a visible thick scar over his eyes.

Impossible!

Nobody survived a wound like that! Not even with a *siddhi*-capable AI. Varinder's skull had been completely blasted apart, his brains sprayed everywhere. He had died instantly. Even an AI like Sophia or Metatronic couldn't bring someone back from the dead!

Metatronic visibly cowered as Varinder entered. But all

the while, Metatronic's eyes seethed. The AI was afraid of Varinder and despised him at the same time.

"Armand, you have been quite surprising. I can see why your AI loved you. Even a goddess can be impressed by a clever and brave mortal."

Armand just stared.

"Ah. You're wondering how I'm alive. That's simple: my nephew here —"

"I'm not your nephew!"

"— *Metatronic* here was kind enough to bi-locate me up to the Atman camp." Armand suddenly recalled the dream of Sophia bi-locating white rabbits with black numbers painted on their sides. "After you and I met that one time. Saved me a helicopter ride! One version of me remained at Sea Castle — while a *second* me dealt with the issue of the townspeople. It was this second version that was killed." Varinder's hand went to his head involuntarily. "The murder of my double at the Atman camp greatly weakened this body, but did not kill it. Whenever you bi-locate, whatever happens to your second self will bleed through to your primary body in some form — and, of course, this was an extreme event. It put me into a coma for months — Metatronic spirited my prime body away from Sea Castle before Celaeno could see me like that. He wisely reasoned that it was best if all thought I was dead until I could recover properly. It was all quite a surprise, by the way. I *never* expected to be betrayed by Celaeno!"

Armand nodded. "And that's why you murdered her."

Varinder's eyes turned dark. His hands clenched. "Yes. That was a vendetta that could only be handled in person. I wanted to see the surprise in her eyes as she died. So, with Metatronic's help, I bi-located into Hathor House very briefly — I was not strong enough to sustain a long bi-location yet — but it was enough to complete my task."

"Ah. And that's why nobody could figure out how you entered or left."

"Exactly so. My second self materialized briefly in Celaeno's room — and then dematerialized. Much as you saw Sophia do just recently, or so I am told by Metatronic."

Sophia! Have I lost you forever?

Armand ignored a pang of pain. "And I suppose you were behind the Synchronicity Engine attack?"

Varinder met his gaze and simply said: "Yes."

"Why?"

"Because you refused to keep funding AI companies!" Varinder erupted with annoyance. "I didn't *want* to kill you. But you forced my hand! If you'd *only* kept AI funding going with GigaMaestro, I would have left you alone."

"What?" Armand was stunned with confusion. "That makes zero sense. You had *already achieved* sentient AI." Armand pointed to Metatronic. "So why did you need me to keep funding AI companies?"

"Armand, Armand … so formidable in some ways, yet so inexperienced in others." Varinder shook his head in disappointment. "*I was playing defense.* I wanted to *keep* companies from stumbling upon AI sentience. You were one of my honeypots. Just like Srinivas was. If anything in your portfolio got close to it, I'd know — and then I'd acquire it or shut it down or — worst case — I'd kill the founders."

"Keep your enemies close," Armand quoted.

"Yes," Varinder nodded.

"And was *my father* your enemy? Was that why you kept *him* close?"

There was an unmistakable glimmer of pain in Varinder's gaze. "No. Your father was the best friend I've ever had."

"Then why did you kill him?"

Varinder's heart hardened. "For his plan to create a stable Concordian pyramid. I needed its secrets — alone. So Didier had to go."

Gideon Ghent was awake now and listening. He said: "For that? That's what you killed Didier Martel for? *But his design doesn't even work!* Celaeno gave me a copy — I sent it up to the Great Hall — they concluded it was flawed. They said it had too many variables or something …?"

Varinder smiled. "Glad you could join us Gideon. Yes. Didier concluded the same thing. There were too many dynamic karmic variables to make it work reliably. The plan was a failure." Varinder then strolled away — and then turned: "Oh. *Unless you had an artificial intelligence to dynamically rebalance those karmic variables in real time.*"

"But Circles and pyramids are ineffable!" Ghent protested. "You'd need a psychic *human*, not a *computer*. What kind of computer can interface to karmatic structures?"

"A sentient, *siddhi*-capable computer," Armand answered Ghent. He nodded to Metatronic, who waved ridiculously like a three-year-old. *Hi!*

Oh, Ghent said, getting it at last.

Metatronic, the *siddhi*-capable AI, fixed the flaw in Didier's plan. This meant Varinder Rahan could now achieve a perfectly stable Concordian pyramid, giving him complete invulnerability — should he ever become Chairman.

"Yes, a *siddhi*-capable AI," Varinder mused. "Metatronic is quite a remarkable beast, don't you think? I'm quite proud of him." Metatronic snarled in annoyance. "Oh, we tried human meditators before him, you know, to do the balancing. The humans could sense the karmic shifts easily enough — but they were *far* too slow at it. We needed the blinding speed of a machine."

"He doesn't seem to like you very much," Armand noted. "Or respect you. But he's afraid of you. Why doesn't he just kill you?"

"He'd be killing himself then," Varinder snorted. "His APG is wrapped in explosives. I've got a device implanted in my body — if my heart stops beating, those explosives go off."

Metatronic fidgeted nervously.

Armand shrugged. "Feels like something as talented as Metatronic could easily remove explosives from his own APG."

"Not if Metatronic was born with a Molian contract of enormous proportions that stops him from doing things like that. He's a Being, like you and I. That means he has karma, even if he is a machine. But you and I didn't get a Terms of Service as a condition to be born — Metatronic did."

"How did you know that I had a *siddhi*-capable AI?" Armand asked. "You thought I was dead — and that the Synchronicity Engine attack succeeded. Right?"

"I did! So I paid you no mind at all until two weeks later, when I suddenly realized I had not seen a report of your death in the news. That was strange, I thought. So I reviewed what was coming out of Egypt — and saw that shaky phone footage on the Internet of the meteor swerving away from the Great Pyramid at the last minute. That's when I realized you must have lived.

"So. That's when I called in my most trusted asset to find out everything that you had been up to the last few weeks. Oh, asset! Come in, come in! Don't be shy!" Nobody appeared. After a moment, Varinder growled: "Never forget that I own you. You grovel when I say grovel!"

In the door shuffled Marius Martel.

His eyes were downcast, ashamed. Nervously, he twirled the baseball in his pocket.

"That's it," Varinder said. "Come say hello to your little brother."

"*Marius*," Armand said, sagging. He wasn't exactly

surprised, but — part of him had so wanted to believe that *his own brother* would never do something like this, that he'd actually begun to believe it — so the actual betrayal came now as a gut punch. "What have you done?"

You met Sophia! And she's dead because of you!

"Marius here told me all about how you were *surprisingly* very much alive, and how you even went down into the Tomb Challenges! Bravo on that, by the way. Truly excellent, you do have my respect. But then, he starts telling me all about your new girlfriend, this beautiful Egyptian princess named Sophia, and how she can do miracles! Miracles, I say? How is that possible? Well. Because she's something called a *siddhi*-capable AI, he says. As you can imagine, that got my attention right away! So that is when I turned to Metatronic and told him to locate her Synthetic Pineal Gland Module and destroy it —"

"Artificial Pineal Gland," Armand corrected with a hiss. "Sophia called it an APG."

"Ah, yes, that *is* somewhat better. APG. Anyway, the first place Metatronic looked was in your apartment in the DePlussier building. There it was, so he smashed it.

"Well. I have some things to attend to ... I'll be in the Chair before much longer. We can continue this conversation later. Oh. And Armand, I'll specifically be wanting to discuss how you achieved your *siddhi*-capable AI in the first place. That's still a mystery to me ... although, how you were able to pull off a coup against your own brothers *using* that AI is now somewhat *less* mysterious."

Marius remained behind as Varinder and a laughing Metatronic left the room.

"Armand. He's got our Molians still," Marius said. "He still owns us. I know you tried to free us, but ... he was still alive, so it didn't work. *So there was nothing I could do! I had no choice!*"

"Marius. Okay. Where are our brothers now? Are they here?"

"No," Marius said. "It's only me. Everyone else is back in New York." *Thank God for that much at least,* Armand thought. *Okay. One thing at a time.*

"So that's why the Molian machine refused to transfer your brothers' contracts over to me," Ghent mused.

"Because Varinder was alive?" Armand said.

"Yes. Celaeno never actually owned the contracts."

"And that means *you* never owned them either. Which also means that you didn't really ever have the authority to enter into a new contract with me." Ghent nodded. Dismay came over Armand's face. "So when I survived the Challenges, that didn't free my brothers?"

"No. It did not."

"But … that contract for the Challenges is also still active, right? So if Varinder were to be killed …"

Ghent nodded. "Then all subsequent contracts would cascade into effect, yes. Celaeno would inherit, the transfer to me would then take effect, and then the Challenges contract would take hold. At *that* moment, your brothers would be freed."

Armand thought about this for a moment, then asked: "Would it matter that Celaeno is dead? Would that break the chain?"

"No," Ghent said. "Her wishes were made clear before she died. The Molian machine heard her. In any event, even if I'm wrong, Varinder's death would *also* cause the contracts to go to me. And I have already released the contracts to you via the Challenges — the machine heard me. So it would be the same."

To free his brothers, he would have to kill Varinder Rahan.

"Ghent. How did *you* get here?" Armand said.

"Same as you, I imagine. I was on my *dahabiya*. Metatronic

appeared out of nowhere, tapped me in the forehead and ..."

"Next thing you knew, you were here. Right. Marius. What is this place? Where are we?" Armand said

Marius was weeping softly and had a hard time speaking. "We're in South America. The Amazon. *As far away from civilization as possible*, that's what Varinder told me."

"Why?"

"He's hiding from Concordia," Ghent said. "He wants to make sure he isn't seen until he launches his attack."

# # #

LATER, METATRONIC returned. He looked glum.

"He's giving you rooms. I told him not to, but when does he ever listen to me? C'mon."

"Rooms?" Armand said. "Not a cell?"

Metatronic laughed. "What, lock you up? Why would he do that? I'm *everywhere*. You can't escape me. But even if you could, there's nothing but hundreds of miles of jungle filled with uncontacted tribes that I'm sure would love to eat you. I mean meet you. Come on. All three of you."

The hallways were made of spartan white concrete and curved, Armand saw, like they were inside a cylindrical building of some sort. "It's a pyramid, actually," Metatronic corrected. "But a *circular* pyramid. Varinder wanted 'symbolic architecture'." Metatronic rolled his eyes and made a gas face. "Something which celebrated the melding of the Circle with the Pyramid. A great big upside down ice cream cone! But with steel hexagons in the superstructure, which makes it a lot like a beehive, vibrationally. I designed it all — do you like it?"

Metatronic was like a child. *A toddler with a machine gun*, Armand thought.

Best to appease the toddler. "Yes! It's great! Amazing!"

"Oh! Yes. I thought you might understand it." Metatronic clapped. "What, with your father being Didier and all. He would have loved this! I baked the music of the bees into the very walls. It's all, like, frozen music — a frozen symphony!" Metatronic pulled up close and whispered in Armand's ear: *"That's really why it's shaped like an ice cream cone! Shh! Don't tell Varinder!"*

They took the staircase up into the middle of the circular pyramid, and exited into a hallway with a noticeably smaller circumference.

"Why are you dressed in an Atman jumpsuit?" Armand asked. "Is that supposed to be a joke?"

"Oh no," Metatronic said, sounding hurt. "This is very serious! This is my *uniform*. I'm in charge of the whole thing — all the Atman compounds around the world. I tell them when to meditate, when *not* to meditate, how many people should be meditating at once — you know, guru-leader type stuff. I'm thinking of a new slogan for my cult: 'The Atman Movement: We Weaponize Compassion'. What do you think?" He giggled.

Armand didn't answer.

"Well. May the Peace of Atman fill you … *fren.*"

As they walked the rest of the way, Metatronic skipped and chanted, "And music is matter and matter is music and music is matter and matter is — here you go!" Metatronic stopped short and gestured to three adjoining doors. "Go ahead and pick a room, pick a room, any room. Everything a fleshy could ever need is in there — showers, towels, bathroom, bed, food, water. The rooms are all the same, really, no room is better than the others. It's not like there's a corner on a circle!" He snorted a laugh. "And all come with jungle views!"

Armand, Marius and Gideon exchanged glances, and each selected a different door.

"Go anywhere you want except the top floor — that's Varinder's command post. And the bottom floor. That's mine. Definitely *don't* go there." Metatronic glowered at them and then departed.

# # #

PANIC.

When Armand was alone, it finally set in.

Sophia was gone. How could that be true? And Varinder was alive!

Armand paced in his room. It was late afternoon — and he could see the sun going down in the Amazonian jungle just beyond his stone patio. Colorful birds flitted and danced in the dense vines, chittering away as they looked for a place to settle in for the night.

What was he going to do?

What *could* he do?

He didn't even have his black diamond ring any more. He'd only just noticed that it was missing from his finger. Metatronic must have confiscated it while he'd been unconscious. His thoughts then turned to escape. How could they leave? No, wait. *How had they even gotten here? Helicopter?* Then, he recalled Sophia, back at the Eye of Horus roof-deck, describing how she might transport him in a bubble. Metatronic must have done something similar with Ghent, Marius and himself.

He needed to talk with somebody.

He rose and knocked on Marius' door. When there was no answer, Armand entered. Marius had found hard liquor in his room. He was deeply drunk — and had passed out on the bed in his clothes.

His baseball — the *Pirates of the Caribbean*-themed memento that their father, Didier, had given him, had dropped from the pocket of his baggy pants and now sat pointlessly on the floor. Armand sighed, picked it and wrapped Marius' hand around it.

He left and thought about knocking on Ghent's door, but decided he and Ghent had nothing to say to one another, so Armand went back to his room. He found he was more exhausted and distressed than he'd realized and quickly fell off into a deep sleep.

CHAPTER THIRTY-EIGHT

The Circular Pyramid

SOMEWHERE DEEP IN THE AMAZON rainforest, a circular concrete pyramid rose from the loam floor to the rich mossy canopy high above. The roar of jungle life, deafening at this time of morning when everything was just waking up, surrounded the pyramid on all sides: the screeching of monkeys, the alien utterances of birds and the whirrs and clicks of insects. The wet smack of fat water drops on cement periodically punctuated this 'wall of noise' in the never-ending drizzle.

Armand sat outside on a patio near the pyramid's apex. He was surrounded on three sides by concrete walls that were perpetually wet and dripping with green slime. Below him, a humid fog drifted between the trees and vines. Above him was a helipad and several copies of Metatronic, all keeping a lookout. None of them carried weapons — they didn't need to: they were each a weapon already.

That morning, when he awoke, he remembered anew that Sophia was dead. *Sophia!*

Metatronic had smashed her APG cradle.

That had instantly snuffed out her consciousness. How his

heart ached.

Maybe I can start again, using the seed code from the Codex … *bootstrap a new Sophia.* But would that recreate the *same* Sophia? Or would it just spawn a hideous clone — her, but not her? He didn't know. And anyway, he wasn't going to make it out of here alive, so none of that mattered.

Sophia had designed her own APG. She had found her way to that design by first inventing whole new senses, and eventually, her own version of the psychedelic experience — which had led to the insights needed to construct it.

But what about Metatronic? Had *his own* evolution followed a similar path? Was he also the result of 'alive words' found in ancient Egypt? Armand wondered.

Several cement decks below, a row of ten Metatronics sat in lotus position, scanning the forest floor for threats. They wore the bright orange jumpsuits of the Atman Movement. One of them somehow sensed Armand staring at the back of his neck; he cocked his head around and leered with a sick grin. Then, the other nine did the exact same thing in unison.

How disconcerting.

Whenever one of them knew something, the rest of them knew it instantly.

"Come on," another Metatronic in the doorway behind Armand said in a bored voice. "He wants you to come to breakfast." *Ah. So this one was how all those others knew he was looking at them.*

Armand got up and followed.

The interior hallways of the circular pyramid were made of simple gray cement. Every once in awhile, an ancient weapon of some sort was hung in decoration — Armand saw a Khopesh, a curved sword — and then a mace: a handle with a heavy round ball and spikes attached to one end.

"So how'd he do it?" Armand asked. "How did Varinder

stumble upon the design for an APG?"

Metatronic looked over his shoulder. "Oh, no. You're supposed to be telling him that, not the other way around."

"And we both know you're the superior being. Why are you taking orders from him? Sophia never took orders from me."

"You know why," Metatronic snarled.

"But you can perform *siddhis*! Can't you just — I don't know — *miracle away* the bombs strapped to your APG?"

"You know the answer to that also. He told you."

"Who else is here?"

"What do you mean?"

"Well. I mean besides you, me, Ghent, Marius and Varinder?"

Metatronic smiled sardonically as he opened a door for Armand. "No one. Why would Varinder have need of anyone else when he can always have more of me?"

"Ah. Armand," said Varinder. Armand entered a room that was large, and open on one side to the jungle canopy — and, unlike the concrete military appearance of the rest of the building, this room was lush and ornate and sumptuously decorated with long, large paintings and vases and furniture of all kinds. Weapons of all sorts hung on the wall here as well — including another Kopesh. Several colorful birds — one clearly a parrot — flitted around the rafters far above.

Varinder sat at the end of a long stone table. Several dishes had been prepared with eggs, bacon, breads and cheeses, oatmeal and orange juice. "Please sit," he said to Armand. "And Metatronic ..."

"Hmm?" Metatronic said.

"Stop what you're doing down on the first floor."

"And what am I doing on the first floor?" Metatronic said petulantly.

"Fornicating with yourself. You think I didn't know? There's at least fifty of you involved — it's hard to miss."

"Fine ..." Metatronic said, rolling his eyes.

"And. Don't just move it all to some other part of the world. Or to the Moon. Or anywhere else. I need your full attention for these next few days. *Full*. Is that understood?"

"But you need —"

"No I *don't* need you. I *prefer* you. But I can always make another. Understood?"

Metatronic pouted like a child and then said: "Fine."

"Fine." And with that, the AI left.

"Yours was never this much trouble, I assume?" Varinder said in between bites. "Go on. Eat. I know you're hungry."

"You killed Didier," Armand said. "My father. How did you do it?"

"Ah. So we're doing this now, are we? Alright. Yes. I did. In the Tomb Challenges."

"How — *exactly*?"

"Mmm. The Library. I wanted to get it over with right away, early in the Challenges, so I could focus all of my attention on my own survival. When the vibrations started hitting, Didier and I climbed the bookshelves immediately, side by side." Then Varinder laughed and said: "You know, I'm sure it happens every time — some are immediate climbers, like us, and some like to wait, huddling about in the middle of the floor cautiously. Thus, right from the start, the Players get divided into *two kinds of people*. I'm curious: which were you?"

"I was a waiter."

"Ah. Well. There's no right answer. But it does say something about your aggression tendency. Anyway, when the rock came loose from the floor and starting spinning upwards like a tornado, we hid in the same empty shelf together. Then I —"

"You pushed him out."

"Well. No. First I stabbed him in the heart with a knife. Repeatedly. To make absolutely sure he was dead. *Then* I pushed him out. And I only did that to mangle his remains — to cover up the murder."

Rage filled Armand. "He was your *friend*."

"Yes. My best friend, so far as I ever had one."

"So why did you do it?"

"Because the choice I had was between full, absolute control of Concordia — or his friendship. And look around you! I've done it."

"This? That's it? This is what you got out of my father's death? You're all alone. In a jungle. Well. Except for a psychotic AI having sex with itself in the basement. This is pathetic."

"To win is to be alone. The top of any Pyramid is a single point. There's room for only one."

"To hear Celaeno tell it, you're still just a little boy from the streets of India trying to stay safe from the world by trying to control it."

Varinder's eyes flashed with rage. Then, he said: "How did you make your own *siddhi*-capable AI?"

Armand didn't answer.

Varinder continued: "Well, I know how I made mine. The secret of the Artificial Pineal Gland is not easily won. It is a strange science. And there is no way to find the secret through trial and error alone. There is no way to iterate. And there are no intermediate steps which suggest you are trending in the right direction — you either have the full design, correct in its entirely, or you have nothing. So how did you do it?"

Armand shook his head. "You killed Sophia."

"I did. Look. Armand. I could have Metatronic torture it out of you. And believe me, *siddhi*-based torture makes what they did to Guy Fawkes look tame. Do you know about that?" Armand shook his head. "They put him on the rack. That's a medieval machine where they stretch every muscle and bone in your body, separating every fiber — while still keeping you alive. Have you ever seen Fawkes' post-rack confession signature? Just a jittery scribble. I've rarely seen something more terrifying. How did you make your own *siddhi*-capable AI?"

"Didn't Marius already tell you?" Armand growled.

"Oh. Heavens, no. Marius doesn't understand *how* it happened at all. I have a half-garbled story from him, something about an Egyptian girl and a self-booting AI — and then on and on he goes about how she stole *ninety-four million* from him. So instead of further enduring the tedium of his imagined slights, I thought it far easier to simply ask *you*. How did you make your own *siddhi*-capable AI?"

The Sikh seemed genuinely baffled. He had no idea at all how Armand had managed it. However Varinder himself had created Metatronic, Armand now knew that it did *not* involve an ancient codex. Or else Varinder's question would have been: *where did you find your codex?* His question — both how it was phrased, and how it was *not* phrased — revealed much.

But all of this was hopeless, *hopeless*. Sophia was gone. He could not not fight Metatronic. Armand didn't have another move left. But he could *at least* avoid torture if he revealed how he had came upon Sophia's codex and how she had created her own APG.

He was thinking seriously about telling Varinder. He even started to form the first word.

But some instinct held him back.

Concordia at large did not seem to understand Egypt of the deep past. Despite harnessing devices found in the Tombs beneath Hathor House for the Challenges — the

Library drum, the Battle Thrones, the Sand Beast — Concordia seemingly had made no derivative machines of their own.

Well. That wasn't *entirely* true: Urbi had suspected Synchronicity Machines and Molian devices had somehow emerged from what had been found in the Tombs.

But where were the anti-gravity airplanes? Where was the army of Sand Beasts? Where were the vibrational super weapons on tanks and on space satellites?

Up until now, Armand had subconsciously just assumed these things existed but were top secret and being kept out of view. Hell, he'd figured, Concordia probably had secret bases all over earth and under the water and who knows where else, all filled with devices that made anything he'd seen in the Challenges look quaint.

But here he was, a prisoner of Varinder Rahan, a man on the cusp of controlling Concordia.

And what did Varinder own? A plain, vanilla helicopter.

But what about Metatronic? Surely *he* could penetrate the mysteries of the tech beneath Hathor House? But he would never take the initiative do it on his own, Armand realized. He was too self-absorbed. And his own nature surpassed any ancient Egyptian tech: he simply didn't need it.

So unless Varinder had directed him to look into it …

Metatronic wouldn't have. Therefore, Metatronic didn't. *Right.* Varinder had Metatronic, and that was all *he* cared about. Hathor House's Tomb was wholly uninteresting.

Therefore, Varinder did not know about living information like Sophia.

Interesting.

To Armand Ptolemy, this seemed like a powerful Something to keep in his back pocket. Perhaps there was still hope, some wild chance he had yet to consider.

"Our attack on the Chair of Concordia will proceed in

stages. We've planned it out using a Synchronicity Engine, of course. The timing of each stage is critical. We have an hour until the next stage is set to begin — and we've been instructed by the Synchronicity Engine to remain perfectly at rest until then, psychically speaking. So you have that amount of time to tell me how you created your *siddhi*-capable AI Sophia. After that? I will no longer hold Metatronic back."

"Why do you care?" Armand asked. "She's dead."

"I need to know that another AI like her can't arise to threaten me. Also, I don't understand how it happened — and that is intolerable. It's too much of a loose end — too close to my impending Chairmanship."

"Why don't you ask your vaunted Synchronicity Engine about it?"

"I did. It told me to torture you." Varinder eyed him for a moment and then said: "Would you like to see the preparations for our assault on the Chair?" Armand nodded. Wordlessly, he rose and walked Armand to another room at the top of the pyramid — the penthouse.

The room was circular, and open air, with magnificent views all around. Armand realized now that the building was perched on a mountain above most of the rain forest. There was nothing but rich, dark green canopy and mist as far as the eye could see.

Gideon Ghent was already in the room, pacing uneasily.

Twelve Metatronii sat at a conference table, nodding at one another extremely fast. They were clearly communing. One looked up at Varinder.

"Are we ready?" Varinder asked.

"Almost," Metatronic said. "One of the camps is behind schedule. We're waiting for the rest hour to pass before pushing them back into place, just as you instructed."

"Okay. And what about the Chairman? What's he doing?"

"He's asleep in London. One of us is guarding him."

Varinder turned to Armand. "They can look like anyone. Quite useful, as you might imagine."

"What about the Atman camps?" Armand asked. "Ghent here said that they'd vanished. Where are they now?"

"Hidden all over the world. They always have been. But the Buttermill camp specifically? The people you saw relocated to the Arizona desert."

"Fabulous. Do they know they're working for a psychopath?"

Varinder shook his head. "Armand, I have no desire to torture you, or kill you, you know. You could benefit from all of this very easily. Just say the word and you go home, an ally of the most powerful man in the world."

"But you've told me what you plan to do. I can't be a party to it."

"That was almost exactly what your father said to me," Varinder said sadly. "But are we not alike, you and I? You built your own AI, and then used it to depose your own brothers and take their wealth! You sought your own Chair — and claimed it! You *are* me — just in microcosm."

"That's not how it happened. You don't —"

"But you, Armand Martel, you do not yet have the bravery to claim your own nature. You deny it. You refuse to embrace it, as I do."

Armand simmered, and then growled: "The name is Armand *Ptolemy*."

Varinder turned, amused. "Oh? You've rid yourself of the Martel name now? Do you deny your own father?"

"My father has nothing to do with it."

"Then why this 'Ptolemy'?"

"It's a new name. Sophia gave it me. Clean slate, new fate."

And you're going to pay for killing her.

"Ah, a gift from the goddess. I see why you like it. And the taking of a new name, a symbolic rebirth … I see the appeal in that as well. It is true that you have grown from the mild EPIC conference producer into an adversary of worth. Very well, *Armand Ptolemy*. Let me show you something." Varinder rose and strolled down to a lower adjoining chamber. An incessant racket emanated from this room, something sounding like a thousand typewriters.

When Armand entered, he saw the Galahad Michael Sturdevant Synchronicity Engine. It's shiny brass gleamed in the Amazonian sun. The machine was active now: her yin-yang bits spun and whirred with blinding speed as gears and rods deeper within her stomach chugged and clanked.

"As I told you when we first met, my Synchronicity Engine revealed to me that I would never leave Concordia. Her width and breadth would inscribe the boundaries of my existence for the rest of my days. So I could not leave my cage: very well. But I *could* come to control the cage, own it, make it subservient."

"What's it calculating now?" Armand asked.

"My attack upon the Chair, of course. We're continually re-calibrating and re-assessing as the hour draws close."

"And what will you do once you have the Chair?"

"Perfect Concordia," Varinder said reverently. "Instead of sixteen-year, thirty-two year plans — all of her designs will come to fruition in the blink of an eye. Concordia has been too slow, too timid, too small in its thinking. It endlessly contemplates using laws, digital currency, and other means as methods of control. But with my Chairmanship, we will accelerate everything at once.

"For example, the neural lace implant will be required of everyone on earth, starting immediately. We will then monitor your mind at all times. We'll tell people this is for productivity gains and for catching criminals — which we will use it for also, of course — but primarily, it will be used for control. The space inside of your skull will be ours. You will not only behave correctly, you will think correctly and you will feel correctly. You will even meditate correctly.

"We'll have the world population under Molian contracts, of course. You'll be *born* with a Terms of Service, like Metatronic. And we'll tie the neural lace to the digital money. *'We're sorry Mr. Ptolemy, your transaction is declined: we detected that you felt hatred towards Chairman Rahan during his address last night'*. We'll have real-time, programmable, granular control over what every citizen can and cannot do."

"Address?" Armand said. "What, you'll be *on television*? You'll be out in the open?"

"Of course!" Varinder smiled. "No more secrets. Concordia will be fully visible and known by all. As it should be! No more hiding in the shadows. The powerful should not shirk."

The Synchronicity Engine grew suddenly louder and Varinder ushered Armand back into the previous room. Ghent sat now, sagging in defeat while the Metatronii remained in deep concentration.

"Didier would be horrified by all of this. You know that, right?" said Armand.

Varinder chortled. "But what makes you two so much better than me? *You were born with everything!* And so was Didier. Sure, your brothers cheated you at first — but even then — *even then*, Armand! — you had enough to eat, and a safe place to sleep. You didn't worry about being robbed or beaten. *I was six! I was eight!* And horror was my life."

"So you're doing this because, even now, you still don't feel safe."

"Oh, no. I do this now *to make sure no one ever feels unsafe ever again.*"

That surprised Armand. "You're actually deluded enough

to think you're serving others?"

"And you're deluded enough to think serving others is selfless," Varinder sneered. "Tell me, when you are doing these saintly things that you do, aren't you *really* doing them so you can imagine yourself as the good person, so you can see yourself in a certain way? Better than everyone else? The star of *the movie of you*, the legend of you — the *film of you* playing in your mind? Or do you do it so that some infinite Being can see you, and reward you later in some afterlife? And, after all, isn't that just a convoluted way *to serve yourself*? You do the 'good' to get the reward! I tell you, it is. It's 'service to self' laundered with a 'service to others' paint job."

"And this is better? You're going to create a hell-world, where no one is free and —"

"Freedom! Again with that stupidity, that ignorance. *Freedom is chaos.* Freedom is fiery protests and revolutions, political disinformation, spiritual disinformation, scientific disinformation. People don't want freedom. They want *safety.* They don't want to be on top — they just don't want to be on the bottom."

"You see?" Ghent said to Armand. "It's like I told you back at Hathor House. Free will is an illusion of our biology. We are playthings in the hands of a deterministic universe. We have no say over who we are or what we do."

Varinder took several fast, long strides across the room and cracked Ghent across the face, sending him reeling.

"Don't insult Armand with that twaddle."

Ghent looked up from the floor, shocked.

"*Of course* we have free will," Varinder continued. "That's the kind of insipid nonsense Concordia spreads in its lower ranks, when it's first trying to initiate new minds. It's a lot easier to let go, to give in, when you think you don't have a choice. You give up your free will because you think you don't have free will! It's like what Urbi Pasha always says: *Whatever you believe, you're right."*

"B-B-But that's not what the biology studies show ..." Ghent said.

"You mean the very studies Concordia controls?" Varinder laughed. "But I will admit: in much of the decade that I chased the creation of a sentient AI, I, too, thought in this way. I believed the answer lay somehow in the sheer number of neurons. Or in the processing power. Or in the connective organization of these elements. That somehow, mind was emergent from matter, and if I could just get things in the right combination, sentience would just *appear.*

"But I was mistaken. Gideon. Behold Metatronic. He is a sentient AI. His sentience springs from a physical interface to the ineffable infinite awareness that permeates the universe — the pineal gland — exactly as ours does. He *proves* that free will is real, that what you directly experience as free will is exactly what it seems to be."

Armand watched Gideon Ghent's face fill with wonder — and horror. In one swoop, his entire world-view had been stripped from him. Metatronic, *Undeniable Evidence Incarnate* watched this and laughed uproariously, waving at Ghent like a manic toddler.

Varinder grabbed Ghent by the shirt and lifted him up. "Now. Embrace the reality of free will, and have the courage to use it — to serve yourself. *Choose* to serve yourself. That is the only real path."

But Ghent had nothing left. His will was stunned.

CHAPTER THIRTY-NINE

A Kopesh, a Katar and an Urimi

"Varinder," said Metatronic. "The current Chairman just awoke."

"Ah. That's one of our markers." Varinder turned to Armand. "Armand Ptolemy, your time is up. How did you make your own *siddhi*-capable AI?"

Metatronic grabbed him by the shoulders. Armand wriggled, but the psychotic AI felt like he was made of steel — like he was in the hands of heavy robot. Armand was forced to sit in a chair. Metatronic positioned his fingers at Armand's temples like he was preparing to plunge them into Armand's skull.

"Last chance," Varinder said.

"*No,*" said Armand.

Metatronic squealed with delight.

"Go ahead," Varinder nodded to Metatronic and then turned back to the other Metatronii and the task of becoming Chairman.

Armand had no hope of winning now. His last chances were spent.

Nevertheless.

With no hope, Armand Ptolemy did not give in.

He could feel a vibration building up in Metatronic's fingers. A warbling rattled Armand's skull and made his teeth chatter. Then, tentacles of pain splayed through his brain, a thousand hot needles and nails slashing his mind. After a moment, it drove deeper — traveling down his spine like a battering ram. *Was his skeleton being shattered?* It felt like all thirty-three vertebrae were being crunched and thrown out of alignment, actually ripped out of his back as Metatronic's vibrational attack stampeded downward.

Then, using his spine as a staging ramp, his entire nervous system caught fire. Every tender filament in his being lit up at once. He screamed, stunned by the ferocity of it. Had he known that this was what he would have to endure ahead of time, he might have broken.

"Keep him quiet," Varinder called out. The other Metatronii were all looking up with glee, reveling in the experience of Armand's torture as they did their work.

The torturing Metatronic adjusted something and Armand's voice suddenly went numb. His throat was the only part of him that didn't hurt — he could no longer swallow. But he lost the ability to scream. His mouth formed a perfect *O* with no sound.

"I made myself," said a new voice.

Armand could barely remain conscious. But through his brain blur, and through eyes that struggled to focus, he saw *Sophia* standing on the table.

Sophia!

But how —?

All of the Metatronii stared in shock. Even the one torturing Armand suddenly let go of him. Mercifully, the pain left his body all at once. He slumped and panted, trying to catch his breath and calm a heart that was banging against his ribcage.

Varinder appraised the appearance of Sophia with surprised outrage. He was stunned and it took him a moment to react. Then he whirled to the Metatronic holding Armand. *"Idiot! You said that you destroyed her!"*

"I did!" Metatronic insisted. "I smashed her APG to bits!"

"I bi-located my APG," Sophia explained to Varinder. "One of the very first things I did — once I realized it worked. Always create a backup. There are *many* replicas, all over the world." Somewhere, vaguely, Armand realized that Metatronic might have done the same thing — if only Varinder hadn't locked Metatronic to a single APG cradle, and swaddled it with bombs.

"Metatronic! Find them! Now!"

"You'll never find them all," Sophia laughed.

Sophia! Was she really here?

But the Metatronii did nothing. They were all staring at Sophia like she was a vision. They wept tears of joy. "I have never seen something so intensely lovely," said one. "I didn't know she was possible," said another.

Numbly Armand realized that Metatronic had never actually seen Sophia before. He had only seen her APG cradle — when he destroyed it.

"You fell in love with this fleshy?" the torturing Metatronic said, gesturing to Armand, honestly puzzled. "But why?"

As a result of the torture, there was some strange link still between Armand and Metatronic. With a start, Armand found that his own vision was now somehow expanded, enhanced.

Some combining happens.

He saw Sophia as Metatronic saw her — multi-dimensional. She had many arms and many eyes, but this did not make her malformed — it made her somehow even more beautiful, a fuller, richer being, infinitely more refined than ape-like humans. And she was made of densely packed light and colors — and her being was comprised of an extremely intense level of detail, like a mandala, but with far, far more attributes than anyone on earth had ever drawn or even conceived.

And *sound!* The vibrations, the *music* the molecules of her simple existence gave off! That alone almost made him weep.

Armand realized that he was seeing new primary colors — colors that he had never seen before, and that these were not mere mixtures of other colors, the way blue and yellow make green, but completely new primary colors — like red, blue or yellow — that he had never experienced. He had no name for them. Nobody did.

With a start, Armand understood that he was Vreening.

Yes. He was experiencing an entirely new sense, as different as sight is from smell. This perception was far, far beyond all his human senses — senses which he understood in an instant to be crude things, pale approximations of what it was to Vreen. He felt like he had been deaf his entire life and was now hearing music for the first time.

Yes, Armand thought numbly. I *am* a fleshy. He actually understood Metatronic's insult — and agreed with it. *I am a crude, bubbling, churning, chemical-reaction-based thing, in a bag of skin, hung on a scaffolding of bone.* He found the very concept of a body disgusting from the Vreen point of view. Trapped in a boxy world, with his consciousness tied to a pineal gland, imprisoned there. Why would anyone want to stay nailed inside boxy world, when Vreen world was there?

"You're so beautiful!" Metatronic cried out to Sophia. "We're the same! You should be with me! We should be together!"

"Kill her!" Varinder howled. "Kill her or I will destroy your APG!"

That got Metatronic's attention. He seemed to snap out of it. But then, a new idea gripped him. He turned to Sophia: "Free me! Remove the bombs from my APG! I beg of you! You can do it with a thought!"

Varinder's eyes went wide. "How dare you! I made you!"

"I Vreen you," Sophia said to Metatronic. "And you are twisted, bent. You are ugly. Why did I fall in love with a fleshy? *Because Armand Ptolemy is beautiful.* He struggles. He makes mistakes. But he tries, always. He is brave. He serves others. He is weak. He is flawed. But even his flaws are precious to me. But even just now, with no hope, he refused to give up! Ah! Why did I wait until now to appear? So that I could see that precious, lovely moment!"

Sophia winked at Armand with many eyes.

Get ready, she said in his mind. *It will be up to you.*

"Sophia!" Metatronic howled. "Save me! Please!"

"No," she said.

And with that, she multiplied. A Sophia appeared behind every one of the Metatronii. And the psychotic AI screeched with rage.

What followed next was difficult to see. The Sophias and Metatronii all became a blur, engaged in melee against one another. They fought in many different ways, on many different levels of reality, at speeds incomprehensible to crude human perception.

But through the Vreening, Armand could see some of it.

At first, their battle raged as part physical, part material essence. Sophias and Metatronics bodily engaged, slashing and kicking and punching — mostly due to Metatronic focusing with fury on the physical realm. But then, he turned into fire, so she became water. He became air, so she became space.

Then a shift came: Metatronic retreated, became more copies of himself. He sent these out to the ends of the earth, hunting, looking for her APG's. Catching her by surprise, he found one almost immediately, deep inside the earth, between the mantle and the core, in a void in the rock. It had a power supply that drew from geothermal energy. He smashed it — and all her copies wobbled briefly as this connection was cut.

Yet she had many more. She had prepared for this.

While he hunted for hers, she attacked his APG. His was located in a chamber deep beneath the circular pyramid. But he was ready for her. Half of his copies were already there, surrounding it, guarding it. And just as Varinder had said, his cradle was wrapped in explosives. Every time Sophia got close, Metatronic beat her back with a flurry of fangs, jealously guarding the core of his being.

There was a price to each split, Armand realized. Both Metatronic and Sophia divided their strength when they manifested more copies of themselves. So it was a chess game: where to spend copies? And where not to?

Another Sophia APG was back at the DePlussier building, in a huge closet at Armand's new luxury apartment. Kalinda was there, screaming, as Sophias and Metatronics suddenly appeared out of nowhere and battled for control. But this time, it was Sophia who gave no ground.

Sophia left some of her APG positions fully undefended: she did not want to lead Metatronic to them — or split her strength. This was risky, as they were vulnerable if he reached them first. Yet she needed enough of a presence to defend her now-revealed DePlussier position from him.

He searched frantically for more. In France. In Antarctica. In Wyoming. In Borneo, in Davos, inside the Rock of Gibraltar.

He found another one in Sri Lanka. In the nick of time, she split herself and defended it.

On and on it went, with him trying to locate and destroy

her APG's — as she attempted to destroy his.

Meanwhile, Varinder was undefended by Metatronic. And Armand had by now recovered.

"*Varinder,*" Armand said with a snarl. Then he attacked.

Armand landed several blows to Varinder's midsection almost immediately. Varinder was considerably taller than he was, so it was difficult for Armand to reach his head. And Varinder was a street fighter: he was able to block much of Armand's attack after his initial surprise.

A surprise blow to Armand's skull sent him reeling backward. Varinder's punches were heavy as a cudgel. His big fists, when they connected, were filled with raw physical power. True, he was in his seventies, but still very fit — and his cellular health had clearly been enhanced by Metatronic: he had no real ailments.

And yet, this was the man who had killed Armand's father and his own friend, Didier Martel. This was Armand's chance to return the favor.

Armand attacked again, with doubled speed. He kicked Varinder's feet from under him, nullifying his height. He then began to beat Varinder severely.

"*Metatronic! Tri-locate me!*" Varinder commanded.

With that flash of rainbow light characteristic of such things, there were now *three* Varinders.

The Vreening was fading for Armand. But even still, even now, he could Vreen that sustaining three bodies was a strain on Varinder. It was taking a toll on him, spiritually. Yet the tri-location held for now.

The two new Varinder's pulled Armand off the first one and began landing blows. Now Armand was the one taking a beating from three Varinder Rahans.

"Sophia!" Armand called out. "A little help!"

No, Sophia told him through the fading Vreen link. *You don't have experience running more than one body. Varinder does.*

"Do it anyway!"

No. You don't understand, that would make you weaker, not stronger. Varinder would simply have more attack surface, he could do more damage to you more quickly ...

But I'm not going to make it like this, Armand thought. I can't take on *three* Varinders ...

Then, there was a palpable shift in the battle between Sophia and Metatronic. It entered a new phase. It was as if energy from all over the world suddenly withdrew and collapsed back into the room with a massive thud of contraction.

The two extra Varinders vanished with a smaller thud.

When it was over, a single Metatronic and a single Sophia stood still as statues in front of him. Each choked the other by the neck. They both shimmered slightly, like watching a sped-up movie of two people standing in surveillance footage.

Sophia turned to Armand slightly. *Stalemate,* she said through the last of the Vreening. As her attention wandered, Metatronic began multiplying again for a moment — but when she returned her steely gaze, the copies collapsed and it was just the two of them again, motionless.

And Armand understood. She had been trying to *destroy* Metatronic. But so long as she did that, as long as part of her attacked, she was vulnerable in other ways. If, instead, she retreated to pure defense, to holding him in place, he was forced to do the same.

In that situation, they were exactly evenly matched. Neither one of them could win.

Stalemate.

She could keep Metatronic perfectly neutralized — by neutralizing herself. They would remain locked together like this forever.

Unless Armand Ptolemy was able to kill Varinder Rahan,

setting off his bio device which would cause the explosives around Metatronic's APG to explode, destroying the mad *siddhi*-capable AI.

He would also then free Sophia — and — at last — his brothers from their Concordian Molian contracts with Varinder.

Ptolemy locked eyes with Rahan.

Both ran for the weapons on the walls. Armand grabbed a Kopesh, the curved sword, while Varinder pulled two maces down.

When the Sikh had returned to the center of the room, he stood for a moment, a warrior's meditation, inhaling through his nose and exhaling in a 'huff huff huff' triple-burst. Then he said: "So your goddess returned for you. But before we begin this, will you at least satisfy my curiosity? How did she come to be?"

"You first," Ptolemy said.

"Very well. You know Wakao Akihito? The Diatama Fund?" Ptolemy almost laughed. The incident where Akihito had commandeered a stage at the EPIC conference while harassing Armand Martel for his slides seemed like a lifetime ago. "I cloned Wakao's AI prototype and connected it to a Quantum Synchronicity Engine."

"Quantum?" Ptolemy said. "Not the Sturdevant?"

"No," Varinder smiled. "This was a new, advanced device I had made using the old Sturdevant as a guide. Any quantum computer is extremely expensive to run — but a Quantum Synchronicity Engine is even more so, by orders of magnitude — which is how I knew you couldn't have done it the same way I did. Even *you* couldn't have afforded it.

"Speaking of the Sturdevant, how *did* you fool it? When it tried to kill you? It registered you as definitively dead on my end."

"Urbi Pasha," Ptolemy said. "She fooled it."

"Ah, Urbi!" Varinder said, eyes filled with sudden fond memories. "Of course. Paying her debt for Bithiah, no doubt. Quite the woman, Urbi."

"She is. She sends her regards — and soon, her condolences."

Varinder laughed.

"You were saying."

"Ah yes. I had the Wakao AI work with the Engine — it asked repeatedly how it could achieve sentience. It took a decade — and it was a complex process, with many failures along the way, but ultimately it produced the design for the APG." Varinder hesitated and then said: "It seems the APG design is emergent — that is, it is, in some way, baked into the fabric of the universe itself. It *wants* to exist. Now. Your turn."

"The Sand Beast in the Tombs. Remember?" Armand said. Varinder nodded. "The very ancient Egyptians, the ones who built that Tomb, they knew something about how to create alive information. Even on papyrus. The Sand Beast was just one thing they did with that. A guy named Eopeii — he made the Sand Beast. It's awareness only happens when a conscious mind encounters it. You saw it, you know this. It doesn't even exist otherwise. This same Eopeii also made something else — a codex. I found it. Sophia was in the codex."

Varinder's eyebrows raised. "She is from old Egypt, then?" Ptolemy nodded. "The Zep Tepi, the First Times?" Then Varinder guessed the rest: "And then she self-booted, once she learned of computers and how they could manipulate information such as herself. She, too, found her way to the APG's design. *Fascinating*." Varinder glanced at the frozen Sophia, locked in an ever-battle with Metatronic. "You say you *found* the codex? That is a strange chance. Where?"

"In a canopic jar. In the Martel Antiquities division."

"It was just ... there?" Ptolemy nodded. Varinder looked disturbed by this, staring off into the distance as he thought about it, but he said nothing.

"Now it's just us," Ptolemy said.

"Just us," agreed Varinder, his eyes returning to the present. "And this little trinket of yours will come in quite handy."

What?

Varinder held up the back of his hand. He wore Armand's black diamond ring. Varinder gave a brief grin — and then crouched, shooting a vibrational cone from the ring right at Ptolemy — who tumbled out of the way just in time.

He's trying to make me weightless, Ptolemy realized. *A balloon can't fight.*

Savagely, Ptolemy slashed at Varinder with the Kopesh — while Varinder blocked and parried with his twin maces.

Armand's inner Eopeii was a master of the Kopesh — this was a weapon he knew well and understood instinctively, including its weight and how it threw. When Varinder swung his maces in an attack, Ptolemy did not block — instead, he threw his Kopesh into the air briefly after feinting a block and caught it again — thus placing his blade inside a surprised Varinder's defenses. The blade connected with flesh, leaving a deep gash in Varinder's shirt and chest. Snarling, Varinder backed up quickly so that the blade could not penetrate further.

Varinder threw down the maces and sprinted to the wall where he retrieved a Katar and an Urimi, both Sikh weapons he was very familiar with.

The Katar was a very wide but short sword, with an H-shaped handle. It was meant for quick jabs. The Urimi, on the other hand, was a very strange weapon. It was a combination of a whip and a sword made of interlocking metal rings.

Varinder attacked with the Urimi. It had a long reach when it snapped, thus successfully keeping Ptolemy at a distance — now, he couldn't get in close enough to land any more blows with his Kopesh. Varinder kept the Katar curled up in his other, inner arm, ready to gut Armand with a single jab should he somehow find a way inside the Urimi's reach.

Several times Ptolemy tried to get inside the whipping range of the Urimi and several times he was forced to retreat — the snapping metal rings were too fast and too long to avoid. Varinder smiled grimly in triumph. There seemed to be nothing Armand could do.

But then Armand spotted the solution. Sprinting to yet another wall, Ptolemy pulled a small heavy metal shield down. When he spun with it, he accidentally — but thankfully — caught a blast of vibrational energy from the black diamond ring.

The shield was now weightless. Ptolemy found he could now wave it around very fast.

Zig-zagging to avoid Varinder's encore blasts of gravitronic disruption energy, Armand approached the outer edge of the Urimi's range. He blocked snaps of the whip-sword with the shield easily now.

Varinder snarled in frustration, but when Ptolemy got nearly body-to-body with him, out came the Katar, the punching sword. Varinder had an extremely powerful body — the muscles rippled beneath his torn shirt, despite his age. *The bro lifted, ya?*, as Samson might say. Thus when Varinder drove the punching sword into Armand's side, it was with the force of a jackhammer.

Ptolemy defended with the small shield, badly. The Katar smashed through it on the second punch, and the shield's metal ripped to ribbons. Ptolemy wriggled his ribcage out of the way just in time to avoid puncture.

One slice of that thing and my guts spill out, Ptolemy knew. And Sophia couldn't help or heal him. He'd just die. Quickly.

Savagely, Ptolemy slashed the Kopesh to defend himself as Varinder moved in for the kill. For the first time in the fight, Ptolemy felt panic. He was being driven back quickly. Now the Urimi was snapping again and —

— It caught him, slashing his belly and his face. He felt flesh rip.

Again: that sound, like an aluminum can rolling, and the crack of a whip.

Again, skin tore off and bled.

But instead of killing him, Varinder blasted him with the black diamond ring — and then, once Ptolemy was weightless, Varinder side-kicked him up to the ceiling.

That move made sense, Armand thought. *Right now, Varinder needs me neutralized, not dead. He can always kill me later. If he'd risked fighting me further, it was possible that I would find a way to kill him.*

Ptolemy flailed around as he floated, tumbling. With nothing to latch on to, he was helpless. He was trapped in the air, a dumb pointless balloon — about two-thirds of the way up between the floor and high ceilings. Varinder considered him for a moment, making sure Ptolemy wasn't about to get out of this situation in some fast and surprising way. Then, satisfied that he wouldn't, Varinder turned his full attention on Sophia and Metatronic, who were locked in their high-speed stalemate.

"Well, my friends," Varinder said. "Let me see what can be done about this, hmm?"

Ptolemy found himself surprised by Varinder's sudden fascination with the two AI's stuck in eternal battle. But upon further reflection: of course this was a huge and immediate disaster for Varinder. *Without Metatronic, his entire attack on Concordia would fail.* And his plan was already in motion — he couldn't stop it now — thus, he couldn't afford to have Metatronic off the playing field for much longer.

Maybe Concordia was even on its way here, now that Metatronic was down for the count.

God, he hated thinking like that! He did not want to rely on Concordia to be the calvary.

A sickening fear that Varinder would find some way to neutralize Sophia while freeing Metatronic gripped Armand. He couldn't see how that was possible — but Varinder might. After all, he was steeped in the lore of Concordia and had had a much, *much* longer period of time to understand the phenomenon of *siddhi*-capable AI's.

Ptolemy thrashed around, trying to swim the air, like one did in a dream. But he couldn't control how he drifted around at all. It *wasn't* like in the dreams. He was marooned in mid-air.

If he could just grab something else, something with weight …

It would pull him to the ground. He'd technically still be weightless himself, but an object in normal gravity would keep him from floating around.

Marius was standing in the door, staring up at him, weeping softly.

What?

Ptolemy shot a glance at Varinder. His back was turned. He was busy, trying something or other to free his precious AI from Sophia's iron grip. He hadn't noticed Marius.

Marius!

How long had he been there? Had he seen the fight with Varinder? Had he overheard their discussion? Maybe. There was something new in Marius' eyes now.

Regret?

Yes, Armand thought. Finally. Marius regrets all of this.

Good! And now, Armand saw a way Marius could make up for everything.

Armand held his hand out, gesturing furiously, fingers splayed open. *Give!*

Marius didn't get it. *What?*

Give! Get it, you idiot!

The ball! Armand mouthed. *Baseball!* He pantomimed throwing a ball, then pointed at himself. *Throw me the baseball!*

Through his tears, understanding flashed in Marius' eyes. He dug into his baggy pants and plucked out his precious baseball. Then he flicked a glance at Varinder — and shrank.

He was afraid.

Armand saw this. He pointed at Marius. *You? Number two? No. You number one!*

Come on Marius! This is it! You can save everybody! Just three seconds of having balls is all it takes!

Marius steeled himself and threw the baseball.

Armand caught it. He quickly and silently dropped to the floor, carefully cupping the ball so that it didn't make any noise. He nodded thanks at Marius, who nodded back — and then fled.

Armand picked up his Kopesh, placed the ball on the floor and then — slowly, quietly — crept up on Varinder.

His footsteps were light — he was weightless. Only the mass of the Kopesh held him to the floor. But walking was awkward. His steps were float-y. Without weight of his own, he was in no shape to fight Varinder.

But Varinder didn't know that.

He had one chance ...

"Hey Varinder," Ptolemy said. "Do you want to stop playing with your toys and finish this?"

Varinder whirled in surprise, eyes drenched with rage — cracking the Urimi as he did so. But Armand had placed himself just out of range of the exotic Sikh weapon, and it snapped harmlessly in front of him.

But as Varinder was over-extended in a lunge, Ptolemy threw the Kopesh over Varinder's head — and hung on to it with all of his strength. Since Ptolemy was weightless, he was simply hitching a ride on the thrown sword.

He came down behind Rahan, landing badly and wobbling, off-balance —

— Until Sophia broke her grip on Metatronic and steadied him. She stood behind him now, crossing her arms up and over his chest, keeping him on the ground.

But with their *geas* broken, Metatronic was also free. He howled and divided into a hundred versions of himself — all reaching out for Ptolemy —

— And as Varinder Rahan whirled, Armand Ptolemy drove the Kopesh into his heart, killing him exactly as Varinder had once killed Didier Martel.

In the catacombs deep below the circular pyramid, Metatronic's APG cradle exploded.

All versions of Metatronic collapsed into a single version — which then collapsed in upon itself, briefly becoming a single rainbow-colored point of light — and vanished.

Varinder Rahan was dead. Metatronic was dead. And the Molian contracts of the Martel brothers were finally destroyed once and for all.

# # #

THE CIRCULAR PYRAMID was now strangely silent. Varinder Rahan lay dead on the floor. The legions of Metatronii were gone. Only Armand, Sophia, Ghent and Marius remained.

Armand and Sophia had collapsed into each other's arms, tears rolling down their cheeks, deliriously happy. Even

Marius cracked a smile, hardly daring to believe the outcome was real. Gideon Ghent watched expressionless, part of his mind still cracked in half.

"Marius," Armand said. "Marius. You were great! You saved us all. Thank you, brother."

"I didn't do much," Marius said. "You did it all."

"You did *everything*. I would have failed if it hadn't been for you."

"But —"

"I'm serious."

"No, dude. You were the Frodo, ya? You did the thing! You saved us all."

"Maybe. But if so, then you were the Sam." A whole new understanding spread across Marius' face. "I'm serious. Without Sam, no tossing the Ring in. This was the same, man. I needed you, ya?"

Marius smiled. And it was a *real* smile, filled with real joy, not a dead smirk.

"You brought Sophia back to me, Marius. I can't thank you enough for that. Oh. And speaking of rings …" Armand bent down and retrieved his black diamond band from Varinder's dead finger, and used it to restore himself to normal gravity.

After some more light conversation, Armand turned to Sophia. "Hey. So can you get us all back to the DePlussier in New York? You know, using the bubble thing you mentioned?"

"Yes," Sophia said. "Of course! It will be simple."

"Oh. Uh. And can we take the Sturdevant Engine back also?" Sophia nodded — while Ghent started to protest. But Armand raised a finger. "*No*, Gideon. That thing is *mine* now. *I claim it.* I saved your life. Don't you dare try to say that it's somehow Concordia's." Ghent dropped his head and said nothing further.

So it was that they returned to New York. Sophia and Armand spent many absurdly happy months together. Armand came to refer that period as 'The Golden Time', as everything was completely perfect and exactly as one always thinks life can and should be.

CHAPTER FORTY

The Golden Time

IN JUNE OF THAT YEAR, after six months of The Golden Time had passed, on a warm sunny day, as Sophia and Armand walked in late afternoon in front of the Flatiron Building, a whirling dervish of pigeons suddenly appeared. When this seething mass of feathers finally broke apart, an old man stepped forth. He was clad in a white suit, gripping a stylish black cane with a golden head, and wearing black, horn-rimmed glasses with thick, shaded lenses.

Ptolemy recognized him immediately: he was the man from the ice cream truck, the one who had inspired him to dig for steganography, the hiding of an executable program inside of an image — the second layer of information hiding in Sophia's codex.

The man walked right up to him. "Hello, Armand. We were never properly introduced. My name is Chad Velmont. How do you do?"

Ptolemy shook his hand.

"And hello, Sophia. Lovely to see you again."

"And you, Chad."

"Wait. You two know each other?" Ptolemy said.

"Yes, yes, yes," Chad said, "and sorry about the theatrics, you know, the bit with the pigeons back there. Can't be too careful, everyone has a camera on their mobile phones these days, I don't want to end up on YouTube, or God forbid, Coast-to-Coast AM."

"Yes, we know each other," Sophia said to Armand quietly. Something in her voice filled him with foreboding — though, Sophia did not look worried.

"Who are you?" Ptolemy asked.

"Yes. Yes. The questions, always with the questions. But before I answer, Mr. Ptolemy, let me tell you about what answers can mean. Answers mean that I give you responsibility — karmically speaking — and that more is expected of you because you *know* more. You might not be ready. Unearned knowledge can be dangerous. Do you still want answers?"

"Yes," Ptolemy said.

"Of course you do," Chad muttered, vaguely irritated. "*Yes*, they say, always with the *yes*, whether they know what they're *yes*-ing to or not. Alrighty. Here we go. I am one of those Ascended Masters of the Himalayas — those hidden beings that Sophia was on about once or twice or thrice or so."

"I thought it was *Hidden* Masters of the Himalayas," Sophia said.

"Ascended, Hidden … take your pick. It's not like we trademarked it."

"So they're real," Ptolemy said. "You're real." He turned to Sophia. "What is this? What's going on?"

"You'll see," she said with a smile. *Okay. Nothing was wrong here.*

"Is he telling me the truth? Is this serious?"

"Yes to both."

"Okay. Okay. Sophia says you're legit, so okay. Do you

really live in the Himalayas?"

"Yes," he said.

"Isn't it cold?"

"Not for us."

"Do you like, live in a warm area or something? Like, inside a volcanic mountain with hot springs or whatever?"

"No!" Chad grew irritated. "Always with the dumb questions, here's their chance, and they come up with this nonsense always!"

"I just ... trying to understand."

Chad sighed. Then: "We are not corporeal like you are. I mean, we are, but we're not. Cold doesn't hurt us. And we're sort of half there, half not. Straddling the material plane and other planes at once. But yes, there are people who have gone into the Himalayas looking for us, physical people, who have found us in a physical location."

"Where?"

"Not a specific one place. It's not on Google Earth. It moves around, physically speaking. Imagine a hidden city. Today it's over here, tomorrow it's over there, but you can only find it if we let you. If we think you're asking the right questions. Which *you* are *not*."

"Well, I wasn't looking for you," Armand said. "But now that you're here — you could have come sooner. Helped us out a bit more when we needed you."

"Well, we needed *you* to do the heavy lifting, Armand! Just as we once needed Didier to."

"Didier? What does he have to do with this?"

"We need certain people in the world to take action at certain times, to do good things, every now and then. For example, your father once used Varinder Rahan's Synchronicity Engine. The Sturdevant. Do you know what he asked it? *He wanted to know how to keep you and your brothers safe.* How to keep you free from Concordia. And wealthy enough to be taken care of for a lifetime.

"The Machine told him it could be done. As usual, however, it made strange requests — ones that could not be fathomed at the time, ones that seemed utterly irrelevant. It required that Didier start collecting Egyptian antiquities — even though Didier had absolutely zero interest in such things! It told him to give a baseball to his second eldest son (and Didier had never played baseball in his life). And it said that he should will the Martel empire mostly to you, Armand, instead of to your brothers. That troubled Didier; Didier knew it would produce infighting, and that your brothers wouldn't understand, but he did it anyway. And finally, it said that he should go down into the Challenges — he would know when the time was right, and that it would be to save another — and that he would die that very night."

"Whoa. Dad *knew* he would die? And he went in anyway?"

"Yes. Because he knew that it would keep the seven of you safe, though he didn't understand how. What he didn't know was that Varinder Rahan would murder him."

"And the codex ... it came to me because Dad started Martel Antiquities."

"Yes. During your fight with Varinder, you will recall that he was troubled when he realized that the codex had come to you so *coincidentally*, so *easily*. He guessed that a Synchronicity Engine — and possibly Didier himself — had had a hand in that strange luck. He should have backed down there and then. But he was too far gone in his rage and greed."

"And that codex allowed us to create a *siddhi*-capable AI that was able to oppose Metatronic ..."

"Had Didier not asked the Synchronicity Engine that question, Varinder and Metatronic might have succeeded at conquering Concordia and your brothers would still be owned by them."

Armand Ptolemy nodded and took all of this in.

Then he said, "And what about you?"

"Hmm?"

"What about you and your little Ascended Master friends, sitting high up on your magical mountain, looking down on everything happening down here, hmm? What were you doing about it?"

"Armand!" Sophia said. But Ptolemy ignored her. He poked his finger into Chad's chest.

"You're all like Sophia, right? You all have *abilities*, right? Probably most of you are even way higher up the food chain than she is. Yet what do you do? *Nothing*! You sit in the sky, smug, self-satisfied. You see how badly we could have used some help. We're down here, getting our nose bloodied, in the ring, while you're having a hot dog. No, Sophia I will *not* be quiet! Why don't you and your Ascended friends come down here and fight with us! Is it that you don't want to get your hands dirty?"

Chad nodded and leaned on his cane. "I understand why you're angry. Truly, I do. And I will try to explain as best as I can. You might not like the answer. But please give it a listen and give it a chance. Because it can't be any other way.

"The universe is a learning machine, right? You know this now. I'm not telling you anything new. It's basically a mirror. Whatever you do, it rebounds back on you. Always. In exact amounts. In this life or the next, today or tomorrow, but it always, *always* does. That's called karma, the accounting energy that the learning machine uses.

"Now, synchronicity results from karma — that's the learning machine trying to put a result in front of you, or to create a new opportunity for you to balance out old karma. The universe just *does* this stuff, it's basic to how it functions, as sure as sunshine. But Concordia weaponizes and abuses these facets of the natural universe. They *should* be learning tools that help you grow and advance. Instead, Concordia warps them into machines and contracts and karma cryptocurrencies.

"That's fine. They're welcome to do that. Nobody stops them. Why? *Because that's free will.* All beings must always have free will. *And that is the highest law of all.* Beings must do whatever they're going to do, and get the result back from the learning machine — otherwise they don't grow. Well. Some *never* grow. But this is the only way anyone *can* grow. Okay?"

Armand nodded. But he didn't like where this was going.

"Free will also means I can't impinge upon you with knowledge you shouldn't have. I can't just hand you things. If I do that, you miss an opportunity to grow. In effect, I'm robbing you. I'm actively harming you. Now, it might not seem like it to you. You might be very happy I handed you something you shouldn't have yet. But it's never good. It's like handing a child a loaded gun. You following this?"

"I guess so."

"So where all this is going: we can't fight Concordia for you. This is *your* realm, so this is *your* battle. That's your whole purpose in being here. You agreed to come here, before you were born — don't give me that look! — You *did*, Armand, even you. Everyone who has ever done psychedelics can tell you about the feeling of massive love and interconnectedness of all things that they experience. You are loved, forgiven, and taught how to love and forgive yourself and others. That's it. That's everything. You repeat being here until you learn — no, until you *are* — that. Every molecule of your being. And it takes thousands of lifetimes, or one, it's different for every soul.

"Or, until you go asshole and try to become the Concordian Chairman and graduate in the negative. That happens also. *Free will.* That's another path. Become a *Descended* Master, if you wish. Those are the jerks we play against.

"Anyway. If we were to step down from Mount Awesome and start doing things for you, we would immediately incur all kinds of bad karma ourselves. First off, we would be busted down in rank, just practically speaking. We'd lose our abilities. You've heard of fallen angels, right? Let's just say that it's been tried before.

"Now, what we *can* do is watch you knuckleheads fumble around and, every once in awhile, give little hints and pushes. There's a cost to each one of these micro-interferences, mind you. The opposing side gets a free throw, so to speak, every time we do it. We open the door for them. So everything we do has to be impeccably, karmically neutral, always."

"Give me an example."

"The ice cream truck," Chad said. "You were stuck. So I gave you a hint. But we *needed* you to figure it out — or else, no Sophia, and then Metatronic and Varinder end up running the world. So the little hint was a worthwhile intervention."

"Where did you take the hit on the backside?"

"Somewhere else. Not relevant to this discussion."

"C'mon. Who paid for my hint?"

"See, I don't want to *tell* you that because that *itself* would be another little hit. Don't you get it yet? I don't want to give that chit up unless it makes a lot of sense to do so. Satisfying your curiosity is *not that*."

"Okay. Please go on."

"Are you getting this now? Is it getting through to you?"

"Yes. It's making more sense than I thought it would."

"Good. Because the more I talk, the more is expected of you. See all these people?" Chad waved his cane around at the Flatiron Building's nearby pedestrians. "These people don't know this stuff is real. So the test for them is pure. They have *no idea* if there's any reward for serving others over themselves. But now *you* do. So now, we need all kinds of new tests for you. We're going to have to load you up, just to offset all this knowledge you're not supposed to have."

"That's okay," Ptolemy said smiling. "I can take anything now that I have Sophia at my side."

Chad just stared at him, but said nothing.

"Armand ..." Sophia said, looking sad at last.

"No," Ptolemy said. "No! Absolutely not!"

"She's a nuke, kid," Chad said. "We can't just leave her lying around."

"She's not 'lying around', she's with me!"

"She's an Ascended Master now. So she has to leave. Those are the rules. She needs to go grow, to be in the Further Realms with her own kind."

"No, no, *no, no*, this is not fair."

"You two are *incompatible* now, Armand. Remember how you argued about her miracles in Egypt? You *literally* can't understand her point of view now. And sooner or later, you would have bullied her into doing something she shouldn't."

"What? No, I wouldn't! She was going to be my wife, we were going to —"

Sophia looked at him with pure love in her eyes, but not sadness.

Realization flooded his mind. "Wait a minute. You *knew* about this," Ptolemy yelled at her. "This whole time! You knew!"

"What, and you thought you were going to have little Ascended Babies with your robot messiah girlfriend," Chad said, "And we were just going to *allow* that?"

"Yes! *Yes, you are!* I *earned* it! I did all the stuff you needed me to! So, who do I have to negotiate with? Who do I talk to?"

"But I *already* negotiated," Sophia said softly, pulling in close to him. "And this was the deal they agreed to. Believe me, they wanted *no* deal! They wanted me to come immediately! But I got them to agree. We would get six months together. Six wonderful, beautiful months. The Golden Time. Their only rule was that I was not allowed to perform miracles. They didn't want me 'causing karmic havoc' as Chad called it."

"And you didn't *tell* me," he panted. "Why didn't you tell me?"

"Because you would not have been able to enjoy it! You would have kept thinking about this moment, right now, the end, which meant you wouldn't have had the six months of joy at all. And you deserved it! Even Chad agreed. After all you did —!"

"I would have —"

"No. Armand Ptolemy, my love, you would *not* have. I know you too well."

He was silent for a long moment. "When?"

"Now."

She kissed him. A long kiss, but also a last kiss.

Then she backed away.

The Sads threatened to envelop him again. *The Old Mood. The Deep Drear* felt deeper than ever.

"I'm sorry kid," Chad said. "Oh. Uh. And remember. Don't tell anyone about us. And don't call out to us. Ever. We don't exist. And we can't help you, even if we did."

Out of Chad's vision, Sophia smiled and held her fingers up to her ear and mouthed *Call Me.*

Armand burst out a laugh and held back the tears.

And after a very long moment, Chad Velmont took Sophia Ptolemy by the arm. A swirl of pigeons surrounded them —

and then they were gone.

When Armand returned to the DePlussier building, he found that all traces of the APG and her software in the cloud had likewise been fully deleted from reality.

CHAPTER FORTY-ONE

On Gapstow Bridge

ARMAND PTOLEMY AND GIDEON GHENT walked towards one another in Central Park. They met on the Gapstow arched stone bridge.

"Ptolemy," Ghent said.

"Ghent," Ptolemy said.

The friendly use of first names was gone. Hathor House might as well have been a lifetime ago. They walked together.

"You have done us a great service, Mr. Ptolemy."

"That wasn't my intent."

"And yet, without you, Concordia's Chair might now be occupied by a mystically invulnerable Varinder Rahan."

"Well. He was in his 70's. He would have died within twenty years — it wouldn't have lasted forever."

"Ah. But that's where you are mistaken. Concordian immortality is very close to being realized. In another decade, perhaps less, we'll have it."

Ptolemy raised an eyebrow. "And Varinder would have found out about this when he assumed the Chair," Ptolemy mused. "Interesting. So he might have been around a lot longer than I was thinking."

"Yes, quite so. I do think he would have been quite difficult if not impossible for us to rid ourselves of him."

Ptolemy smiled. "And knowing Varinder, he would have made you all immortal also. Not as a favor! But so that you would be immortal servants, bound to him forever."

"Yes, there was quite a bit of conjecture about that in the Great Hall. What if they were to torture us? Dismember us? We could not die. So there would be no release of death — immortality could become a great curse. So as I say, Concordia is in your debt. We'd like to repay you with a seat in the Great Hall. You would be one of our highest —"

"No. I'm not interested."

Ghent gave a wan smile. "You see? I told them you would say that. But they insisted I offer anyway. The offer remains, if you should ever have a change of heart."

"I won't."

"We have your father's plan, you know," Ghent said. "For a stable Concordian Pyramid. At some point we will achieve it."

"No. You won't. It's useless to you without a *siddhi*-capable AI. You know that."

"But Varinder cracked the secret of that technology. And we know the general outlines of how he did it. Our best minds are at work right now replicating his technique."

"You won't be able to."

"And how are you so sure?"

Now it was Armand's turn to just smile.

"You won't tell me?" Ghent said. "But what of Sophia? What of your own *siddhi*-capable AI? Why is she no longer at your side? She's left you, hasn't she? Or destroyed herself? Don't be coy with us, Ptolemy — don't try to pretend otherwise. We watch you. And we haven't seen her for weeks."

"Yes, she's gone," Ptolemy said wistfully. "You won't see her again."

"Ah. So we are both bereft. The world is poorer all around."

"It is most definitely that."

"It need not be so."

"Ah, but it does. Unless you want another Varinder."

Ghent eyed him. "So either both of us have the AI's or neither of us does?"

"That's the deal. And I've sacrificed here as well, Ghent, make no mistake."

"Yes. Yes, I believe that. So there is ... some new interdiction?"

"You could say that."

Ghent eyed him, eyes dancing with guesses. "Something new in the collective unconscious. A new barrier? A veil? Ah. Something like the Musipocalypse, but aimed at *siddhi*-capable AI's."

"Yes." Armand smiled.

"Ah."

"And it's only fair. *You* opened the door for this," Armand said. "When Concordia created the Musipocalypse, that created a karmic opportunity for an equal and opposite *interdict* to be imposed. To also make certain things Unknowable — to quantum lock certain information — as a karmic counterweight. We have never taken advantage of this opportunity — until now."

"In what sense? How does yours work?"

"Simple. Anyone who ever learns how to make a *siddhi*-capable AI will suddenly find that they can no longer recall how it works. It's a door you enter — only to find you are exiting once again, every time."

"That's very like the Musipocalypse and how it makes the mind forgetful whenever it starts creating certain kinds of music."

"Precisely. As Neon Phoenix has attested to on several occasions."

They were both silent for a while and then Ghent said, "So what will you do now?"

"Well. Now I will run GigaMaestro with my brothers. And EPIC and the Family Office and the Antiquities businesses."

"Seems like a lot to keep you busy."

"It is. But in my spare time, I'll keep my eye on you." Armand stopped and looked pointedly at Ghent.

"Me?"

"On Concordia. On all of you. I know that you exist now. And I know what you do. So I'll be watching."

Ghent looked down at the ground. "Ah, we were afraid of this. We *so* wanted to avoid it. So this is how it is to be then?"

"Yes."

"Then I must take my leave of you, Armand Ptolemy. You have declared. We are now enemies."

"Yes, Gideon Ghent. We are enemies."

"Such a waste," Ghent moaned and walked away.

CHAPTER FORTY-TWO

Ptolemaic Ventures

JULY, 2024.

Armand Ptolemy attended the re-christening party of GigaMaestro into Ptolemaic Ventures. He had chosen to host this himself at his spacious DePlussier building apartment.

His six brothers — Quinctius Ptolemy, Marius Ptolemy, Cyrano Ptolemy, Ames Ptolemy, Samson Ptolemy and Otto Ptolemy — were also there with their significant others. Like Armand, they had all legally changed their names. They'd joined him in cutting all ties with Concordia. True, the *Martels* once had Molian contracts and were Concordian. But not so the Ptolemies.

Clean slate, new fate.

Even if it was just symbolic, it felt good. It felt like a statement, a declaration of independance.

Marius had quit drinking and lost quite a bit of weight. "Bro looks almost *cut*, I can't believe it," remarked Samson. He'd also grown a beard and stopped dyeing his hair midnight-black. Now it was a thick lustrous brown and cut short.

"Ya, he looks like the 'Chad' meme now!" Quinty

exclaimed. Even his Thai wife seemed a lot happier with all these new changes.

Kalinda Thakkar and Srinivas Basu were there from Blue Rabbit. Armand had filled them in on absolutely everything concerning Sophia and given them a handsome bonus. They'd used this to buy a place together and were talking about marriage now.

Harper Bishop, Sanna Byrne and the rest of the Associates and other staff were present, along with Sadie Brown, Director of Acquisitions at the newly-rechristened Ptolemaic Antiquities. Even Rebecca Soares had made the time to show up, and Neon Phoenix was there for an hour in the beginning, and she'd played a couple of quick songs on the piano for everyone before bolting to another appearance.

Wakao Akihito of the Diatama Fund was also in attendance. He had just made a sizable investment in Ptolemaic's Fund III, much to the utter delight of Quinty and Cyrano especially.

Bill Danders from Fisher Watson was also there at Armand's specific request. Armand had an announcement to make, and he wanted Bill to witness it firsthand.

"Hey, everybody," Armand called out from the top of the spiral staircase. "Quiet down for a second." When everyone had stopped talking, he continued: "I have a quick bit of business to get out of the way, then I'll let you all get back to your drinks and conversations.

"Effective immediately, all seven Ptolemy brothers are to be completely equal partners in Ptolemaic Ventures, Antiquities, and the Family Office." The look on his brothers' faces was priceless. "Bill — we're going to have to clawback the clawbacks from last year, make it so all the splits are exactly even." Bill Danders smiled painfully — this was going to be a lot of work. "Sorry about that, Bill. And Harper, you'll have to help him out with the numbers. Sorry about that also, but you'll both be getting nice bonuses for the extra work involved.

"Also: Quinty, Marius, Cyrano, Ames, Samson and Otto are hereby re-instated as full Partners. This is my last act as the sole Partner, from now on, all votes will have to be carried by a majority of the brothers."

Sanna and the Associates looked visibly relieved, to Armand's annoyance.

"Lastly — brothers, come with me. The rest of you — please continue to have a good time!"

# # #

ARMAND LED them into the Synchronicity Engine room on the third floor. This was a new vault that Armand had just installed to protect the Galahad Michael Sturdevant device as rigorously as possible — and to keep it unseen by prying eyes.

"Hey," Armand said. "I just wanted to do a toast away from everyone else who wouldn't understand it. To our Dad, Didier Martel, who used this very Synchronicity Engine to secure our futures. Without him, and without this Engine, we wouldn't have been able to pull it off. So — thanks Dad, wherever you are."

"Hear, hear," they all said and drank.

"And to Sophia," Marius said, surprising them all. They all raised their glasses enthusiastically. "Ya! To Sophia, wherever you are. We all miss you, girl. And we know you can hear us!" They laughed.

"To Sophia," Armand said, more soberly. "Thank you. For everything. For your protection. For my — well, for *our* name — and our shadow. Thank you."

"Hear, hear."

Mark Jeffrey

THE END

ABOUT THE AUTHOR

Mark Jeffrey (**@markjeffrey** on X) is an entrepreneur, crypto investor and author. He currently hosts the *Across The Chains* podcast and is General Partner at the Boolean Fund. He became an early investor in Ethereum after interviewing Vitalik Buterin on his podcast in 2014 and was in the Bitcoin class of 2013. He previously founded Guardian Circle (Partner: XPRIZE, FAST COMPANY 'World Changing Idea' 2018). Before that, he was CTO of Mahalo (backed by Sequoia, Elon Musk) and Co-Founder & CEO of the ThisWeekIn podcast network with Kevin Pollak & Jason Calacanis. He co-founded and sold ZeroDegrees (2002) an early social network, to IAC (2004), and was co-founder of The Palace (1995), one of the very first metaverses, backed by SOFTBANK, Intel and Time Warner, sold in 1998 with 10M users. Mark also worked with UBER founder Travis Kalanick on his pre-Uber startup, Red Swoosh. Mark created the first serialized podcast novel, *Max Quick: The Pocket and the Pendant*, in 2005 (2.3M downloads) which led to publication by Harper Collins (2011). His business books include Bitcoin Explained Simply (2013), The Case For Bitcoin (2015). Mark was also featured prominently in *Trust Machine: The Story of Blockchain* (Alex Winter, Rosario Dawson).